ON DANGEROUS GROUND

NEW YORK TIMES BESTSELLING AUTHOR

SHARON SALA

Previously published as *A Place to Call Home* and *Grayson*

Recycling programs for this product may not exist in your area.

ISBN-13: 978-1-335-40646-0

On Dangerous Ground
First published as A Place to Call Home in 2000.
This edition published in 2021.
Copyright © 2000 by Sharon Sala

Grayson
First published in 2011. This edition published in 2021.
Copyright © 2011 by Delores Fossen

This edition published by arrangement with Harlequin Books S.A.

For questions and comments about the quality of this book, please contact us at CustomerService@Harlequin.com.

Harlequin Enterprises ULC
22 Adelaide St. West, 40th Floor
Toronto, Ontario M5H 4E3, Canada
www.Harlequin.com

Printed in U.S.A.

CONTENTS

Sharon Sala is a *New York Times* bestselling author. She has 123 books published in romance, young adult, Western and women's fiction and in nonfiction. First published in 1991, she's an eight-time RITA® Award finalist. Industry awards include the following: the Janet Dailey Award; five Career Achievement Awards from *RT Book Reviews*; five National Readers' Choice Awards; five Colorado Romance Writers Awards of Excellence; the Heart of Excellence Award; the Booksellers' Best Award; the Nora Roberts Lifetime Achievement Award presented by RWA; and the Centennial Award from RWA for recognition of her 100th published novel.

Books by Sharon Sala

Secrets and Lies

Dark Hearts
Cold Hearts
Wild Hearts

Forces of Nature

Going Gone
Going Twice
Going Once

The Rebel Ridge novels

'Til Death
Don't Cry for Me
Next of Kin

The Searchers

Blood Trails
Blood Stains
Blood Ties

Visit the Author Profile page at Harlequin.com for more titles.

A PLACE TO CALL HOME

Sharon Sala

I dedicate this book to all of my readers
who have vanquished the monsters
that slept under their beds.

Chapter 1

"Goddamn it, Hanna, you aren't listening to me."

Detective Judd Hanna of the Tulsa Police Department gave his captain a look that would have quelled a lesser man. Roger Shaw threw up his hands in defeat.

"And don't give me one of those 'spare me' looks, either. This is serious."

Judd let his gaze shift from his captain's face to a spot just over his shoulder, and then the window beyond. There was a window washer halfway up the building across the street. Judd wondered absently why a man would choose such a dangerous occupation.

Shaw saw Judd's focus shift. He turned, following Judd's gaze, saw the man on the scaffolding across the street, and then strode to the windows and deftly dropped the shades. When he turned, Judd was heading for the door.

"I'm not through with you," Shaw snapped. "Get back here now, and that's an order."

Judd sighed. Short of mutiny, which he was considering, disobeying an out-and-out order was beyond him. He turned, wishing that this feeling of helplessness would just go away. He felt aimless…almost out of control. And of all things, Judd Hanna had to be in control. It was the only way he could function.

"What…sir?"

Shaw took a deep breath and then popped a mint in his mouth to keep from cursing again. He'd lost his temper more in the last ten minutes than he had all month. God only knew what his blood pressure was doing right now. He shuddered and pushed the thought from his mind.

"Look, Hanna. I'm serious. This is Vice. We do things here as a team. You can't keep playing cowboy every time we go out on a raid. Use your radio. Call for backup. Depend on your partner. That's why he's there."

Judd's eyes narrowed. "My partner is dead," he said shortly.

Shaw shoved an angry hand through what was left of his thinning hair. Even though Judd had been assigned a new partner over a month ago, he had yet to acknowledge his presence.

"I know it was rough losing Myers the way we did. We all liked Dan. But life goes on. David Sanger is your partner now, and you will, by God, treat him as such."

Judd didn't blink and wouldn't answer. None of them knew the guilt Judd carried. Three days away from retirement, Dan Myers had taken a bullet meant for Judd. Instead of a retirement party, they'd attended Dan's funeral. Judd hadn't slept the night through since.

Shaw glared at the implacable expression on Hanna's face. Never in his life had he wanted to shake anyone as badly as he did right now. And yet looking at him, Shaw knew that was the last thing a sane man would do. At three inches over six feet, and with an attitude that wouldn't quit, Judd Hanna was a man you didn't want to piss off. Shaw sighed, then tried a different approach.

"Hanna, you know as well as I do that the rules are in place for everyone's safety. Not just yours. I don't want to attend another funeral, namely yours."

Judd muttered something that, to Shaw, sounded suspiciously like, who the hell cares.

"That does it!" Shaw snapped. "Turn in your badge and your service revolver. I'm placing you on medical leave until you get your head screwed on straight."

Finally, Shaw had Judd's attention. "You can't!" Judd argued. "We're too close to finding Dan's killer."

Shaw pointed a finger in Judd's face. "That's what I mean," he shouted. "Dan Myers's case belongs to Homicide. We're Vice."

Judd swallowed as panic started to intercede. He couldn't let go just like that. Why couldn't Shaw understand?

"Look, Captain, Dan was my partner. He took a bullet meant for—"

Shaw shook his head. "You heard me. As of this minute, you're on leave…with pay, of course. You will report to Dr. Wilson at nine o'clock tomorrow morning, and every morning thereafter until he pronounces you fit for duty again."

The department shrink? Judd's nostrils flared.

"Like hell."

Shaw leaned across his desk, glaring into Hanna's face.

"Hell it may be," he snapped. "But you don't come back until Wilson says it's okay."

Judd straightened. Just the notion of letting go of the devils he lived with was impossible to consider. He tossed his shield on the desk, then laid his revolver down beside it. Without saying a word, he headed for the door.

"Hanna—"

He stopped but didn't turn around, leaving Shaw to say what must be said to the back of his head.

"Nine o'clock tomorrow morning."

Judd slammed the door behind him. It was all the comment he was capable of making.

Shaw grabbed the phone and punched in a series of numbers, frowning as he waited for an answer.

"Dr. Wilson…it's me, Shaw. I've just put Judd Hanna on medical leave. He's due in your office at nine in the morning. Yes, he's borderline now. I don't know what's wrong, but I want it stopped before I lose him, too."

He hung up, then leaned back in his chair and closed his eyes. It hadn't been easy being tough on Hanna. He liked the man, even admired him. And losing a partner of fifteen years would have been difficult for anyone. At least now things were on the right track.

But for Judd, everything was off balance. For the first time since he took the oath of office, he had nowhere to go but his apartment. He hesitated on the street outside the station house, then headed for the bar down the street. His apartment wasn't home. It was just where he slept, and it was far too early to go to bed.

The bar was cool and fairly quiet. The afternoon crowd had yet to arrive. Judd slid onto a stool and combed his fingers through his hair in frustration. How in hell had his life gotten so mixed up?

"What'll it be?" the bartender asked.

"Bourbon," Judd muttered.

The bartender slid a bowl of pretzels his way and then went to pour the drink. Judd pushed the bowl aside. He didn't need to eat. He needed to forget.

"Here you go, buddy," the bartender said.

Judd grabbed the shot glass and lifted it to his lips, and as he did, he caught a glimpse of his own reflection in the mirror over the bar. But something happened between recognition and focus. Instead of seeing the man that he was, he saw the boy that he'd been. His belly knotted and his heart suddenly ached as he let himself remember.

The pink slip in Joe Hanna's back pocket rode his conscience like a hot poker. Overwhelmed at being fired from another dead-end job, he'd spent the last four hours, and what was left of his money, drowning his sorrows at the local bar. The only thing he had left was a constant, burning rage at the disappointments life had dealt him, and the burden of a ten-year old son he had never wanted.

As he started up the walk to his house, it occurred to him that the house was dark. He squinted against the glare of streetlights and cursed. That damned kid. If he wasn't home from school, he would tan his hide.

It never occurred to Joe that more than seven hours had passed since his son, Judd, would have come home from school, or that he'd come home to a house with no food. Joe felt no guilt for his lack of concern. He kept a roof over their heads, which was more than his daddy had done for him.

He stumbled as he started up the steps, falling forward and then catching himself on his hands and knees just before his face hit the porch. A sharp pain pierced the palm of his right hand. He got up swearing and staggered into the house, turning on the lights, room by room.

"Boy! Where the hell are you?"

No one answered. Joe cursed again as he stumbled to the kitchen sink. He looked down at his hand. It was bleeding. He wiped it on the front of his shirt, then reached for the cabinet. The second shelf down from the top was where he kept his liquor. He needed a drink, but there was nothing there.

He slammed the door shut with a bang. "Goddamn it, Judd Hanna! You answer me, boy! What did you do with my whiskey?"

Again, the rooms echoed from the sound of Joe's voice. Rage grew. His belly burned and his head was swimming. In a minute, he was going to lie down, but not before he got his hands on that damned kid.

Joe started through the rooms, shouting Judd's name. Doors slammed. A lamp tumbled to the floor and shattered into pieces, and still no sign of the boy. He was furious. The shame of being fired, coupled with the frustrations of his life in general, had boiled into a rage. He staggered back into the kitchen, swaying where he stood and staring around the house in disbelief.

It took a while for him to realize that the door leading down to the basement was slightly ajar. A cold smile broke the anger on his face. Seconds later, he stood at the landing, shouting Judd's name into the darkness below.

The basement walls were damp with condensation, the odors a choking blend of dust and mold. Something scurried in the darkness beneath ten-year-old

Judd Hanna's feet and he stifled a gasp. Yet the fear of the unknown was far less sinister to him than the man standing at the landing of the stairs.

"Judd... Judd, boy, I know you're down there. Answer me, damn it."

Judd held his breath, afraid to swallow for fear he'd be heard.

When his father started down the steps, every muscle in Judd's body went tense.

No, no, no... God, don't let him find me.

"Answer me, you sorry little bastard. I know you're down there," Joe growled.

Judd squeezed his eyes shut and shrank a little farther against the wall. If he couldn't see his father, then his father couldn't see him. It was a game he'd played in his mind for more years than he cared to count. Sometimes it worked. Sometimes it didn't.

"What did you do with my whiskey, boy? Answer me, you hear? Don't make me come down there and get you."

Judd gritted his teeth, struggling against the need to cry. It had been years since he'd given his father the satisfaction of knowing he could be hurt.

Joe cursed beneath his breath and reached for the light switch. But nothing happened. He cursed even louder, unaware that Judd had taken the bulb out in hopes he wouldn't be found. But to Judd's dismay, his father started down the steps, fumbling his way through the dark and cursing with every breath.

Judd slid silently to the floor and doubled over on himself, trying to become invisible. His eyes were closed, his breathing almost nonexistent.

"I know you're here," Joe whispered.

Judd's heart was pounding and the bitter taste of fear was in his mouth.

Please God, if you're out there…take me away. Take me away.

"You can't hide from me. Come out now and take your punishment like a man."

Bile rose in the back of Judd's throat. *Please, God, please. Not again. Not again. Don't let him—*

"Gotcha!" Joe said.

When the hand closed around the back of Judd's neck, he knew it was over. He did not go willingly. Fighting against the pain of his father's grasp, he struggled to pull free. If he could get to the stairs, he could get away. He would be safe after that. His father was bound to pass out soon. He always passed out. Those were the only times Judd ever knew peace.

Joe backhanded his son, wincing when one of Judd's teeth accidentally cut the back of his knuckle.

"Don't you bite me, you little bastard," Joe snarled.

Judd's mouth was already swelling as he tried to break free of his father's grasp.

"I didn't mean to, Daddy, I swear."

"Don't lie to me," Joe snapped, and backhanded him again. "Why didn't you answer me when I called you? And what the hell did you do with my whiskey?"

Reeling from the force of the blows, Judd couldn't think, let alone answer. All he could do was duck and hold up his hands, trying to dodge his father's fists.

It was futile.

Joe was too far gone in his rage to think about what he was doing. In his mind, he was striking out at the man who had fired him and the bartender who'd refused him a last drink. He saw the woman who had laughed at him as he stumbled out of the bar, and himself in a cycle of self-destruction with no way out.

He hated what he saw.

It was the painful jolt of flesh against flesh that finally sank through his senses. Slowly, he became aware that the skin on his hand was stinging. He paused, his arm raised above his head, and looked at the boy who was his son. The child's face was covered in blood. Joe shuddered, his stomach suddenly roiling as the adrenaline rush started to crash. He needed to lie down.

"Now, then," he muttered as he staggered back against the wall. "Let that be a lesson to you."

He expected Judd to run. When he didn't move, Joe shrugged, then turned, grabbing at the stair rail to steady himself. From the faint light spilling out from the stairwell above, he could see that Judd hadn't moved. In fact, the boy's silent demeanor was starting to get to him.

"It's your own fault," he mumbled.

Judd's only response was a slow, careful breath. He would die before he let Joe Hanna know that he hurt.

Joe watched a thick drop of blood gathering at the corner of Judd's nose. He began to get nervous. Tomorrow was a school day. If Judd went to school in this condition, someone might decide to butt into their business. And at this point in Joe's life, he had too much to lose to let that happen.

Joe's wife was dead, worn out by the years of living with the man who had been her husband. And while her death had left him with the burden of raising their son all alone, there had been a benefit to the loss that Joe hadn't expected. Until Judd reached the age of eighteen, he received a monthly social security check on his mother's behalf. And, as Judd's legal guardian, the check came to Joe. It kept a roof over their heads and beer in his belly.

Yet even in the state he was in, Joe had sense enough to realize that if he lost custody of his son, he would lose access to the money. He couldn't let that happen. So, instead of apologizing to his son, he angrily pointed a finger in Judd's face.

"Don't think you're gonna go running to those damned teachers you're so fond of and tattle on me," Joe snarled. "They won't help you. You know why? 'Cause you're white trash, boy, and people don't give a damn about white trash."

Judd's hands curled into fists. A red haze was spreading between himself and his father, and he couldn't think past the heat in his belly. The urge to hit was overwhelming. The urge to wipe that look off his father's face forever was even stronger.

Joe snorted. The kid was a loser. He wouldn't even speak up for himself.

"I'm tired. I'm going to bed now."

Then he started up the stairs. Halfway up, Judd's voice came out of the silence.

"Daddy."

Joe turned, blinking owlishly into the darkness below. Judd was only a vague outline in the shadows.

"What?"

"When you go to bed…say your prayers."

Joe frowned. "What the hell did you say that for?"

"When you sleep, I will kill you."

Joe's lips slackened. The statement was so ludicrous he couldn't think of what to say. But when Judd stepped into the light spilling down from the kitchen above, Joe took an instinctive step back. The hate on his son's face was too real.

He tried to laugh. Judd was just a kid. A ten-year-old kid. But the laughter wouldn't come. Suddenly, he found himself stumbling up the steps and into the light of the kitchen, his heart pounding, his belly lurching. He swayed where he stood, aware that he was only moments from passing out.

When you sleep, I will kill you.

The words still echoed in his head. Suddenly the sound of footsteps coming up the stairs sent him into a panic. Within seconds, he was staggering down the porch steps and running through the bushes of their backyard.

A cat scrambled out of a garbage can, hissing and spitting as Joe stumbled into the alley. The commotion set the neighbor's dog to barking. Joe's blood ran cold. If Judd wanted to, he could find him by the noise trail alone.

Joe paused and looked back. Something moved in the shadows. His heart skipped a beat. He turned and ran and never looked back, passing out some time later beneath some trees in the city park.

When he woke the next morning, his only concern was that he'd outrun his fate. Days after, when the Kentucky authorities came and took Judd away, Joe couldn't bring himself to feel anything but relief.

And Judd Hanna didn't care that his father was out of his life. In his mind, he'd been alone for years. His last refuge had been God, and that night under the stairs, even God had deserted him.

A loud sound outside the bar startled Judd's reverie. He blinked several times as his thoughts refocused. Once more, he found himself staring at the man in the mirror, and at the glass of whiskey only inches away from his lips. He shuddered. Damn. He wasn't far from the man he'd learned to hate.

At that moment, something inside of him snapped. He set the drink down without tasting it, tossed some money on the bar, and headed for the street. His captain had been right. He *was* taking chances with his life, only he didn't know why, but one fact remained that he couldn't ignore. If he wanted to live, it had to stop now.

He walked the streets for hours, weighing his options. His rent was paid until the first of the year and his utility bills were deducted directly from his bank account. He had no one to answer to but himself, and no intentions of spilling his guts to a shrink. In Judd Hanna's mind, that left him only one option, and he was going to take it before it was too late.

Captain Roger Shaw's satisfaction in dealing with Hanna's problem was short-lived. At nine-thirty the next morning, a call from the department shrink verified the fact that Judd Hanna was a no-show.

Furious, he called Judd's apartment and got a disconnect message on the phone. He stared at the receiver in disbelief, then dialed again, certain that he'd made a mistake. Again, the prerecorded message came on, saying that the number he had dialed was no longer in service. By six o'clock that evening, it was obvious that Judd Hanna was gone.

Late August, Call City, Wyoming

Judd Hanna glanced at the map on the seat beside him and then shrugged his shoulders, trying to alleviate some of the tension in his neck. It was the driving. Driving always made him tense. He looked at his watch. It was almost five o'clock. Even though it was a few hours away from nightfall, an early night sounded good. Maybe tonight he would be able to sleep. Maybe tonight the dreams wouldn't come. God, he hoped so. He was tired. So tired.

As he topped a steep hill, he saw movement in the pasture beyond and slowed down to look. It only took a moment for the unfolding scene to register. A little girl of no more than two years old was toddling through the grass. Beyond her, and more than one hundred yards away, was a young woman, running at full stride, with her mouth open in a scream he couldn't hear. To their right, and converging between them and gaining speed with every lope, was a huge black bull. It was obvious to Judd that the baby was the intended target, and that the mother would never reach her in time.

Without thinking, he stomped the accelerator to the floor. Tires spun on pavement, leaving behind the scent of burning rubber. He bounced across the shallow ditch and then straight through the five-strand barbed wire fence, leaving a tangle of mangled wire and broken fence posts behind him as he went. His grip tightened on the steering wheel as he focused on the dwindling space between the baby and the bull.

Today was laundry day. Two-year old Rachel Franklin loved the days that her mother, Charlotte, pulled all the clothes from the clothes hamper to separate for wash. Charlotte—Charlie to her family—loved her baby more than life, but there were days, like today, when she could have done without her help. She'd already separated the colored clothes twice, each time pulling her red T-shirt from the whites. Rachel did love that red T-shirt, but Charlie didn't think her brother, Wade, would be too fond of pink underwear, especially since he was Call City's chief of police.

"Rachel, give Mommy the shirt," Charlie said.

Rachel picked the red T-shirt from the pile and gave it to Charlie. The smile on her face was so precious that Charlie dropped the clothes she was carrying and picked her daughter up instead, nuzzling her nose against the baby-soft skin beneath Rachel's ear.

Rachel cackled and squealed with delight, then threw her arms around Charlie's neck.

"My mommy," Rachel said, and squeezed as tight as she could.

Charlie returned the hug. "My Rachel," she said, her throat tight with emotion.

The child was her life. The only good thing to come from loving Pete Tucker, their neighbor's son. He'd played loose with Charlie's feelings, then skipped out on her when she was two months pregnant to chase his dreams on the rodeo circuit. A month before Rachel was born, he'd crawled on a bull that, in a matter of seconds, had put an end to Pete Tucker's dreams.

Charlie had grieved, but only for the loss of Rachel's father. Charlie's love for Pete Tucker had died the day he left her to bear the burden of their affair all alone.

"Want down," Rachel muttered.

Charlie sighed as she put her baby back on her feet. Her daughter's independence was inevitable, but she couldn't help the spear of regret. She tousled Rachel's curls.

"You go play in your room, baby girl. Mommy is

going to put these clothes in the washer. Get them all clean for Uncle Wade."

"Unca Wade?"

"Yes, these are for Uncle Wade."

Rachel toddled off, satisfied with her mother's explanation. Next to her mother, Wade Franklin was her favorite person.

Charlie picked up the pile of clothes, careful not to include the red shirt, and headed for the utility room off the kitchen. A couple of minutes later it dawned on her that the house was entirely too quiet and she started back through the rooms in search of Rachel.

"Rachel, where are you?" Charlie called.

She got no answer.

"Rachel, answer Mommy, where are you?"

This time the silence hit hard. Trying not to panic, she retraced her steps, searching in all of Rachel's nooks and crannies, certain she would find her in one of her favorite places.

It wasn't until she'd made the second trip through the house that she noticed the screen door in the living room was slightly ajar. She dashed out on the porch, telling herself to stay calm.

"Rachel, where are you?"

The silence that came afterward was unnerving. She wasted another precious minute running around the house and calling Rachel's name, certain she'd find her playing in the sandbox under the trees in the backyard. But she wasn't there, either.

Now she was beginning to panic. It wasn't until she turned around that she noticed Everett Tucker's black bull was in their pasture again. This wasn't the first time it had happened, and her brother, Wade, had warned

Everett more than once to fix his fence. She stood for a moment, staring at the bull's curious stance. His head was up, his body almost motionless in the way animals are when they sense something trespassing on their territory. And then it hit her.

"Oh, God…oh, no," Charlie moaned, and started to run, just as the bull began to charge.

She ran without focus, searching the pasture with a frantic gaze, all the while praying against hope that she was wrong. Then she saw Rachel, toddling through the grass with a handful of flowers. She bolted across the cattle guard, running as she'd never run before, and screaming aloud Rachel's name.

She didn't feel the heat of the sun upon her face. She didn't even hear the sound of her own screams. All she could do was focus on Rachel's curly head and remember how soft her baby's curls were against her face, and how sweet they smelled after a shampoo.

The bull's angry bellow shattered the air and Charlie screamed again, trying to divert his attention. It didn't happen, and it occurred to her then that she would watch her daughter die. As fast as she was running, the bull was still gaining on Rachel, and there was nothing she could do to stop it.

Then out of nowhere, a black Jeep suddenly appeared in the pasture, flying across the ground at breakneck speed. Before she could absorb the implications, she stumbled and fell. The next thing she knew, she was flat on her face. Dirt was in her eyes, and her leg was afire with an unbearable pain. And yet as quickly as she fell, she was struggling to her feet and rubbing at her eyes, desperate to see. Had Rachel died while she was facedown in the dirt?

Through a blur of tears, she looked up to see the Jeep come to a sudden halt only a foot or so from where Rachel was standing. The door opened. She saw a man lean out and yank Rachel inside only seconds before bull and Jeep collided. The heavy thud of bending metal was like music to her ears. She dropped her head and took deep, calming breaths. Nothing mattered any longer. Rachel was safe.

Judd was numb. The rush of adrenaline that had gotten him this far was receding as swiftly as it had come, leaving him weak and shaken. The baby in his arms looked as startled as he'd been moments earlier when he'd seen the scene unfolding. The bull had already done a job on the passenger side of his Jeep and was now butting against the radiator as hard as he could. Judd sighed, watching the steam spewing up from under the hood. No telling what was busted, but it really didn't matter. For now, the child was safe.

He began running his hands over the little girl's body, desperate to assure himself that she had come to no harm. He'd yanked her pretty hard when he'd picked her up, but there hadn't been time for gentle introductions. When he was satisfied that she was all right, he glanced at the bull, who had taken an angry stance a distance away.

So far, so good, Judd thought, and looked around for the woman he'd seen running earlier. Then he saw her on her knees a distance away. It was obvious from the expression on her face that she was in pain.

Beyond the Jeep, the bull began pawing the earth, sending showers of dust into the air. Every now and then, the air would shift from the force of an angry bellow.

Judd eyed the woman nervously. If the bull figured out she was there, she could very well be its next target. Saying a prayer that the Jeep would still move, he grabbed the little girl to keep her from falling, then put it in gear.

"Okay, baby, let's go get your mother."

The little girl stared at Judd with a solemn expression.

"Mommy," she said, pointing with the flowers she still held.

"I see her, honey. And I have a suspicion she would like to see you, too."

The Jeep moved forward amid a spewing mist of steam. He drove slowly, hoping the bull would stay his ground.

Charlie saw them coming, and her heart skipped a beat. The bull stilled, watching intently as the Jeep began to move. She started to get up, and then realized that motion—any motion—might set the bull off. She held her breath, almost afraid to blink. The fire in her ankle was spreading up her leg. When the Jeep stopped beside her, she tried to stand up, then dropped back to the ground from the pain.

A deep, gravelly voice suddenly rumbled close to her ear. "Easy there, lady, let me help."

Charlie was starting to shake. "My baby—"

"She's fine," Judd said. "Put your arms around my neck."

Charlie reacted instinctively, clutching at the collar of his shirt as he picked her up. She had a vague impression of a hard body, dark hair, and a muscle jerking at the side of his jaw as he set her into the driver's side of the seat. Charlie winced as she slid over to the passenger side, grabbing at Rachel as she moved.

"Mommy," Rachel said, and crawled into Charlie's lap as if this was an everyday occurrence.

Charlie clung to her baby in desperation and buried her face in her neck. Seconds later, the door slammed and she knew that the man had climbed back inside. She needed to thank him. She needed to look in his eyes and see the man who had given her back her world, but she couldn't seem to focus on anything but the child in her arms.

Finally, she looked up. Rachel was smiling that sweet baby smile, unaware how close she'd come to getting them both killed.

Charlie stared at a smear of pollen on Rachel's cheek, as well as a crushed petal stuck to the corner of her lip, and didn't know whether to laugh or cry. Rachel hadn't just been picking the flowers; it looked as if she'd been eating them as well.

Tears welled, spilling down Charlie's face as she wrapped her arms around Rachel, flowers and all, and rocked her where she sat.

"Mommy cwy?" Rachel asked, feeling the streaks on Charlie's cheeks.

Charlie choked on a sob and buried her face in Rachel's curls. "Yes, baby, Mommy's crying. You scared me."

"Fwowers, Mommy. Picked you fwowers."

Charlie nodded and tried to smile, but it was impossible.

Judd saw her distress. The woman was in pain, both emotionally and physically. He looked toward the cluster of buildings just beyond the fence and put the Jeep in gear.

"Hang on, lady. I'm taking you home."

Chapter 2

The farmhouse looked old, but well-cared-for. The single-story white building was a perfect square, with a deep wraparound porch framing the exterior walls. A brown brick chimney rose above the rooftop on the north side of the house. Judd suspected that on a cold winter day the smoke from that chimney would rise high above the grove of surrounding trees.

The woman beside him was still crying, although silently now. He couldn't blame her. For a while there he'd felt like crying himself. As he crossed the cattle guard, the Jeep began to sputter. By the time he got to the house, it was barely moving, but it didn't matter now. They were safe. He killed the engine, then glanced at the woman to his right. There was dirt on her face and blood on her knees, and her fingers were trembling as she brushed at the baby curls tumbling around the little girl's face. In his line of work, he'd seen plenty of people in shock, and he wanted to get her inside before she started coming undone.

"Ma'am, if you'll allow me, I'll help get you inside, and then I'll be needing to use your phone to call for a tow."

Then, what the man had sacrificed to save them hit Charlie. She glanced up, and for the first time, she really looked at him. His eyes were blue—so blue they were almost transparent. His features were even, his jaw strong. There was just a hint of a crook to his nose, an indication of it once having been broken, and there was a small jagged scar on the right side of his jaw. And he was big, so very big. His shoulders spanned almost half the width of the seat. She remembered the feel of his hands closing around her waist and pulling her up to safety, and she shuddered.

"Please, call me Charlie."

He smiled. "I knew a Charlie once, but he wasn't as pretty as you."

It was just the sort of silly remark Charlie needed to gather herself together. "It's short for Charlotte… Charlotte Franklin."

Judd extended his hand. "Pleased to meet you, 'short for Charlotte.' My name is Judd Hanna."

Charlie hesitated, but only briefly. His grasp was firm but gentle, and again, the ordinary gesture took another bite out of her unsettled nerves. She sighed, then pointed to the hood of his car and the smoke spewing out from beneath the hood.

"Mr. Hanna, I'm so sorry about what happened to your car."

"Judd, please," he said, and then looked at Rachel.

"As for the damage, it was worth it. Now, let's see about getting you two inside."

He took Rachel out of Charlie's arms and then carried her to the porch.

"Wait right here, honey. We've got to help Mommy, okay?"

"Help Mommy," Rachel echoed, and then sat down on the steps, the wilting flowers still clutched in her hand.

Charlie scooted across the seat and then out from under the steering wheel, but when she tried to stand, her ankle gave way. Before she could argue, Judd picked her up and started up the steps. A little nervous that a total stranger had taken charge of her life, she began to fidget.

"Mr. Hanna, I—"

"Judd."

She sighed. "Judd, this is embarrassing."

He paused. "Lady, allow me the honor of helping one of the bravest people I ever saw."

She flushed. "I don't know what you—"

His voice grew quiet, and the look in his eyes hushed her words.

"You would have both died. You know that, don't you?"

She glanced down at her daughter, who was pulling the petals from a flower, and her expression crumpled.

"Life wouldn't have been worth living without her."

Breath caught in the back of Judd's throat. Logically, he accepted the fact that there were people who would willingly die for another, but Charlotte Franklin's willingness to put herself in harm's way for her child was the first example of that selfless dedication he'd ever seen. He supposed that his mother might once

have loved him like that, but he didn't remember it.
He glanced back at Rachel, who was still sitting on
the steps.

"Yeah. I can only imagine," he said softly. Then he
raised his voice a notch. "Come on, little girl, it's time
to go inside."

To Charlie's surprise, Rachel minded the stranger
and followed them in. As soon as Judd put her down,
Rachel crawled up in Charlie's lap and laid her head on
her mother's breast.

"Is she okay?" Judd asked.

Charlie nodded. "Just a little confused, I think.
She'll be all right." Then she pointed toward the phone.
"There's a phone book in the drawer underneath."

Judd shook his head. "You come first. If you don't
mind me prowling a bit, I want to put some ice on your
ankle."

"The kitchen is that way," Charlie said. "There are
some plastic bags in the drawer beside the sink and
there's an ice maker in the top of the fridge."

Judd headed for the kitchen, returning shortly with
a bag full of ice wrapped in a towel. Charlie winced
when he laid it on her ankle.

"Sorry," Judd said. "Does your husband work
nearby?"

The tone of Charlie's voice never wavered. "I don't
have a husband."

Judd glanced at Rachel, then at Charlie, then fussed
with the bag of ice just for something to do.

"I'm sorry, I didn't mean to bring up painful memories. It's just that you can't be here by yourself. Is there
anyone I can call for you?"

Charlie sighed. The man was getting the wrong

impression, and while it really didn't matter what he thought, she felt obligated to explain.

"I am not a widow. To the contrary, I have never been married. And yes, there is someone—my brother, Wade. If you don't mind handing me the phone, I'll give him a call."

Judd turned, then stopped and stared. "There's a police car coming down your driveway."

A wave of emotion suddenly washed over Charlie. Wade was hardly ever home on time. Thank God this was one of those rare days. To her surprise, she felt tears threatening again.

She took a deep breath, trying to still the tremble in her voice. "That would be Wade. He's the police chief in Call City."

Judd stiffened, then made himself relax, accepting the irony of the situation. He'd driven halfway across the country to get away from law enforcement, and the first time he lingered long enough to exchange names, they were tied to the same damned branch of government.

A few moments later, the officer who'd been driving the car came through the door, his eyes wide with concern. Judd braced himself for the confrontation.

Wade had been looking forward to an easy evening until he'd seen the destruction to the pasture fence. His mood had taken a quick swing downward and was far from level when he came through the door. Seeing Charlie's tears and the stranger standing next to her, his hand automatically slid to the butt of his gun.

"Charlie...honey...what the hell happened?"

"It's okay," Charlie said, and then started to cry in earnest.

Judd sighed. She'd been bordering on hysteria ever since he'd pulled her out of the dirt. It was inevitable that she would finally break down. What surprised him was the urge he had to comfort her.

Wade moved toward Charlie, but his attention was completely focused on the man standing next to her.

"Easy, buddy," Judd said, "I'm the good guy here." Then he offered his hand. "My name is Judd Hanna."

Wade nodded, but reserved the right to the handshake until after he knew some more facts. Judd shrugged. He couldn't really blame him.

"What the hell happened to the fence?" Wade said, looking straight at Judd. "Did it run into your car?"

Judd laughed out loud. Even Charlie managed to chuckle through tears. Rachel giggled, too, although the joke was over her head, and then she pointed out the door.

"Big bull."

Wade frowned. "What bull, honey?"

Charlie choked on a sob. "Oh, Wade. Tucker's bull... it was in our pasture again. I couldn't find Rachel, and then I saw her...and the bull was charging...but I couldn't outrun...if it hadn't been for...he drove through the fence and... I fell and it was...oh, God, Wade, the bull would have killed her."

She shuddered, then buried her face against the back of Rachel's neck.

All the color faded from Wade Franklin's face. He looked at Judd, and this time, he was the one who offered his hand.

"Mister, I suppose we'll sort out the details later, but if I'm understanding the situation here, you just saved their lives, and if that's so, then there aren't enough words to thank you."

Judd shrugged, a little embarrassed at being the sudden focus of attention. "I just happened to be in the right place at the right time."

Too overcome to speak, Wade impulsively hugged him. Judd was still reeling from the impact of being royally thumped on the back when Wade let him go and shifted his focus to Charlie.

He squatted down beside her and lifted the ice from her foot. "I think you need to see a doctor," he said, then took out his handkerchief and wiped at the tears and dirt on her face as if she was a child.

Charlie caught his hand. "No, it's just a sprain. I'll be fine."

Judd's heart twisted again. The closeness between brother and sister only served as a reminder of what was missing in his life.

"About that phone call," Judd said. "If you'd recommend a towing service and a motel, I'll be out of your hair."

Wade rocked back on his heels. "There aren't any motels in Call City, and the only tow truck is out on a call. I know because I sent him."

Then he glanced at Charlie. She nodded. They had no options but to offer their home to the man. After all he'd done, it was the least they could do.

"Charlie and I would consider it an honor to put you up for the night."

Judd shook his head. "That's not necessary. I've slept in my car plenty of times. It won't hurt me to do it again."

"No," Charlie said. "You'll stay in the house, with us."

He took a deep breath and looked down. Even with the dirt on her face, Charlotte Franklin was a good-looking woman, but it was the expression in her eyes that swayed him. She needed to make reparation. Whether he wanted to or not, he felt obligated to accept her hospitality.

"Then I thank you," he said. "And just to make sure you folks don't feel the need to sleep with a gun under your pillow, would it make you feel better to know I'm a cop?"

Wade's smile was one of relief as he stood abruptly. "Why didn't you say so sooner?"

"Probably because I'm AWOL from my precinct," Judd said. "And, before you assume the worst, I'm not in trouble, I just got fed up."

Wade's gaze narrowed thoughtfully. "Yeah, that can happen."

Judd handed Wade a card with the phone number on it.

"Call the Tulsa, Oklahoma, P.D. Ask for Captain Roger Shaw. He'll vouch for my honesty, if not my sanity."

Charlie flinched, then held her baby closer, suddenly unsure of having this stranger in their house all night. Judd caught the look.

"Ma'am."

She looked up.

"I swear to you that the only person I'm capable of hurting is myself."

Charlie stared intently. She had no reason to trust his word, other than the fact that he'd saved their lives. It would have to be enough. Finally, she nodded and managed a smile.

"Then that's that," Wade said. "And before you call a mechanic, I need to use the phone. I've got to talk to a man about a bull."

Wade stalked to the phone and punched in some numbers before taking the portable with him as he strode out to the porch.

Charlie combed a shaky hand through her hair as Rachel wiggled to be put down. Through the open doorway, bits and pieces of Wade Franklin's conversation could be heard.

"Don't give a good damn about why…nearly killed… going to be hamburger if you don't get the son of a…"

Charlie looked at Judd and then sighed. "Wade has a bad temper."

Judd shrugged. "I don't blame him. If it had been me, I would have probably shot the son of a bitch and worried about the complications later."

Startled by his matter-of-fact tone, Charlie could think of nothing to say. When Judd turned away, she found herself watching his every move.

"Potty," Rachel suddenly announced.

Charlie groaned. With her bad ankle, she'd never make it to the bathroom with Rachel in time.

"Wade! Come quick."

Her call brought her brother running.

"What's wrong?" he asked.

"Rachel needs to go to the bathroom."

Wade laughed and tossed the cell phone on the cushion beside Charlie as he picked up his little niece.

"Come on, shortcake, let's hurry."

Rachel giggled. "Hurry, hurry," she repeated.

Charlie rolled her eyes and then glanced at Judd. He was grinning.

"Potty training," she explained. "There's never much time between her and disaster."

His grin widened.

"As soon as Wade comes back, he'll show you where you can sleep. After I wash some of this dirt off myself, I'll see to fixing supper."

"No, ma'am," Judd said. "We'll cook. You just sit there and look pretty. It'll make us all feel better."

Charlie blushed. Moments later, Wade was back. He helped her to her feet and then down the hall to the bathroom, leaving Rachel and Judd alone.

Judd squatted until he was eye to eye with the little girl, and then reached out and pulled a flower petal from the side of her face.

"These any good?" he asked, and licked it.

She giggled and ducked her head.

As she smiled, the knot in Judd's belly shifted slightly. Maybe this detour wouldn't be so bad, after all.

Within the hour, Judd realized how unimportant haste was in Call City. It would be morning before the mechanic would come get his car. Even if he'd been willing to pay the extra money to have it hauled in tonight, it would solve nothing. The garage wouldn't be open until 7:00 a.m., so there was no need to hurry just to have it parked.

Resigned to his fate, he'd taken his suitcase out of the Jeep and headed for the room he'd been given. It was small but clean, and the furniture was sturdy. The fact that he'd have to share a bathroom with a baby and two other people seemed a small price to pay for the comfort of a home-cooked meal and a place to wash some clothes.

A short while later, Judd saw a pickup truck coming down the driveway and pulling a trailer. The owner of the runaway bull, he assumed. He watched from the window as Wade met the man in the drive. Again, harsh words were traded, and while he was debating with himself about getting involved before someone threw the first punch, he overheard something that stunned him. The man called Tucker wasn't only the owner of the bull, he was Rachel Franklin's grandfather, as well. What made no sense was that he was so belligerent about the fact.

"He's not a happy man," Charlie said, pointing toward the man in the truck.

Startled, Judd turned. "Who, Wade?"

"No, Everett Tucker."

Judd turned away, a little embarrassed at being caught eavesdropping, but he supposed it was the cop in him, always wanting to know the why of everything.

"I didn't intend to pry," he said.

Charlie shrugged. "It's no secret in these parts that Everett doesn't like us." Then she turned and looked at Rachel, who was playing on the floor in front of the television. "He especially doesn't like Rachel."

"But why?" Judd asked.

"Because she's all there is left of his only son, Pete, and I guess it hurts him too much to look at her."

"I'm sorry," Judd said. "Again, I seem to be stepping on ghosts."

Charlie glanced at him and managed a smile. "No. All my ghosts are laid, Mr. Hanna. It wasn't in me to grieve for Pete's death when he'd already walked out on me for getting pregnant."

Judd paled. "Look, I know I keep saying this, but

I'm sorry. And for what it's worth, the man must have been a purebred fool."

Charlie sighed. "Pretty much."

Uncomfortable with the emotions tumbling around in his head, Judd stared at her for a moment, then strode out the door.

The sun was hanging low in the west before Judd came back in the house. He'd helped Wade mend the fence, but did little more than watch as the livestock were fed. Country life was something foreign to his world.

After washing up, Wade had handed him a bowl of potatoes and a paring knife and then headed for the door with a platter of steaks. Now he stood at the sink peeling potatoes while Wade tended to the meat cooking on the grill outside. Judd watched as Rachel ran from the swing set to her uncle and back again, talking nonstop without care if anyone answered. He paused with a potato in one hand and the paring knife in the other, imagining himself in such a family tableau. Then reality surfaced and he returned to the potatoes, removing the peelings in angry chunks. It was obvious as hell that he couldn't take care of himself, let alone a wife and kids, so why want something he couldn't have?

In the midst of his anger, it dawned on him he was no longer alone. He pivoted. Charlotte Franklin was standing in the doorway, using the facing for a crutch. He dropped the knife and potato and bolted toward her, wiping his hands on his jeans as he went.

"You shouldn't be on that foot. Let me help you to a chair."

Grateful for his strength, Charlie started to lean on

him, when Judd slid an arm beneath her shoulders and lifted her off her feet.

"This is getting embarrassing," she muttered.

Judd grinned, trying to put her at ease. "Now, Charlie, you wouldn't deny a man such a golden opportunity. It isn't every day I get the excuse to hold a pretty woman."

"Not even your wife?"

Judd found himself caught in her gaze. For a long moment, neither moved—neither spoke. Damp tendrils of her freshly washed hair brushed the backs of his hands. Her eyes were wide and questioning, her expression tense, as if she were holding her breath for an answer she didn't want to hear. Then he shook off the thought. This was crazy. She was a stranger.

"Not married," he said, and then added, "No significant other, either. Being a cop isn't conducive to permanent relationships."

"You can put me down now," she said.

Judd blinked, a bit startled by the abrupt change in their conversation, and then continued his trek across the floor, gently lowering her into a chair.

"Thank you," she said.

He nodded. As he started back toward the sink, she spoke.

"Mr. Hanna…"

He sighed, then turned. Obviously she wasn't going to call him Judd until she was ready.

"Yes?"

"It isn't the job, it's the man inside the uniform that controls his own life."

Reeling from the brutal truth in her words, he was still struggling for an answer when Wade came inside.

"Steaks are done," he announced, carrying the platter before him as if he were bearing pure gold.

"The potatoes aren't," Judd said, and headed for the sink.

Charlie stared at the stiff set to Judd's shoulders, and ignored her brother's curious gaze. Obviously, her comments had touched a nerve.

"No matter. These will keep," Wade said. "I've got to fish Rachel out of the sandbox, anyway." He set the plate down on the table near Charlie's elbow and headed back out the door.

The evening meal came and went, but long after Judd had gone to bed that night, Charlotte Franklin's words still rang in his ears. *It isn't the job, it's the man inside the uniform that controls his own life.*

If that was true, then no wonder he thought he was going crazy. That night he dreamed of his partner, Dan Myers—laughing one minute, then the next, drowning in his own blood from the bullet that had exploded inside his chest.

Judd was in the country, so awakening to the crow of a rooster didn't surprise him. But he wasn't expecting to feel soft baby breath on the side of his face. One heartbeat he was drifting toward consciousness and the next second he was wide-awake and staring into a pair of round brown eyes. Before he could move, Rachel Franklin stuck her finger up his nose.

"Nose," she said.

He laughed. It wasn't the soft, easy chuckle that his buddies in the department would have recognized. In fact, if he'd heard a replay of it, he wouldn't have recognized himself. It was a deep, from-the-belly laugh that echoed within the silence of the house. The little girl giggled and ducked her head behind the blanket wadded up in one arm, then peeked out at him again.

He reached down and picked her up, sitting her on the side of the bed. Soft baby curls straggled down in her eyes, and she was missing a sock. But she smelled sweet and the smile she gave him was even sweeter.

"So, you're an early bird, are you, punkin?"

"Bird," Rachel said, and pointed out the window.

Judd's grin widened. She wasn't just pretty. She was smart, too. It shouldn't have mattered, but the knowledge pleased him.

"Yeah, that's right. Birds live in trees."

She wiggled her bottom a little closer to the warmth of his leg beneath his covers, and pulled her blanket up under her chin just as Charlie came hobbling into the room.

Her hair wasn't in much better shape than her daughter's, but that was where the similarities ended. Devoid of all makeup and with eyes still heavy with sleep, she had the look of a woman who'd spent the night in a loving man's arms. He had a moment of insanity wondering what it would be like to make love to her, and then tossed it aside.

"I am so sorry," Charlie said as she made a grab for Rachel. "She's just started getting out of her baby bed by herself."

Judd grinned. "If you could bottle her action, she'd make alarm clocks passé."

"I'm afraid to ask, but what did she do?" Charlie asked.

Judd grinned. "Let's just say that, if it wasn't before, I'm pretty sure my left nostril is clean."

Charlie rolled her eyes. "Oh, Lord."

Judd started to laugh again. "It wasn't so bad. It's better than the barrel of a .45, any day."

Charlie grimaced. "You cops have a weird sense of humor. Now, if you'll excuse us, we'll leave you to your sleep."

Judd stretched and yawned. "Never was much good at sleeping in," he said. "If you don't mind, I'll make some coffee."

Charlie's pulse gave a leap as the sheet slipped down toward his belly. It was all she could do to answer.

"Uh…yes… I mean, no, I don't mind. Make yourself at home. Wade is in the shower but he'll be out in a few minutes."

Judd glanced down at her ankle as she moved toward the door. It was still swollen and starting to bruise. Without thinking, he started to get up and help her, then remembered he had nothing on. He waited until they were gone, then got up and dressed, keeping it casual. He put on his last pair of clean jeans and a slightly wrinkled T-shirt bearing the logo of the Tulsa P.D.

As he headed for the kitchen, he could hear Charlotte's voice, soft and coaxing as she helped her daughter dress, as well as the occasional rumble of Wade Franklin's voice. From what he could hear, the police chief was already on the phone, dealing with the business of the day. Just for a moment, he regretted the fact that he wasn't getting ready for the job, then reminded himself that it was because of the damned job that he was here. Somehow, he was going to have to find a way to forgive himself for not dying along with Dan Myers.

A couple of minutes later, he was digging through

the cabinets for the coffee when Wade walked into the kitchen. He turned.

"I asked Charlie if it would be okay to make coffee," he said.

Wade shrugged, obviously preoccupied. "Have at it," he muttered.

Judd filled the carafe with water then measured out the coffee, all the while keeping an eye on Wade. Once the coffee was on and brewing, he turned.

"Got trouble?" he asked.

Wade nodded. "Probably."

"Want to talk about it?"

Wade reached for a bottle of painkillers. "Bad knee," he said, and downed a couple without water.

Judd waited. If the man wanted to talk, he would do so when he was ready. Then Wade looked up, and Judd felt himself under sudden scrutiny.

"I talked to your captain," Wade said.

Judd grinned wryly. "What did he say?"

"That he was glad to know the son of a bitch was still alive and to tell him to get his ass back to Tulsa."

Judd shrugged. "He loves me. What can I say?"

Wade almost grinned, but there was more on his mind than Judd's defection.

"He also said you're a hell of a detective, which brings me to my question."

Suddenly, Judd sensed he wasn't going to like what was coming.

"Looks like I've got myself a problem in Call City," Wade said, then poured them each a cup of coffee before continuing. "A man named Raymond Shuler, who is president of the local bank, is missing. His wife said he went to a meeting last night and never came home.

My deputy found his car, still parked at the town hall where the meeting was held, but Shuler is nowhere to be found."

Judd frowned. "This ever happened before?"

Wade shook his head. "That's just it. Shuler isn't the type to pull any stunts. It's obvious something has happened."

"Like robbery, or maybe another woman?"

Wade shrugged. "Could be any number of things. I'll find out more when I get to the office."

"What's that have to do with me?" Judd asked.

Wade paused. Judd could see the hesitation on his face.

"It's just that my deputy, Hershel Brown, is getting married tomorrow and leaving on his honeymoon. He won't be back for at least two weeks, maybe more. I can hardly ask the kid to postpone his wedding because of this, and I'm damned sure not going to tell him he can't go on his honeymoon, but I'm going to be real short-handed until he gets back."

Judd stiffened. "How many other deputies do you have?"

Wade grinned. "None, and since you're going to be stuck here until your Jeep is fixed, I thought you might consider helping me out with this case. I could probably work a small consultation fee into the budget, although it wouldn't be much."

Judd sighed. This wasn't what he'd planned to do, but like the man said, what other options did he have?

Then Wade added the kicker. "And, since you'll be staying on here until your vehicle is up and running…"

"Okay," Judd said. "But no fee is necessary. Technically, I'm still employed in Oklahoma."

Wade grinned. "Thanks, man, I really appreciate this."

"Don't thank me yet," Judd said.

Wade shrugged off the warning, but before he could comment, someone honked outside.

Wade refilled his coffee cup and then motioned with his chin. "That will be Tooter Beel."

"Tooter?"

Wade grinned. "Don't ask." Then he added, "He'll tow your car to the garage in town, but you'll have to wait until tomorrow to talk to the mechanic."

Judd frowned. This meant another day's delay added on to the rest. Then he sighed. Why wasn't he surprised?

"Why tomorrow?" he asked.

"Because today is Monday and Harold doesn't open the shop on Mondays."

Judd knew he shouldn't ask, but the question came out, anyway.

"And why doesn't he open on Mondays?"

Wade's grin widened. "Because he's usually sleeping off a weekend drunk. Even if he came in and unlocked the shop, you wouldn't want him working on anything. He's real mean until the liquor wears off."

"So, all that's going to happen today is my Jeep gets parked in town?"

"That's about the size of it."

"Fine. Then I'll stay here and help Charlie."

Wade looked nervous. This wasn't what he had in mind.

"Uh, I don't think…"

"Is there anyone…maybe a neighbor, or a friend, who can come stay with her?" Judd asked.

Wade frowned. "No."

"Maybe you were planning to stay here and help her?" Judd asked.

"Not with Shuler missing. In fact, I should already be at the office," Wade said.

"So, what's-his-name can tow my car and I'll stay here and help. Maybe by tomorrow the swelling in her foot will be down."

The horn sounded again. Wade was out of excuses. He set his coffee cup down and headed for the door.

"Fine," he said shortly. "I'll tell Tooter to hook 'er up and pull it into town. You can talk to Harold tomorrow about repairs."

"Sounds like a plan to me," Judd said, and wondered why he'd been so bent on baby-sitting a woman and a kid. It wasn't like him. In fact, it wasn't like him at all.

Chapter 3

Judd couldn't remember ever wanting to touch a woman as much as he wanted to touch Charlotte. Her skin, an even golden tan, was glistening with a faint sheen of perspiration as she crawled around on her knees, weeding the flower garden in front of the house. She wore her hair in a thick rope of braid, and the warm chestnut color glowed from the heat of the sun. The braid hung over her shoulder as she worked, and each time she straightened to rest her back, it would bounce against the thrust of one breast. Her shorts were old and frayed at the hems, the denim fabric faded by countless washings, and the logo on her T-shirt was completely illegible. He kept staring at the slender curve of her neck and the high, delicate instep of her small bare feet, and telling himself to focus on something else. He didn't listen.

Beyond the sandstone walk, the baby played, carrying a small bucket of dirt from one pile to another, then scooping it up and doing it all over again. Overhead, a lone turkey buzzard circled high in the sky, looking for something to eat. Judd glanced up, past the buzzard to the jet trail far above, and thought of the faceless people in that plane. They didn't know it, but at this very moment, they were flying over heaven.

"Judd, would you hand me that small rake, please?"

He grabbed at the rake with a guilty conscience. Could she tell he'd been thinking about her? Would it show on his face?

"Thanks," she said, and began pulling it through the dirt, loosening the soil around the roots of some bushes.

"I would have been happy to do that for you," Judd said.

Charlie paused, giving him more than a casual glance. His shoulders were straining at the shirt he was wearing, and from where she was sitting, the muscles in his legs weren't too shabby, either. She wondered if he was a fitness freak, and then discarded the thought. It shouldn't matter to her what he was.

"Do you know the difference between marigolds and weeds?" she asked.

He hesitated and then grinned. "No."

"Then if you don't mind, I'll do it myself."

Judd laughed. "You don't trust men much, do you?"

She never looked up. "I haven't had much reason."

Judd's smile faded. He glanced at Rachel, watching the way her baby curls bounced as she toddled from place to place, and he thought of the fool who'd denied her.

"No, I guess you haven't at that," he said softly,

watching as Rachel came toward them, still carrying her shovel but leaving her little bucket behind.

"Mommy, I sirsty."

"Just a minute, sweetie," Charlie said. "Let Mommy get up and I'll get you a drink."

Judd put his hand on her shoulder. "I would be happy to take her for you."

Charlie hesitated, then smiled. "Thanks, but I'd better do it. She probably needs to go to the bathroom, too."

Judd started to argue, then thought better of it. He couldn't blame her. If it was his daughter, he wouldn't want a strange man taking her to the bathroom, either.

He nodded, then slid his hands beneath her armpits and pulled Charlie to her feet. For a second, they were face-to-face, gazes locked.

Then something happened.

Charlie would think later that it was a recognition of souls, while Judd would not remember the thought in his mind, only the yearning to kiss her.

He moved.

She lifted her face and held her breath.

"Mommy…"

Rachel's plea yanked them back to reality, a vivid reminder that they were not alone. Desperate to put something between them, Judd picked the child up, then slid his free arm around Charlie's waist and helped her into the house. Oddly enough, she leaned on his strength without fuss, taking his help as it was meant to be given. When they were inside, he set Rachel down in the hall outside the bathroom door. Charlie moved past him without comment. Judd watched the door closing between them while thinking he should have gone into town with Wade, after all. Staying alone in this house with Charlotte Franklin hadn't been a good idea. He already admired her. He didn't want to like her—at least, not so much that it would matter when it was time to leave.

Raymond Shuler came to in the dark and thought at first he'd gone blind. Then he felt the blindfold on his eyes and fought an urge to throw up. A whimper of protest came up his throat, but never got past the gag in his mouth. The ropes around his wrists and ankles were rough and binding, but those were the least of his worries. He'd been kidnapped. He was going to die.

Time passed. His mind was clearing as he recognized a current of air moving across his skin. A few seconds later it hit him. My God, he was naked!

Fear sliced through him, leaving him sick to his stomach as he struggled to pull free. The smell of dust was thick in the air and his throat felt dry, his lips cracked and burning.

Something rattled—then rattled again. At the sound of footsteps, he stilled. Was this it? Was this the moment he was going to die? He thought of his wife, of his family, of the debts that he owed and the secrets he'd kept and wondered how the world could go on without him. A low whimper slid up his throat, hanging just behind the gag stuffed in his mouth.

Hands yanked him roughly, rolling him from his back to his belly. He started to cry, mutely begging for a mercy that never came. Suddenly, something hot was thrust against his hip and the scent of burning flesh was in the air. Shocked by the unexpected stab of piercing pain, he arched up off the floor and then blessedly passed out before it was over. He never knew when the syringe full of antibiotic went into his arm, or when the sound of footsteps receded. It would be another day before he awoke, and by that time, the deed—and the damage—had been done.

"So, what do you know about the missing banker that you didn't know this morning?" Judd asked as he cleared the table from the supper they'd just had.

Oblivious to the seriousness of the conversation going on around her, Rachel crawled up on her uncle Wade's lap and began unbuttoning his shirt—a new and favorite pastime.

Wade looked down at his niece and grinned as her tiny fingers worked the buttons out of the holes.

"Not much," he said. "Only that it looks like a real abduction, but there's been no demand for ransom."

"Does he have money?" Judd asked.

Charlie snorted lightly. "He's got plenty of ours," she muttered.

Wade patted Charlie on the hand, then looked at Judd. "Sometimes it's hard to meet the mortgage payments and Shuler isn't exactly a 'good old boy' when it comes to extensions." Then he answered Judd's question. "Yeah, he's got money. Inherited it from his old man."

Judd frowned. "Maybe you're not the only people who don't like the way he does business. Would you say he has enemies?"

Charlie's snort was a little more pronounced. "It would be easier to count his friends. There're fewer of them."

Judd grinned at her. Damned if he didn't like her spunk. "That bad, is he?"

She grimaced, then looked at Wade and sighed. "Am I being dramatic again?"

"Yes, honey, but that's part of why I love you."

She grinned. "And the other part is?"

He looked down at the imp in his lap. His chest was bare clear down to his belt. When she started twisting the hair on his chest around her little fingers and pulling, he yelped, then handed her to Charlie.

"I suppose that would be Miss Rachel here, although I must be a masochist for thinking it. Every night I suffer the tortures of the damned with those tiny fingers." He looked at Judd and grinned. "With Rachel, who needs a razor?"

"Or a handkerchief," Judd added.

Charlie thought of the way Judd had been awakened this morning and started to laugh.

"What did I miss?" Wade asked.

"While you were in the shower this morning, Judd had a rather rude awakening."

Wade started to grin. "Not the finger-up-the-nose trick?"

Judd chuckled. "Oh, yeah," he said. "But it was the exploratory twist before she pulled it out that got my full attention."

Wade chuckled as Charlie squeezed Rachel close in her arms, burying her nose against the little girl's neck.

"You're such a mess, baby girl. What is Mama going to do with you?"

Judd leaned over and patted the tousle of curls on Rachel's head. They felt like loops of silk against his palm.

"Just love her," he said softly. "These days, the age of innocence is far too short."

Wade's smile slipped. "Amen to that," he said, and then out of curiosity, decided to change the subject. "So, you know how my day went. What did you two do?"

"Not much," Charlie said, and began fussing with the ties on Rachel's tennis shoe.

"She did a little gardening," Judd added, and stacked the rest of the plates in the sink.

The stilted tones of their voices set Wade on alert. For a moment he sat, staring at them in disbelief. Charlie was tying Rachel's laces in knots and Judd began splashing water far too forcefully for the small stack of dishes that had to be washed. Concern crept into his thoughts. Despite the fact that the man was a cop and had saved Rachel's life, he was still a stranger. Had he done something to Charlie while he was gone?

The chair squeaked across the linoleum as he suddenly stood.

"That's the biggest bunch of nothing I ever heard and I've heard a lot. What went on out here that no one wants to discuss?"

Charlie stood, meeting her brother's angry gaze. "Oh, for Pete's sake, Wade, do you honestly think that if Judd had been less than a gentleman, he would be standing in my kitchen in one piece? I thought you knew me better than that."

Judd was almost as angry, but at himself for getting into this position.

"Look, you two. Just give me a ride into town and I'll be out of your lives for good."

Panic hit Charlie hard as she turned toward him, and in that moment, she accepted the fact that she didn't want him to go. But before she could speak, Wade shrugged and grinned.

"Sorry I jumped to conclusions. I guess it's my suspicious nature. I've been a cop too long." Then he added,

"Besides, you can't go. You promised to help me with the Shuler case."

Judd nodded without comment. The way he figured, the less said, the better. Technically, Charlie was right. Nothing had happened. But they both knew it could have, and that was where the guilt began.

Morning of the next day dawned gray and overcast. Charlie slipped out of bed, gingerly testing her weight on her ankle. It was markedly better, which was, to her, a relief. Having Judd Hanna for a houseguest was difficult enough when Wade was around to play buffer, but being alone with him had been worse. There was something about him that she couldn't let go. At first, she thought it was gratitude for the fact that he'd saved their lives. But that theory hadn't lasted past the first time she'd thought about kissing him. She'd been grateful to a lot of people in her lifetime, but she hadn't once wanted to kiss them the way she'd wanted to kiss Judd Hanna.

All night she'd struggled with her conscience. Sometime around morning, she had decided that she didn't want to be thinking of a man. The last time she'd let her guard down with one, she'd wound up with a baby and no husband. That wasn't happening to her again.

She dressed quietly, hoping to get into the kitchen and start breakfast before Rachel woke up. Considering the weather, she opted for a pair of blue jeans rather than shorts, and tucked her T-shirt into the waistband before giving herself a last look in the mirror. Her hair was neatly braided, her clothes were old but clean. She'd even managed to get an old sandal onto her swollen foot without too much discomfort. But as she exited her bedroom, she kept feeling as if she was leaving something undone. And then Judd walked out of his room and for a startled moment, they were alone in the hallway.

Judd started to speak, when Charlie put a finger to her lips and shushed him before leading him into the kitchen.

"Rachel," she explained, pointing back down the hall. "She's a light sleeper."

He nodded, but his thoughts were on the uneven row of tiny curls already popping out from her neat hairdo and feathering across her forehead.

Charlie reached for the coffeepot and began filling it with water. He was making her nervous.

"Did you sleep well?" she asked.

"Yes."

The silence between them was noticeable.

"How's your foot?" Judd finally asked.

She turned, a fake smile on her face. "Better, thanks."

Now the lull in the conversation was uncomfortable.

Finally, they both turned to speak at once, then laughed uncomfortably.

"You first," Charlie said.

Judd shook his head. "No, ma'am. Ladies first."

She set a skillet on the stove, then took a bowl of eggs from the refrigerator.

"Scrambled okay with you?"

He grinned wryly. "It pretty much fits the description of my brain, so I guess that sounds about right."

Charlie stopped. This wasn't the first time he'd made light of his exodus from his job. She suspected he wasn't really as carefree about it as he claimed.

She set the eggs down. "Can I ask you something?"

He shrugged. "Have at it."

"What happened to you?"

His smile faded. "Hell if I know," he said, and turned away.

"I'm sorry," Charlie said. "It's really none of my business."

Judd sighed and made himself face her again. "My partner died on the eve of his retirement. He took a bullet meant for me and I can't get the memory of his wife's face out of my head."

"Oh, Judd…"

He grimaced. "That's exactly what she said when I told her Dan was dead."

"Being a cop is a dangerous occupation," she said. "He knew the risks. So did his wife."

Judd digested her answer. Logically, he knew she was right, but logic and emotions rarely went hand in hand.

"Charlotte?"

Charlie looked up. Rarely did anyone call her by her full name, but hearing the syllables roll softly out of Judd's mouth gave her shivers.

"Yes?"

"Can I ask *you* something?"

She hesitated, then managed a smile and nodded. "Sure, why not?"

"Did you love Rachel's father?"

Her smile twisted bitterly. "Once, when I was still naive enough to believe people meant what they said."

Judd flinched. He understood her anger, but was surprised by the answering chord he felt within himself. He knew firsthand the pain of abandonment and lies. Impulsively, he touched the side of her face.

"I'm sorry."

Charlie froze, telling herself to ignore the warmth of his palm against her cheek and the tenderness in his voice.

"You have nothing to apologize for," she said shortly, and turned away before she made a fool of herself.

Judd sighed. He felt sad, frustrated, even though he understood her unwillingness to compromise. She'd done it once and look what had happened.

And then the sound of little footsteps pattering down the hall broke the mood. Moments later, Rachel came into the kitchen, her blanket bunched under her arm like a sack and her thumb in her mouth. Her curls were in tangles and, once again, she was missing a sock. She was so endearing, he reached down and picked her up. Without thinking, he nuzzled his nose against the side of her neck, inhaling the sweet baby scent, and gave her a soft kiss on the cheek.

"Good morning, punkin. What's that you have in your mouth?"

Then he teased at her thumb, tugging gently without intending to remove it from her mouth. The unexpected game brought a giggle out of Rachel that warmed Judd's heart.

Charlie was mesmerized by what she was seeing. The trust her daughter had just given to Judd was surprising, as was the lump in Charlie's throat. All she could think was, so this was what their lives would have been like if Pete Tucker had been a different man. Rachel would have had a father and she would have had a—

She inhaled sharply and reached for the eggs, angrily breaking them one by one into a bowl. Stop it, she warned herself. Stop it right now. Fantasizing was one thing, but letting it go too far could be dangerous.

Wade came in on Rachel's heels, and soon the kitchen was full of noise and laughter and Rachel begging for something to eat. And in the midst of it all, Judd sat, quietly watching and absorbing the love that bound them. Wade left soon afterward in his patrol car, leaving Judd to ride into town later with Charlie. The day was already full of things to be done. Charlie had shopping to do. Rachel had a checkup at the doctor's. Wade had a missing man to find, and Judd needed to see a man about fixing his Jeep. Ordinary things on an ordinary day. But why, Judd wondered, if it was so ordinary, did he feel as if he was on the brink of discovery?

Waves of pain rolled across Raymond Shuler's leg and up the muscles in his back. He'd lost track of time. Living behind the blindfold and gag was disorienting. Day turned to night, then back to day again. Every time he began to come to, someone poked a needle in his butt and sent him back to La La Land, which was fine with him. Lack of consciousness made his situation more bearable. He knew little more than he had when he'd first been taken, other than the fact that he was still naked, and whatever they'd done to his hip was probably infected. The heat from the wound permeated his entire body, often racking him with fever and chills. The mattress on which he was lying belly-down smelled like chicken feathers and dust. If he hadn't been so sick, he would have been starving. Except for water, not a morsel of sustenance had passed his lips since this nightmare began. Every now and then when lucidity came, he would try to figure out who could have possibly done this to him.

In his business, he made enemies, but it went with the territory of being a banker. However, as hard as he had tried, he couldn't think of one single man he'd pissed off who had enough guts to carry this through. So where did that leave him? Tied up and hurting in some godforsaken place, that's where. All he could do was pray that, one way or another, it would soon be over.

Judd exited the body shop, satisfied that his vehicle was in good hands. Now all he had to do was exhibit some patience. It would take a week, maybe longer, for the parts to come in, and then time after that for Harold to repair the damage. Ordinarily, such a delay would have been frustrating, but for some reason, he felt as if he'd been given a reprieve. At least he had a valid excuse for staying on in Call City, instead of passing through as he'd planned.

He glanced up at the sky, gauging the building cloud bank against a possible threat of rain, and then looked around for Charlie's car. When he'd seen her last, she'd been going into the doctor's office with Rachel. Sure enough, the car was still in the parking lot. He paused, debating with himself about checking in on her first or going on to the police station. Truth be told, his curiosity over the missing banker was starting to grow. But he thought of Charlie, trying to cope with a wiggly baby and a sore ankle, and opted for the doctor's office first.

The street was nearly deserted. A couple of cars were parked two blocks down on his left and there was another in the parking lot beside Charlie's car. An old red hound ambled out of an alley and started across the street, sniffing along the pavement as it went. Several blocks away, a hulking figure of a man was coming up the street toward him, pulling a child's red wagon as he went. Every now and then he would stop and dig through the trash cans at the edge of the curbs, obviously searching for recyclable cans.

Judd grinned to himself. This was a far cry from the big-city atmosphere of Tulsa. He stood for a while, watching the fervor with which the man searched. It was only after he'd come a bit closer that Judd realized the man was quite young, and obviously slow, both in mind and body. The childlike expressions that crossed the man's face were quite touching, and his heart went out to the man-child who would never grow up.

A couple of minutes passed. Finally, the man was only a few yards away.

"Looks like you've got quite a load," Judd said, pointing to the bed of the wagon and the rattling cans.

The man looked up, startled by the presence of a stranger.

The moment Judd spoke, he regretted the impulse. It was obvious the man was frightened.

"My name is Judd Hanna," he said. "I'm staying with Wade and Charlie Franklin. Do you know them?"

The man's face lit, from the inside out. "Rachel," he said, nodding eagerly.

Judd smiled. "Yes, and Rachel," he added. "So, she's charmed even you. What's your name, son?"

"Davie. My name is Davie."

Judd held out his hand. "Hello there, Davie. Pleased to meet you."

Davie hesitated, but only for an instant. He knew about handshakes. He just hadn't been offered one before. He wiped his hand on his shirt and then clasped Judd's hand, giving it a vigorous shake.

Judd noted that the man's clothes were clean, and his hair, while in need of a cut, was definitely not shaggy. Someone was taking good care of him.

"I'm going to work now," Davie announced, and reached for the wagon tongue.

Judd smiled as Davie moved past him. "Good hunting," he said.

But Davie was already focused on more important matters, like the next untested garbage can and the treasure trove of cans that might be waiting.

Judd started across the street to the doctor's office as the sound of rattling cans faded behind him. He entered to the sound of a baby's cry, and to his dismay, saw Rachel in tears with Charlie not far behind. Ignoring the curious stares of the others in the waiting room, he hurried toward them.

"What's wrong with her?" he said, cupping the back of Rachel's head.

Charlie looked up, her eyes filled with sympathetic tears.

"It was time for her last booster shot. She's pretty unhappy with me and the world right now."

"Bless her heart," Judd muttered.

Upon seeing a new and sympathetic face, Rachel set up another howl and held out her hands for Judd to take her.

"Do you mind?" Charlie asked. "I need both hands to write this check."

Judd grinned and lifted the baby out of Charlotte's arms.

"It would be my pleasure," he said. "Come with me, little girl. Let's go see if we can see any birds."

Rachel hiccuped on a sob, hushing almost instantly. "Birds?"

He grinned. "Yeah, punkin. We're going to look for some birds." Then he winked at Charlie. "We'll be outside, scanning the skies."

She smiled gratefully.

"Tweet-tweet," Rachel said, mimicking the bird sound she'd been taught.

Everyone in the waiting room laughed. Rachel didn't know what was so funny, but being the instant center of attention was a lot better than getting a shot. She gave everyone a teary smile and clung to Judd's collar as they started out the door.

"Here, these might help," Charlie said, handing Judd a plastic sandwich bag full of miniature marshmallows.

"She likes these?" Judd asked.

Charlie rolled her eyes. "Oh, yes. Just don't let her put them all in her mouth at one time."

"Right," he said, looking a little nervous as Rachel reached for the bag.

A few moments later, they were gone.

"Who was that?" the receptionist asked as Charlie handed the woman her check.

Charlie glanced out the window. From where she was standing, she could just see the back of Judd's shirt and the top of Rachel's head, but they were both looking toward the sky. She looked back at the receptionist and stifled a smile. Curiosity was eating her up.

"Oh, you mean Judd? He's the man who saved Rachel and me from Tucker's bull."

Every gaze in the waiting room swerved toward the man outside. They'd already asked about Charlie's limp and learned of their brush with death. But now, to actually see the hero of the moment was too much to ignore.

Then Charlie added, "Actually, he's a policeman from Tulsa, Oklahoma. He's staying at our place while his vehicle is being repaired, and he's graciously agreed to help Wade with the Shuler case."

The receptionist gasped, then stood and leaned across the counter for a better look at the man on the lawn outside.

"He sure is good-looking," she said.

Instantly on the defensive, Charlie dropped her ballpoint pen into her purse and snapped it shut. She'd endured comments from plenty of people about the fact that Pete Tucker had knocked her up and then left her behind, choosing the rodeo life instead of her. Of course, there were plenty more people who thought that when Pete Tucker broke his neck on that bull, he got no more than what he deserved, but that didn't help Charlie's conscience one bit. There was no denying the truth of it all. She'd let a man get too close and come away burned. There was no way she'd let that happen again.

"I'll call you about Rachel's next appointment when it gets closer to time," Charlie said.

The receptionist had been put neatly in her place and she knew it.

"Sure thing, Charlie. You take care of that ankle now, you hear?"

Charlie nodded and started toward the door. All the way across the room, she felt the people's stares and knew she was being judged yet again.

Once outside, she breathed a slow sigh of relief, then gave herself permission to focus on something besides her sordid past.

Unfortunately, the only thing there to focus on was her child and the man who was holding her. The sight of them together tugged at her heart. It occurred to her then that her life was spiraling out of control.

At that moment, Judd turned and Charlie found herself caught in his stare. A long, silent moment passed, and all she could think was, *Lord, don't do this to me again.*

Chapter 4

Charlie pulled out of the parking lot and onto Main Street, but her attention to driving was being distracted by the man beside her. Judd was sitting sideways in the seat and laughing between mouthfuls of marshmallows that her daughter was poking into his mouth. Every other bite that he took, he made a pretend growl and nipped at her baby fingers, which seemed to Rachel to be the height of hilarity. Charlie sighed. That laugh was so like her daddy's, God rest his sorry soul. Then she turned a corner and began slowing down.

"I need to get a prescription filled," she said, and parked in front of the pharmacy.

"I'd be glad to do it for you," Judd said. "Save you an extra step or two."

She hesitated, then gratefully agreed. "Just tell Judith Dandridge, the pharmacist, to bill Wade at the office."

"Will do," Judd said, then he winked at Rachel. "Be back in a minute, punkin. Don't give Mommy all my marshmallows."

Rachel dropped the sack and held out her hands. "Wanna go."

Judd glanced at Charlie. "I don't mind if you don't," he said.

Charlie hesitated, but only briefly. "I suppose it's okay," she said. "But don't let her talk you into anything. She's had enough sweets, and whatever you do, don't put her down. The last time we were in there, she tipped over an entire rack of condoms. When I bent down to start picking them up, she began poking them in my purse."

Judd threw back his head and laughed. He was still chuckling as he pulled Rachel out of her car seat.

"Come on, kiddo. You sound like my kind of girl."

Charlie handed him the pill bottle to be refilled and managed a smile, but her knuckles were white from gripping the steering wheel too tightly as she watched them disappearing into the pharmacy. The image of a big strong man carrying a tiny child was too touching to be ignored. And the smiles of delight on each of their faces only added to her fears. At that moment, she would have liked nothing better than to sit there and cry. But letting go of her emotions was a luxury she couldn't afford.

God, please take away this feeling. I don't want to want that man.

Then she sighed again and looked toward the street, trying to focus on something besides the lump in her throat. Unfortunately, the near-empty street was a mirror to her own life. Granted, she had a brother who loved and cared for her, and she had her child. There was nothing Charlie loved more than being Rachel's mother. But a valid part of her life was missing. She took care of Wade and Rachel and their home—but there was no one to take care of her. She slept alone and wept alone, and for the most part, considered it her just due. But every now and then, something or someone would come along and remind her of how lonely her life really was. It was those times, like now, when she would have traded almost anything to be held in a man's loving arms.

Had Judd been aware of Charlie's feelings, he would have had an entirely different set of thoughts in his mind. But he was too busy fielding Rachel's chatter and grabbing at her busy little hands to worry about the woman they'd left behind. When he got to the prescription counter, he glanced at the pharmacist's name tag as he set the bottle on the counter and wondered about her stern expression. Dandridge. Not Judith, or Miss or Ms., just Dandridge. She was tall, almost as tall as he, and although she didn't look to be more than forty or so, her thick straight hair was iron-gray with a mannish, military cut. Once, he thought, she would have been considered an attractive woman, but now it was hard to see past the bitterness on her face.

"Ma'am," he said, handing her the empty pill bottle. "Charlotte Franklin wants this refilled, please, and she asked me to tell you to bill it to Wade at his office."

The woman took the bottle, noted the name, then gave Judd a considering stare before looking over his shoulder to the window behind him. Only after she was satisfied that Charlotte Franklin was truly waiting outside in the car did she step back.

"What's wrong with Charlie?" she asked. "Why didn't she come in?"

"She's got a sprained ankle."

Judith nodded, then reached for a bottle on a shelf behind her.

As they waited, Rachel patted Judd on the cheek. When he pretended to growl at the little fingers inching toward his mouth, she giggled.

Judith turned. A faint smile broke the somberness of her expression.

"Rachel is a sweet baby, but she's a handful."

Judd nodded. "I'm finding that out."

She poured a number of pills into a small tray and began counting them out.

"Are you kin?"

"No, ma'am. Just passing through."

The smile disappeared almost instantly. "Men have a way of doing that," she muttered.

Judd arched an eyebrow, but wisely kept his thoughts to himself. Obviously, this woman wasn't enamored of the male sex.

A couple of minutes later, she handed him a small white sack. Then, almost as an afterthought, handed Rachel a lollipop.

Suddenly shy, Rachel took it, then turned her face against Judd's neck. Judd froze. The soft baby breaths against his cheek were almost his undoing. Never in his life would he have imagined that a female this small could make him feel so weak. He swallowed around a knot in his throat and gave the woman a brief nod.

"Thank you, ma'am."

Clutching her lollipop, Rachel glanced up at the woman and gave her a bashful smile.

"Sank you, ma'am," Rachel echoed.

Judd chuckled, then to his surprise, saw a slow smile finally break the somberness of Judith Dandridge's face.

"Come on, punkin, let's go find Mommy."

"Mommy," Rachel echoed, and clutched tightly at the collar of Judd's shirt as they started for the door.

Charlie thought she was prepared for their return, but when they came out the door and headed for her car, her heart skipped another beat. From his long, sure stride, to the breadth of his chest, Judd Hanna was about as much man as she'd ever seen. And although his face was half-hidden by the brim of his cowboy hat, the sensuous curve to his lower lip was a tease. Would he make love with as much force as he moved through life? Probably. She shuddered, then shoved the thought from her mind.

"Well, that was entertaining," Judd said as he slid into the seat after buckling Rachel back in hers.

Charlie looked startled. "Did Rachel misbehave?"

"I was referring to the pharmacist."

Charlie started the car, but hesitated before putting it in reverse.

"I'm sorry. I didn't think. Judith is a little different. Did she give you a hard time about filling the prescription?"

Judd shrugged. "It wasn't that. I just had the feeling the whole time I was in there that I could have cut my own throat in front of her and she would have stood and watched me die."

"I don't get it," Charlie said.

"I mean, she doesn't much like men."

Charlie put the car in gear. "I can understand how that might happen."

Judd blinked, suddenly reminded of Charlie's history with Rachel's father and decided that the wisest path at the moment was to keep his mouth shut. However, Charlie seemed to be filled with a new curiosity.

"Judd."

"Yeah?"

"Did she say anything about… I mean, what did she say when you asked her to…uh—"

Judd sighed. He suspected what she was trying to say, but until she did, second-guessing her did neither of them any good.

"Just spit it out, Charlotte."

Charlie stopped for a red light and gave Judd a glare.

"All right, fine," she snapped. "Did she act like she thought something was going on between us?"

Judd's gaze raked Charlie from head to toe. It was only after he refocused on her mouth that he spoke.

"You mean, do I think she thinks we're sleeping together?"

Charlie flushed, but nodded.

"Hell if I know," he said softly, careful that Rachel didn't overhear his answer.

Charlie's shoulders slumped. "She probably does. My reputation hasn't been all that good since Pete— "

Judd interrupted angrily. "I think you judge yourself harsher than others judge you."

Charlie glared back. "You don't know what you're talking about," she snapped. "You don't know what it's like to be the butt of everyone's jokes, or to hear a noisy room come to instant silence when you enter."

Judd thought of his childhood and his expression went flat. "Oh, lady, but yes I do. And in ways you can only imagine, so don't start feeling all sorry for yourself. You're not the only one life has kicked in the teeth."

Charlie went pale. Her thoughtless words had obviously struck a nerve, which reminded her she knew virtually nothing about the man except his name.

"Look, I'm sorry, I didn't mean to—"

"Just drop it," he said shortly, then glanced at his watch. "I'll help you with Rachel while you're getting groceries, and then I'd better start making good on my promise to Wade to help out with the Shuler case."

"Of course," Charlie said, and put the car in gear.

Even though she knew separating herself from this man was all for the best, she felt regret, even guilt, that he seemed anxious to leave her presence.

An hour later, Charlie was on her way home and Judd was going through the evidence Wade had collected pertaining to the missing banker.

"Is this all?" Judd asked as he sorted through the half-dozen photos and the pages of notes.

Wade nodded. "Told you I didn't have much to go on."

Judd whistled softly beneath his breath. "This isn't 'much,' this is nothing. No fingerprints, no tracks, no witnesses, no blood, no motive, no ransom note. Lord have mercy, my friend, what you need here is a miracle."

Wade dropped into his chair with a solid thump, his expression as morose as his attitude.

"Like I don't know that," he muttered.

But the facts didn't put Judd off. He had always liked a challenge. This should make him happy as hell.

He stood and walked to the front windows overlooking the street.

"How about grudges or angry clientele from the bank?"

Wade shook his head. "Raymond has lived here all

of his life. He wasn't the most popular person in town, but definitely also on no one's hit list." Then he added, "That I can tell."

Judd nodded. "What did Mrs. Shuler have to say? Did you check her angle? Does she have money troubles? Is there a big life insurance policy against Raymond's life? Maybe she's got someone on the side."

Wade snorted softly. "Betty? She's beside herself. Not only does she care for the sorry so-and-so, she wouldn't want to lose her social standing in the community. As for cheating on him, hell, no. There are no secrets in a town this size. Everyone knows everyone else's business. Being the bank president's wife gives her major clout within the women's circles."

Judd turned around. "So you're saying that Raymond Shuler is every woman's answer to a successful marriage?"

Wade frowned. "No…yes…hell, how do I know. From where I sit, Shuler is almost bald, about twenty pounds overweight and has a tendency to use his power to bend people to his way of thinking." Then he sighed. "But there's no law against being a bully, and to my knowledge, he's never laid a hand on his wife."

"Okay, so that's what you know. Now let's start at the beginning…again. You say Shuler was abducted as he was getting into his car?"

"We think so," Wade said. "He was reported missing, and then we found his car. The driver's-side door was open, the dome light was still on, and the keys were in the ignition. The briefcase he'd had with him at the meeting was on the front seat and there was even a couple of dollars in plain sight in the ashtray. Basically, the only thing missing was Raymond."

"I'm assuming you impounded the car?"
Wade nodded.
"I want to see it."
Wade stood, grinning slightly. "That, I can do."

It was daytime. Raymond could tell that much from the temperature in the hot, airless room. His hip still pained him, but less than it had. He wondered what they'd done to him, and then stifled the thought for a more pertinent concern. It wasn't so much what *had* happened as what *had yet* to come.

The fact that the kidnappers had yet to feed him was another fact against his hope for release. Obviously, they didn't care if he lived or died, and then he remembered they had given him water and, besides the stuff that made him sleep, some sort of antibiotic to offset his injury.

He flinched as something lit on his hip and then began crawling around on his flesh. Moments later, he realized it was only a fly. He flexed a muscle, trying to shoo it away, but the pain of the motion was too great. Moments later, he felt it light again, and it occurred to him then that the fly could, at this very moment, be looking for a nice nasty place to lay some eggs. He thought of the festering wound on his hip and groaned beneath his gag. Dear God, maggots! What if he got maggots in the wound?

He began to moan and thrash, trying to pull himself free from his bonds, but nothing budged. In the midst of his panic, he heard footsteps. He paused, listening intently, trying to decipher the length of stride and any accompanying sounds. When the hinges on the door suddenly squeaked, he flinched. Whoever it was had

come back. Was this it? Would they finally let him go—
or had they come to kill him?

Inside his mind, he was screaming. Then he smelled
something sharp and tangy, like the scent of an orange
being squeezed, and felt the familiar prick of a needle.
Soon, cognizance began to slide. On the verge of un-
consciousness, he heard something familiar—something
he'd heard a hundred times before. It buzzed and buzzed
in a rapid, repetitive fashion.

He sighed. Everything faded, and the imminent revelation was lost.

A ripple of thunder ripped through the sky, rattling
the windows near Judd's bed. His sleep was restless,
his dreams filled with places that, in daytime, his mind
refused to go. Outside, the darkness of the night was a
mirror to the terror he was reliving. Although he was
safe and dry inside the Franklin household, his mind had
taken him back to the place of his youth where, crouched
beneath the cellar steps and hovering in the shadows,
he prayed he wouldn't be found. The scent of mold and
dirt was thick in his nostrils and the thin fabric of his
T-shirt was drenched in sweat born of fear. In the brief
ten years of his life, he'd been through more hell than a
soldier in war. Through all the fear and hunger—all the
pain and suffering at Joe Hanna's hands—he was like a
rat in a maze with no way out.

Outside, the gusting wind from the oncoming storm
whipped a tree limb against the house, pulling it across
the siding in a teeth-grinding scratch. But in Judd's
mind, the sound had become a floorboard suddenly
creaking above his head. A shudder racked his body as
he held his breath and slid quietly onto the floor.

A distant flash of lightning briefly lit up the Wyoming sky, but he was seeing the pie-slice of light spilling down the stairway from the kitchen into the cellar below.

Outside the Franklin household, a water bucket bumped against the fence post on which it was hanging, caught in the gusty front. But to Judd, it was the thump of footsteps on the stairs just above his head.

A faint wail of distress from Rachel's bedroom suddenly broke the silence within the old farmhouse, only Judd heard the wild shriek of Joe Hanna's voice as he dragged him into the light. He didn't hear Charlie come running down the hall, or see the light come on in Rachel's room. Instead, he groaned audibly and prepared himself for the blows.

It was the sudden silence that yanked him out of the dream. He sat straight up in bed, his heart pounding, his body slick with sweat. His boots were right beside the chair he'd sat in as he'd taken them off. His jeans were on a hanger on the back of the closet door, and his Stetson was on a hook near the window. It took a few moments for reality to surface—for him to realize that he was not in the cellar, and that he hadn't seen his father in more than twenty-five years.

"Son of a bitch," he muttered, and crawled out of bed.

Across the hall, he could hear the soft, soothing timbre of Charlie's voice as she put her baby back to sleep, and one door down, the familiar sound of Wade's intermittent snores. Unwilling to stay in the room with his ghosts, he put on his jeans and then slipped out of his room. He needed some air.

But as he opened the front door and stepped out on the porch, he flinched. A storm was brewing and he hadn't even noticed. He lifted his chin, as if bracing himself for a blow. The unsettled elements fit his mood—dark, stormy, threatening. With a muffled curse, he took several deep breaths and then closed his eyes, willing the memories away.

Charlie sat in the old pine rocker, looking down in the lamp light to the baby asleep in her arms. Whatever had disturbed Rachel's sleep was past. Longing for the comfort of her own bed, Charlie sighed wearily, then stood and laid Rachel down, covering her with her blanket before turning out the light. Giving the room one last glance, she tiptoed out. It was only after she was standing in the hall that she realized Judd's door was ajar. She glanced in. His bed was empty. Thinking he'd probably gone to the bathroom, she started to go back to her own bed when she became aware of a draft on her bare arms and legs. She frowned. Had she left a window open somewhere? If she had, it would surely rain in before morning. The thought of cool sheets and soft pillows drew her, but she stifled the urge and went in search of the open window, instead.

She didn't expect to see the front door wide open, or the man standing in the dark out on the porch. But the moment she saw him, her heart skipped a beat. There was something about the thrust of his chin and the way he was standing that made her think of a man facing a firing squad, defiant to the end. Her instincts were to go to him, to put her arms around him and take away his pain, but self-preservation kept her motionless. And then he turned. His expression was shadowed, but she could tell by the jerk of his shoulders that he was surprised by her presence.

"Judd?"

He took a step backward.

She moved toward the screen door, pushing it wide as she stepped onto the porch.

"Did Rachel's cries awaken you?"

He didn't answer.

She frowned. "Are you all right?"

Then she saw his face. Her first instinct was to run, her second was to express empathy. The latter won. She took a step forward.

When she moved, he panicked. Her sympathy would be his undoing.

"I'm fine," he said briefly, thankful that his answer stopped her. She was already too close.

Charlie frowned. "If you're sure…"

Judd laughed, but the wind caught the sound and carried it away. She shuddered. Somehow, she didn't think the laugh came from joy.

Judd shoved his hands in his pockets to keep from reaching for her. He needed her to leave—now—before he made a fool of himself.

"Sure? Am I sure? Hell, Charlotte, the only sure thing in this world is that life will kick you in the teeth if you smile."

Charlie gasped. The bitterness in his voice hurt her heart. Not even at her lowest, when she'd known Pete Tucker was never coming back, had she felt as bereft as he sounded. The urge to soothe him was strong. This wasn't the man she'd seen laughing with Rachel over marshmallows, or even the man who had pried too close to her own secrets. This was a man she didn't know.

"Is this about your partner…the one who died?" she asked.

"*This* isn't about anything," he said shortly, and pivoted and stepped off the porch onto the grass. The blades felt cool beneath his bare feet, but he knew better than to go too far. Snakes were night crawlers, and he wasn't looking to add to his troubles by getting bitten.

Charlie hesitated, then followed him off the porch.

He didn't hear her coming, and when her fingers curled around his arm, he jumped, steeling himself to stay calm.

"You shouldn't be out here barefoot," he said.

"Neither should you."

He sighed, then combed a hand through his hair in frustration.

"Look, I couldn't sleep. Thought I'd get a little air, that's all."

The wind was getting stronger now, whipping loose strands of Charlie's hair around her face and neck and plastering her sleep shirt to her body. He tried not to look, but it was impossible to ignore the generous thrust of breast and slender curves beneath the soft fabric.

Charlie glanced up at the sky. A streak of lightning tore through the darkness. Thunder belched. The storm was getting closer. She slid her hand to his wrist, then grabbed his hand and began to tug.

"Please, Judd, come inside. The storm is getting closer."

Her gentleness was his undoing. He shrugged free of her grasp, only to cup her face with his hands. To her credit, she stood her ground.

He moved closer. His need to forget what he'd dreamed was all wrapped up in his desire to lay claim to her, to see if her lips were as soft as they seemed.

"Charlotte, I…"

Her hands suddenly splayed in the middle of his chest. He froze. The storm was closer now; the first drops of rain were just beginning to fall.

"Judd…please," she begged.

He took a deep breath. "Please what?" he whispered.

A shaft of lightning split the night, somewhere between the house and the barn.

"Run!" she cried, then grabbed his hand and bolted for the porch.

He had no option but to follow.

Moments later, they were inside and she was locking the door. Before anything else could be said, Wade was coming up the hall with his boots in his hands.

"What's going on?" he asked, giving them a curious stare.

"Rachel had a bad dream," Charlie said. "She woke Judd up. Didn't you hear her?"

Wade sighed wearily as he dropped down on the sofa to put on his boots.

"Hell, no, I didn't hear anything but that phone ringing in my ear. There's a wreck just off the main highway outside of town that's blocking the road. I'll be back when it's cleaned up."

"Need any help?" Judd asked.

Wade glanced at Charlie, then shook his head. "No, I'd rather you stayed here with my girls," he said softly, and gave his sister a hug. "Turn on the television and keep track of the weather, honey. This time of year, you never know what it's going to do."

"Okay," she said, and then locked the door after Wade as he left.

Now the house was quiet. Too quiet. Charlie glanced at Judd. He was staring at her. Breath caught in her throat. She lifted her chin, meeting his gaze. He took a step toward her and then stopped as Rachel began to cry in earnest.

"She's afraid of storms," Charlie said, and bolted down the hall, thankful for the interruption.

A few moments later, she came back into the room, carrying Rachel and her blanket, then sat down in Wade's easy chair and began to rock.

And so they sat, staring at the flickering lights from the television screen because it was safer than looking at each other.

Chapter 5

Wilma Self had been born and raised in Call City, and since the death of Francis Belcher more than seventeen years ago, she had been their only librarian. Rain or shine, like the postman, Wilma considered it her duty to open the doors promptly at 8:00 a.m. She was big on duty and short on patience, which could have been part of the reason she'd never been married. Every day except Sunday, she walked the four blocks from her house to the library, using the back entrance. It gave her time to put away her things and smooth down whatever flyaway strands the wind might have tugged from her hairdo. Wilma was also rather fond of coffee, and always started a pot brewing upon arrival, to have with the sweet rolls she would bring from home.

And, as always, after her coffee had been poured and she'd changed the date on the check-out stamp at the front desk, she went to unlock the front door. She was short and plump, and pushing forty, but her step was light. Moments later, she turned the dead bolt and opened the door. After last night's rain, the day was clear with only a few floating clouds overhead. But it wasn't the sunshine that bugged Wilma's eyes. It was the naked and unconscious man on the steps that set her pulse to hammering. She recognized him at once. It was Raymond, all right. Dirty, and in places, even bloody, but in all his natural glory. She gasped, then pressed her fingers to her lips, torn between the knowledge that she must notify the police and the urge to stare at that which she'd never seen—namely, the male body in naked form. Her face flushed as she fought the urge to lean closer. Moments later, the corners of her mouth turned down in disappointment. After all the fuss, she'd expected so much more. Then Raymond began to stir, and Wilma regained her senses by letting out a scream that carried all the way to the gas station two blocks away on the corner.

The attendant came running out from the garage with a wrench in his hand, ready to do battle. Even from that distance, he could see that Wilma was out of her element. He yelled at the kid pumping gas to call the police, then started running. It would be his first visit to the library in more than twenty-two years.

Wade was on his way out the door when the telephone rang. He paused, knowing that at this time of the morning, it was usually for him. He looked back, watching Charlie's expression as she answered the phone.

"Wade, it's Martha. She sounds hysterical. Can't make too much of what she's saying other than it's about Raymond Shuler."

Wade bolted for the phone as Judd entered the kitchen, his hat in hand. Today was to be his first full day on the job and he was surprisingly eager.

"What's up?" he asked.

Charlie shrugged, and then spun to rescue the baby's milk cup before it fell off of her high chair.

"This is Wade. What's up?" Then he frowned and interrupted the caller. "Martha... Martha...listen to me. Take a deep breath and start over."

The daytime dispatcher did as she was told, and in the process accidentally swallowed her chewing gum. After a short coughing spell, she regained her momentum.

"You better get here quick," she said. "Raymond Shuler just turned up on the steps of the library."

Wade's heart skipped a beat. "The hell you say. Is he dead?"

Martha giggled. "No, but he was butt-naked. Wilma Self ain't never gonna be the same." Then she added, "He had some sort of injury to his hip. Oh, and Chief, just thought I would remind you that today is Hershel's wedding, and he ain't gonna be any help to you at all."

Wade sighed. On a good day, the young man who was his deputy caused more problems than he solved. He could only imagine the kid's state of mind today.

"It doesn't matter," he said. "For God's sake, don't call him in. I've already got backup in place until he gets back." Then he added, "Did you send for an ambulance?"

"Yes, sir. One's already on the way from Cheyenne."

"I'm on my way," Wade said, and disconnected. Then he turned to Judd. "Better fasten that Stetson down real tight," he muttered. "Our missing banker just showed up naked on the library steps. Other than some sort of injury to his hip, he seems to be fine."

Charlie grinned. "That I would have loved to see."

"Well, according to Martha, Wilma Self got more than an eyeful. Says she'll never be the same."

Judd stifled a grin as Charlie laughed aloud.

"I'll call you later, sis. If you need anything, just give Martha a buzz. She'll know where to find us."

Charlie nodded, watching as Wade bent down to kiss his niece goodbye.

"Unca Wade," Rachel cried, waving her spoon toward his nose.

"Hey, shortcake, watch where you're waving that thing," Wade said, and removed the spoon from her hand before kissing her cheek. Then he handed back the spoon and tweaked her nose for good measure.

They started to leave when Rachel let out a screech. Everyone stopped, then turned to see what was wrong. Rachel was holding up her arms toward Judd, just as she had the day he'd taken her into the pharmacy with him.

"Wanna go! Wanna go!" she cried.

Judd looked startled while Wade and Charlie stared. He glanced nervously at Charlie, then walked back to where the little girl was sitting.

"Hey, punkin, you can't go with me today, but if you're a good girl for Mommy, when I come back, I'll bring you a surprise."

Rachel frowned. Only a few of Judd's words sank in. One of them was *can't,* the others were *good girl* and *surprise.*

"Surprise," she suddenly stated.

Everyone laughed, which brought forth a wide grin.

She giggled, and when Judd bent down to kiss her, she sopped the side of his face with the milky spoon.

"Best kiss I've had all day," Judd said as he straightened.

"Here," Charlie said, handing him a towel to wipe his face. "I don't know whether to thank you for hushing the fit, or give you a lecture for bribing her to be good."

Judd wiped his face and then gave her a slow, studied look.

"She might be little, but she's still female. I didn't do anything to her that I wouldn't have done to you."

Charlie blinked, a little startled by his answer. "Exactly what do you mean by that?"

Judd never broke a smile. "I don't pretend to know diddly about what makes women tick, but I have learned over the years that to get along with one, I have to keep her in a good mood, and honey, if bribery is what gets me off the hook, then consider yourself forewarned."

Wade was grinning from ear to ear.

Charlie was momentarily speechless. The sexual tension between them was growing with every passing day. She'd been sleepless for hours after the episode on the front porch last night, trying to tell herself to leave well enough alone. But her heart kept overriding her head. Now he was playing with her, and she knew it. But unless she chose to reveal her own frustrations to Wade and the rest of the world, she was stumped.

"Oh…you're such a man," she muttered.

At that point, Judd laughed. It was a quiet, secretive sort of chuckle that held promises only Charlie understood.

"Guilty as charged," he said, and then followed Wade out the door.

* * *

Betty Shuler was sobbing profusely when Wade and Judd exited the hospital elevator. Judd's first thought was that the man must have died. They hastened their steps to get to her.

Wade touched the brim of his hat with his forefinger in a gesture of respect, then introduced Judd to Raymond's wife. In spite of her tears, the woman took time to give Judd a curious glance. She'd heard all the gossip about the good-looking stranger staying out at the Franklin place, but she hadn't really believed he was a cop until Wade introduced him as such.

"Oh, Wade, you should see Raymond's poor hip. It's awful…just awful."

Wade frowned. "What's wrong with it? Was he shot?"

She set up another wail and poked a wad of tissues beneath her nose to stem the flow.

"No," she cried. "The doctor said he's been burned."

Judd grabbed a handful of fresh tissues from a box on the table and handed them to her. She took them, nodding gratefully.

"Ma'am, did he know his captors? Has he said anything to you about where he's been?"

She shook her head. "No, and he says he doesn't remember a thing." Then she frowned. "And that…that mark…it will be there forever."

"What mark, ma'am, the burn scar?"

She rolled her eyes. "Not just a scar. A brand. Those horrible people branded my Raymond."

Wade and Judd exchanged looks, then Wade led the woman to a chair and quieted her down while Judd waited. Judd accepted the fact that this was Wade's territory. He would be the one to call the shots.

A few minutes later a doctor emerged from the room across the hall. Wade identified himself, then introduced Judd.

"When can we talk to Raymond?" he asked.

The doctor shrugged. "Other than the fact that he's been sedated, anytime should be fine, as long as he gives his consent."

"Exactly what are his injuries?" Judd asked.

"Dehydration, a few bumps and bruises, and one hell of a sore on his hip."

Wade frowned. "Mrs. Shuler said it was a brand?"

The doctor shook his head. "Damnedest thing I've ever seen. It's the letter *R*...for Raymond, I suppose. But why someone would kidnap a man just to slap a brand on him is beyond me."

"Thanks, Doc. If we have any other questions, we'll let you know."

The doctor shook their hands and walked away, leaving them with the next step in their investigation—to interrogate the victim himself.

Shuler was propped lying on his side, but he was cognizant enough to appreciate the fact that his hands and feet were no longer tied. His injured hip had been cleaned and bandaged, and the stuff they'd given him for pain was making him woozy, but he remembered that he'd been found. What he couldn't figure out was how. The last thing he had remembered was another knockout shot in that filth, and then coming to on the steps of the library. His ears were still ringing from Wilma Self's screams.

He flinched as the door to his room suddenly opened.

"Raymond, it's me, Wade. Feel like talking to me a bit?"

Raymond sighed. The police chief. Thank God.

"Yes, sure," he mumbled.

When Judd moved into Raymond's line of vision, he saw fear in the man's eyes.

"Sir, I'm Detective Judd Hanna, from Oklahoma."

Shuler frowned, trying to compute in his drug-induced mind why a policeman from Oklahoma would be in Wyoming, and then he sighed. He didn't give a damn who was here, as long as they caught the people who'd done this to him.

Wade put his hand on Raymond's arm, making the man focus his attention.

"What can you tell us about your abduction?"

Raymond started to move and then moaned.

"Easy, Mr. Shuler," Judd said. "Is there something I can get for you?"

"A drink of water."

Judd promptly obliged, waiting patiently while the man took several sips.

"That's better," Raymond said. "Thank you."

"Sure thing," Judd said. "Now, as Wade was saying… what do you remember?"

Raymond frowned. "Nothing except a pain in my head and waking up to realize my clothes were gone and I'd been blindfolded and gagged."

"Did you ever hear their voices?" Wade asked.

"No. Not ever. I don't even know how many were involved. All I do know is that after they burned me, someone kept giving me shots that put me to sleep. I ran a fever. Probably from some infection. They gave me something for that, because the fever finally went away."

"Do you know why you were taken?"

Raymond looked a bit startled. "What do you mean? Wasn't it because of a ransom?"

Wade shook his head. "No, sir. We had no contact with them whatsoever."

Raymond paled. "They never asked for anything?"

"No, sir."

"Then why did they turn me loose?"

Wade's expression changed from serious to stunned. "You mean you didn't escape?"

"No," Raymond muttered. "Hell, I couldn't have crawled from here to the door, let alone gotten myself into town."

At this point, Judd interrupted. "Mr. Shuler, I'm going to ask you a question, and I want you to think very hard before you answer."

"Okay," Raymond said.

"Do you have any enemies?"

Shuler snorted, then winced when the motion caused him pain.

"I'm a banker, sir. Of course I have enemies." Then he added, "But none that I think capable of this."

Judd persisted. "Think back. Before you worked at the bank, what did you do?"

Shuler frowned. "I was in college. Before that, I was in high school. My father owned the bank. I came to work straight out of college and took over when he died."

Wade interrupted. "Judd, exactly what are you getting at?"

"This was never about money," he said.

Both men looked startled, but Raymond was the first to speak.

"I'm sorry, but I'm afraid I don't understand."

Judd never took his eyes from Shuler's face. "What happened to you was a case of pure revenge. Whoever took you wanted you scared and miserable, and the brand is so that even after you're well, you will never forget."

Shuler blanched, while Wade congratulated himself on bringing Hanna into the case. This was an angle he hadn't considered.

"But who?" Shuler whispered.

Judd leaned closer. "You tell us, Mr. Shuler. Think back—five, ten, even twenty years. Have you ever done something you weren't proud of? Something that hurt someone else, maybe not physically, but socially or financially? Enacting revenge is a crime of passion, and the public humiliation they wanted you to suffer is all too obvious."

Shuler looked angry, as if he was insulted by the very notion of what Judd had asked.

"No, of course…" Suddenly, Shuler froze. His eyes glazed over and his mouth went slack. To Judd's surprise, Shuler looked away. Judd knew without asking that something had occurred to him—something he didn't want to admit.

"What?" Wade asked. "Did you think of something that might help?"

"No," Shuler snapped, then closed his eyes. "I need to sleep now."

"Yeah, sure," Wade said. "We'll talk later."

"There's nothing more to tell," Shuler muttered.

Moments later, the two lawmen were standing in the

hall with their hats in their hands as Betty Shuler bid them goodbye and went into Raymond's room.

"Well, that wasn't much help," Wade said.

Judd shook his head, then set his Stetson firmly on his head.

"Oh, I don't know about that. If I read the man right, I think he remembered something he'd rather forget."

Wade shrugged. "Maybe so, but that's all we're going to get out of him for now. He'll be released soon. We'll talk with him some more after he comes home." Then he grinned. "And speaking of home, it's time we were heading back. No telling what sort of mischief has been going on in Call City with me out of town."

They headed for the door, their long legs matching strides. As they reached the police cruiser, Judd paused.

"Wade?"

"Yeah?"

"What's it like being the only cop in town?"

Wade grinned. "Busy."

"Did you ever think of working in a larger place? You know…where you would at least have someone to work another shift. From what I can see, you're basically on call twenty-four hours, seven days a week."

Wade nodded. "That's about the size of it, and while a competent deputy or two would be nice, nothing would be worth what I'd lose if I lived somewhere else. Call City suits me, and even more, it suits Charlotte and Rachel. I don't want that baby growing up in the big city and getting lost in the hell that goes on there."

Judd nodded as he got into the car. He reached for the seat belt and then paused.

"I know what you mean, but it seems to me that

you've got your own sort of hell going on right now with Shuler."

Wade frowned. "Yeah, you're right. You know, I really appreciate your input on this. I might have thought about that revenge angle somewhere down the road, but not this soon."

"What do you think?" Judd asked.

"I think maybe you've gotten too close to some of old Raymond's skeletons. He sure did turn off the congeniality when you started asking about his past."

Judd nodded. "Maybe when we get back to headquarters, we can do a background check on the man. I have a feeling that your answer is somewhere in Shuler's past."

"Good idea. We better get cracking. I want to find out who was responsible for this. The last thing I need is a repeat performance by the perp."

A few miles down the road, Judd turned to Wade.

"Before we go home tonight, I need to stop by the grocery store and get Rachel's surprise. Even though she's only two, I have a feeling she won't have forgotten it."

Wade gave Judd a considering look.

"She sure has bonded with you, and that's unusual."

"She's a great kid," Judd said.

"Got any of your own?" Wade asked.

Judd's expression went flat. "No, but if I did, I damn sure wouldn't have bailed out on them like that son of a bitch did to Charlie and Rachel."

Judd's indignation on Charlie's behalf was food for thought as Wade continued toward Call City. On the one hand, he liked Judd Hanna, was even learning to trust him. But on the other, he sensed that the man wasn't the kind who would stay in a place as small as Call City, which led him to his next concern. He was beginning to suspect that Judd and Charlie were interested in each other. His sister was a grown woman. He wasn't about to tell her how to live her life.

But…if Judd Hanna hurt Charlie in any way—

He gritted his teeth and kept on driving. No need to borrow trouble. There was always plenty of the real stuff on hand to keep him busy. As for Judd and Charlie, the safest bet would be to wait and see.

Less than an hour before Wade Franklin's normal quitting time, a jailbreak occurred in Cheyenne. According to reports, the three escapees were last seen heading toward Call City and points north. With the help of the state police, a roadblock was set up on the highway in and out of Call City. Once everything was in place, the officers sat down to wait. Judd's surprise for Rachel, a large bag of multicolored miniature marshmallows, lay on the seat beside him. The longer they waited, the more tempted he was to tear into the bag and sample some of them for himself. But he kept picturing her delight and the powdered sugar that would color her smile, and he just leaned back in the seat and stretched his legs, instead. Almost an hour had come and gone before it dawned on Judd that he was actually content. In Tulsa, being static for this length of time would have gotten on his nerves. He put his hands behind his neck and flexed his shoulder muscles, wondering what it was about this place that made it seem different. Was it the slower way of life, or the people themselves?

In the distance, he could just make out the high school band, practicing on the football field. Off to his right, a herd of cattle was grazing near the highway, oblivious to the unfolding drama only a few yards away. A young girl on a bicycle came pedaling down a dissecting street and was quickly turned back by an officer from the state police. It was calm—almost too calm.

He turned his attention toward the highway stretching out in front of him and stared, watching the meager flow of approaching traffic. Already they'd let a couple of eighteen-wheelers through, a farmer with a truckload of hay, and a school bus loaded with junior high football players en route to a neighboring school. There was always the chance that the escapees would take another route, but until they knew for sure, here they sat.

A few minutes later, the silhouette of another eighteen-wheeler appeared on the horizon. At first, he thought little of it, but as he continued to watch it, he began to tense. He pulled himself straight in the seat, then leaned forward over the steering wheel, staring intently at the way the truck was moving. He got out of the cruiser, then a few seconds later, his hand moved to the butt of the handgun he wore on his hip.

"Wade."

Wade Franklin turned from the conversation he'd been having with one of the state police.

"Yeah, what's up?"

Judd nodded toward the truck. It was less than a quarter of a mile from the roadblock with no signs of slowing down. As they watched, a sudden belch of black smoke puffed from the smokestack. The trucker had shifted gears, all right, but up, not down. The truck was bearing down on them with increasing speed.

"Oh, hell, he's gonna run it," he yelled, waving to the officers.

Men scattered, taking cover behind their vehicles as

they all pulled their guns, waiting for the order to shoot. Tension continued to build as the roar of the diesel engine filled their ears.

Then suddenly, from behind them, came the persistent squeak of an unoiled wheel. Tin rattled and the men turned in dismay to see the lumbering man-child with his little red wagon, standing in the middle of the highway and staring curiously.

Wade broke free from the group and started waving his hands.

"Run, Davie! Get off the highway."

The men groaned in unison when Davie just waved back.

Wade glanced toward the approaching truck. The engine was wide open now and running hot. He looked back at Davie, then made an instant decision. God willing, he just might make it. "Open fire!" Wade shouted. "I'm going after him."

"Aim for the tires," someone yelled, but Judd knew that if they waited for the truck to reach them, it would be too late—for both Davie and Wade. Without thinking of the consequences of his actions, he darted out from behind his vehicle and began running toward the truck, moving parallel with the highway.

When the truck was only a couple of hundred yards ahead, he stopped and took aim. Through the windshield, he could see the figures of three men. The one by the passenger side of the window suddenly leaned out, aimed a rifle across the hood of the truck and fired. Judd flinched at the sound but stood firm. It was just like qualifying at target practice, only this target wasn't paper, and if he missed, the consequences were deadly. Behind him, he could hear the sounds of men running and knew that some of the other officers had picked up on his plan.

His first shot hit the outside tire on the driver's side, ripping through the rubber with deadly force. By the time the tire blew, sending shards of steel-belted rubber into the air, he had already fired his second shot into the tire beside it.

Suddenly, the truck swerved, and Judd could see the three men in the cab scrambling to hang on. As the cab began to tilt, Judd pivoted quickly, then ran up the slope of the shoulder toward a nearby fence, vaulting it with room to spare, before turning and emptying his gun into the tires on the back axle. Other officers followed suit, moving in desperation to get clear of the truck cab that was already on its side and being pushed against the concrete by the momentum of the trailer behind it. Moments later, the trailer followed by falling onto its side. The metal surface of the cab and trailer skidded along the pavement in a high-pitched scream, sending sparks into the air like shards from a welder's torch. It hit the first two police cars in the roadblock, buckling them like empty pop cans. Men were shouting and running, and the stench of diesel fuel was everywhere.

Judd looked back. The little red wagon was right where Davie had been standing, but Wade and Davie were nowhere in sight. Something popped, and a police cruiser burst into flames. He flinched and dropped, covering his head as burning fuel shot into the air. In the distance, the sound of sirens could be heard, and he knew that someone had called the volunteer fire department.

Seconds later, he raised his head. The truck had stopped. Exhaling slowly, he got to his feet.

"You okay, buddy?"

Judd nodded at a highway patrolman who'd taken cover not far from him.

"Damn, that was something," the patrolman said, and then parted the fence wires for Judd to crawl through. He did so, then returned the favor before they headed for the wreck.

Three police cars, as well as the truck, had been totaled. Smoke was spilling out from beneath the hood of the truck cab as the passenger's-side door began to open. A man looked out.

"Don't shoot," he yelled. "I give up."

"Throw out your weapons," someone yelled.

Two handguns and a rifle were promptly ejected.

"I'm comin' out," the man yelled, then, with effort, managed to pull himself out of the overturned cab before dropping to the pavement below.

Another man followed his lead, dropping to his knees and putting his hands behind his head as soon as he got on the ground.

"Artie's dead," the man said as a state policeman cuffed him.

"Artie should have used his brakes," the policeman said, and escorted him to a waiting patrol car.

Judd squinted his eyes against the blowing smoke and circled the wreck, stepping over fire hoses and looking for Wade at the same time.

Then he saw him, standing at the edge of the highway a short distance away, with his arms around Davie, patting him gently on the back. As he neared the little red wagon, he reached for the tongue, then pulled the wagon along with him. The intermittent squeak of the unoiled wheel seemed almost comical after everything else that had occurred.

At the sound, Davie turned. Judd could tell that he'd been crying. *Poor kid. He must have been scared to death.*

"Davie, here's your wagon, all safe and sound."

Davie grabbed the wagon tongue and then dropped to his knees and began frantically counting the cans inside. Judd squatted down beside him, his heart going out to the man who could not count past the number three.

"They're all there, son. Just like you left them, okay?"

The calm, ordinary tone of Judd's voice seemed to help settle the young man's panic.

"All there?" Davie asked.

The lost, vacant look in Davie's eyes struck an echo in Judd's heart. Davie looked like Judd sometimes felt. But before he could say anything more, they heard a woman screaming Davie's name.

They stood. Only Judd seemed surprised by the woman's appearance. It was the steel-jawed pharmacist, Judith Dandridge.

"Davie! Davie!" she shouted as she raced toward them.

Davie began to get nervous all over again. "My aunt Judy is crying," he said, his voice shaking with every breath.

"She's okay," Wade said. "You just scared her, that's all."

Judith reached them moments later and grabbed Davie by the shoulders in a desperate embrace.

"What happened? What happened?" she cried.

"Some prisoners escaped out of the Cheyenne jail.

Davie wandered into the middle of a state police road-block, but he's okay."

Judith paled as she pulled Davie's head down to her shoulders and patted him on the back.

"Davie, darling, you could have been hurt."

"Cans, Aunt Judy. I was lookin' for cans."

Judd watched a muscle jerking at the side of her jaw as she struggled to maintain composure. When they suddenly made eye contact, Judd was struck by how different she appeared now from the woman behind the counter.

"Take him on home," Wade said. "I think he's had enough excitement for one day."

Judith Dandridge nodded, then, taking Davie by the hand, they walked away, accompanied by the rattle and squeak of the little red wagon.

"Damn," Wade said as he watched them walk away. "It's times like these that make me so grateful that Rachel was born healthy and whole."

"So she's his aunt?" Judd asked.

Wade shrugged. "Not really. Judith's parents kept foster children. Davie was the one that never left, so to speak. I think they adopted him when he was around seven, maybe eight. Anyway, her father, Henry Dandridge, owned the pharmacy. After college, she came back to work with him, but when her parents were killed in an accident, she inherited his business...and Davie."

"Hell of a load," Judd muttered.

"Her shoulders are broad," Wade said, then clapped Judd on the back. "Gutsy move back there, going after the truck like you did. It bought me enough time to get Davie out of harm's way." Then he added, "Let's see what's left to do here. Personally, I've had just about enough of this day."

Judd glanced around, taking note of the fact that the police car he'd been driving had come out of the mess unharmed. He thought of Rachel's marshmallows, and of the little girl waiting back home for her surprise.

"Yeah," Judd said. "Besides, I've got a date with a certain little angel and a bag of marshmallows."

Chapter 6

Wade was quiet on the long drive home, and without the need for constant conversation, Judd had the time to appreciate the sunset from the front seat of the car. Tomorrow, the repairs on his Jeep would be finished, but he wouldn't be leaving—not until Wade's absent deputy got back from his honeymoon. He'd promised. Even though the initial condition of his stay had hinged upon the missing banker who had since turned up, Judd knew he wasn't ready to leave. Using the deputy's honeymoon for an excuse did both him and Wade a favor.

As he watched, a bright streak of orange began appearing across the sky, adding a new layer to the purple-hued clouds on the horizon. He sighed. It would be a long time before the images of this day faded from his mind. From the moment he'd walked into the kitchen and had seen Charlie making breakfast and laughing at her child, to the image of Wade standing at the edge of the highway with his arms around Davie's shoulders, it had been a day like no other. The bag of marshmallows he'd bought for Rachel was on the seat beside him. He picked it up, imagining the baby's delight when he handed it over. An awareness came suddenly, like a fist to the gut, frightening him more than any shootout had ever done. He was letting himself become attached— too damned attached—to Wade Franklin's family. In their eyes, he was just a man passing through. But sometime during the past few days, he'd let himself ignore the fact that he'd be moving on. He stared at the sky, watching until all light was gone and there was nothing to see but the first evening star. A distance ahead, a coyote suddenly ran across the highway in front of Wade's car, momentarily caught in the glare of the headlights, and then it was gone. A loner—just like him.

A few minutes later, Wade began slowing down and Judd noticed that they were almost home. As he looked to his right, the headlights revealed the ruts his tires had left as he had spun out through the bar ditch and then through Wade's fence, trying to beat a bull to a little baby girl. That single action, done without a second thought, had changed his life forever.

Then Wade topped the hill just above the old house. There, shining in the window was a lamp, like a beacon to the lost.

Judd pointed. "Charlie must be reading to Rachel. The lamp by your easy chair is on."

Wade chuckled. "No. That's just a family tradition that Mom started years ago when our father worked away from home. She turned on that lamp every night about dusk, and didn't turn it off until Daddy was home."

A shiver ran up the back of Judd's neck as he stared at the warmth of that yellow light piercing the surrounding dark.

"You mean Charlie leaves that on for you every night until you're home."

"Yeah."

"*Every* night?"

Wade nodded.

A knot formed in the back of Judd's throat. He kept thinking of the years of his childhood, and the countless times he'd come home to a dark and empty house to fend for himself. Not once had he ever known that kind of safety. He glanced at Wade and tried not to covet that which was not his. But as they drove into the yard and then parked, Judd knew he was fighting a losing battle. He got out of the car with the marshmallows in his hand and took a deep breath. In his heart, he suddenly knew this was what had been missing. He wanted to be loved—and missed—and trusted like this. And he wanted it bad.

When Charlie saw the headlights of the approaching car, her heart skipped a beat. They were home! It didn't occur to her until she was moving toward the hall mirror to check her hair that she was doing something she never did for Wade—checking her appearance. Added to that, she was wearing a dress and she'd put up her hair. Ignoring the implications of her own actions, she looked at herself in the mirror, making sure she was still in one piece.

The woman looking back seemed scared—but she also looked more alive than she'd been in years. Just for a moment, she let herself imagine what it would be like to welcome Judd Hanna home every night—to be enfolded within his embrace and feel the warmth of his breath on her face…just before he kissed her hello. Angry with herself, she frowned. This was stupid. She'd played with fire once and had gotten burned. But Judd Hanna was a far cry from Pete Tucker. Something told her his fire would consume her. As footsteps sounded on the porch outside, she bit her lip and then turned away.

"Rachel! Uncle Wade is home!"

A faint squeal, accompanied by the pitter-pat of stocking feet, sounded up the hall. Moments later, Rachel came into the room, her face wreathed in smiles as the two men came inside.

Wade grinned and swung her up in his arms, burying his nose in the place below her ear and kissing it soundly, which sent Rachel into giggles. Charlie watched, a smile on her face as the familiarity of the scene played out before her.

But Judd was caught in a very different web—not Rachel's, but Charlotte's. Then he realized the connotation of what he'd thought and almost grinned. Charlotte's web. Wasn't that some children's book—about a pig and a spider? Yes, that was him. Caught in the web of Charlotte Franklin's love. But what dug at him most was that the joy on her face was for her brother and her child, not for him.

So, truth hurts, he reminded himself, but it wasn't going to kill him. He could still store up the memories of Charlotte Franklin—from the way her eyes crinkled at the corners when she laughed, to the way she chewed on the lower edge of her lip when she was trying to be stern.

As he watched her, it occurred to him that her hair looked different tonight. It was the first time he'd seen it up off her neck. It made her look younger, more vulnerable. And she was wearing a dress, instead of her usual T-shirt and jeans. It was made of something yellow that clung to her body as she moved, and he decided that yellow had become his new favorite color. The thrust of her breasts against the fabric was nothing less than a taunt, and he could have spanned her waist with his hands. Her bare arms and neck were a warm, golden tan, as were the sandals she was wearing. He knew, if he moved just the least bit closer, he would smell perfume, as well.

"Sorry we're late," Wade said.

Charlie grinned. "Like this is the first time?" He looked a little guilty, which made Charlie add, "I heard about the roadblock from the dispatcher. I'm just thankful you're both all right."

She glanced at Judd then and smiled, as if finally giving herself permission to look at him, too, when, in fact, she'd been all too aware of him from the moment they'd entered the room.

Judd knew he was staring, but he couldn't make himself stop it.

"Lady, you're sure something to come home to," he said.

Wade looked startled, only then noticing that Charlie was wearing a dress and that her hair was different. Guilt hit him again.

"Yeah, Charlie, you look nice. What's the occasion?"

Charlie could have willingly strangled her brother. "There is no occasion," she muttered. "And I didn't dress up. This dress is at least five years old."

"Maybe so," Judd said. "But it has certainly withstood the test of time."

Then he glanced at Rachel and tweaked a lock of her hair.

"Hey, punkin, I brought your surprise, just like I promised."

When he held out the bag of marshmallows, Rachel squealed with delight and went from Wade's arms to Judd's without a backward look.

Wade arched an eyebrow as his niece abandoned him. "Just like a woman," he drawled, and then laughed. "If my own niece will abandon me for nothing more than a bag of marshmallows, then it's no wonder I'm not married."

Charlie grinned. "We have our priorities," she said, then turned away, ignoring a spurt of jealousy for the fact that her daughter had the luxury of testing Judd Hanna's hugs when she did not. "I kept supper warm," she said. "I'll have it on the table by the time you two wash up."

That night, Judd slept without dreams, secure in the knowledge that for a while, he was safe within these walls in a way that he'd never been before. It wasn't until day was breaking that he roused, and when he did, he lay for a moment, trying to figure out what had wakened him. He cocked his head, listening to the soft scraping sounds in the hallway beyond his door, then the ensuing silence that came afterward. A few seconds later, he heard a distinct thump and then another sound he couldn't decipher. It wasn't Charlie, that much he did know. Over the past few days, he'd learned to distinguish her movements apart from everyone else, like the lightness of her step, the methodical manner in which she prepared all their meals, even the gentleness of her reprimands as she dealt with the messes her baby often made.

As for Wade, he couldn't have been quiet if his life depended on it. He was big and noisy and moved through rooms the way he moved through life. So, Judd thought, that left only one other person who could be making those sounds. Unless there was a burglar in the house, Miss Rachel was up for the day.

He smiled to himself and then rolled out of bed, curious as to what a two-year-old would be bent upon doing at this hour of the morning. He put on his jeans and then slipped into the hall, moving soundless through the house on bare feet. He peeked in the living room, thinking she might have headed for the television, because she'd only recently learned how to turn it on, but she wasn't there. Another thump sounded, this time, accompanied by a small squeak. He spun around. The sound was coming from the kitchen, but when he got there, she was nowhere in sight. Curious as to where she had gone, he stood for a moment, listening.

"Rachel…where are you?" he called.

Total silence.

"Rachel…it's me, Judd."

Still nothing.

A niggle of concern pulled him farther into the room. That was when he noticed that the pantry door was ajar. He turned on the lights, then moved toward it.

She was sitting in the corner of the pantry with her blanket around her neck and the bag of marshmallows in her lap. Already a rim of powdered sugar encircled her lips, and her little chipmunk cheeks were full to overflowing with the mouthful she was trying to chew. She looked up at him and smiled, and as she did, one small syrupy-looking drool slipped out of the corner of her mouth.

For the second time in less than a week, Judd Hanna found himself falling in love. He grinned as he walked inside, then surprised himself, as well as her, by sitting down right beside her.

"Whatcha got, baby girl?"

"'Mallows," Rachel said, talking around the ones already in her mouth.

"Can I have one?" Judd asked.

Pleased that she had an excuse to dig into the sack for more, Rachel crammed her hand into the sack, then poked the tiny marshmallow she pulled out into his mouth.

"Mmm-hmm," Judd said, making a big pretense of smacking his lips and licking her fingers.

As she ducked her head and giggled, another dribble of syrup oozed out of her mouth.

He swiped at it with his thumb, then winked. "Better swallow that bite you've got in there," he said, poking gently on the sides of her cheeks.

She quickly obliged, then before he could stop her, she filled her mouth back up again. It was all he could do not to laugh.

Then to his surprise, Rachel crawled onto his lap, her blanket still around her neck, and continued to dig through the sack, every now and then bestowing him with another bite. Humbled by her trust, he became so focused on watching her that he didn't realize they were no longer alone.

With the instinct of a natural-born mother, Charlie knew without looking that something was amiss with her daughter. Dressing quickly, she slipped out of her room without making a noise, but when she got to Rachel's room, both she and her blanket were gone. Charlie sighed. This new spurt of independence was to be expected, but it was worrisome, just the same. As she started up the hall in search of her daughter, she noticed Judd's door ajar. When she peeked in, she saw that his bed was empty, as well. A bit of her tension eased and she was all the way into the living room before it dawned on her that she was beginning to trust the man—even enough to know that if he and her daughter were together, then that would mean Rachel was safe.

Longing hit her square in the belly, then straight up to her heart. This was getting scary. She didn't know whether to be glad Judd Hanna had awakened her emotions, or worry about what would come next. Either way, it was too late to fret. Awake they were.

A sound came from the vicinity of the kitchen—a soft giggle. Rachel's—she would know it anywhere.

Then an answering chuckle, deep and rumbling. Judd's—she had heard it before, even in her sleep.

She frowned. But what were they doing?

As she stopped at the doorway, she saw them almost immediately, sitting in the shadowy corner of the deep walk-in pantry. She felt like a voyeur. The camaraderie between the pair was impossible to miss. Judd's head was bent to Rachel's tousled curls. His pleasure was obvious, but not nearly as apparent as the joy on her little girl's face.

My baby...she's crossed her first threshold and given her heart to a man.

The moment she stepped into the room, Judd seemed to sense her presence and looked up.

"Uh-oh. Mommy's up. Looks like we've been made."

Rachel fisted the loose edges of the bag as Charlie came toward them.

"Pease?" Rachel said.

Charlie tried to look stern. "Rachel Ann, aren't you asking permission just a little bit late?"

Judd looked almost as nervous as Rachel was acting. "Uh… I heard her and I…then we—"

"Save the excuses for someone who'll believe them," Charlie drawled.

Judd started to get up, when Charlie put her hand on his shoulder.

"Is there room for one more at this table?"

The surprise on Judd's face was impossible to miss, but it was soon followed by a gleam in his eye that made her a little bit nervous.

"Darlin', for you, there'll always be room."

Having set her heart atwitter, he moved his long legs to one side, giving her a place to sit down. To his ever-lasting delight, she did.

The intimacy of sitting side by side and facing each other in the shadowy closet set a mood neither would have dared to suggest. Even with the baby between them, there was an energy impossible to miss.

"So…what's on the menu?" Charlie asked, a little surprised at her own audacity and trying to make light of what she'd done.

Judd peered over Rachel's shoulder into the bag, and then frowned.

"Well, looks like we have 'mallows. Green 'mallows, pink 'mallows, even white 'mallows." Then he added, "But no dry 'mallows. Today, all our 'mallows are being served with a sauce."

Charlie took one look at the mess on her daughter's face and hands and then threw back her head and laughed. It was a hearty, from-the-belly-first laugh that echoed through the house.

Judd listened to the sound coming out of her mouth as his gaze raked the tender curve of her neck. She looked as if she'd combed her hair with her fingers, and her T-shirt and shorts were quite old, but at that moment, he was certain he'd never seen a more beautiful or sexy woman in his life.

"Hey, what's going on in here?"

They looked up, laughter still on their faces. Wade was standing at the pantry door, staring down in disbelief.

Charlie patted the floor and scooted a little closer to Judd, making room for her brother to come in.

"Breakfast is being served," she said. "This morning, Rachel has chosen 'mallows as the menu of choice. Will you have pink ones or green ones, or are you going to be a purist and stay with the white?"

Wade arched an eyebrow, then grinned. "You're all crazy," he said, then lifted Rachel out of Judd's lap. "Sorry, baby girl, but Uncle Wade needs caffeine, not sugar, to get him awake, and you need a bath. However, we'll settle for a good wash at the sink, okay?"

When the weight of her little body left Judd's lap, he felt oddly bereft, even though it was past time to put an end to their snack. He stood, then reached down and offered Charlie a helping hand. After a moment's hesitation, she took it, trying not to concentrate on the way his fingers curled around her hand and wrist, or the breadth of his bare torso.

At the sink, Wade was chuckling beneath his breath as he tried to wrench the sack of marshmallows from

Rachel's grasp, but inside the pantry, another sort of war was in progress.

Charlie was standing now, but Judd refused to let go of her hand. Charlie bit the edge of her lower lip and then looked up. There was a faint smudge of sugar on the side of his cheek, probably from one of Rachel's indiscreet caresses. Without thinking, she reached up to wipe it away when Judd grabbed her hand. For a heart-stopping moment, she was caught. She saw his nostrils flare as he took a deep breath, and instinctively, she closed her eyes for the kiss she knew was coming.

It was brief but tender and Charlie stifled a groan. Even though it was only a kiss, she'd given away more than she should.

All too aware of Wade only a short distance away, Charlie glanced nervously in his direction. To her relief, he hadn't seen a thing.

"Why did you do that?" she whispered.

Judd dropped her hands and then cupped the side of her face. "Just to see if your kisses were as sweet as Rachel's."

Her heart fluttered. "And?"

He leaned forward until his breath was just a whisper against her face. "Lady, I'm going to be on a sugar high all day."

"Hey, what are you two doing in there?" Wade yelled.

"I'm kissing your sister," Judd said. "Do you mind?"

Charlie gasped, her eyes wide with shock. She didn't want Wade to know—not yet. Not when she wasn't even ready to face what she'd done.

Then Judd turned around, tore a length of paper towel from a roll on the shelf and began methodically picking up the marshmallow remnants on the floor.

Charlie stared at the back of his head in disbelief. How could he be so calm? If he knew Wade like she knew Wade, he should be running out the door about now. She stalked out of the pantry, her head held high, and marched straight past Wade to the refrigerator.

"Scrambled or fried?" she asked, yanking a bowl of eggs from the shelf.

Wade gave her a long, considering look, then dried Rachel's face and hands and set her down on the floor.

"How about scrambled?" he asked. "Sort of fits the mood of the moment, wouldn't you say?"

She ripped a wire whisk from a nearby rack and pointed it at Wade.

"Don't say it!" she muttered. "Just don't say a word."

Judd came out of the pantry, tossed the paper towels and marshmallows into the trash, then went to the sink to wash his hands.

Wade gave him a cool, considering look.

"You are a nervy son of a bitch, aren't you, Hanna?"

Judd looked at them then, judging the embarrassment on Charlie's face against a hint of anger on Wade's.

"Yes, I guess I am," he finally said. "But I learned it the hard way. When I was a kid, no matter what I did, I used to get the hell beat out of me on a regular basis, even though I tried to do everything right. I stayed in school. I didn't complain—not even when there was no food in the house, not even when there was no heat or light. When blood was running out of my ears and nose, I lied to my old man and said it didn't hurt. When he didn't come home for days on end, I pretended I didn't care. But no matter what I did, it wasn't enough. And one day, I realized that the only way I was going to survive was to quit worrying about making him happy and take care of myself."

The revelation had come out of nowhere, and Charlie wondered how long this had been festering inside of him. Her embarrassment gone, she reached for his arm. When he smiled coldly, she stepped away.

"Sorry, Charlotte. I'll take almost anything from a woman but sympathy."

She winced but wouldn't back down. "It's called empathy, Judd Hanna, and do you want your eggs scrambled, too?"

Startled by her gutsy change of subject, he blinked, then took a deep breath, making himself relax.

"Sorry, I don't know where that came from."

Wade shook his head. "It's okay."

"No, it's not okay," Judd said. "It's called abusing your hospitality, and I can promise you it won't happen again."

He started out of the room when Charlie called him back.

"Judd!"

He stopped, then turned.

"Yeah?"

"Your father…did he ever change?"

A dark look came and went in Judd's eyes. "Don't know. Haven't seen him since the night I threatened to kill him."

Charlie paled. Wade gritted his teeth.

"Damn, Hanna, when was that?"

"When I was ten." Then he glanced at Charlie and made himself smile. "Don't fix any eggs for me. I'm too full of 'mallows."

She bit her lip to keep from crying as he walked out of the room.

"Oh, Wade…"

Wade sighed, then put his arms around Charlie's shoulders.

"We were lucky, weren't we, sis?"

Then they both looked at Rachel, who was playing in a puddle of sunlight on the bare kitchen floor. Suddenly, tears sprang to Charlie's eyes and she picked her daughter up from the floor and hugged her fiercely.

"Mommy loves you s-o-o-o-o much," she said softly, kissing the little freckle below Rachel's left ear.

Rachel giggled.

After Judd's revelation, it was a bittersweet sound.

Chapter 7

Nothing more was said about what had happened in the kitchen, but the truth of it rode between the two men all the way into town. Judd Hanna was a man with baggage, who had obvious designs on a woman with baggage of her own. And while Wade never said it, Judd sensed his judgment just the same. Basically, it came down to one fact. If Judd was any kind of a man at all, he would resolve his own mess instead of adding to Charlie's.

As they neared the outskirts of Call City, Judd finally spoke.

"If you'd drop me off at the garage, I can pick up my Jeep. As soon as I settle up with the mechanic, I'll come to the office. You can tell me where you want me to go from there."

Wade gave him a considering look. "I appreciate the

fact that you've agreed to stay on, even though Shuler turned up."

Judd shrugged. "It's no big deal," he said softly. "I had no destination in mind when I got here. I still don't. One place is as good as another. Besides, you still don't know who snatched Shuler, or if it will happen again."

"Don't even say that," Wade muttered, and then he shifted the topic of conversation to something else Judd had just said. "What did you mean by having no destination? Aren't you planning to go back to Tulsa?"

Judd shrugged. "I doubt it. Once something's over, I don't ever go back."

Wade's hands tightened around the steering wheel as he thought of Charlie.

"Don't hurt her," he said as he pulled up to the garage and parked.

Judd opened the door, then paused before getting out. He looked down at the ground, taking absent note of the few blades of grass persistently growing between a crack in the blacktop, then nodded without saying a word. Judd closed the door behind him with a solid thump. Wade watched until he'd gone into the office, then he backed out of the drive and headed for the P.D.

Raymond Shuler was home and healing nicely. The infection in his hip was almost gone and his attitude, at least on the outside, was positive. Friends, neighbors and colleagues came on a regular basis, each wanting to hear all about his ordeal. He was basking in the notoriety of being a five-minute celebrity, but at the same time, was struggling with the shame of being found naked and unconscious on the library steps. Only one other time in his life had he ever been that disoriented—or suffered that much loss of control—and he'd been a senior in high school, only a couple of months away from graduation. To this day, he didn't remember a damn thing about what he'd done, only that he'd started the night by celebrating homecoming at a football game and wound up facedown near a creek the next morning, waking up to a squirrel chattering in the trees overhead and suffering from the worst headache he'd ever had in his life. He'd rolled to his knees and puked up his guts, then crawled to the creek and stuck his head in the water, hoping to alleviate some of the pain. It hadn't worked. But when he'd come up for air, he'd seen something in the water that had given him chills.

It was a shoe. A woman's shoe.

The moment he'd seen it, an image had flashed through his mind of a girl running, and then screaming. At that point, another wave of nausea hit. When it was over, the fleeting bit of memory was gone, too. He'd made his way home, half expecting some girl's daddy to be waiting on his daddy's porch with a shotgun in his hand, but the only one standing on his porch had been his mother. She'd burst into tears upon seeing him, and then he'd been grounded for the rest of that month.

When Monday came, he'd gone to school with a knot in his gut, certain that the proverbial ax had yet to fall. But after a few weeks had passed with no revelations, he had convinced himself nothing had happened, after all.

Now here he was, more than twenty years later, experiencing the same set of symptoms. Only this time, pretending wouldn't make his nightmares go away. Every time he closed his eyes, he felt the darkness closing in around him—then the pain on his hip, then choking on the dust and the filth in which he'd been lying. He was convinced that somewhere beyond the safety of his home, danger still waited. Waited for him to show signs of weakness—waiting for the moment when he would drop his guard once again. Only this time, if they took him again, he wouldn't survive.

So when Betty announced that a deputy wanted to talk to him, his gut knotted. On the one hand, he wanted the perpetrators caught, but on the other, he kept wondering if, in aiding in their capture, he wasn't releasing a Pandora's box of his own.

"Raymond, dear…you remember Mr. Hanna? He was at the hospital with Wade. He's filling in for Hershel Brown while he and Mindy are on their honeymoon."

Raymond gave the big man a nod, then waved toward a chair.

"Yes, I remember. Have a seat, Mr. Hanna. Betty, would you bring Mr. Hanna something cold to drink?"

Judd shook his head. "No thanks, ma'am. Nothing for me." Then he turned to Raymond. "Let's forget the formalities, okay? Call me Judd."

Raymond smiled magnanimously. "Then Judd it is. Do you have any news for me?" he asked.

"No, sir, I'm afraid that I don't. And actually, that's why I'm here. So far, there's nothing to go on except the brand on your hip."

Raymond's face turned a dull, angry red.

"I'd rather you didn't refer to it as a brand."

Judd leaned back and took a small notepad from his shirt pocket.

"I stand corrected," he said softly. "Then we'll call it the wound."

Raymond nodded.

"Okay…the *wound* is shaped like an *R,* is that correct?"

Again, Raymond's face flushed. Judd spoke up before the man could argue.

"Look, Mr. Shuler. I know this is painful. But there's only one way to get at the truth, and that's to tell it like it is. According to the medical report, someone branded your hip with the letter *R,* for Raymond, I assume. From the way it was shaped, your doctor was guessing it had been done with an electric branding iron. Do you remember hearing anything?"

"No," Shuler said shortly.

Judd tried another tack. "Think hard. You were blindfolded the entire time, right?"

Shuler nodded.

"Okay, then maybe there was a scent, or something you felt, that you can remember?"

"No," Raymond said shortly. "Don't you think that if I remembered something, I would have told you?" Then he glanced at Betty. "Dear, I believe I would like a glass of lemonade. Do you mind?"

"No, of course not," she said, and quickly left the room.

Judd watched the man's face, well aware that there was something he wasn't saying, maybe something he didn't want his wife to hear.

"You'll forgive me for asking," Judd said, "but I need to know if there is an angry husband somewhere who might be trying to teach you a lesson?"

Shuler's forehead wrinkled in a frown. "I don't follow."

"Were you having an affair?" Judd asked.

"Hell, no," Shuler spluttered. "I've never cheated on my wife and don't intend to start. She's a good woman. I wouldn't disrespect her that way."

"Sorry," Judd said. "But I had to ask."

Shuler made himself relax. "I know," he said, and

gave Judd a weak smile. "It's just hard to accept that you're only asking what dozens of people are probably already thinking." He sighed. "But I swear to you, nothing could be further from the truth."

"What about enemies? As a banker, you must have made some people mad, especially on things like foreclosures."

Shuler shrugged. "Honestly, there haven't been all that many in my years as an officer. However, if you'll call my secretary at the bank, she can give you a list. I'll let her know you'll be coming by to pick it up."

Judd nodded, then made a note to himself to pick it up later. When he looked up, he caught Shuler staring.

"You know, the only stranger to come through this town in years that wasn't just passing through is you," Shuler said.

Judd immediately caught his drift and grinned. "Sorry, Mr. Shuler. But if my facts are correct, I was asleep in Wade Franklin's spare bedroom when you were abducted. Besides, if I was ticked off at someone, they'd know it. Blindfolds and branding irons aren't exactly my style."

Shuler flushed. "It was just a thought," he muttered.

Judd nodded. "And not a bad one, except for one thing."

"What's that?" Shuler asked.

"What happened to you is a case of revenge, pure and simple."

Shuler went still. Judd watched as all the blood suddenly drained from the man's face. Shuler's chin began to quiver, and it was all he could do to speak.

"Revenge?"

"Yes. So if you can think of anything in the next few

days that might pertain to those facts, I would say it's to your advantage that you let either Wade or me know. Revenge is an odd emotion. Sometimes the reason for it eats at people for years before they decide to get even."

The tone of Shuler's voice shifted into a higher octave. "Years?"

Judd nodded. "It wouldn't be the first time," Judd said. Then he stood as Shuler's wife came back into the room. "Well, sir, I'll be going for now. Remember what I told you. If you can think of anything…anything at all, just let us know. In the meantime, you enjoy that lemonade, you hear?"

Charlie parked in front of the police department and got out, then turned and lifted Rachel into her arms. Before she could get to the curb, she heard someone calling her name. When she turned, she saw Davie coming up the street, pulling his wagon and waving wildly. She smiled and waved back, then hugged her baby just a little bit tighter, thanking God that she'd been born healthy and whole. She couldn't remember a time when she hadn't known Davie Dandridge. They were close to the same age, and while he'd long ago outgrown her in size, his grasp of reality was still that of a five- or six-year-old. Some people in town called him names, some looked down upon Judith Dandridge for not putting him away with others of his kind, and then there were those like Charlie who were satisfied to let Davie be. He was what he was. A twenty-something man with the mind of a child.

"Charlie girl, look at my clock!" Davie cried, pointing into the bed of the wagon he'd parked at her feet.

She looked down. As usual, the wagon was half-full of crushed aluminum cans. Davie dug between them, grinning widely as he pulled a man's watch from the bottom.

Charlie's eyes widened. "My goodness, Davie, that's some watch," she said. "May I see it?"

Davie hesitated. "You give it back?" he asked.

"I promise," Charlie said. At that point, Rachel wiggled to be put down. "Just a minute, baby girl," Charlie said. "Let Mommy look at Davie's nice watch."

It was a Rolex. Not something one would expect to *find* on the side of the road. She turned it over, masking a gasp as she read the inscription.

To Raymond with love. Betty.

"Oh, my gosh, it's Mr. Shuler's watch," she muttered.

Davie frowned, then snatched it out of her hand before she realized she'd spoken aloud.

"No!" he said abruptly. "It's Davie's watch now."

He tossed it in the wagon with his cans and started up the street. Charlie hesitated briefly, then bolted into the police department. She had to tell Wade. Only it wasn't Wade that she ran into. It was Judd.

Judd grabbed her by the shoulders to steady her on her feet as they collided at the doorway.

"Whoa there, ladies, what's the rush?"

He ruffled the little girl's hair and wished he could have kissed Charlotte Franklin again, just to ruffle her feathers a bit, too. But he'd promised himself he'd back off from Charlie. Now was no time to change his mind.

"Sorry," Charlie said. "I wasn't watching where I was going. Where's Wade? I need to talk to him fast."

Judd frowned. "I think the dispatcher said he went to pick up Harold down at the co-op."

She groaned. "Oh, no. That will take forever. Harold must be drunk, and he always wants to fight when he's drunk."

"What's wrong?" Judd asked. "Maybe I can help."

She hesitated, but only briefly. "Right! I don't know what I was thinking," she said. "I'm so used to running to Wade for…" Then she grabbed him by the arm and started tugging him toward the street. "Out there. Just now. In Davie Dandridge's wagon with the cans."

Judd stopped. "Calm down. You're not making any sense. Take a deep breath and start over. Now, what's in Davie's wagon that's so important?"

"Raymond Shuler's Rolex watch."

The smile on Judd's face slipped. "You're sure?"

She nodded. "He showed it to me," she said. "It had an inscription on the back from Betty to Raymond."

Judd bolted out onto the street with Charlie right behind him, but the street was deserted. He stood, listening for the squeak of the wagon's wheel, but heard nothing but the engine of a passing car.

"Where did he go?" Judd asked.

Charlie shrugged. "That way," she said.

"Go tell Martha to radio Wade. When he gets back, tell him what you just told me."

She nodded, then stood for a moment, watching as Judd started walking down the street at a rapid pace. By the time he got to the corner of the block, he was running.

Davie was scared. Charlie girl said the watch wasn't his—but he knew better. Finders keepers, losers weepers. It was his watch now. He ducked down the alley between the florist and the barber shop, running as fast as he could. The cans in his wagon were bouncing like popcorn in a pan, up and down, up and down.

He reached the end of the alley, turning right and then ducking into the service drive of the beauty salon. A delivery van was just pulling out and he ducked in behind it, afraid to look back, afraid to slow down.

Suddenly, someone called out his name. In panic, he stumbled, falling forward onto the pavement and skinning both his elbows and knees as he braced himself against the fall.

"Davie, Davie, darling, are you all right? Why were you running?"

He looked up. "Aunt Judy... I fell down," he said, and when he saw droplets of blood beginning to ooze through the skin, he started to cry.

Judith Dandridge wrapped the big child in her arms, aching for the pain on his face.

"Yes, sweetheart, I see that," she said. "Come with me. We'll get you cleaned up."

"My wagon," he said, pointing behind him.

She sighed. "Bring it along," she said gently. "We'll put it in the back room of the pharmacy, okay?"

He nodded, then followed along behind her in his pigeon-toed shuffle with the wagon bumping against his heels.

A few minutes later, he was sitting on a stool in the back room. His jeans were rolled up past his knees and he was sucking on a lollipop as his aunt began to doctor his wounds. Every now and then he would wince, and she would stop and blow on the spot until the hurt eased. Only after she was through and the bandages were in place did she resume the questions she'd started.

"Davie...sweetheart...why were you running? Did someone scare you?"

His lower lip trembled. "Yes."

Judith Dandridge's ire rose. She'd spent the better part of her adult life standing between Davie and the world, and the older he got, the harder it was for her to protect him.

"Who?" she asked.

"Charlie girl. She scared me," Davie said, and then poked the sucker back into his mouth.

Judith rocked back on her heels. It was hard to believe that someone as soft-spoken as Charlotte Franklin would be unkind to Davie.

"Are you sure?" she asked.

He nodded vehemently. "Yes, Aunt Judy. I'm sure."

"Exactly what did she do?" Judith asked.

Suddenly, Davie looked away, busying himself with the sucker. Judith's eyes narrowed thoughtfully.

"Davie..."

He sighed. When Aunt Judy got that tone in her voice, he knew he had to mind.

"Yes, ma'am?"

"What was it Charlie did that frightened you?"

Davie's chin jutted mutinously. "Tried to take my clock," he muttered.

Judith stared. "What clock?" she asked.

"Just my clock," he said, then pointed to a spot on his elbow. "It's still bleeding," he said. "See?"

Judith took him gently by the arm. "Davie, you know never to lie to Aunt Judy, right?"

His chin dropped to his chest and his shoulders slumped.

"Yes, ma'am."

"I want to see your clock."

He sighed, then slid off the chair and shuffled to his

wagon. Moments later, he pulled the watch out from the cans and handed it to his aunt.

Judith took the watch, looking at it in disbelief, then absently turned it over. Suddenly she went pale.

"Where did you get this?" she hissed, and grabbed Davie by the arm.

He cringed. "I found it, Aunt Judy. I found it."

"Where?"

Confusion colored his expression. "Don't remember."

"You have to give it back," she said. "It's not yours."

"No, Aunt Judy. I found it, now it's mine."

"It has someone else's name on it, Davie. That's how we know it's not yours. Now, you have to come with me. We'll find Wade and ask him to give it back."

Davie sat back down on his stool and started to cry again, only this time it wasn't from the pain of skinned knees and elbows.

"But Aunt Judy, he wasn't using it anymore. You said that…"

Judith Dandridge interrupted. "You know better than to take other people's property and you have to give it back."

"But you…"

"That's enough," she said sharply. "I don't want to hear anything more about the subject. You can't have something that doesn't belong to you."

She took him by the hand and led him toward the front of the store.

Charlie was running up the street, searching alleyways and doorways for a sign of Judd. Wade had been notified, then she'd left Rachel with Martha, the dispatcher, playing beneath the desk at her feet. If Judd hadn't found Davie by now, she had an idea of where he might be.

Suddenly, she saw Judd step out of the barber shop and look down the street.

"Judd!" she yelled, waving as she started to run.

Judd paused, then waved back, waiting as Charlie started toward him. There was an urgency in her movements, just as there had been the day he'd first seen her, running across the pasture toward certain death.

"What's wrong?" he asked.

"Have you found Davie yet?"

"No."

She exhaled slowly, then took a deep breath. "I'm out of shape," she muttered. "There was a time when I could have run the distance of a football field without breaking a sweat."

"I don't know. Your shape looks pretty good to me," Judd said.

Charlie blinked. Suddenly the conversation had jumped from Davie's whereabouts to something far more personal. She chewed on the edge of her lower lip and then looked away, refusing to acknowledge his taunt.

"I think I know where Davie might be," she said.

Judd's attitude shifted. "Where?"

"The pharmacy with his aunt."

Understanding dawned. "That's right. Judith Dandridge is his aunt, right?"

She shrugged. "Not really, but close enough. Come on. Let's go see if I'm—"

Charlie paused in the middle of her sentence to stare at the pair coming out of the doorway a half a block ahead. Judd turned, following her gaze. It was Judith, and she had Davie by the hand.

"Charlie, I'm glad I found you. We need to clear something up," Judith said. "Davie knows you weren't trying to take his clock, don't you, Davie?"

He ducked his head and nodded.

Judd saw a fleeting expression of pain come and go in Judith's eyes, and then she was all business.

"We're on our way to the police department. Davie found something that doesn't belong to him. He wants to give it back, don't you, Davie?"

Again, Davie nodded, but Judd could tell he was doing it reluctantly. His heart went out to the man, trying to imagine what it must be like to live in an adult's body, expected to cope within the parameters of an adult world, yet not able to understand the rules.

"That's great, son," Judd said quietly, and patted Davie on the back. "Mind if I walk with you?"

Davie gave Judd a nervous glance, but when he saw the smile on Judd's face, his expression lightened. He glanced at Judith.

"Can he, Aunt Judy? Can he walk with us?"

Judith shrugged. "If he wants."

The morose expression on Davie's face lightened considerably, and when Charlie patted him on the arm, he broke into a smile.

"I'm sorry I scared you, Davie. I didn't mean to," Charlie said.

"It's okay, Charlie girl. You can still be my friend."

Tears came to Charlie's eyes. "Thank you, Davie. You are a good friend to have."

Happy that all the earlier turmoil was behind him, Davie impulsively threw his arms around Charlie's neck and gave her a hug.

"Charlie is my friend!"

Judd watched the way Charlotte Franklin hugged the young man, gentling him with her touch as well as her words.

"That's good, Davie," he said softly. "You don't want to lose friends like her."

Again Judd's voice wrapped around Charlie's senses, making her long for something unnamed. When Davie let Charlie go, she had to fight the urge to place her cheek against Judd Hanna's heart and let those strong, able arms hold her close, just as she'd been holding Davie.

A couple of minutes later, they entered the front of the police department, just as Wade came from the back.

"I'd better get Rachel," Charlie said, and headed toward the dispatcher's cubicle where the strident sound of a little girl's chatter was mixing with thumps and laughter.

Judith strode forward, taking the initiative.

"Wade, Davie has something he wants to give you."

Wade stood, waiting for Davie to come forward on his own, but his mind was racing. The dispatcher had told him what had been happening. This was the first clue they'd had regarding Shuler's disappearance. If only Davie was able to remember the details of where he'd found it, it could be the break they'd been waiting for.

"Hello, Davie. Let's see what you found."

Judith took the watch from her pocket and handed it to Davie. With only a slight reluctance, he handed it over.

Wade's eyes widened. It was, indeed, Shuler's watch. Considering it was the only Rolex in town, it wouldn't have been hard to identify. Not only that, but he'd been at the Shuler's anniversary party when Betty had presented it to Raymond. He turned it over, running his thumb across the words engraved upon the back.

"Well, now, this is fine, just fine," he said. "You did a good thing, did you know that, Davie?"

Davie's eyes widened and he grinned. Only a few minutes ago, he'd been in trouble, but now someone was telling him he'd done a good thing. He wasn't sure how, but he liked this much better.

Wade took Davie by the shoulder and led him to a nearby chair.

"Where did you find it?" he asked.

Davie started to look nervous. He glanced at his aunt Judy. She was frowning. That meant he'd done something bad again, only he didn't know what.

"I don't remember," he said, and ducked his head.

Wade sighed, masking his frustration, and came at the questioning from a different angle.

"Could you show us where you found it?"

Davie's lower lip slid forward and he began picking at a button on the front of his shirt.

"He just said he doesn't remember," Judith said. "So how can he show you if he doesn't remember?"

Wade gave Judith a wary glance, wishing he could tell her to take a hike. She was making Davie nervous. Hell, Wade thought. That frown she's wearing could make anyone nervous, even him.

"Was Shuler wearing the watch when he disappeared?" Judd asked.

Wade looked up, a little surprised that he hadn't thought to check that fact himself. If he hadn't been, then where Davie found the watch was moot.

"He was never without it," Wade said. "But I'd better check. Everyone sit tight for a moment while I make a call."

He disappeared into his office, leaving the others to wait.

Davie glanced at Judith Dandridge. "Aunt Judy, am I in trouble again?"

"No," she said shortly. "And I don't see what all the fuss is about. He found something. He came to give it back."

"The fuss is all about solving a crime," Judd said.

"What crime?" Judith asked. "I understand no money was exchanged and that Shuler was let go loose without harm."

Judd frowned. "I wouldn't call abduction or branding harmless."

She sniffed. "I suppose, but it's not as if he was disfigured in any way. It was on his butt, for God's sake. If he keeps his pants on, no one will ever know." Then she turned away, as if refusing to discuss the incident any further.

Judd frowned. In his opinion, that last remark was full of innuendos regarding Raymond Shuler's inability to do just that. Shuler had claimed faithfulness to his wife and Judd had believed him. But what if the man was lying? What if there were people in this town who knew something Betty Shuler didn't? He made a mental note to himself to talk to some other people about Shuler's private life. The possibility of an angry husband was still a good theory.

But before he could pursue the thoughts any further, Wade came back into the room.

"Shuler *was* wearing the watch when he was abducted," Wade said. "He's on his way down to the department to identify it."

Judith took Davie by the hand. "We've done our duty. If there's nothing else you need, we'll be going now."

"Wait," Wade said, and then added, "Please."

Judith frowned, ready to argue, and then Rachel came running into the room with Charlie right behind her, and Davie's fears were completely forgotten in his joy at seeing the little girl.

"Rachel! Look, Aunt Judy, it's Rachel!"

He dropped to his knees and hugged Charlie's daughter. Judd watched, amazed at the transformation. The gentleness with which Davie held her was evident. Rachel had a handful of crayons in one hand and a coloring book in the other. She thrust it in Davie's face and grinned.

"Color?"

Immediately, they sprawled on the floor with the coloring book between them.

"Sorry," Charlie said. "I can take her on home if—"

"No, that's fine," Wade said, grinning. "In fact, it's perfect. We needed a diversion."

Judith Dandridge's ire disappeared as she stared at the backs of the two children's heads. The fact that almost twenty years separated them in age was moot, because their delight was still the same. She drew a deep breath and then looked away.

But Judd was watching her, trying to imagine the strength of character it would take to care for someone who would forever be a child—especially when it was not a child of your own. His estimation of the woman rose. Obviously, her attention to Davie ran far deeper than duty. Despite the fact that he'd been her parents' foster child, in her own way, Judith Dandridge had come to love him.

Chapter 8

Raymond Shuler entered the police department, walking with the aid of a cane. His limp was pronounced and so was the frown on his face. Everyone scattered to make room for his entrance, including Charlie, who scooped Rachel off the floor, and Davie, who ran to stand behind Judith.

"What's this about finding my watch?" he announced.

Wade held it out. "This is just a formality, but I need you to identify this for me."

Shuler all but snatched it from Wade's fingers, then turned it over. His face reddened as he spoke in an accusatory tone.

"It's mine, all right! Where did you find it?"

Wade pointed to Davie. "He found it," Wade said. "He and Judith just turned it in."

Raymond's gaze scanned past Davie as if he didn't exist.

"Where did you find it?" he asked.

Judith frowned. "I didn't, Davie did. It's him you'll be needing to thank."

Raymond looked flustered, obviously resenting the fact that he'd committed a social faux pas. He stared at the lumbering man-child standing beside her and tried not to let his true feelings show.

"Yes…well…thank you for finding my watch."

The man's angry voice seemed frightening. Davie turned his face against his aunt Judy's shoulder and refused to look at him.

Raymond flushed, taking Davie's behavior as a personal affront, and started to leave, muttering beneath his breath that people like him should be put away.

Judd heard just enough of what Shuler said to get mad.

"I suppose it's a damn good thing he wasn't or you wouldn't be standing there with that watch in your hand."

Shuler glared at Judd, but Judd held his ground. Finally Shuler relented.

"Yes…well, I apologize. I didn't mean to speak out of turn, but this hasn't been a good week for me, you know."

Judith drew herself up to her full height of nearly six feet and took Davie by the hand.

"If you think your life is tough," she snapped, "try walking a mile or two in Davie's shoes." Then she headed for the door.

Judd felt bad, both for Judith and for Davie, who had started to cry.

"Hey, there," he said, patting Davie on the back. "You weren't going to leave without your reward, now, were you?"

Davie blinked. He wasn't sure what that meant, but the man's voice was nice.

Judd took off his own watch and then slipped it onto Davie's wrist.

"How's that?" he asked. "Does it fit okay?"

Davie smiled widely and quickly lifted the watch to his ear to listen for the tick.

Judith Dandridge sighed. "That wasn't necessary, Mr. Hanna."

Judd shook his head. "I disagree. I think it was very important that Davie be rewarded for his honesty."

Raymond Shuler realized too late that the offer should have come from him. He reached for his pocket and pulled out his wallet in haste.

"Yes, of course," he said, thrusting two twenty-dollar bills in Judith's face. "Here, buy the boy something nice."

Judith backed up from the money as if Raymond had tried to hand her filth.

"That's what's wrong with you, Raymond Shuler. You always did think that money could buy anything, including a good reputation."

Then she turned and walked away, taking Davie with her.

Shuler flushed angrily, then stuffed the money back in his wallet.

"Damned woman," he muttered. "She's always been a cold bitch. It's no wonder she never married."

"Known her long, have you?" Judd asked.

Shuler snorted beneath his breath. "We were in school

together," he said. "Always thought she was better than everybody else." Then he patted his pocket, making sure his watch was still there, and nodded to Wade. "I don't suppose that retard could help you any with my case?"

Wade flushed angrily, but held his temper. "Davie didn't remember where he'd found the watch, if that's what you're asking."

"Figures," Shuler muttered. "Well, I'll be getting on home now. I'm not supposed to overdo it, you know."

"Wait a minute, Raymond," Wade said. "Technically, your watch is evidence. I need to keep it in—"

"Whatever for?" Shuler snapped. "You're never going to find who did it."

Judd jumped on the comment before Shuler could leave. "Why do you say that, Mr. Shuler? Do you know something we don't?"

Shuler pointed his cane at Judd with an angry jerk.

"I don't like what you're insinuating, mister."

Judd refused to comment, leaving Raymond to think what he chose. A few moments later, he stomped out of the office, leaving a wake of anger behind.

The moment the door slammed behind him, Wade pivoted and threw his keys across the room where they hit the wall with a splat.

"Sometimes this job is hell, and keeping my opinions to myself, even harder. That son of a bitch. Whoever took him should have branded him with an *A* for asshole, not *R* for Raymond."

Charlie was at the window, watching the banker making his way across the street toward his car. Calmly, she turned, giving the two men a cool glance.

"In my opinion, they could have gone either way and still been right. The two are synonymous with Shuler.

As for changing the brands, that would have been stating the obvious all over again. Raymond—asshole. Asshole—Raymond."

Judd pivoted suddenly, staring at Wade and Charlie in disbelief.

"Well, I'll be damned."

"What?" they both echoed.

Judd pivoted and headed toward the file of notes he'd laid on his desk.

"What she said. Maybe that's what we've been missing."

"I don't get it," Wade said.

But Charlie immediately tuned in.

"I think I do," she said. "What Judd's saying is that we've never considered the fact that the *R* on Raymond's backside might stand for something else."

Judd grinned, pleased that she'd caught on so quickly.

"You're good," he said. "Maybe Wade should have hired you for a detective and sent me on my way."

"No way," Charlie said. "Now, I'm going to take my daughter and myself home and leave you two to your work."

"See you this evening, sis," Wade said, and gave Rachel a quick kiss. "Judd, we need to talk. Wait here while I tell Martha we're leaving."

He left, leaving Charlie and Judd momentarily alone. Rachel was almost asleep on Charlie's shoulder, and when Charlie turned, the afternoon sunlight caught in the curls on the little girl's head.

"Damn," Judd whispered, unaware that he'd spoken aloud until Charlie stopped and turned.

"What?" she asked.

He just shook his head and then reached out and

touched their heads—first one, then the other—lightly palming some of Rachel's curls before running his hand over the sleek ponytail Charlie had made of her hair.

Charlie's heart skipped a beat. At that moment, if she hadn't been holding Rachel, she would have hurled herself into this man's arms and damned the consequences later.

"Why did you do that?" she asked.

There was a knot in his throat that made his voice tremble.

"Just then…you and your baby…standing in that sunlight." He tried to smile, but it wouldn't come. "You look like a painting I once saw. I think it was called *Madonna with Child*."

Charlie's breath caught at the back of her throat.

"Oh, Judd, I—"

He put a finger across the curve of her lips.

"Don't."

Charlie closed her eyes, absorbing the feel of his hand on her mouth, then she inhaled slowly, masking a moan.

The abrupt tap of Wade's boot heels on the floor signaled his return. They turned away. Judd pretended great interest in the papers he'd picked up, and Charlie readjusted her hold on Rachel as she started toward the door.

"Okay, I'm ready," Wade said.

Charlie was halfway across the room when Judd noticed the way she was walking.

"Charlie!"

She turned.

"You're limping again."

She shrugged. "It's just been a long day."

"Here," Judd said, taking the sleeping baby out of Charlie's arms. "At least let me carry her to the car for you."

As they passed the baby, their gazes met, then momentarily held. Judd could see his own reflection in the pupils of her eyes, and the image of his own vulnerability was startling. Then he gritted his teeth and settled Rachel upon his shoulder.

"Lead the way, Charlotte. It's time to get this little curly-head home."

Long after Charlie was home and had put Rachel down for her nap, she kept thinking about the gentleness of Judd's hand on her hair, then the pressure of his finger upon her mouth. But no matter how hard she tried, the images wouldn't go away. She knew what was happening and it scared her to death. She was falling in love with Judd Hanna.

Raymond Shuler watched his wife leaving for her afternoon club meeting, then turned away from the window and hobbled to the door, making certain she'd locked it behind her. He was tired, so tired, but there was no way he was going to lie down until he was sure that he was safely locked in.

A few minutes later, he made it to the bedroom and stretched out on their bed, careful not to put pressure on the healing wound on his hip. As he closed his eyes, the events of the afternoon began to replay in his mind, from receiving the phone call about his watch, to the dressing-down that he'd received from that uppity stranger Wade had taken into his office. What was his name? Oh yes, Hanna. Judd Hanna.

Raymond frowned. He didn't like the way Hanna had talked down to him, and first thing the next morning he was going to give Wade Franklin a piece of his mind. After all, he'd been part of the city council who'd voted to hire Franklin. He could be fired just as well.

A slight breeze was moving the limbs of one of Betty's shrubs up against the house. The scratch, scratch, scratch reminded him of the sound his fingernails had made as he'd clawed against the hard earthen floor. He shuddered, then carefully rolled over onto his belly, pillowing his cheek against his hand. In another part of the house, Betty's grandfather clock chimed the half hour. It was half past three.

His thoughts drifted, scattering like seeds in the wind, when suddenly, something clicked in his subconscious. His eyes popped open and he rolled abruptly, ignoring the pain on his backside as he reached for the phone. His hands were shaking with excitement as he dialed the police department.

"Call City P.D., how can I help you?"

"Martha, this is Raymond! I need to speak to Wade immediately."

"Sorry, Raymond, but he's out of the office."

"Then do whatever it is you do to contact him and tell him to get to my house right now! This is an emergency! I just remembered something about the people who kidnapped me!"

Martha gasped. "Yes, sir! I'll radio him now."

Raymond hung up, then leaned against the headboard of his bed, weak and shaking. He'd been so certain there was nothing to remember. Now he wondered what else might come as time passed.

Less than five minutes later, he heard a car stop

abruptly in front of his house. With a groan, he dragged himself up from the side of the bed and hobbled to the door. He was turning the lock as Wade banged on the door.

"Raymond! This is Wade! Open up!"

He pulled the door wide, his gestures jerky with excitement.

"Come in, come in," he said.

Judd moved in behind Wade, surprised by the change in the man's demeanor. Earlier, Shuler had been nothing short of hateful, and now he was almost ebullient in his greeting.

"What's up?" Wade asked. "Martha said it was an emergency."

Raymond waved them toward the living room.

"Sit, sit," he ordered. "I have news regarding my captors."

Judd stopped and turned, his eyes narrowing. "Has someone contacted you?"

Shuler frowned. "No. Why would they contact me now when they've already let me go?"

"I don't know," Judd said softly. "You tell me."

Shuler frowned. Again, this man seemed to be insinuating things about him he didn't appreciate.

"What I will tell you," Raymond said, "is that I remembered something that happened while I was being held captive."

"Like what?" Wade asked.

"A pager! I heard the sound of a pager going off, and when they moved past me, I smelled oranges."

Wade's expression fell. "Is that all?" he asked.

Shuler glared. "What do you mean, is that all? Isn't that enough to get you started in a positive direction?"

Wade sighed. "Look, Raymond, as you said earlier, you've had a rough week. But you've got to be serious for a minute. Do you know how many people in this town carry pagers? Besides half the kids in high school, the vet does, the mayor does, all of the city employees carry them. I think both pharmacists carry them, and for that matter, I have one, too, and I damn sure didn't snatch you."

Shuler dropped onto the couch with a thud, only afterward remembering his sore backside, but by that time it was too late to ward off the pain.

"Damn!" he moaned, then leaned over on his good hip and put his head in his hands. "What about the scent of oranges?" he muttered.

"Maybe your captor is a fruit freak."

He looked up, his expression filled with disgust. "That isn't funny."

Wade's lips twitched. "Sorry, Raymond, but what else can I say? It's not against the law to eat oranges, and I'd hate to have to sort through the people who've bought oranges at the supermarket over the past few weeks, trying to find a kidnapper."

"It might not even be oranges you smelled, but just the scent of orange, instead," Judd said. "You know... like lemon-scented furniture polish, coconut-scented tanning lotion, peppermint-scented toothpaste—you get the picture."

"Get out!" Shuler muttered, dragging himself to his feet.

"Now, Raymond, there's no need getting mad at us," Wade said. "Look on the positive side of this. If you remembered this much, there could be even more. Maybe some of it will be more helpful."

"Just get out!" Shuler said. "No one is taking this seriously. Everyone is laughing at me because I've got a sore on my ass. They weren't scared half out of their minds, thinking they were going to die. They didn't think they'd never see their family again."

Judd's sympathy for the man overrode his earlier disgust as he put a hand on Raymond's shoulder.

"Look, Mr. Shuler, I know this has been tough on you. Have you considered counseling? It might help to talk to a—"

"Oh, sure, that's just what I need," Raymond drawled. "Do you know how many people would withdraw their money from my bank if they thought their president was seeing a shrink?"

"I think you're exaggerating," Judd said. "And I don't think you're giving your friends the benefit of the doubt."

"I don't have any friends!" Raymond shouted.

"Now, Raymond. You know better than that," Wade said. "Why, there were dozens of people who came to see you after you got home from the hospital."

"They were snooping, that's all, just snooping," he cried. "They aren't really my friends. If they were, they wouldn't be making jokes about what happened to me."

Judd glanced at Wade and shrugged. "If what you say is so, Mr. Shuler, then have you ever asked yourself why?"

Shuler blanched. "Why what?"

"Why do you believe you have no friends? Have you treated that many people unfairly? Have you cheated someone enough to make them seek retribution?"

Shuler leaned forward, then buried his face in his hands, his earlier outburst forgotten.

"I don't know," he moaned. "I honestly don't know." When he looked up, his expression was haggard. "The entire time I was tied up, I kept trying to think who hated me enough to do that, but a face wouldn't come. Sure, I've been tough on some of the bank's customers, but I have to. It's my job to protect the interests of the depositors."

Judd glanced at Wade, silently asking permission to continue his interrogation. Wade nodded.

Judd slid onto the couch beside Shuler, waiting until he was calm enough to listen.

"Mr. Shuler, I'm going to ask you a personal question, and I want you to think very hard about it and then tell me the truth, no matter what."

Raymond sighed and then nodded.

"Do you really want these people caught?"

Raymond jerked, then looked up, stunned by the question. Not because he was insulted, but because he'd asked himself the very same question more than once. He glanced away, studying the pattern on the carpet as he tried to find a way to answer without making himself look guilty. Finally, he folded his hands in his lap and met Judd's gaze.

"Honestly... I don't know." Then he added, lest he be misunderstood, "It's not that I liked what they did, but they did let me go. I *am* home." He hesitated, then continued. "I don't know if you can understand this or not, but I have the strangest feeling that if I ever find out, my life will never be the same."

Judd put a hand on Raymond's shoulder. "That's just it, Mr. Shuler. Maybe you have yet to accept it, but your life has already changed."

Raymond's shoulders slumped. "What do you want me to do?"

"Tell us the truth," Judd said.

"But I did," he argued.

"Then why do I keep getting the feeling that there's something in your past that might pertain to this incident—something that maybe no one knows?"

Shuler blanched. Hanna was beginning to frighten him. It was as if the man saw past all of his defenses to the weak, scared creature beneath.

"I don't know what you're talking about," he muttered.

Judd sighed. "As the saying goes, It's your funeral." Then he stood. "I'm through here, Wade. Unless you have something else you wanted to ask Mr. Shuler, I think our business is done."

"Nope," Wade said. "Don't get up, Raymond. We'll let ourselves out."

"Be sure and lock the door," Raymond said, hating the panic in his voice.

Judd paused and looked back. "One more question, Mr. Shuler."

Raymond flinched. "Yes?"

"This is a small town. You've lived here all your life. Before you were abducted…did you always lock your front door?"

Raymond's mouth went slack. Silently, he shook his head no.

"Like I said…your life has already changed. What if next time, they take your wife instead of you? Are you going to be willing to forget it then?"

Raymond's heart skipped a beat, and when the sound

of the lock suddenly sounded in the silence they'd left behind, he covered his face and burst into tears.

The house still smelled of fried chicken, although they'd already eaten and cleaned up the kitchen more than two hours ago. Wade was down at the barn, checking on a cow that was due to give birth, and Charlie was taking a load of towels out of the dryer.

Judd was lying on the living room carpet on his stomach while Rachel climbed on and off of him, as if he were a playground toy. Fresh from her bath and dragging her blanket, she smelled like toothpaste and powder, but her little elbows and knees were beginning to take their toll. He grunted as she walked up the middle of his back and then sat down across his backside as if it were a saddle. When her heels dug into his sides, he pretended to buck.

She giggled, then stretched out along the length of his back and pulled her blanket up over them both.

Judd stilled, listening to her baby mutterings, waiting for her to make the next move. But she didn't. He didn't know when he realized that she'd gone to sleep, but once he had, it would have taken an army to make him move. He felt humbled by the little girl's trust, and wished that her mother was as easy to reach.

He heard her sigh, then felt her fisting a part of his shirt, subconsciously anchoring herself to his back. Judd smiled. He was tired, but it was a good tired. Charlie was bound to come back into the living room pretty soon. All he had to do was wait until she came looking for Rachel.

The steady hum of the air conditioner was hypnotizing. He took a slow breath, careful not to disturb Rachel's rest, and then closed his eyes.

Charlie put the last of the towels on the shelf in the linen closet, then shut the door. Only after she peeked into Rachel's room did she realize that the little imp had crawled out of her bed again. She turned, intending to call Rachel's name, when the silence of the house overwhelmed her. She glanced toward the windows. It was already dark. Rachel was afraid of the dark, so she wouldn't have gone outside. And then she reminded herself, when it came to Rachel, there was always a first time for everything.

She started through the house, checking room by room, telling herself she was making a big deal out of nothing. More than likely, the little imp had snuck back into the pantry for more 'mallows. But then she entered the living room and froze, unable to believe her eyes.

Judd was on the floor asleep, his cheek pillowed by his hands, while Rachel lay asleep on his back, her precious blanket covering them both.

"Sweet Lord," she whispered, and reached for the wall behind her for support. Then she moved slowly, dropping into a nearby chair, unable to take her eyes from their faces. Judd looked more vulnerable, even younger, in his sleep. There was a slight frown right between his eyebrows, and Charlie wanted to kneel down beside him and smooth it away. Rachel's mouth suddenly pursed and then made sucking noises. When Rachel put her thumb in her mouth, Charlie sighed. If thumb-sucking would make her life easier, she might consider it herself. She leaned back in the recliner, careful not to make any noise, then sat without moving, watching them as they slept.

Some time later, Wade came in the back door and went straight to the sink to wash up. It wasn't until he was reaching for a towel to dry off that the unnatural quiet of the house suddenly dawned.

Frowning, he tossed the towel on the cabinet and stalked through the house, only to come to an abrupt halt as he reached the living room. He didn't know what struck him first. The image of Judd and Rachel, both asleep on the floor, or the look on Charlotte's face as she sat watching them sleep. He took a deep breath as a knot formed in his belly. If he wasn't mistaken, his sister was in love, and with a man they knew precious little about.

Chapter 9

The loss of warmth on Judd's back was the first incli-
nation he had that the baby was gone. Blinking sleepily,
he raised his head and saw Wade carrying Rachel out of
the room. He groaned, then rolled over and stretched. It
wasn't until he started to sit up that he realized he wasn't
alone in the room. Charlotte was sitting in the chair by
the window. His pulse skipped a beat. How long had she
been sitting there?

"Charlie…"

"You are a dangerous man, Judd Hanna."

He frowned. "What do you mean?"

Her chin was quivering, and there was a brightness
to her eyes that looked suspiciously like tears.

"My daughter has fallen for you, I think. It makes
me worry how she'll react when you leave us."

If he stood up, he was afraid she would bolt and run, so he turned to face her instead.

"What about her mother?" he asked softly. "Is she going to care, too, or is she going to be glad to see the back of my head?"

Charlie stood abruptly. "This isn't a game. Playing with people's feelings isn't funny, Judd."

He got to his feet and walked toward her, stopping only inches from where she stood.

"You don't see me laughing, do you?"

Charlie tilted her head, staring intently into his eyes, trying to interpret what was going on behind that dark, secretive gaze. Finally, she shook her head and then sighed.

"I don't know what I see, but I know, as sure as my own name, that you're going to make both of us cry."

Judd winced. The thought was obscene. He shook his head and then cupped the side of her cheek with his hand.

"No, honey, I wouldn't do that to you—to either of you."

"Oh, but you will—the day you pack up and leave."

Angry with herself for giving away so much of her feelings, Charlie ducked her head as she stood, then started to leave when Judd grabbed her arm.

"Wait," he pleaded.

She paused.

"I don't know what to say," he said softly. "I've never mattered to anyone before in my life."

At that moment, Charlie saw past the man to the little boy he'd been, waiting in the dark for his father to beat him. She knew what she felt, but telling him the truth would be giving him even more ammunition with which to break her heart. And yet lying to him now, at his most vulnerable, was impossible.

"You don't have to say anything," she said. "Just know that your absence will leave a very painful hole in our lives."

Then she walked away, leaving him to digest what she'd said.

Only Judd's mind wasn't processing anything past the fact that when he left, Charlotte Franklin would cry. Something inside of him started to give way—something old, and scarred, something ugly that he'd kept hidden. He took a deep, shaky breath and headed for the porch. At the least, he needed some air.

A few minutes later, he found himself at the far end of the corrals and looking back toward the house. At first, all he could see was the dim outline of the rooftop and the faint glow of lights showing through the kitchen and bedroom curtains. Then one by one, the lights in the house went out, leaving it in total darkness. He shoved his hands in his pockets, letting the vast emptiness of the land envelop him.

Off to his right was the pasture where Tucker's bull had trespassed. It seemed like a lifetime ago since the incident, and yet barely a week had passed. Seven days ago he'd been running away from everything he'd known, rather than face the truth about himself. Now here he was, faced with a truth older than time, and he felt himself withdrawing even further. How could he let himself love Charlotte Franklin when he didn't know how to love himself?

His shoulders slumped as he turned back toward the house, and as he did, he saw something that stopped him cold. There was a light in the living room window, burning bright against the night. It took him a moment to accept what it meant, and when he finally did, he felt a lump forming at the back of his throat. What was it Wade had said about that lamp? Something about the lady of the house always leaving it burning until all those she loved had come home?

Wade Franklin was in bed, so that left only one other man for whom that light burned. He swiped a hand across his eyes, angry for the sudden shift of tears.

"Oh, God, Charlotte, don't love me like this."

But she wasn't there to argue, and he had nothing left to say to himself. A few minutes later, he entered the house, pausing to lock the front door behind him. He started toward his room and then paused and went back, turning out the light that she'd left burning for him. Later, as he was drifting off to sleep, the image of that lamp in the window moved across his mind, lingering long enough to give his heart ease. And he slept.

Just after midnight, the phone beside Wade's bed started to ring. Trained to wake up at a moment's notice, he answered before he even opened his eyes.

"This is Franklin," he mumbled.

"Wade, this is Della."

The voice of the night dispatcher at the police department was enough to drag him the rest of the way awake. He sat up.

"What's up?"

"Sorry to wake you, but I think you need to come in. There's a federal marshall here wanting to use our jail for the night, and with Hershel on his honeymoon, we don't have a jailer on duty."

"Tell him to hang tight. I'll be right there," Wade said, then hung up and reached for his pants.

A couple of minutes later he exited his room, carrying his boots. His service revolver was on a shelf in the hallway. As he stopped to retrieve it, he heard a door open behind him. He looked back. It was Judd.

"Trouble?" Judd asked.

"No, I just have to play jailer tonight. Tell Charlie I'll call in the morning."

Judd frowned. "I could do that for you," he said.

Wade gave him a cool look. "Want to explain to a federal marshal why you're pretty much AWOL from your own department?"

Judd grinned wryly. "Not really."

"That's what I thought," Wade said. "It's no big deal, and it's not like I haven't done this before. There's a cot in the office. I'll be fine."

"Okay, but if you need me…"

Wade nodded. "I'll know where you are."

Judd walked him to the door, then locked it behind Wade. He stood, listening until the sound of Wade's cruiser was no longer evident. Then he reached down and turned on the old family lamp, smiling to himself as he turned to go. But the smile died on his face, leaving him weak-kneed and suddenly breathless.

Charlie was standing in the shadows, and even though her nightgown was decent enough, the vague outline of her body beneath the soft, worn fabric made him ache for what she could offer.

"I didn't see you," he muttered.

"Where was Wade going?" she asked, ignoring his remark.

"Said something about having to play jailer for some federal marshal."

She sighed. "He needs more help," she said. Then she glanced at the lamp. "So you know," she said softly.

"Wade mentioned the family tradition the other day."

She nodded and looked away, rubbing her hands against her arms, as if she were suddenly chilled.

"Charlotte."

She looked up, drawn by something in the tone of his voice.

"What?"

"Thank you."

"For what?" she asked.

"For leaving that light on for me."

She sighed, as if giving up some internal struggle.

"You're welcome," she said softly.

He started toward her, and to her credit, she stood her ground, but when he got closer, he could tell she was trembling. He stopped.

"Hell, Charlotte, please tell me you're not afraid."

"I can't," she whispered.

Her honesty pierced him, sharper than any knife could have done. He shook his head in disbelief.

She was visibly shaking now, so much so that Judd thought she might faint.

"You can't think I would hurt you?"

"I've already told you, I know you will hurt me, Judd Hanna. But not in the way that you mean."

"Then what *are* you afraid of?"

"That someday I'll think of you and won't be able to recall your face."

Her words were like a kick in the gut. Without thinking, he reached for her, thrusting his fingers through her hair and tilting her face to his.

"God help us both, lady. If you intend to run, do it now."

But Charlotte didn't run. On the contrary. She took a step forward, and then another, until she could feel the warmth of his body against the thrust of her breasts.

"Are you going to make love to me?" she whispered.

"Only if you want me, Charlie."

She sighed. "I must be out of my mind."

"Not yet," Judd said. "But you will be."

He lowered his head.

It was nothing like Charlie had expected. Having based her entire experience on making love with Pete Tucker's gropes and kisses, she wasn't prepared for this man. Somewhere between their first kiss and her next heartbeat, she lost her voice and what was left of her mind. The heat of his mouth pulled at her senses. His hands, moving upon her breasts, then across her shoulders and down her back, lay claim to all that they touched. He moved, pinning her between the wall and his body, then lifted the hem of her gown and cupped her backside with both hands. The hard ridge of him rode between the juncture of her thighs, and as she arched against the pressure, she thought she might die. So long—it had been so long.

In the midst of their passion lay a truth Judd couldn't ignore. He wanted to make love to this woman more than he'd ever wanted anything in his life, but he wasn't prepared to protect her. He clenched his teeth and closed his eyes, willing himself not to explode, yet when she wrapped her legs around him, he buried his face against the curve of her neck and groaned.

"Oh, Charlotte."

Her breath was little more than brief gasps. Her head was tilted back, exposing the slender column of her throat. The knowledge that she was so far gone this fast was almost more than he could bear. But while he wouldn't let himself take that last step with her, there was no way he was going to deny her the ride. He slid his hand between them until he heard her gasp.

Seconds later, she let out a soft moan as she followed the path of his touch, and when, moments later, she collapsed in his arms, he scooped her up and carried her down the hall to her bed.

The aftermath was uncomfortable for both of them. Judd was still aching to the back of his teeth, needing a release he wasn't going to get, and Charlie was stunned by her uninhibited response to a man who'd given her pleasure while taking none of his own. The moment he laid her down on the bed, she covered her face.

"Why?" she whispered. "Why did you let me do that alone?"

Judd moved her hands, forcing her to look at him.

"I wasn't prepared to protect you," he said. "And I damn sure wasn't going to leave you in the same condition Pete Tucker did."

She groaned. What must Judd think of her? She was the one who would have suffered the consequences, yet one touch from this man and her good sense had completely disappeared. She rolled over, then sat up on the side of the bed, smoothing her hair and her gown at the same time, too embarrassed to face him.

Judd sighed.

"Charlotte?"

She stilled, waiting for the rest of his question.

"Look at me…please."

She bit her lip, then looked up.

"For the love of God, don't be sorry that happened."

She shook her head in disbelief.

"How can I?" she asked. "You gave me more than just a physical release. You made me remember something I'd almost forgotten."

"What's that?" he asked.

"That I'm not just Wade's sister, or Rachel's mother. You gave me back my sense of self, Judd Hanna, and for that, I will be forever thankful."

Judd groaned, and then took her hand and pulled it to his lips, kissing the curve of her palm before he pushed himself off of the bed. He was halfway to the door when he stopped and turned.

"There's just one other thing you should know," he said.

She held her breath, almost afraid to listen.

"The next time you experience that sense of self you were talking about, I'm going to be so deep inside you, you won't know where you stop and I start."

It wasn't until he closed the door quietly behind him that Charlie realized she was still holding her breath. With his promise still echoing within the silence of her room, she exhaled on a slow, shaky sob and then lay down and pulled the covers up over her head.

Long after Charlie had gone back to sleep, Judd was still in the shower, standing beneath the pounding of a cold, steady spray. Oddly enough, when he finally made it back to bed, he fell asleep almost instantly, sleeping without dreaming until the sun coming in the window woke him to the day.

Judd smelled the coffee and stretched, reveling in the luxury of getting up to something other than the strident peal of an alarm. Yet when he rolled over to pick up his watch to check the time, he remembered he didn't have a watch anymore. He'd given it to Davie Dandridge. He made a mental note to stop in at the pharmacy today and pick up another one. It didn't have to be fancy. All he needed was for the darn thing to keep time.

He heard the phone ringing as he was getting dressed. Probably Wade. He'd promised to call. He stomped his feet in his boots and headed for the bathroom to wash his face, tucking his shirt in as he went. A short while later he was reaching for a towel when he realized he was no longer alone.

"Well, now, good morning, little girl. Did you get out of bed by yourself again?"

Rachel nodded sleepily, then draped her blanket over one shoulder and lifted her arms to be held.

Judd reached down, lifting her into his arms and cuddling her close to his chest. Still sleepy, she snuggled, laying her head on his shoulder and shifting until the crown of her head was directly beneath his chin. In spite of the bony jut of his collarbone, that seemed to be her favorite spot to lie.

"You're sure something, you know that?" he said softly, and because no one was looking, he gave himself permission to snuggle her back.

Her tousled curls tickled his nose, and once again, he felt her latch on to his shirt with her fist. He knew if he looked, she would probably be sucking her thumb, too. Sweet baby moments. Who would share these with her when he was gone?

Then he sighed. Wade, of course—and Charlie. Who better to watch her grow up than a doting uncle and a loving mother? He started out of the bathroom with her still in his arms, but the closer he got to the kitchen, the more anxious he became. But what if she needed some-one and Wade wasn't around? What if she got away from Charlie again as she had before? Who would res-cue her then? By the time he got to the kitchen, his gut was in a knot. Last night, he'd held Charlie in his arms and felt this same damn way—this gut-wrenching panic that they would one day need him and he wouldn't be around.

But before he could sort through his feelings, Char-lie saw them and smiled. After that, the knot in his gut took another hitch.

"Good morning," Charlie said. "Did she wake you again?"

"No, she just came to watch me shave."

Charlie's smile slipped a bit. "I used to love to watch my daddy shave," she said, then reached for a cup. "Ready for some coffee?"

"Oh, yeah," he said softly, and then he cupped the back of her head, forcing her to look at him. "About last night…"

"Don't," Charlie said. "Don't apologize. Don't make excuses. Just…just…don't ruin something that was spe-cial to me."

He hesitated, then Rachel squirmed and the subject was changed.

"'Mallows?" she asked.

Judd grinned as Charlie shook her head.

"No, baby, we don't eat marshmallows for break-fast," Charlie said. "How about some scrambled eggs and jelly toast?"

Her lower lip slid forward. Just as she was beginning to argue, Judd interrupted her train of thought.

"That sounds good to me," he said. "Can I have some of your scrambled eggs?"

The idea of sharing food with this man was intriguing. They'd shared 'mallows. Sharing eggs should be okay, too.

"Ekks," she said, nodding her okay. "With toas."

Charlie giggled. "Ekks and toas it is," she said. "Judd will put you in your high chair while Mommy fixes your breakfast, okay?"

"Do you care if I take her with me to the barn instead? We need to see if that old mama cat had her kittens yet, don't we, baby girl?"

"Let me take her to the bathroom first, and you've got a deal," Charlie said.

Judd poured himself a cup of coffee while he waited for them to come back. And all the while he was sipping and staring out the window, he kept trying to picture himself in this role for at least the next fifty years. Oddly enough, the thought didn't panic him as it once might have. What would it be like, he wondered, to go to bed and wake up beside this woman for the rest of his life? To laugh with her and cry with her and even grow old with her?

"Here you go," Charlie said. "One busy little girl, ready to start your day."

Judd picked her up and started outside. The moment they got off the porch, he swung her up on his shoulders, letting her straddle his neck.

"Hang on tight, baby girl," he said, and planted both his hands in the center of her back to keep her steady.

Rachel laughed aloud and fisted her hands in his hair to hang on.

"Ouch, ouch, ouch," he yelped. "Don't pull Daddy's hair."

The moment it came out of his mouth, he groaned, thankful that no one had heard the Freudian slip.

The word *daddy* was foreign to Rachel, and the notion of being this high off the ground was too exciting for anything else.

"See da cows?"

Judd sighed. "Yes, honey. I see the cows. Now, if I could only see what was wrong with this mess inside my head, we'd all be a lot better off."

A short while later, they headed back to the house to tell Mommy that the Franklin homestead was four kittens richer than it had been last night.

But when they got inside, Judd learned that Charlie had some news of her own. Once Rachel was eating, Charlie served them, as well.

"Looks great," Judd said. "I feel sorry for Wade, missing out on all of this."

Charlie shrugged. "He's used to my cooking. It's nothing special to him."

"If he had to live on his own, he'd think differently," Judd said. "By the way, didn't I hear the phone ring earlier?"

Charlie was shoving her eggs around on her plate, trying to think of a way to bring up the idea she'd had. His question gave her just the right spot.

"Yes, it was Wade. Said he'd be home to shower and change after nine." Then she pushed her plate aside and leaned forward, ready to state her case before Judd could change the subject. "I had an idea this morning."

Judd started to smile, but the seriousness of her expression changed his mind.

"Oh? About what?" he asked.

"I've overheard you and Wade talking about Raymond. You know, about the fact that maybe someone from his past is responsible for what happened to him."

"That's right, although it is just a theory," Judd said.

"And a good one," Charlie added. "Which brings me to my idea. I wondered how you were going to check that out? Are you going to interview people he grew up with, or just talk to Raymond again?"

"Probably a little of both," Judd said. "Although, to be honest, I doubt we're going to get much more out of Shuler. I get the feeling he's not telling us the whole truth, but he's definitely not ready to talk about it."

"I could help," she said.

Judd looked startled. The idea of putting Charlie in any sort of danger, however remote, wasn't happening.

"Oh, I don't know," he said, and then the disappointment on her face made him add, "What did you have in mind?"

"The library."

"What?"

"The library. There're more than fifty years of newspapers on microfiche, and I think there's a copy of every Call City Cougar since 1907."

"What's a Call City Cougar?" Judd asked, intrigued in spite of himself.

"The school yearbook. I know it's a long shot, but maybe it would be a place to start."

Judd started to smile.

Charlie sighed. "Don't laugh at me," she said.

"No, you misunderstand," Judd said. "It's a damned good idea. In fact, it's better than the one that I had. So how about we do this together?" Then he remembered Rachel. "What about her? I don't think she'll do too well in a place where she's supposed to be quiet."

Charlie was so excited that he'd agreed that she was almost giggling.

"Oh, we have a neighbor a couple of miles down the road. Mrs. Miller? You know the place. She lives in that green-and-white house with the two cedar trees in the front yard. She loves to baby-sit for me. I've already called her...just to make sure she was free."

"Okay, then, Nancy Drew. It's a date."

Charlie looked a little surprised, and then chuckled. Nancy Drew, indeed. Granted, her idea to research the town's written history was hardly on the same level as the renowned fictional sleuth, but it was heady stuff just the same.

Chapter 10

"Wow," Charlie muttered as she and Judd entered the library. "Would you take a look at Wilma!"

Judd looked at the woman behind the check-out counter. "I see her, but what am I supposed to be looking at?"

"That red hair used to be mousy brown with some big streaks of gray. And I don't ever remember seeing her dress like that."

Judd still didn't see anything particularly unusual. "You mean that purple flowered thing?"

"It's so short!" Charlie hissed. "I can almost see her knees."

Judd grinned. "Now, Charlie, you're complaining to the wrong person. I've always been a leg man."

Charlie blushed. "That's not what I meant," she said. "I wasn't criticizing her, I was just surprised, that's all."

At that point, Wilma looked up, then smiled and waved.

"Good morning, Charlotte," she said. "Did you come to pick out some more books for that little sweetheart of yours?"

"No, ma'am," Judd said. "I thought I'd pick them out for myself this time."

It was hard to say who looked more shocked, Charlie or Wilma. And then Judd grinned and Charlie regained enough sense to introduce him.

"Wilma, this incorrigible man is Judd Hanna. He's acting deputy while Hershel is on his honeymoon."

Wilma's eyes suddenly rounded. "Oh! I know who you are," she cried. "You're the man who saved little Rachel from that awful bull."

This time it was Judd's turn to blush. "It's a pleasure to meet you," he said, then quickly changed the subject. "We need to look at everything you might have pertaining to Call City and its citizens over the past twenty... maybe even twenty-five years."

Wilma pivoted sharply, patting her hair as she went, just to make sure it was all still in place, and headed for the microfiche. Her step was light and there was a slight sway to her backside that hadn't been there before. The changes in her appearance were to be expected, of course. After all, she was no longer a virgin. She'd looked upon the naked male form and survived. She was now officially a woman. As for her hairdo, Audie Murphy, the World War II hero-turned-movie-star, had always been her idea of a real man. The change in color was her own personal "red badge of courage" for seeing Raymond Shuler naked.

She flipped on the power to a microfiche screen and then turned.

"Any particular thing you'd be looking for?" she asked.

"Any stories or articles pertaining to Raymond Shuler," Judd said.

She gasped, then put her hand to her bosom, much in the same way she'd done when she'd opened the front door and seen him lying on her steps.

"Oh, my! Does this have to do with his abduction? Is this part of the investigation?"

Judd hesitated. "In a way."

Wilma looked at Charlie, as if she'd suddenly become a stranger, and lowered her voice.

"Is it all right…to talk in front of her, I mean?"

Judd grinned. "Yes, ma'am. In fact, this angle of the investigation was actually Charlie's idea."

"Well, now," Wilma said, eyeing Charlie with renewed respect. "And all this time I thought you were just a sweet little thing with that darling baby." Although they were the only three people in the library, she looked over her shoulder before she spoke. "If there's anything else you need…anything at all…just ask me. I'll stand watch at the front desk. If I see anyone coming, I'll tap three times."

It was all Judd could do not to laugh. "Uh…maybe the better idea would be for you to play it cool, ma'am. You know…go about your business as if we weren't here?"

Wilma's little round eyes widened even more. "Yes! Right! That way word won't get out and the criminal will be caught unaware!"

"That's the way it usually works," Judd said. "So, if you don't mind, we'll get to work."

"Wilma, isn't there a complete set of Cougar year-books in the library?" Charlie asked.

Wilma clapped her hands. "Yes! Good idea, Charlotte. Follow me."

"I'll be over there," Charlie said, pointing to a nearby table as Wilma bustled away. Then she realized there was something she hadn't asked. "Uh... Judd?"

"What?"

"Exactly what am I looking for?"

"Start with the years Shuler would have been in high school," he said. "Anytime you find mention of his name, mark it. We'll look at the stuff together, later."

She nodded and started to walk away when he called to her.

"Charlie."

She turned.

"You're the first person I've worked with since Dan was killed."

Her expression froze. "Oh, Judd, I didn't..."

"No, it's not that. In fact, it feels pretty good to have someone like you backing me up."

She smiled, then lifted her chin. "I can't shoot worth a plug nickel, but I'm okay with my fists."

He nodded, remembering the selfless way in which she'd been willing to run down a bull to save her child.

"Yeah, lady, I'll just bet that you are."

They stared at each other in silence—remembering. It was Wilma's stage-voice hiss that broke the spell.

"Charlotte... I have everything ready now."

Charlie blinked, then pointed toward the table where Wilma was waiting. "I suppose I should—"

Judd took a deep breath. "Yeah, and I need to—"

Neither felt the need to finish the sentence they'd started, and by some unspoken word of mutual agreement, they parted company, leaving Judd on his own at the microfiche screens. But as the morning passed, the sound of flipping pages and the occasional sigh from the woman behind him was reminder enough that he wasn't really on his own—not anymore.

It was getting close to noon when Judd looked up. Rubbing his neck, he wearily rolled his head and then stood and strolled over to the table where Charlotte was sitting.

"Find anything?"

She shrugged. "Plenty of pictures, but I don't know if they mean anything. How about you?"

He shook his head. "Nothing that seems to connect," he said, adding, "Shuler's old man was a power in this town, wasn't he?"

Charlie frowned. "I guess. I don't really remember him. I think he died when I was a little girl."

"Well, let's see what you've got," Judd said, and dropped into a chair beside her.

There were the usual group photos.

Raymond at the county fair with his FFA steer.

Raymond as a sophomore on the Cougar baseball team.

Raymond as a junior and starting quarterback of the Cougar football team.

Raymond as a senior and captain of the basketball team.

Judd paid particular attention to the candid photos of the students, looking for a continuing thread, but there didn't seem to be anything other than the fact that Raymond Shuler was a big man on campus.

"He must have been quite a ladies' man," Charlie said.

Judd paused, his interest piqued.

"Why do you say that?" he asked.

"Just look. He's in lots of pictures with lots of girls, but never the same girl twice."

Judd stared, then started to grin. "Like I said, lady. You're really good at this."

Charlie was pleased by the praise. "Does it mean anything?" she asked.

"I don't know," Judd said. "But it's definitely a character trait that he's either overcome or kept hidden."

Her eyes widened. "Oh! I see what you mean!" Then she pointed to one particular picture. "Look, isn't this Wilma?"

Judd pulled the yearbook closer, peering at the small typeface beneath the photo.

"Damned if it's not," he said, then looked up at the librarian, eyeing her with renewed interest. "Hey Wilma, got a minute?" he called.

She spun, instantly pressing her finger to her lips to indicate quiet, then bustled toward him. Judd grinned. Again, the need for quiet seemed moot, since they were the only ones in the room.

"Sorry," he said.

Her lips pursed as she smoothed the fabric of her dress across the front of her belly.

"Did you find anything?" she whispered.

"Nothing obvious," Judd said, and then pointed to the picture in the yearbook Charlie was holding. "Isn't this you?"

She peered over his shoulder, then frowned. "My goodness, I haven't looked at that thing in years. Yes, it's me. I was president of the debate club that year."

"Isn't that Raymond with his arm around you?"

She peered closer, then blushed. "Why yes, I suppose that it is."

Judd watched her closely. She seemed suddenly nervous, when before she'd been so assured.

"Did you two date?"

She began to stammer. "Not really... I mean we never...uh, we barely kissed...and that was only once or twice." Then she regained her composure, reminding herself that she was a grown woman. So she had a past. All women of the world had pasts. "Raymond was a ladies' man," she said loftily. "He passed briefly through my life. It meant nothing."

Charlie stifled a grin and turned her attention to another yearbook, but Judd wasn't through pursuing the issue.

"How about these?" he asked, pointing to the other photos in which Raymond was either hugging or kissing a different girl. "Where are they now?"

Wilma looked a little closer. "Well, let's see. That was Anna Mankin—she's Anna Stewart now. I think she lives in Dallas. And this one, oh...what was her name? Mary Lee, that's right, Mary Lee Howards. She's dead. Died in a car wreck about ten years ago."

Judd made a few notes now and then, but mostly just listened as Wilma regaled them with stories of Raymond Shuler's past. And the longer he sat, the more convinced he became that somewhere within the pages of these books was the answer to what had happened to Raymond. He was just at the point of stopping the stories when she mentioned a name that caught his interest again. Not because he suspected a culprit, but because the woman on the page was so foreign to the one he knew now.

"This is Judy," Wilma said. "You know her."

Judd looked at the tall, elegant girl with dark brown hair and frowned, trying to place that vivacious smile with someone he'd met. She looked vaguely familiar, but the recognition didn't come.

"No, ma'am, I don't think I do," he said.

Charlie clutched his arm. "Sure you do, Judd. That's Judith Dandridge. You know… Davie's aunt."

"You're kidding," he muttered, and pulled the book closer. "She's certainly changed."

Wilma frowned. "I hadn't thought of it, but I suppose you're right. Of course, she's a pharmacist now, and that's almost like a doctor. She has a responsibility to look her professional best. It's a matter of trust, don't you know?"

Judd nodded. "Yes, ma'am. I suppose that's so."

Charlie was still leafing through the pages of Raymond's senior year when she paused.

"Uh, Wilma, wasn't Judith in the same class as you and Raymond?"

Wilma nodded.

"How come she doesn't have a senior picture?"

Wilma frowned. "Why, that can't be. She graduated with us. I remember because she stood in front of me during the processional and I couldn't see over her head. She's very tall, you know."

Wilma turned through several pages, flipping back and forth. Suddenly she stopped.

"Oh, I remember now. Judy and her folks were in

some sort of accident, I think. She was bunged up pretty good. I remember she had a lot of scratches and bruises. I think the last two months of our senior year, she was home-schooled."

"What does that mean?" Judd asked.

Charlie answered. "For whatever reason, a student is identified as having some sort of handicap that prevents them from attending regular school, so a teacher is assigned and the student does all of his or her lessons at home, with tutorial sessions from the assigned teacher, of course."

Judd's eyes narrowed thoughtfully. Maybe that was what wiped the smile off of Judith Dandridge's face.

"It must have been a pretty severe accident," he said. "Lucky it didn't cripple her. Were her parents hurt, too?"

Wilma frowned. "No. That was the strange part. Judith was the only one who was injured. Maybe she was in the back seat or something. If I knew at the time, I'm afraid I don't remember now." And then she added, "I do remember that they got a new car afterward."

Judd nodded, accepting the plausibility of the story, but unable to get over the change. It was like looking at two separate women. One with long, flowing hair and a form-fitting dress, the other with greying hair shorn and straight, with no-nonsense clothes. Somewhere along the way, life had wiped the smile right off her face.

He looked at the boy who was in the picture with her. "So, Raymond and Judith dated, too."

Wilma frowned. "Not really. In fact, as I recall, Judy had a boyfriend in another town. I think it used to bug Raymond." Then she added, "Raymond's daddy spoiled him, you know. He had everything he ever wanted."

She looked at the picture and amended her statement. "Except Judy, of course."

"Wonder why she never got married?" Charlie asked.

Wilma's frown deepened. "There's nothing wrong with the unmarried state. I had offers, but I stayed single."

"Guess you never found that special someone, huh?" Judd asked, and then glanced at Charlie before turning away.

Charlie's heart skipped a beat. What had that look meant? Was he trying to tell her something about the case—or was it something entirely different? Something that had to do with her and him? She pushed her chair back, then stood.

"I need to stretch my legs."

Judd watched her go, saying nothing about the abruptness of her departure. He looked back at the picture of Raymond, standing beneath a large shady tree with his arms around a young, smiling girl. Poor Judith Dandridge. He could relate. Life had kicked him in the teeth a few times, too. He shoved the book aside and leaned forward, rubbing his eyes with the heels of his hands.

"Do you have a headache?" Wilma asked. "It's probably that microfiche screen. It always gives me a headache."

"Yes, ma'am," Judd said. "It'll go away once my eyes are rested."

"I have some over-the-counter painkillers," Wilma said, and hurried toward the back room, anxious to please. A few moments later, she was back with a plastic cup full of water and an industrial-size bottle of pills. "Here you go," she said. "Help yourself."

A faint but pleasant scent of something citrus wafted past her as she handed him the bottle.

"Nice perfume," he said as he shook some pills out in his hand.

Wilma blushed and patted her hair. "Why, thank you, but I'm not wearing any today."

"Really?" Judd said. "I thought I smelled citrus."

"Oh! That's the liquid hand soap in the bathroom. I washed my hands before I got your medicine. Can't be too careful, you know. Germs live on everything."

Judd nodded. It wasn't until the pills were halfway down his throat that he remembered what Raymond had said about smelling oranges when he'd been tied up. He choked, then took another sip of water.

"Are you all right?" Wilma asked, thumping him firmly on the back.

When Judd could speak without coughing, he nodded. "Just swallowed them the wrong way, I guess."

She smiled, pleased with herself that she'd been standing right there when he'd choked. She couldn't get over what a change her life had taken since she'd seen a naked man. From her hair to her clothes, and now this. He'd been choking a lot. If she hadn't been there to pound his back, there was no telling what might have happened. Today she could go home and write in her journal that she'd saved a man's life.

"So…where did you get that hand soap?" Judd asked.

Wilma frowned. She'd been preparing herself for gratitude, not another question. Then she shrugged. This was another good reason why she'd never married. There was no predicting the intricacies of the male mind.

"I believe I purchased it at one of the pharmacies. It was on sale."

Great, Judd thought. That meant almost anyone could have some.

He nodded. "It's nice."

Then Judd noticed Charlie going out the front door. From the way she was moving, something had obviously caught her attention. He stood, curious as to what it might be.

"I see Charlie's about ready to leave, and I think we've exhausted the possibilities here. Thanks for your help, Wilma."

She nodded importantly. "I'll keep it under my hat," she said, and then grinned and patted her hair. "Figuratively speaking, of course."

Judd grinned back, then followed Charlie out the door. By the time he got outside, she was on her knees in the grass, playing with a small brown puppy.

"Who's your friend?" he asked.

Charlie glanced at him, and then the puppy suddenly barked and she refocused her attention to the dog.

"Isn't she the cutest thing you ever saw?"

Judd squatted down beside her, playfully scratching the small puppy's ears while looking at Charlie's face.

"Yes, she sure is," he said softly.

It took a moment for the compliment to sink in, and then when it did, she blushed, hesitating for the right thing to say.

"Judd, can I ask you something?" she finally asked.

"Sure."

"Are you just playing with my feelings?"

He hadn't expected to be put on the spot so succinctly, but since he'd known Charlotte Franklin, he'd come to expect nothing less than total honesty from her. He rocked back on his heels.

"Hell, Charlotte, I would have thought what happened between us last night was a little more than playing."

Her blush heightened. Remembering the wantonness of her behavior was hard to face, but she wasn't sorry that it had happened.

Someone yelled at the puppy from across the street. They watched as it ran back to its yard, then Charlie stood and brushed off the knees of her pants.

"Are we through?" she asked.

He was a little taken aback that she'd dropped the subject so quickly.

"Yeah, we're through," he said.

She lifted her head, shading her eyes from the afternoon sun as she swept a stray lock of hair away from her face.

"That's what I thought," she said, and got into his Jeep without another word.

It took him a moment to realize that there was another connotation that could have been put on her question and his answer, and when he did, it angered him. As far as he was concerned, the "we" in their relationship had yet to happen, so there wasn't any damned way that "they" could be through.

He got into his Jeep and slammed the door shut with a bang.

"Thank you for your help in there today."

She nodded.

He wanted that earlier camaraderie back, but it was nowhere in sight. Silently cursing himself and the world in general, he reached down and started the engine, then put it in gear.

"Is there anything else you need to do before I take you home?"

"I'd like to stop by the pharmacy. I need to buy a couple of birthday cards."

He backed into the street, then shifted gears and took off, leaving a strip of black rubber on the pavement behind him.

Charlie wisely kept silent all the way to the store.

After spending the morning researching Raymond Shuler's history, it was a little disconcerting to see him getting out of his car. His wife, Betty, was behind the wheel, obviously chauffeuring him around. The look on his face was just shy of furious, and Charlie wondered what had happened to set him off.

"There's Raymond," Charlie said. "But he doesn't look very happy."

Judd looked up. Sure enough, the man was getting out of his car and then hobbling up the curb and onto the street.

"You're right, he doesn't," Judd said. He'd seen that look on men's faces before, and it had usually ended in a shouting match or a fistfight. "I think I'll go inside with you, just in case."

Charlie frowned. "Just in case of what?"

But Judd was already getting out of the vehicle. She had no other option but to follow.

They could hear Raymond shouting before they opened the door, and not even the jingle of the entry bell was enough to slow him down.

"I'm telling you for the last time, you keep that retard away from my house. I'm sick and tired of having my view spoiled by the sight of him digging through my garbage like some damned animal."

Judith's face was completely devoid of color, and although she had yet to speak, he could tell she was livid. The veins in her neck were protruding, and her fingers were curled into fists. When she made a move toward a display of crutches and canes, Judd bolted.

"What's going on here?" he asked, aiming his question at Shuler.

"Nothing that concerns you," Raymond said.

"That's where you're wrong, Mr. Shuler. I could hear shouting all the way out on the street, which definitely constitutes disturbing the peace. And when I came in, I witnessed you verbally abusing Miss Dandridge. There's a place and time for everything, Shuler, and this is definitely not it."

Shuler's face flushed a dark angry red as he pointed a finger in Judith's face.

"That boy she keeps is trespassing on my property. He goes through the garbage cans on the block like some animal. I warned her before that if it didn't stop, I was going to have him committed."

Judith took a deep breath, and Judd could tell it was all she could do to remain civil.

"He was only looking for cans," she said. "And he wasn't stealing. Betty said it was all right for him to take them."

Raymond waved his cane in the air, unaware of any agreement and unwilling to admit he was wrong.

"I don't know anything about an agreement between you and my wife, but I'm telling you now, for the very last time, if you don't keep him off my property, you'll be sorry."

Judd grabbed the cane out of Shuler's hand.

"Give me that," he said shortly. "Now, you listen to me, or you're likely to be the one who winds up sorry. It sounds to me like you need to get your facts straight before you make accusations. If your wife gave Davie permission to recycle your aluminum cans, then it seems to me he was within his rights to be on your property. It doesn't take a lot of guts to threaten a woman, but you're welcome to try that on me."

Raymond blinked, taken aback by the suggestion.

"Don't be ridiculous," he muttered. "I have no quarrel with you."

"You don't have one with her, either," Judd said, pointing to Judith. "Now, I suggest you apologize to Miss Dandridge, then you take yourself home."

Shuler was so angry he was shaking. He didn't like to be thwarted, and he didn't like to be told what to do, but Judd Hanna had done just that, and without raising his voice. He glared at Judith, then turned to Judd.

"My cane," he said, holding out his hand.

Judd handed it back to him, then stepped aside, watching as the man stomped out the door.

The moment he was gone, Charlie rushed to Judith's side.

"Judith, are you all right? Is there anything we can do?"

But Judith didn't answer. Instead, she stood without moving, watching until Shuler was out of her store. Just as he was getting into his car, her pager went off. She unclipped it from her pocket and read the display, then looked up.

"Is there something I can help you with?" Judith asked.

Charlie realized Judith was not going to acknowledge her offer.

"No, I think I can find what I need on my own," she said.

"Take your time," Judith said. "I have to return this call, then I must go look for Davie. He's probably frightened."

"I'll go," Judd said.

Judith looked startled. She glanced at her pager again and knew the call was probably important. Her duties as a pharmacist were warring with her duties to Davie. Finally, she relented.

"I would appreciate it," she said, and hurried away.

As soon as she was gone, Charlie turned.

"Now do you see what I mean? Poor Judith—and poor Davie. I'll bet Raymond scared him to death."

Judd frowned. "When you get through here, do you mind walking down to the P.D.?"

"Of course not."

"I'm going to let Wade know what happened, then see if I can find Davie. I'll take you home later."

"If I'm not in the office, I'll be across the street at the café. It's almost noon and I'm starving."

Judd looked startled and glanced at his watch, only to realize he still didn't have one. That was something else he would do, but later, when he had more time.

"Sorry," he said. "I didn't mean to forget to feed you."

She shrugged. "I can take care of myself. I've been doing it now for years."

Judd left, wishing they hadn't parted on such stilted terms. He sighed as he slid behind the steering wheel and started the engine. As always, it seemed that when he was needed most, he was always running away.

Chapter 11

Judith came from the back of the pharmacy. When she realized Charlie was still there, she looked uncomfortable, as if she didn't know whether to remark on what had just happened or not. But when Charlie calmly inquired about a particular item, she began to relax.

"Are these all the men's watches you have?" Charlie asked, pointing toward a small display on a rotating stand.

"No, there are some in this case over here," Judith said, and pulled a key from her pocket as she moved across the room.

Charlie followed, leaning against the counter and peering down through the glassed-in top, then smiling to herself as she saw the merchandise there.

"That one," she said. "The one in the upper right-hand corner. May I see it, please?"

Judith took it out and laid it on the counter, watch-

ing curiously as the grin on Charlie's face continued
to widen.

"How much?" Charlie asked.

Judith upended the box to look. "It's on sale—$39.95."

Charlie did a little mental math, calculating what
she could cut on the grocery items, and knew she could
swing it.

"I'll take it," she said.

Judith didn't comment on her choice, and Charlie
didn't bother to explain.

"Wrap it up, will you?" Charlie asked.

"Certainly," Judith said, and then hesitated as she
reached for the wrapping paper. "Is it a birthday gift?"

"No. Just a replacement for something lost."

At that moment, Judith realized who this was for.

"I'm sorry," she said stiffly. "I didn't realize. I can
give you a bigger discount."

"No," Charlie said. "It was already on sale. Besides,
in this case, I think the man is well worth the money."

For a moment, the two women stared at each other,
then as if by some unspoken sign, they looked away.
Charlie sorted through the birthday cards she'd come
to buy while Judith wrapped the watch. A few minutes
later, Charlie paid for her purchases and left. Somewhere down the street, there was a cheeseburger and
fries with her name on it and a man who'd stolen her
heart.

Call City wasn't all that large, but there were a lot of
alleys and shortcuts that Judd wasn't familiar with. He
figured his best bet was to start at Shuler's house and
work his way back downtown toward the pharmacy,
where he suspected Davie would eventually end up.

When he began his search, he was confident that, before long, he would see Davie. But when ten, and then fifteen minutes had passed with no sign of him, he began to worry. He tried to put himself in Davie's shoes, but couldn't summon the image. Davie would always be an innocent, and even at six, Judd had been worldly and hardened far beyond his years.

He rolled down the windows and slowed his vehicle to a crawl, listening intently for the sound of a squeaky wheel or the rattle of cans. But he soon realized that he would not be able to hear anything over the sound of his engine. It would take longer to search on foot, but he didn't see any other options.

He parked at a curb in front of the veterinary clinic, then killed the engine and got out. He stood for a couple of minutes, eyeing the lay of the area and trying to see it through the eyes of a child.

Where would I go...if I was sad...and I was scared... and I was six?

He started walking, moving in and out of the patches of shade dappled along the sidewalk. Up ahead, a woman was on her knees, digging in a flower bed. Judd paused.

"Ma'am, have you seen Davie Dandridge?"

She leaned back and pushed her hat off her forehead.

"Who?" she asked.

"Davie Dandridge...the man who collects the aluminum cans?"

"Oh, you mean that simple boy? No, not today."

Judd tipped his hat and hid a frown as he continued up the street. *Simple.* The word had rolled off the woman's tongue without thought, rather callously describing someone who didn't quite fit in this world. But as

Judd walked, he realized it could be a good word, after all. There wasn't really anything wrong with Davie. He wasn't so different; his life was just simpler. He wondered if Davie's mother had known there was something wrong with her baby—if that's the reason she gave him away. Then he shrugged off the thought. There was no reason to feel sorry for Davie when he didn't feel sorry for himself.

He kept moving, stopping now and then to question people in their yards, and some who were walking down the streets. It wasn't until he neared the junkyard at the south edge of town that he saw a narrow set of tracks on the shoulder of the road. Tracks from a little red wagon. Davie couldn't be far.

He walked until he came to the six-foot board fence surrounding the yard, then followed the wagon tracks east. A short distance away, he could see a large gap in the fence where several boards had been removed. He stopped and looked in. There, in the distance, he caught a glimpse of something red. He took off his Stetson, then slipped through the fence. When he was on the other side, he settled it firmly back on his head and stood, examining the lay of the land.

It wasn't a particularly safe place for a child to be, even if the child was over six feet tall. The rusting hulks of car bodies were stacked two, sometimes three high, and in other places, salvage had yet to be stripped down. He moved through the narrow alleyway, keeping his eye on the little red wagon and listening for the sound of voices. It wasn't until he got a bit closer that he realized he could hear someone crying. He frowned. Damn Raymond Shuler's sorry hide. He *had* scared the kid—scared him half to death.

And then Judd saw him, sitting behind the wheel of a '57 Chevy, hunched over a broken steering wheel and staring intently through the opening where the windshield had been. He took a deep breath and started toward him.

"Hey, mister, could you give me a ride?"

The sound of Judd's voice startled Davie. In the middle of a sob, he suddenly jumped, his eyes wide and tear-filled, his mouth slack with fright. He recognized the man. It was the man who'd given him his clock. And then he looked closer. The man was making a fist with his hand and was holding up his thumb. Davie suddenly smiled. He knew what that meant.

"Yes. I can give you a ride," Davie said. "Get into my car and I will drive you away."

Ignoring the layers of dirt and rust, Judd stepped across a thick patch of weeds and crawled into the passenger side of the seat.

"Nice day for a drive, isn't it?" Judd said.

Davie nodded. "I'm running away," he said, and shifted pretend gears—the gearshift had long disappeared.

"Why?" Judd asked. "Won't your aunt Judy be sad?"

Davie's faint smile crumpled. "I love Aunt Judy," he mumbled, and then lay his head on the steering wheel and sobbed.

Judd scooted across the seat and put his arms around Davie's shoulders.

"Then why are you running away from her?" Judd asked.

"Not running away from her," Davie said, sobbing. "That man scared me. I tried to tell him it was okay, but he wouldn't listen."

At that moment, if Raymond Shuler had been anywhere in sight, Judd would have decked him. Damn him for what he'd done to this boy.

"Well, your aunt Judy and I had a long talk with Mr. Shuler," Judd said. "He's sorry he yelled, and he won't be scaring you anymore."

Davie's sobs stopped as suddenly as they'd begun.

"He's not mad at me?"

Judd ruffled Davie's hair and smiled. "No, son, he's not going to be mad at you, I promise." Then he took a handkerchief out of his hip pocket and handed it to Davie. "Here, wipe your eyes and blow your nose and I'll walk you back to the pharmacy."

Davie did as he was told, then crawled out of the car and held out his hand as he'd been taught, waiting to be led to safety.

Judd grinned, but there was a lump in his throat as they began walking out of the junkyard. No wonder Judith Dandridge was so protective of this boy. He was far too trusting for the ugliness of this world.

Charlie had just taken her last drink of iced tea when she happened to look out the window of the café and breathed a quick sigh of relief. It was Judd and Davie, walking hand in hand down the sidewalk. She tossed some money on the table and grabbed her things, heading for the door. Outside, she could hear the faint squeak of that wheel and the rattle of cans as Davie pulled his little wagon behind him. She started toward them across the street.

Suddenly, Judith burst out of the pharmacy.

"Davie! Oh, Davie, I was so worried about you," she cried, and pulled him into her embrace. "Where have you been? You know if you get scared, you're supposed to come to me."

But Davie was beyond explanations. He was too happy to be where he belonged.

Charlie bolted up on the sidewalk, her voice light with relief.

"Judd! Where did you find him?"

"Yes, where was he?" Judith asked.

Judd hesitated, knowing that he was probably going to give away one of Davie's secret places, but it was for the kid's own good.

"At the junkyard. He'd commandeered a '57 Chevy. In its day, I imagine it was a real hot ride. In spite of a few missing parts and no wheels, I think he thought he was getting the hell out of Dodge."

Judith groaned. "Davie, darling, you know you aren't supposed to be in that place. You could get hurt."

A corner of Judd's mouth turned up in a smile. "Yeah, and you're going to have to talk to him about picking up hitchhikers, too. However, you don't need to worry about his driving. He keeps his eyes on the road when he's behind the wheel."

Davie lifted his head and smiled at Judd.

"I gave him a ride, Aunt Judy, and then he brought me home."

Charlie inhaled sharply, then looked at Judd, as if seeing him for the very first time. Tears shattered her view of the world. She knew he was tough, and she knew he was strong, and she'd seen him burst into laughter quite often, especially at something Rachel had done. But imagining him in a rusted-out hulk of a car, letting Davie take them on a wild pretend ride? She'd had no idea, until this very moment, how truly gentle this big man must be.

"Well, now," Judith said softly. "That's fine, just fine, Mr. Hanna, and I thank you…more than you will ever know."

Judd smiled and ran his hand over Davie's head, smoothing down that thick shock of flyaway hair.

"It's just part of the job, ma'am," he said, and then looked at Davie. "Besides, he's a pretty interesting kid when you get to know him."

Judith suddenly clenched her jaw. She nodded briefly.

"Yes, he is," she said. "It's just a shame that everyone can't see that. Davie's life would be so much easier." Then she took Davie by the hand. "Come along, Davie. We'll have our lunch now. Tell the deputy thank you for bringing you home."

"Thank you," Davie parroted.

"You're welcome," Judd said. "But remember what we talked about. No more running away, okay?"

Davie nodded, more concerned with food than with remembering promises.

Judd stood on the street, watching as the pair disappeared into the pharmacy. Now that the little drama was over, he felt out of sync and oddly bereft.

"Judd?"

He turned, nervously eyeing the tears in Charlie's eyes, but when she slid her hand into his, the world settled.

"I thought you were ticked off at me."

She arched an eyebrow. "I still may be. I haven't decided. But that doesn't keep me from being proud of you, too."

"Why?"

"You gave Davie something today that I doubt he's ever known before," she said.

"What?"

"Dignity. When you've had it and then lost it, it's a precious thing to get back."

Suddenly, Judd suspected that they were no longer talking about Davie, but about her, instead. He pictured her pregnant and unmarried, having to face down people who knew she'd been dumped. Before he thought, he opened his arms and pulled her close to his chest. Moments later, his voice was shaking as he let her go.

"You're a dangerous woman, Charlotte."

Still reeling from the embrace and unwilling to let him see how much he affected her, she steadied herself by suddenly clutching her purse to her chest.

"I'm think you've been out in the Wyoming sun a little too long," she said. "Dangerous is the last thing I'll ever be."

But Judd shook his head. "That's where you're wrong. A woman can cry *because* of a man—because of what he did or didn't do to her, as the case may be—but when she sheds tears *for* him, it's a dangerous thing."

"Dangerous to whom?" Charlie asked.

"To the man, darlin', to the man. It's then he knows she's seen his weaknesses. After that, there's no defense."

"Have I seen your weaknesses, Judd Hanna?"

His expression darkened. "You've seen enough," he muttered.

"I doubt that," she said, then grabbed his hand. "Now it's time for you, and you're coming with me."

"Where are we going?"

"To get you some food."

The moment she said it, he realized how hungry he was.

"Okay," he said. "But afterward, I need to have someone take me to my Jeep."

Charlie looked around, only then realizing it was gone.

"That's right," she said. "You and Davie walked here. Where is it? Why didn't you drive?"

"It's somewhere on Henson Street, and we walked, because Davie wanted to hold my hand."

The words hit Charlie's heart, just like the sight of her baby's smile. It was all she could do to speak.

"You know what, Judd Hanna? So do I." She held out her hand. "Are you game?"

Judd stood, stunned by the thunder of his own emotions. It was a moment before he could move.

"Hell, yes," he said softly, then his fingers closed around hers with a jerk, as if he were afraid that she'd suddenly disappear.

Charlie exhaled. She didn't know how long this man would stay in their lives, but she'd made up her mind to take whatever he would give and be happy for the gesture.

Wade was sitting at the kitchen table, downing the last of a sandwich, when they walked into the house. Charlie took Rachel to her room to play, while Judd went to the sink to wash his hands.

"How did the day go?" Wade asked. "Did you find Davie okay?"

"Yes, I found him, but I'm not having as much luck with the Shuler case."

Wade shrugged. "For two cents, I'd chuck the whole investigation, but the cop in me knows I can't do it. Besides, I'm sort of curious as to who hated him enough to put that sore on his ass."

Judd nodded. "The man's a real piece of work, all right. He scared that kid so bad, he was trying to run away."

Wade frowned. "Damn." He stood, then gathered his dirty dishes and carried them to the sink. "You know, I always felt a little sorry for Raymond and Betty that they never had any kids, but now I'm thinking it was probably a good thing. He doesn't have a compassionate bone in his body. On another note, I'll be staying in town at night…at least for the next few days until everything settles down."

"After Raymond came back, I thought everything was settled," Charlie said. "Why do you have to stay in town?"

The men turned, unaware that she'd entered the room.

"In hopes of staving off a damned panic," Wade said.

"What kind of panic?" Judd asked.

Wade started to grin. "Well, it started with Harold Schultz's wife. You remember Harold? He's your mechanic, and the guy I brought in drunk the other day."

Judd nodded.

"Anyway, old Harold went missing again today. I tried to tell his wife that he was probably somewhere sleeping off a drunk, but she'd convinced herself that he'd been snatched, just like Raymond. Then, before the hour had passed, some woman had called the department and reported seeing a UFO. One thing led to another, and before I knew it, Mrs. Schultz had theorized that aliens were responsible for Shuler's kidnapping and subsequent return, and that they'd now taken her Harold. From that, hysteria boiled." He glanced at his watch. "And, if I had to guess, I'd say that right about now, all the members of the Call City Southern Baptist

Church are together at the church, praying in earnest for Harold's safe return."

"Lord have mercy," Charlie muttered.

Judd laughed aloud. "You're kidding, right?"

Wade shook his head. "No, I'm not."

"But Wade, if the alien theory is to hold any water, exactly what does Harold's wife think the brand is about?" Charlie asked.

Wade chuckled. "Funny you should ask. The story highest on the list at the moment is that it stands for the planet they're from. I tried to tell her that living beings from other planets most likely didn't use our alphabet, so putting an *R* on Shuler's butt made no sense. However, by that time, Mrs. Schultz wasn't making any sense, either, so it stood to reason no one would listen to me."

"Are you sure you don't want me to spell you off tonight? After all, you stayed in town last night," Judd said.

"Thanks, but I think a familiar face is best. Hell, if you stepped into this controversy right now, they'd probably find a way to accuse you of being the alien."

"You're probably right," Judd said. "And in a way, they'd be right. I am a stranger."

"Not anymore," Charlie said quietly.

"That's right," Wade said. "As far as I'm concerned, you could call up that captain of yours back home and tell him you quit, that you're taking a job in Wyoming."

Judd wondered if he looked as startled as he felt. All the while he'd been staying here, he'd been focusing on the day he would leave. A little unsure of his feelings, he tried to laugh off the comment.

"Yeah, right."

"You laugh," Wade said. "But I'm serious."

Judd turned away, reaching into the cabinet for a glass and filling it with water from the faucet.

"It's something to think about," he said, then took a long drink, purposefully ignoring the startled glance Charlie gave him.

"Well, I'm off," Wade said. "If I go missing, you'll know where to look for me." He pointed up to the sky, then exited the house, still chuckling beneath his breath.

The silence he left behind him was stark and uncomfortable. Charlie began digging through the refrigerator, leaving Judd on his own.

"Need any help?" he finally asked.

"No, I'm fine."

He shoved his hands in his pockets. "If you don't mind, I guess I'll go see what Rachel is up to. I missed seeing that little face today."

Charlie stood, staring down into the sink at the potatoes she was going to peel, and then took a deep breath. *Stay calm. Don't get your hopes pinned on anything resembling a man. That way you won't get yourself hurt.*

It wasn't long before she heard the sound of his laughter and her baby's giggles coming from the back of the house. She picked up another potato, peeling furiously. Damn the man. He was so under her skin, and she was so going to be hurt.

Charlie came out of the bathroom, fresh from her shower, and peeked in on Rachel. The little girl was sound asleep on her tummy with her rump in the air. As usual, she'd wrapped her blanket around her neck and Charlie slipped inside long enough to pull another one up over her feet.

"Good night, baby girl," she said softly, and blew a kiss into the air before closing the door behind her.

Up the hall, she could hear the faint sounds of a television program in progress, and every now and then, the rattle of a newspaper. She smiled to herself. Just like a man. Trying to do two things at once. Then she amended the thought. If there was anyone who could pull that stunt off, Judd Hanna just might be it.

She smoothed her hands over her hair, then tugged at the hem of her knit pajamas. She started to go back for a robe and then stopped. If she did, she would be too warm, and the pajamas were decent, covering everything that a T-shirt and jeans would cover. She didn't take into consideration the softness of the fabric and the way it clung to her body, or the just-washed soap-and-powder scent she brought with her as she entered the room. She picked up a basket of mending on her way toward her chair, then absently turned on the lamp as she sat.

Judd looked up from his reading, taking careful note of her fresh-scrubbed appearance, as well as the tender curve of her neck as she bent to her task. All evening, he'd been tense, even a little uneasy, wondering how this "family" evening was going to play out. Just he and she—and a baby—it was almost too perfect.

Yet as he sat, looking at her there in the lamplight, a yearning came upon him so strong that it made his heart hurt. Just for a moment, he let himself pretend that this was his life—that Charlotte was his woman, and the baby, their child. It was the pain that came afterward that stunned him. Pain that came from knowing it was only a dream.

He sighed, then made himself return to his reading.

Only the words no longer made sense. He couldn't think past the woman on the other side of the room.

Charlie knew he was watching her. She could feel the heat of his gaze, but she was afraid to look up. Too much had been going on between them today to ignore, but she wasn't sure if she was ready to be the instigator. Finally, she gained a sense of control and laid her mending down in her lap. If nothing else, she just needed to hear the sound of his voice.

"Judd?"

He looked up so suddenly, she could tell he hadn't been reading after all.

"What?"

"What makes some people so mean?"

Her question struck a nerve and he flinched. While he suspected she was thinking of Raymond Shuler, his mind automatically went to his own past, and to the man who'd been his father. It was all he could do to answer.

"I don't know."

"Do you think that people are born that way, or do you think it's a thing that they learn?"

Judd sighed. She wasn't going to give up until she got an answer that satisfied her.

"Maybe a little of both," he finally said. "What do you think?"

Her forehead furrowed, and then she dumped her sewing in the basket on the floor and folded her legs up beneath her.

"I think that life does it to them."

He frowned. "What do you mean?"

"Well, I don't think that babies are born with anger and viciousness, do you? I mean—think about it. At first, they're all brand-new—little angels straight from God. It's what happens to them after they get here that cripples their minds and scorches their wings."

Tears suddenly blurred Judd's vision of her face, and he had to focus on something else to keep from crying. The image she'd painted was too real to bear. If he'd ever had wings, they'd been burned off long ago in the fires of his father's hell.

"I guess you're right," he said, and made a fuss with straightening the paper he'd been reading.

"Look at Raymond. According to Wilma, he was born with the proverbial silver spoon in his mouth, and yet it hasn't made him happy. So, you have to ask yourself why. Maybe the things he was taught were self-destructive. Maybe that's why he has this constant need to be the one in control. But the way he treats Davie... I just don't understand it. There's no way a person like Davie could pose any threat."

Judd tossed the paper aside, pinning her with a hard, even stare.

"In spite of the disappointments life has handed you, Charlotte, you have still lived a very sheltered life."

She flushed. "That sounded like an accusation," she muttered.

Judd stood abruptly. "You know, you're right," he said. "You didn't deserve that, and I'm sorry."

Angry with himself, he started to leave when she called out his name.

"Please, Judd...don't go."

He sighed, then stuffed his hands in his pockets and turned to face her.

"Why? You don't deserve to suffer the effects of my moods."

Charlie stood, too, then took his hand, tugging until he returned to his seat.

"Okay," he said wryly. "I'm here. Now what?"

"Talk to me…tell me about you."

He gritted his teeth. On a good day, talking about himself wasn't a thing that he did easily, and tonight, he knew it was the last thing he needed to do. But the look on her face and the plea in her voice kept him seated. He didn't have it in him to deny her a damned thing.

"What do you want to know?"

"For starters, how old are you? Where were you raised? Why have you never married?"

"Thirty-three. Boyington, Kentucky. Didn't find the right woman."

Charlie folded her hands in her lap like a perfect child.

"Well, now," she said. "That was painless, wasn't it?"

He laughed, but something told him she was just getting started.

Chapter 12

"Have you ever been engaged?" Charlie asked.

"No."

She leaned back, eyeing the clean, muscular lines of his body. Then her gaze shifted to his face. Closed expression, dark eyes, strong chin. But, oh so intriguing. Finally she arched an eyebrow and shook her head.

"Are all the women in Tulsa blind, or are they just plain fools?"

"Talk like that could get you in trouble," he said softly, hiding a grin.

Charlie knew she was playing with fire, but she was cold from the inside out and it had been such a long time since she'd been warm.

"What do you do for fun?" she asked.

He frowned. Truthful answers were going to be too revealing, yet he didn't have it in him to lie to her. He sighed. Better tell her the truth and turn her off now than wait until they wound up hurting each other somewhere down the line.

"Not much," he said.

Charlie hesitated. "What do you mean, not much? Do you mean you don't have much time for your hobbies, or are you telling me that you don't indulge at all?"

"Damn it, Charlotte, why does it matter?" he growled

"Because I never slept with a man I didn't know, and I don't intend to start now."

He froze. *Have mercy. How does a man get past a woman like this?*

Charlie pretended she wasn't flustered by his silence, but the truth was, she was at the borderline of panic. *Oh, God, don't let me lose my nerve now.*

"So, what you're telling me is you do not allow yourself pleasure?" she said.

He couldn't quit staring. Damn the woman, but she was picking him apart at the seams.

"Doesn't look like I need to tell you anything," he muttered. "You're doing a hell of a job on my psyche all by yourself."

Her composure fell. Now she'd done it! She'd made him mad. But the woman inside her wouldn't let up. She stood abruptly, motioning for him to follow.

He eyed it nervously. "What?"

"Come with me."

Muttering under his breath as to the wisdom of letting her call all the shots, he stood.

"Where are we going?"

"Out to play," Charlie said. "It's good for the soul."

Sweat was running from Charlie's hairline and down the back of her neck. Her pajama top was stuck to her body and there was a big dirty handprint on her shoulder where Judd had tried to push past her on his way to the basket.

"Had enough?" she asked, bouncing the basketball up and down at her feet.

Judd was bent at the waist and clutching his knees, struggling for every breath that he took. His legs felt like jelly and sweat kept running into his eyes, burning and blurring his vision. Charlie, on the other hand, wasn't even breathing hard, and there was a glint in her eyes that warned him she wouldn't give in until he gave up. Finally, he groaned and sat the rest of the way down.

"Was this supposed to be fun?" he muttered.

She grinned. At least now she had his attention. She tossed the ball into the shrubs by the back door and then ambled over to where he was sitting and plopped down beside him.

A cloud of bugs had gathered beneath the halo of light by which they'd been playing. Every now and then, one would make a mistake and fly into the heat, and Judd knew just how they felt. For the first time in his life, he'd taken on more than he could handle. Who the hell could have known it would come in such a deceptive package?

"Are you all right?" Charlie asked.

Judd groaned. "I'll let you know tomorrow."

"I suppose this means you're too tired to mess around?"

He looked up, caught the gleam in her eye, and then laughed. The sound surprised him. He didn't think he'd had that much oxygen left in his brain, but the moment he heard it, he realized how good he felt. Not in his body, but in his heart.

Impulsively, he grabbed her by the shoulders and wrestled her to the ground.

"There isn't a man walking who will admit to that," he said, and pinned her beneath him.

"Eeww," she said. "You stink."

He grinned. "You don't smell so good yourself, sweet cakes. And those pajamas are done for."

She grimaced. "This means another bath. I beat you, so I get to go first."

His grin widened as he rolled off of her and dragged himself to his feet.

"You sure you want the first shower?" he asked.

She frowned. There was a gleam in his eye she didn't like.

"I guess."

He turned and walked toward the side of the house.

"You're sure?" he repeated.

"Yes, for God's sake, I'm sure I want the first bath," she yelled.

She rolled over, intending to get up, but only got as far as her hands and knees before the first blast of water struck.

"Judd! Stop! It's cold! It's cold!"

She darted toward the shadows, but he was right behind, aiming the garden hose straight at her back.

"Because of you, I've been taking cold showers ever since the first night I spent in this house. They won't kill you. Trust me," he yelled.

Charlie was caught. She ran from her car to behind the tree. Once she tried to make a run for the house and got a dose squarely in the face. The chill of the water was no longer an issue. It was justice she wanted now— and she knew just how to get it.

In the middle of a blast, she stopped. Ignoring the shattering cold to her back, she slowly turned, facing Judd without flinching. She watched the grin freeze on his face as she pulled one arm out of her pajama top, and then the other, performing a slow striptease beneath the basketball goal. When she pulled the wet garment over her head and tossed it on top of a nearby bush, the grin on his face slid out of sight.

Her nipples peaked in the chill night air, taunting him from a distance. He groaned and dropped the hose. Water began pooling at his feet, then running toward the bottom of the driveway.

Charlie hooked her thumbs in the waistband of her pajama bottoms and started toward him, letting the natural sway of her hips entice him even further.

When she was close enough to feel his breath on her cheek, she lifted her face, offering him whatever he wanted. She saw him shudder, and when he blinked, she made her move. Seconds later, the water hose was in her hand. Before Judd could move, she had him dead to rights.

Water went up his nose, in his eyes and down the middle of his belly. He coughed, then laughed, and then choked again when the water went down his throat.

"You will be sorry," he croaked, and darted off to the side.

But her aim was as good as his had been. Before long, Judd was soaked to the skin. Finally, he held up his hands in defeat.

"You win, darlin', in every way known possible to man. I secede. I give. I'm crying uncle and wolf...even Tom, Dick and Harry."

Charlie grinned. "Those last three don't match the others."

"What do I have to do?" he begged.

She turned off the water, then turned. "Talk to me," she said softly. "Tell me why you don't ever play."

He stilled. Didn't she ever give up? Then he knew by the look on her face that she would stand there all night until he answered.

"Because the noise would have made Joe Hanna mad. And when he got mad, he took it all out on me."

Charlie didn't have to ask who Joe Hanna was. The look he wore now was the same expression he'd had that day in the kitchen when he'd admitted his father had beaten him every day of his life.

"Oh, Judd, I am so sorry."

"It wasn't your fault."

"That's right, it wasn't," she said softly. "So the next time I offer you friendship, don't be afraid to accept. I'm not going to hit you or curse you. In fact, I've been trying to love you for several days now, but you're making it very difficult. I'll admit, I'm scared half to death of being hurt again myself, but there's something I know that you don't."

"What's that?"

"People can and will hurt you. It's happened to me. That's the ugly part of life. But there are also those who will love you—so much so that you can't even imagine the joy. However, if you're afraid to trust again, if you quit on yourself, then whoever hurt you ultimately wins, even if they're no longer in your life."

Judd stood, stunned by what she'd just said. And in that moment, he felt purged of a horrible weight.

"How did you get to be so smart?" he growled.

"I'm not smart. Just a woman who knows how to love."

His heart skipped a beat. He could hear the words coming up his throat before they ever came out of his mouth, yet once uttered, he knew he'd never be the same.

"Charlotte."

She took a step toward him. "Yes?"

"If I ask you a question, will you tell me the truth?"

She blinked, a little startled by the way he'd turned the tables on her. Then she nodded.

"Yes, I will do that."

"If I asked, would you make love with me?"

She took a deep breath and then lifted her chin.

"If you asked, I might."

He started to smile.

"Charlotte?"

"What?"

"Will you make love with me?"

She held out her hand.

Somewhere between the back door and his bedroom, they came out of what was left of their clothes. The soft, even sounds of the baby's breathing were evident as Judd picked Charlie up and carried her across the threshold into his room. He laid her on the bed and then turned and locked the door. The message was clear.

"Now it's just you and me, babe," Judd whispered.

Charlie reached for him, pulling him down until they were lying side by side, looking intently into each other's face. Strands of her wet hair still clung to her cheek and he brushed them away, then ran his hand along the curve of her cheek, then the length of her neck, and finally, the thrust of her breast.

She arched toward him, offering herself in every way.

He grunted briefly, as if he'd gotten a sucker punch to the gut, and then gave himself up to the dance. He stole the first kiss, she gave up the second. After that, there was no keeping track. Time ceased, becoming nothing but a bridge to the next caress. Whispers passed between them in the dark, taking pleasure to a new and dangerous level. Judd was moving into a place where thought ceased, and there was nothing on which to focus except the drumbeat of his blood, hammering against his ears. Her hands were on him now, stroking, urging, pulling him toward a sweet wall of pain. There was something he needed—needed to do. Protection. He needed protection—for her. With his last bit of sense, he sheathed himself, then parted her legs and plunged inside.

After that, there was nothing but the ride and the destination.

Sometime before morning, Judd woke to find himself alone. After what they'd shared, the pain of abandonment was almost physical. He got out of bed and walked into the hall. The wet clothes they'd shed last night were nowhere in sight. The faint but steady hum of the washing machine told him what she'd been doing. Cleaning up so they wouldn't be caught. He wasn't sure whether he felt indignant that she wanted to hide what they'd done, or grateful that he wouldn't have to face the inevitable confrontation with Wade.

He looked in her room. It was empty. A faint light up the hallway led him into the living room. As he neared, he realized it was the lamp in the window. Left on, he supposed, for Wade, who had yet to come home. He shoved a hand through his hair in frustration. Where the hell could she be?

And then it hit him. Rachel. She must be in Rachel's room.

He backtracked his steps and peeked in the half-open door. Sure enough, she was there, dressed in a T-shirt with her long legs bare, rocking her sleeping baby by the beams of moonlight coming through windows. At his entrance, Charlie looked up.

"Is she all right?" he whispered.

She nodded, mouthing the words *bad dream.*

He smiled. He'd had a few of those in his time, himself. He pointed to the clock, mouthing the word *coffee* back at her.

She smiled to herself as he left. He was stark naked. She wondered if he realized it yet.

A few minutes later, she laid Rachel back in her crib, then tucked the favorite blanket under her chin. Rachel snuggled into it, rooting like a baby pig until she was satisfied with the feel, and promptly went back to sleep.

Charlie sighed with relief and tiptoed from the room. This didn't happen often, but when it did, nothing helped but a cuddle. She could hear Judd in the kitchen. Like a typical man, he was making more noise by trying to be quiet than he would have done if he'd behaved in a normal manner. She hugged the familiar sounds to herself, storing them in her memory for the time when he would be gone. As she started up the hall, she remembered the gift that she'd bought for him at the pharmacy and did a backtrack to her room.

Judd was pouring his first cup of coffee when Charlie entered. He set it down and immediately held out his arms. She went willingly, hiding the small box in her hand.

"I didn't hear you get up," he said, then added, "I missed you."

She closed her eyes, savoring the tenderness in his voice.

"I hated to get up, too," she said. "I've never had the pleasure of sleeping next to such a warm body."

He frowned. "Didn't you and—"

She didn't let him finish. "No. Pete wasn't into sleeping with his women. Just screwing them."

Judd frowned. Her bitterness—when it came always surprised him. She did a good job of hiding her pain.

"Sorry," he said softly. "I didn't mean to bring up bad memories."

She shook her head and smiled. "After last night, I don't have room for any bad memories. From a woman's point of view, you are perfect, Judd Hanna, in every way that counts."

He took a deep breath. "Thank you, sweetheart."

"Oh, no. Believe me, the pleasure was all mine."

He grinned.

She poked at his bare belly in a teasing manner, then tucked her finger in the waistband of his jeans and gave them a tug.

"I have something for you," she said.

His smile widened. "Again?"

"Not that," she muttered. "Open your hand."

"What?"

"Just open your hand," she said, and then grabbed his wrist.

He obliged as she ordered, frowning slightly as she set a small box in the palm of his hand.

"What's this?" he asked.

"Open it and you'll see."

Oddly excited about the unexpected gift, he tore off the paper and tossed it aside, then opened the box. At once, his eyes widened and the grin on his face slipped and fell.

"Do you like it?" she asked, and without waiting for him to answer, took the watch out of the box and slipped it on his wrist. "If the band doesn't fit, you can take it to the pharmacy and Judith will fix it for you."

"It's Mickey Mouse," he said, swallowing past the lump in his throat, then tracing the path of the second hand with his finger as it swept around the face.

He was being so quiet, Charlie suddenly feared that he was embarrassed by the gift and didn't know how to tell her it was stupid.

"I know it's sort of silly, but I thought you could use a little fun in your life."

"When I was a kid, there was this fund-raiser contest at school. The student who sold the most candy bars would get a Mickey Mouse watch. I wanted that watch. More than I'd ever wanted anything in my life."

Charlie waited, knowing that the reason for his behavior would soon be clear.

"So, I peddled those candy bars up one street and down another, working after school and on weekends until I'd sold twenty-seven boxes."

He shifted the watch so that it would catch the light, staring in fascination at the little black mouse with the bright red pants.

"I knew I had it won. My closest competitor had only sold twelve. The day the contest came to an end, we were to turn in our money to the teacher. I was so excited I could hardly sleep. I could see myself walking to the front of the class and claiming my prize."

Charlie was starting to tense. She could see the end of this story coming and the pain on his face nearly broke her heart.

"The next morning, as I was getting dressed for school, I went to the dresser to get the money, but it wasn't there. I'd been so careful, putting it in the same place every day when I came home. And even though I tore that room apart, telling myself that I'd just put it somewhere else by mistake, I already knew it was gone…and I knew who had taken it." He took a deep breath. "It was one of the few times I ever yelled at him. I cursed and I cried and I screamed until my head was pounding. But it was no use. He couldn't have given it back to me if he'd wanted. He'd already spent it…on booze."

"Oh, Judd. What happened?"

"I got in trouble at school. Everyone thought I'd either eaten all the candy myself, or sold it and kept the money. I was nine years old and I spent the rest of the semester cleaning toilets after school to pay back what he'd stolen."

Then he looked at her, standing in the kitchen with no makeup and an old T-shirt on. Here was where the bloom was supposed to fall off the rose. Unfortunately for him, he thought she'd never looked better. At that point, he knew he was in trouble.

"There are no words to express what I'm feeling right now," he said gruffly. "But I feel it only fair to tell you that you could tick me off for the next twenty years, and it still wouldn't be enough to use up my joy."

She smiled. "See what you get when you give self-lessly?"

"Yeah," he said. "The real dynamic duo…you and

Mickey Mouse." He pulled her into his arms, crushing her close against his chest. "Damn woman, this is getting scary."

She sighed. "I know, Judd. I know."

It wasn't until a couple of days later that the UFO scare died down. By then, Judd and Charlie were feeling the desperation of the relationship. She woke up each morning, scared to death that this was going to be the day he would tell them goodbye, while he fell deeper and deeper in love. Somewhere in the midst of it all, something was going to have to give. And it did, right in the middle of Main Street at five minutes after twelve.

Judd sauntered out of the police department and headed for the café. He'd just gotten off the phone from talking to his captain, Roger Shaw, back in Tulsa. After Shaw had finished cursing at him, they'd settled down and had a fairly decent conversation. Bottom line, Judd had just let himself off the hook by turning in a verbal resignation, with a promise of a written one to follow. Now all he had to do was see if Wade had been serious about the job offer he'd made. And while he had yet to run it by Charlie, he was pretty sure she wouldn't mind if he stayed. Leaving Call City had become a thing of the past.

His step was light as he jogged across the street. Just as he got to the other side, he heard someone calling his name. He turned and then grinned. It was Davie, obviously on his way to the pharmacy, where Judith would be waiting to feed him his lunch.

"Hey, fella, how you been doing?" Judd asked.

"Got cans. Lotsa cans," Davie said, pointing into the wagon with pride.

"That you do," Judd said. "What are you going to buy with all that money?"

Davie frowned. "Something."

Judd sensed another secret looming, similar to the junkyard car that he'd favored.

"I keep secrets pretty good," Judd said. "Want to tell me?"

Davie shook his head. "No, I don't think so."

"That's all right," Judd said. "You're getting to be a big boy now, aren't you?"

Davie's face lit. "Yes. I'm a very big boy. Aunt Judy even let me use the lighter to burn the naked man's clothes."

Judd heard the words, but for a second, couldn't bring himself to respond. He took a deep breath, then squatted down, pretending to sift through the mound of crushed cans, giving himself time to think. But the longer he thought, the more certain he was that the mystery of Shuler's abduction had just been solved.

"So you burned them, did you?"

Davie nodded, but he was starting to frown. He'd just remembered he wasn't supposed to talk about this.

"I have to go now," he said.

"Is that where you found Raymond's watch? The one you had to give back? Was it with the clothes your aunt Judy let you burn?"

"I'm not supposed to talk about this," Davie said, and started to cry.

Judd felt sick, both for what he'd just learned, and for the fact that two people he'd come to admire were at the bottom of a pretty serious crime.

"I know, son. I know."

He hesitated. Making a big deal out of this in the middle of the street would serve no purpose.

"You run along now. Your aunt probably has your lunch ready and waiting."

Davie looked relieved. "Yes. I will eat now." And he darted across the street without looking.

"Hey!" Judd yelled.

Davie stopped. When he turned, the innocence on his face made Judd sick.

"What?" he yelled.

"You forgot to look both ways before crossing the street," Judd warned.

"Oh! Yeah! I forgot. I will be careful again."

"Okay, buddy. Now, go eat your lunch."

As soon as Davie made the other side of the street to safety, Judd pivoted sharply and headed for the café to get Wade. No need being the only one who'd just had his lunch ruined.

Wade looked up from his BLT, grinning as he chewed. "I waited," he said, talking around a bite.

"I see you did," Judd said, and slid into the seat opposite to the one where Wade was sitting. Then he leaned forward, lowering his voice so that he wouldn't be overheard. "We've got trouble," he said softly.

Wade rolled his eyes and then swallowed his bite, quickly washing it down with a big drink of iced tea.

"I almost hate to ask," he said.

"If you want Shuler's kidnappers, they're across the street at the pharmacy."

Wade sat up straight, his eyes wide with shock.

"The hell you say!" he yelled, then realized what he

done. "Sorry," he said, tipping his hat to a couple of women in the next booth to apologize for his language. "The hell you say," he repeated in a much softer voice.

Judd waved a waitress away. "I'm not ordering," he said. "And he'll be needing his check."

Wade's mind was spinning. "We're not talking hostage situation here, are we? Do I need to notify the state police? Hell's bells, Judd. Tell me what's going on?"

"Let's get out of here," Judd said. "This is going to be public knowledge soon enough, but better later than now."

"My God," Wade muttered, and tossed some money down on the table as he followed Judd out the door.

As soon as they were alone on the street, he pulled Judd to one side.

"Talk to me."

Judd sighed. "I was talking to Davie just a couple of minutes ago. He was talking about secrets and buying things with his can money and accidentally blurted out that his aunt Judy let him burn the naked man's clothes."

Wade was speechless. He was hearing what Judd was saying, but his mind was not processing the facts.

Judd continued. "I asked Davie if that's where he found Raymond's watch. You know…in the clothes he was going to burn."

"What did he say?" Wade muttered.

"He got scared, realized he'd spoken out of turn and bolted for the pharmacy. I let him go. Figured the least I could do was let them have one last meal in peace before it hit the fan."

Wade wiped his hands across his face, then took off his hat and ran his fingers through his hair in disbelief. "I have to be honest here, Judd. I don't quite know how to handle this. Yes, we could haul Davie in for further questioning, but in the eyes of the law, he's incompetent, so nothing he says will be of much use."

"But Judith might not know that," Judd said. "If you bring Davie in, I can guarantee she'll come to his rescue. If there's anything to what he just said, she'll tell the truth herself before she lets him suffer."

Wade nodded. "You're right about that."

"So, let's get this over with," Judd said.

Their hearts were heavy as they started across the street.

Chapter 13

Judith Dandridge knew before they opened their mouths that something was wrong. She'd never seen Wade so pale, and the new man, Judd Hanna, kept staring at Davie as if he were eating his last meal.

Suddenly, her heart skipped a beat. She didn't know how, but somehow, they knew. A strange calm came over her. Instead of panic, she felt an odd sense of relief.

"Gentlemen, how can I be of service?"

Wade was the one who spoke. "Judith, I'm going to have to ask you to bring Davie down to the police department."

The mention of Davie was a shock. Her voice started to shake.

"Why? What has he done?"

"We have reason to believe that he was involved in the kidnapping of Raymond Shuler."

"No," she moaned. "That's not so."

Davie heard the change in her voice and looked up, his sandwich forgotten.

"Aunt Judy…are you getting sick?"

She turned, the expression on her face pale and strained.

"No, dear. Finish your lunch."

"Yes, ma'am," he said, and took another bite.

"Please," she said. "You must be mistaken."

Judd shook his head. "No, ma'am, I'm not. A few minutes ago he told me that you let him start the fire that burned the naked man's clothes. So, unless you can produce proof that there's been another 'naked' man situation in this town in the past few days, I'm afraid the both of you are going to have to come with us."

Before she could answer, something crashed on the next aisle over. They turned in time to see a customer scurrying up the aisle toward the front door.

Judith swallowed a groan. That was Sophie Bruner, the biggest gossip in town. Within the hour, everyone would know. She glanced at Davie, in a panic as to what would happen to him when they took her away. But she didn't show her fear when she turned to them.

"If you'll give me a moment to gather up Davie's food, we'll be happy to come along."

Judd made no attempt to hide his surprise. She showed no remorse or fear. Then he thought of the altercations he'd witnessed between Judith and Shuler. While he didn't agree with what she'd done, he could almost understand it. The only thing that still puzzled him was the brand. What the hell did an *R* have to do with… He stopped in mid-thought. Revenge? Was it the symbol she'd left for revenge?

He watched her gentleness with Davie as she began packing up his food, making it seem as if they were going on a picnic so as not to frighten him. Poor Davie— the world that he'd known was about to take a terrible turn.

"Gentlemen," Judith said. "We're ready."

Wade opened the door for her. Judd followed them up from the rear. Judith held Davie's hand as they walked down the street, her expression revealing nothing of her emotions, just as she'd been doing for the last twenty years.

A few minutes later, she was seated at Wade's desk. Judd watched from the doorway, waiting for some sign of remorse. But Judith Dandridge's main concern of the moment seemed to be that Davie not spill his juice on Wade's floor.

"Judith, I'm going to be taping this," Wade said, setting a tape recorder on his desk.

She shrugged. "Do what you have to do." Then she grabbed for a chip that tumbled out of Davie's hand. "Careful, sweetheart," she said softly. "We don't want to get Wade's floor all dirty, do we?"

"Okay, Aunt Judy. I'll be careful."

"That's a good boy," she said softly, then looked back at Wade, waiting for him to begin.

Wade glanced at Judd, his heart in his eyes. Judd could only imagine how difficult it was for him to arrest someone he'd known and respected for all these years. Then Wade's eyes narrowed as he turned on the recorder.

"This is Chief Wade Franklin, recording the interrogation of Judith Dandridge and her foster brother, Davie Dandridge."

Judd watched a strange expression cross Judith's face, but it came and went so quickly he thought he'd imagined it. He glanced over his shoulder to the outer room, checking to make sure they wouldn't be disturbed, then nodded to Wade.

Wade took a deep breath.

"Judith Dandridge, you have the right to remain silent. If you choose to—"

She held up her hand. "I understand my rights," she said. "And I waive my right to have an attorney present."

He frowned and then shook his head. "As an officer, as well as your friend, I'm advising you to reconsider that last statement you made."

"I don't need a lawyer," she said. "All they do is make deals with other lawyers. No one pays any attention to the law as it is written anymore. If they had, none of this would be happening."

Judd felt sick to his stomach. There was a part of him that completely agreed with her. He couldn't think how many times he and his partner had arrested a perp, only to have him back out on the street before the day was over. He shoved the thought aside and refocused on the interview in progress.

"Judith, where were you on the night of August 5 of this year?" Wade asked.

"There's no need to pussyfoot through all of these questions," she said quietly. "I am the one responsible for teaching Raymond Shuler a lesson." Then she leaned over and wiped a bit of mustard from the edge of Davie's mouth.

Wade blinked. The admission wasn't exactly what he'd expected.

"You did more than teach him a lesson, Judith. You

abducted him, held him against his will and inflicted bodily harm. Basically, that's called kidnapping, and it's a federal offense. Once we have your confession on tape, I'll have to notify the FBI. The case will be tried in federal court."

"I tend to disagree with your description," she said. "I didn't kidnap him. Nothing was asked for, or traded for his release. When I thought he'd learned his lesson, I let him go. However, there's no need for a trial. I did it. I'll take whatever punishment the judge hands out."

Wade cursed and got out of his chair, then turned off the recorder in frustration.

"Damn it to hell, Judith, have you completely lost your mind?"

She lifted her chin in a gesture of defiance. "Once, years ago," she said. "But I got over it."

Davie began plucking at Judith's arm and trying to get her attention. All the yelling and tension was making him nervous.

"Aunt Judy... Aunt Judy... I need to go to the bathroom."

"I'll take him," Judd said. "Come on, buddy. I'll show you where it is."

"Thank you," she said, and then made Davie look at her. "Don't forget to wash your hands when you're through, and you come right back here to me."

"Yes, ma'am," Davie said, and let Judd lead him away.

Judd stood in the hall outside the bathroom door, waiting for Davie to come out. And even from where he was standing, he could hear Wade, still yelling, and Judith, still answering in a calm, monotone voice. A few moments later, Davie emerged. He took Judd by the hand.

"Is my aunt Judy mad at me?" he asked.

Judd shook his head. "No, Davie. If I had to guess, I'd say she's mad at herself."

"Okay," Davie said. "I'm ready now."

Halfway back to Wade's office, Raymond Shuler burst into the front door of the police department. His face was flushed in anger and he was already yelling before his wife, Betty, could shut the door behind them.

"Is it true?" he yelled. "Is Judith Dandridge the one responsible for my abduction?"

Judd bolted, trying to grab him before he barged into Wade's office, but he was too late to stop him.

"Get out, Shuler!" Wade said. "You have no business here."

"On the contrary," Judith said. "Let him stay. I don't mind."

Raymond stared. "You're crazy! Certifiably crazy!" he yelled, then waved his cane toward Davie, who'd come scurrying into the shelter of his aunt Judy's arms. "It's no wonder he turned out like he did."

Judith flinched but stood her ground.

Betty Shuler began to cry. "Judith, I just don't understand. I thought we were friends. Why on earth would you do something so horrible to my Raymond?"

Judith didn't bother to respond. Her attention was focused on Davie, who had started to sob.

"Look, Shuler," Judd said. "You've got a choice. Sit down and be quiet, or you're going to be arrested for disturbing the peace."

Betty dropped into a nearby chair, taking Raymond with her. He followed Judd's orders, but reluctantly.

Wade rolled his eyes. "This is the most unorthodox investigation I've ever seen."

"It was an unusual case," Judd said. "So far, it's sort of been resolving itself. Why don't we let it continue and see what happens?"

Wade picked up the recorder and waved it in everyone's face. "This will be on. Remember to mind your damned manners." He flipped the switch, then sat on the edge of his desk. "Judith, I'm going to ask this one more time, and by God, I want an answer. What prompted you to abduct Raymond Shuler?"

Judith turned, and the look she gave the banker made Judd's heart skip a beat.

"He was abusing his own son."

Raymond threw up his hands in disgust. "See, I told you, Wade. She's crazy. Everyone knows Betty and I have no children."

"I wasn't talking about you and Betty," she said. "I was talking about the baby I conceived after you raped me."

Raymond grunted audibly. Betty gasped. Wade and Judd looked at each other, then at Davie. And what was even more interesting to Judd was the fact that Raymond Shuler hadn't bothered to deny a rape had happened. In fact, the guilt on his face was obvious. Not only had he not denied it, but he couldn't bring himself to even look at the boy sitting beside Judith. Suddenly it was beginning to make sense. The *R* on Raymond's hip stood for *rapist*.

Wade touched Judith on the shoulder, waiting until she looked at him.

"Start at the beginning…please."

Judith sighed. "It was so long ago."

Her eyes lost focus, and Judd could tell she was no longer here with them, but in a time when she'd still known how to smile.

"Everyone in school knew that Billy Ray Shuler always had to have his way." Then she looked up. "That's what we called him then... Billy Ray. He didn't become Raymond until he went to work at the bank. Anyway, he'd asked me out several times, but I wasn't interested."

Raymond finally regained his equilibrium enough to speak.

"I don't remember any rape," he muttered.

"I don't doubt that," Judith said. "I wish I could have said the same. It was homecoming night, two months before our senior graduation. You were blind drunk and mad because I'd gone out with Ted Miles instead of you."

She paused and looked up, explaining to Wade. "Ted was from Cheyenne. He came up from time to time to take me out. We were going to go to the university together."

Again, her gaze turned inward. Judd watched as her hands began to shake.

"Ted had been to the dentist that day. He wasn't feeling well and had gone home early from the game. I'd driven Daddy's old truck into town, so after the game was over, I started home." She took a deep breath, struggling with the panic that came from remembering. "I had a flat," she muttered. "Sometimes I wonder if I hadn't had that flat, what my life would have been like."

Then she shuddered. "Anyway... I had the flat, but no spare. We lived in the country then, out on the old Hamish place. I wasn't more than a mile from home, so I started to walk. It was a nice night. A three-quarter moon—nice breeze. I was actually enjoying the walk. And then the car came."

Her hands suddenly fisted in her lap. "It was Billy

Ray, drunk out of his mind, and driving in the middle of the road. I got into the ditch, afraid that he was going to run over me." Her lips twisted bitterly. "Looking back, that would have been preferable."

Then she took a deep breath. "He stopped. Offered me a ride. I told him no, that I didn't want to ride with him because he was drunk. The refusal angered him horribly. He got out of his car and started toward me, yelling about how I thought I was too good for the boys in Call City. I kept expecting him to pass out, but he didn't. I started to run. He caught me."

Then she looked up, and the complete lack of expression in her voice was more horrible than any hysteria could have been.

"He broke my jaw and two ribs. He raped me in a foot of water and left me for dead. My daddy came looking for me around 3:00 a.m. He found the car first. They said I came stumbling out of the woods, bloody and in shock. That, I don't remember." She leaned forward, her gaze piercing Shuler with fierce intensity. "My last memory was of his face and the pain between my legs as he tore into my body."

Betty Shuler slid to the floor in a faint. Raymond was so stunned by what had been said that he sat and watched her fall. Oddly enough, it was Judith who offered advice.

"I have some smelling salts in my pharmacy. Should I get them for you?"

Wade sighed. "No, ma'am. I think there're some in the first aid kit." He looked at Judd. "Hold down the fort. I'll be right back."

Judd nodded.

Raymond kept shaking his head, as if he couldn't accept what she'd said.

"Why didn't you say something?" he asked. "Why didn't you tell?"

"Oh, I did," she said. "I told Daddy. I expected justice, you see."

Raymond looked up at her then. "I don't get what you mean."

"Daddy didn't go to the police. He went to your father. Two weeks later, the mortgages on our home and Daddy's business were paid off and we had a new car."

A dark flush slid up Raymond's neck. "Are you saying my father paid your father off to keep his mouth shut?"

She sneered. "You're a banker, Raymond. Do the math."

Judd felt sick. He could identify with every injustice Judith Dandridge had suffered. As a child, he'd expected protection and justice from a parent, only to be the one to suffer at his hands, and had known that there was no one out there who would believe. He put his hand on Davie's shoulder.

"Judith, I'm assuming this is why you were home-schooled until graduation."

She nodded. "It was all I could do to make it through the ceremony. Every time I got around people, I became physically sick."

"Didn't your parents get you any counseling?"

She smiled bitterly. "Back then, counseling was for crazy people, and there was nothing wrong with me. I'd only been raped, remember?"

"There is no such thing as only rape," Wade said as he came back into the room. "Judd, help me get Betty onto this sofa."

Together, they lifted Shuler's wife off the floor, then Wade broke the cylinder of smelling salts beneath her nose. Almost instantly, she roused. Once cognizance returned, she started to cry.

"Betty, I'm sorry," Raymond said. "You have to understand, I was just a kid. I didn't know what—"

"Shut up, Raymond," she said, sobbing. "You're always blaming someone else for your troubles, but this time, there's no one left but you to blame." Then she stood abruptly. "Wade… Mr. Hanna…if you will excuse me, I need to go now."

Wade shrugged. There was no reason she had to be there.

"You need a ride home?" he asked.

She clutched her purse to her chest, unable to look her husband in the face.

"No, it's Raymond who's going to be afoot when this is over."

Raymond looked startled, and it occurred to him then that he might be facing more than a revelation here. He might be facing divorce.

"Betty, you need to give me a chance to—"

"I don't need to do anything," she said, then turned to Judith. "I know it's not much, but I'm sorry," she said, and then walked out of the room.

Raymond struggled to his feet, torn between the need to follow his wife, and the fear of what else might be said if he left. He glanced at Wade.

"I don't intend to press charges," he said abruptly.

Wade sighed. Somehow he wasn't surprised. He looked at Judith. Her composure was frightening. She was far too cool for his peace of mind.

"That still doesn't eradicate the fact that she committed a crime," he said.

"I won't testify against her," Raymond muttered.

Judith sat quietly listening to the decisions men were making of her life. Then Raymond looked past her, for the first time since the revelation, to stare at the face of his child.

To his surprise, he actually recognized bits of himself. The dark hair. The nose, a little too short for the size of his face. The slight cleft in his chin. He blinked, surprised that he found himself crying.

"Boy."

Davie wouldn't look and Raymond couldn't blame him. He thought back to the treatment the boy had suffered at his hands.

"Boy, look at me…please," Raymond said.

Finally, he did.

"I promise I will never be mean to you again."

The slow smile that came on Davie's face shamed Raymond more than he could say. Then he looked at Judith.

"Sorry will never be enough," he said. "If there is ever anything I can do for you…or for him…"

"Davie. His name is Davie," Judith said shortly.

Raymond flinched as he spoke the name, for the first time in his life, saying the name of his son aloud.

"Davie. If there is ever anything I can do for Davie, all you have to do is ask."

"Just leave us alone," she said.

His shoulders slumped. He walked out of the department, a lesser man than when he'd come in.

Judd looked at Wade, waiting for him to make the call.

Wade leaned forward.

"Judith, you know you need some help."

She shrugged. "Once I needed help and no one came."

Judd's belly turned. With that one sentence, he was yanked back to that place beneath the stairs where he'd prayed to God for help that never came. He took a deep breath, fighting the nausea that came up in his throat.

"That may be so," Wade said. "But I'm talking about now. Who's to say you don't fly off the deep end and do something worse the next time?"

"There won't be a next time," she said. "I accomplished what I set out to do."

Judd's breath was coming faster now. He could feel himself coming undone. Everything Wade was saying to Judith, his captain had said about him. He'd ignored it then, refusing to believe it of himself. But now, faced with the evidence of what suppressed anger could do, he knew his troubles were not over. Not until he faced his own devil as Judith Dandridge had done.

"I don't intend to argue about this," Wade said. "I'm going to recommend that you start some counseling. Only after I'm convinced that you've channeled your need for revenge into something positive, I'll consider the case closed. Do we have a deal?"

Judith stood. "Since I have no say in this matter, I suppose we do." Then she began gathering up the remains of Davie's lunch.

"Is the picnic over, Aunt Judy?" Davie asked.

She stopped, staring at him for a long, silent moment, then she ruffled his hair.

"Yes, dear, I believe the picnic is finally over."

Judd couldn't be there any longer. He needed to move, before he came undone.

"I'll be at the house," he said shortly, and stalked out of the office before Wade could object.

All the way home, he kept seeing himself as a child, storing away the hate because it was all his father could give him. He thought of Charlotte, and of Rachel's sweet baby face. Always laughing, in constant mischief. Neither one of them deserved to live with a ticking time bomb, which is what he knew he was.

By the time he turned in the driveway, he knew what he had to do.

Charlie was still in shock when Judd pulled up in front of the house and parked. Wade's call wasn't unusual, but his news had floored her. Not only had he called to tell her that he wouldn't be home until he was certain the news didn't start a riot in the streets, he'd felt obligated to warn her that Judd had bolted out of the office without an explanation and was on his way there.

She heard Judd get out, then heard the car door slam shut. She glanced at the clock. It was just after one. Rachel would nap for at least another hour, maybe longer. That was good. She and Judd could talk. He was obviously upset about something, or he wouldn't have left so abruptly. She wouldn't let herself think of the inevitable— that the mystery was solved and he would be leaving. She wouldn't think about that at all.

She heard the kitchen door open. She turned. Judd was standing in the door and she could tell by the look on his face that he had come to say goodbye.

"This isn't fair," she whispered.

"Life rarely is," he countered, and took her in his arms.

She clung to him, stifling an urge to throw herself at his feet and beg him to stay, but her pride was all she had left. It would be what held her together when he was gone.

"Wade told me what happened."

Judd shook his head. "It was unbelievable."

She pushed out of his embrace and then turned, reaching for a dish towel to have something to hold besides him.

"I suppose you came to pack your things." And then her chin quivered. "In a way, I've been expecting this," she said. "Only not quite so sudden."

Judd sighed. Of course she was going to misunderstand. If only he could make her see.

"It's not what you think," he said softly.

She turned, clutching the dish towel against her belly, her eyes nearly blind with tears.

"Then make me understand," she said. "Because I'm thinking that I just might die from this pain."

He groaned. "God, Charlotte, I need to do this or I'll wind up like her."

She frowned. "Like who?"

"Judith. Judith Dandridge. If I don't get rid of the hate that's inside me, I'm afraid that one day I'll explode as she did—only you and Rachel would be the ones who would suffer."

She blanched. Suddenly, things were starting to make sense. This wasn't about him leaving her. It was about finishing the journey he'd started before they met.

She swiped at her tears with the flats of her hands.

"I have a request to make of you."

"Ask," he said.

"Go bury your demons and lay all your ghosts, Judd Hanna, but when you're through, will you come back to me?"

"In a heartbeat," he said, then pulled her back into his arms. "Now I have a request to make of you."

"Ask."

"Lie with me, love."

"Always," she answered, and wrapped her arms around his neck.

Two hours later, he was gone. Charlie was still crying when Rachel woke up from her nap. She toddled into the room, dragging her blanket behind her as she went and crawled into her mother's lap.

"'Mallows?" she asked, and then laid her head on Charlie's breast, uncomfortable with the tears on her mother's face.

Charlie hugged her close, struggling to remember where her priorities lay.

"Okay, sweetheart," she said. "We'll go get you some 'mallows."

Rachel grinned, pleased with the answer. "Judd have some, too?"

Charlie stifled a sob. "Not today, honey. Judd went bye-bye. He'll have to eat his 'mallows somewhere else."

Chapter 14

More than a week had passed since Judd's exit from Call City. He'd stopped in Tulsa on his way through and tied up the last of loose ends. The news that they'd arrested the perp who'd killed his partner was a huge relief. Everyone at the police department had seemed genuinely glad to see him, but he'd already felt the mental distance between them. He'd abandoned them. They'd gone on with their lives. It was the way things were.

After that, it had taken him a couple more days to pack up his apartment and put the stuff in storage. Now there was nothing standing between him and Charlie but the laying of ghosts.

The next day, he'd packed up his car and headed east, telling himself that the anxiety he felt was all in his mind. Yet the minute he crossed the border into Kentucky, his belly started to knot. He couldn't see the rich green of the mountains or the deep, endless valleys for the memories that came flooding back. It had been fifteen years since he'd gotten on that bus in Paducah, determined that life would not turn him into a replica of his father. And in a manner of speaking it had not. But something had happened to him along the way that he hadn't expected. His father had given him up, but Judd had never given up the hate that bound them. Normally, one would expect the years to fade a child's memories, but not so Judd's. Some of the foster homes he'd been put in were good, some not so good. But nothing had ever come close to the hell of his first ten years.

He stopped at a gas station along the highway to refuel. And as he waited for the car to fill up, his gaze fell on a telephone booth beside the store. Immediately, his thoughts went to Charlie. Was she okay? How long would it be before Rachel would forget him? He sighed. The deputy was probably back from his honeymoon by now. Oh, God, please don't let Charlie have second thoughts now that I'm gone.

The pump kicked off and he replaced the nozzle before going to pay. The day was warm, the wind, gusting. When he got inside, he went to the cooler to get something to drink, then strolled past the small grocery aisle to pick up a bag of chips. As he did, a display of marshmallows caught his attention and he immediately thought of Rachel. She was quite a charmer. If they had a houseful like her it would be great.

Then he stopped, overwhelmed by the idea of family, and of knowing that he would always be loved. The concept was staggering to a man who'd never known it before.

"Will that be all, mister?"

Judd looked up. The woman behind the cash register was waiting. He set his purchases down on the counter, then pulled out his wallet. A short while later, he was back on the road. If he'd figured correctly, he would be in Boyington by midafternoon. Soon enough to find a motel—and call Charlotte. He just needed to hear her voice. After that, he would take it one day at a time.

Wade sat at the kitchen table, helping Rachel eat a bowl of spaghetti, while eyeing Charlie's every move. He knew she was worried. It had been a week since Judd's departure and they had yet to hear from him. But every time he brought up the subject, she gave him the same explanation, saying Judd would be back.

"How do you know?" Wade had asked, and her answer was always the same. "Because he said."

She was running on nerves and he could tell it, but there was nothing he could say to make it better.

A short while later, they were just sitting down to their supper when the phone began to ring. Charlie jerked, dropping a fork she'd been about to put in the salad, then turned, staring at the phone as if she could will it to be Judd.

"I'll get it," Wade said, and reached for the phone. "Hello, this is Wade."

"Is Charlie there?"

Wade let out a sigh of relief. "Breathing down my neck. I suppose you want to talk to her instead of me."

"Sorry," Judd said. "But you just don't have what it takes."

"That's not what the new waitress at the Call City café thinks," Wade said.

Judd laughed in his ear. Wade grinned as he handed the phone to Charlie.

"For you, sis."

"Hello?"

"Charlotte, is your brother still listening?"

Weak with relief, she leaned against the wall and cupped the phone against her ear.

"No."

"Good," Judd said. "Because what I have to say to you isn't fit for other ears."

She grinned. "I'm listening."

Moments later, her eyes widened, and then her heart skipped a beat.

"Is that possible?" she muttered.

"Oh, yeah," Judd said. "And after that, I'm going to…"

Charlie moaned beneath her breath.

"Are you all right?" Wade asked.

She nodded, then laughed out loud. "I am now."

Judd smiled to himself, listening to the joy in her voice and knowing that he'd made the right decision to call.

"I miss you, Charlotte. I miss seeing you, and touching you. I miss your smile, and the way you chew on your lower lip when you're bothered."

"I miss you, too," she said, echoing his sentiments. Then she added, "Are you okay? I mean…have you found what you were looking for?"

He glanced at the phone book, and the name he'd circled in red.

"Not yet, but I'm close."

She sighed. "Take care and hurry home."

The words wrapped around him. Home. Hurry home.

"Keep the bed warm for me," he said softly.

"Always," she said.

Moments later, he was gone.

Wade was grinning. "So he called. So I was wrong. So sue me."

Charlie sat down at the table, then sighed. She wasn't going to relax until he was back in her arms.

Morning was a long time coming. Judd had walked the motel floor until long after 1:00 a.m., psyching himself up. More than once he found himself standing in front of the mirror, staring at his reflection.

He was a big man—well over six foot tall. His shoulders were broad, sometimes too broad for the clothes on the racks. He'd been shot once and broken his leg twice. Once while running down a perp, and the second time, falling off a dock at Lake Tenkiller while fishing for crappie. He'd had two partners in his law enforcement career, and both were dead. One of natural causes, the other died on the job. Both times, he stood at the gravesite, dry-eyed and stoic. He was the iron man. The man who never gave up.

Finally, he turned away from the mirror, unable to look at himself anymore. If he was so damned tough, then why was he scared to death to go face the bogeyman down? He wasn't a kid any longer. On a daily basis he had arrested worse men than Joe Hanna and had never flinched. But Judd was overlooking one very important fact. His only knowledge of Joe had come when he was a child, too small to fight back. There were no mental boundaries for the man Joe was today.

He reached for his jacket and started to put it on, then decided against it and tossed it back on the bed.

"Just get it over with," he muttered, and headed for the door before he could talk himself out of the trip.

An hour later, he was cruising through the streets, checking addresses and looking for something—anything—that might prove familiar. But it had been a long time. Things change. People move. Houses get remodeled and some even burn down, which was the case with the house he'd just passed. He slowed, leaning forward and peering out the windshield as he checked the house numbers for 122. And a few minutes later, he saw it, then tapped the brakes and wheeled up to the curb.

The house was old, like the one they'd lived in when he was a kid, but it was different. He didn't recognize anything about where he was—not the neighborhood, not the landscape, not any of the nearby businesses he'd passed. Maybe he had the wrong man, or the right man and the wrong address, or maybe he was just delaying the inevitable. He sighed. Most likely the latter.

He got out, slamming the door shut behind him, then stood for a moment, his hands on his hips, his Stetson pulled down low across his forehead. Even though he had parked in the shade, the air was already hot. He was glad he'd left his jacket behind.

The house at 122 May Avenue was in need of paint. The screens on the windows were rusted, giving the gray, peeling house the appearance of having black eyes. Large trees shaded the small, postage-stamp yard, and tall, overgrown bushes in desperate need of trimming bordered the old concrete porch. There was a narrow opening in the bushes that led to the steps, and then the front door. He fixed his gaze and started toward it with purpose in his step.

By the time he got to the front door, he was sick to his stomach. He kept picturing a large, angry man looming over him in the dark. He made a fist and started to knock, when he was startled by a voice to his left.

"What's your business?"

He jerked, his hand automatically going for a gun that wasn't there. He squinted, peering into the shadows, and could just make out the silhouette of an old man in a chair.

"I'm looking for a man," Judd said.

The old man snorted. "One of them kind, are ye?"

Judd frowned, ignoring the allusion to homosexuality. "His name is Joe Hanna. Do you know him?"

This question seemed to set the old man into hysterics. He slapped his leg and guffawed until he made himself cough. Then he hacked for another minute or so until Judd thought he was going to have to call an ambulance.

"You all right?" Judd asked.

The old man pounded his chest, wheezing and gasping as he shook his head.

"Hell, no, I ain't all right. I'm dying," he muttered.

"Still got your sense of humor," Judd said.

The old man grinned. "Well, I ain't dead yet."

Judd started all over again. "About Joe Hanna. The name in the phone book lists him at this address. Do you know how long he's been gone?"

The old man laughed again, slapping his leg and rocking back in his chair.

Judd rolled his eyes, waiting for the mirth to subside. Obviously, the old fellow knew something that Judd did not.

Finally, the old fellow calmed. Judd asked him again.

"Please, mister. It's important to me. Do you know where I can find Joe Hanna?"

The old man leaned forward, pointing at Judd with a long, bony finger.

"Who wants to know?" he asked.

Judd pulled out his ID, wishing at the moment that he still had his badge, but he'd already turned that in to the captain back in Tulsa.

The old man waved Judd's wallet away.

"I can't see nothin' anymore. Talk to me, boy. I ain't in the mood to read a book."

"I'm a cop. My name is Judd Hanna, and I'm looking for a man named—"

"Joe."

"Right," Judd said. "Joe Hanna."

The old man's expression was suddenly haggard. Judd wondered what it would be like to accept the imminence of death, to take each breath knowing it could be the last. He watched as the old man dragged himself to his feet, then began an odd little scoot and sidestep toward where Judd was standing.

But the closer he got, the more tense Judd became. He didn't know when he finally realized his search was over, but as he did, a bonus came with it. The fear he'd been saving for all of these years wasn't there. Joseph Hanna, the snarling demon who'd plagued his life and his dreams, didn't even have his own teeth anymore. Judd took a deep, cleansing breath, then looked down into the face of his father.

"I didn't figure on ever seeing you again," Joe said.

"I didn't plan to come."

The abruptness of his son's answer wasn't what Joe expected. Like Judd, he didn't know how to relate. This wasn't the little snot-nosed kid who'd caused him so much trouble. This man was tall, much taller than Joe had ever been, and there was an edge to his manner that Joe envied. A "like me or leave me alone" attitude he'd never been able to cultivate. In that moment, he would have sold his soul for the ability to stand straight once again. And then he amended the thought. Hell, he couldn't sell something he'd already lost.

"So…if this little surprise ain't no accident, then what are you doing here?" Joe asked.

Judd thrust his hands in his pockets.

"Laying ghosts."

Joe frowned. "I don't get it."

Judd shrugged. "Somehow, that doesn't surprise me, old man."

"Yeah, you call me old now, but once I was big and strong and—"

"And you beat the hell out of me for no reason. Every day of my life, just because you could. Yeah, you're right old man, once you were a real, big son of a bitch."

Joe looked flustered, then became defensive.

"I did the best I could," he said. "It wasn't easy raisin' no kid by myself."

"You didn't raise me. I took care of myself."

"You don't know nothin'," Joe muttered.

Judd sighed, suddenly exhausted, as if he'd been awake forever.

"Maybe you're right. But what I do know is that I guess what I came for was to tell you goodbye."

Joe blinked. "But you just got here."

"You're wrong. I never left—at least, not in my mind. It's past time I let it all go."

He settled his hat a little firmer upon his head and turned away.

"Where you goin'?"

Judd paused, then turned. "I'm going home, where I belong."

Joe followed him to the edge of the steps, watching the vigor with which Judd was walking, and in that moment, resented him more than he'd ever resented him before.

"You think you're something, don't you?" Joe yelled. "You think because you're bigger and meaner now, that you're top dog. Well, I got news for you. You'll never be like me, boy! Never!"

Halfway down the sidewalk, Judd stopped and turned, and there was a look on his face that had never been there before.

"Thanks—Dad. That's the best news you ever gave me."

Then he got in his Jeep and drove away. The farther he got, the lighter his heart became. He'd buried his demons—conquered his fears. It had taken him twenty-three years, but he'd vanquished the monster under the bed.

He'd been on the road for two days, driving almost nonstop. The urge to get back to Charlie was fierce, far stronger than the one that had taken him away. He glanced at his watch, judging his exhaustion against the time it would take him to reach Call City. He groaned. At the least, it was another three hours of hard driving. Ahead, a line of thunderstorms were lighting up the sky—ripping apart the heavens with bright angry threads of pure energy. If he kept going, he'd be driving straight into the mess. There was a small town up ahead. He remembered it from before, when he'd first come this way. It had a motel. He could stay there for the night and get an early start tomorrow. But the thought of being only a few hours away from Charlotte's arms was enough to keep him driving.

Another hour passed, and true to his prediction, he had driven into the storm. The force of the wind was whipping his Jeep all over the road, and it was all he could do to keep it in the right lane. The frenzy of the windshield wipers scraping back and forth across the glass beat a rhythm he couldn't ignore.

Char-lie. Char-lie.

Everything whispered her name.

"Just get me home," Judd said, unaware that he'd said the words aloud until the sound of his own voice startled him.

And as he focused on what he'd just said, his heart skipped a beat. Dear God. While he'd been a little vague about who he'd been asking, he'd just said a prayer. Something he hadn't done since that night under the stairs.

Granted, as far as prayers went, it wasn't much, but for a man who'd all but given up on God, it was a giant step in the right direction. The emotional upheaval of the revelation left him stunned. Where had the urge come from?

Was it something as simple as going home to Charlie? Was that what he had needed to regain his faith? Or was it the fact that he'd turned loose of his hate and would no longer be haunted by visions of Joe Hanna's face? He cleared his throat, a little stunned that his eyes had filled with tears.

"Are you there, God? It's been a real long time since I acknowledged your presence."

His heart stayed silent. If there were answers, Judd couldn't hear them.

Suddenly, a bolt of lightning hit the ground a short

distance ahead. Judd swerved, almost running off the road. As he guided the vehicle from the shoulder, then back to the highway, he breathed a quick sigh of relief, realizing he'd just gotten an answer.

"Thanks," he said softly. "I owe you one."

He continued to drive, never taking his gaze from the yellow line that was leading him back to Charlie.

The thunderstorm had passed through hours ago, washing everything clean. Outside the Franklin homestead, water stood in puddles, reflecting the moon glow overhead. Except for Wade's occasional snore and the tick of a clock, the house was silent.

And then in the middle of a breath, Charlie sat bolt upright, looking around the room in sudden panic. What? What was it she'd heard?

She threw back the covers and raced out of the room; her first instinct, as always, was Rachel. But her baby was asleep, motionless beneath the wrap she'd made of her blanket. She stood in the hallway a moment, listening closer, yet heard nothing but Wade's gentle snores. She turned, looking nervously up the hall. Something was going to happen, she just knew it, but what could it be?

Hugging herself quickly, she started to go back to bed, but the moment she turned her back on the hall, the feeling came over her again.

"God, I know that you're here…but I don't know what you're trying to say."

Knowing now that sleep would be impossible, she tiptoed up the hall, following the glow from the living room lamp, and curled up in one of the chairs. Her eyes were wide, transfixed by the darkness beyond the windows as she waited for the answer to be revealed.

* * *

Judd's eyes were heavy, his body weary from lack of sleep, but the urge to keep moving was strong—so strong. Two packages sat on the seat beside him, each wrapped in a different color of paper. In the pink one, all covered with ribbons and curls, was a small baby doll with its very own blanket and wide brown eyes, just like a certain baby he knew. The package of miniature marshmallows it was pillowed on was probably getting squashed, but Judd knew she wouldn't object.

The white package was small and unadorned, but to Judd, it held the greatest treasure of all—Charlotte's ring. He'd dreamed of putting it on her finger, of watching the expression on her face spreading from surprise to joy. It was to be the final connection needed that would bind him to these people for the rest of their lives.

A ring, two simple words, and a preacher. That's all it would take. And the only thing left between them was a slow but diminishing distance.

Suddenly, Judd straightened in the seat as he realized he was beginning to recognize landmarks. Even in the dark, he could see the outline of Old Man Tucker's barn. And down the road was the tree with three forks. His heart skipped a beat.

Another mile, then another, and without warning, the road was there. He took the turn, following the beam of his headlights as they cut through the night. In the midst of his anticipation, it hit him that, although he had reached his destination, they would all be asleep.

And then he topped the hill leading down toward the house, and his heart caught in his throat. There, shining through the old farmhouse window, was that lamp, burning bright against the night. Tears shattered his vision, bringing him and the Jeep to a halt. In the distance, he could see the faint outline of Wade's patrol cruiser and Charlie's car. Everyone was home—except him. He took a deep breath. With the lamp as a guide, he began to move.

Charlie was staring blindly through the windows when she first saw the headlights top the hill. And the moment she did, she was on her feet and running for the door. This was her answer. This was why she'd wakened so abruptly in the middle of the night.

She ran outside, standing at the edge of the steps and watching as the vehicle came to a stop. She bolted off the porch as the man inside emerged. Within seconds, she was in his arms, crying and laughing as she fielded his kisses.

"You're home! You're home! Thank God, you're finally home."

Judd's heart was full to overflowing. A thousand words were running through his mind and all he could do was hold her. The softness of her body, the tenderness of her touch—even the laughter she had saved for him—were almost more than he could bear. He kept taking deep breaths between kisses, wanting to tell her, needing her to know that she was his true partner, that she had saved him, as surely as if she'd stood armed at his back, but nothing came out of his mouth but her name.

Charlie paused in the middle of a kiss, laughing as she cupped his face with her hands.

"Yes, Judd Hanna, it's me. Welcome home, my darling, welcome home."

* * * * *

Delores Fossen, a *USA TODAY* bestselling author, has written over one hundred novels, with millions of copies of her books in print worldwide. She's received a Booksellers' Best Award and an RT Reviewers' Choice Best Book Award. She was also a finalist for a prestigious RITA® Award. You can contact the author through her website at deloresfossen.com.

Books by Delores Fossen

Harlequin Intrigue

The Lawmen of McCall Canyon

Cowboy Above the Law
Finger on the Trigger
Lawman with a Cause
Under the Cowboy's Protection

HQN Books

Lone Star Ridge

Tangled Up in Texas
That Night in Texas (ebook novella)
Chasing Trouble in Texas

A Coldwater Texas Novel

Lone Star Christmas
Hot Texas Sunrise
Sweet Summer Sunset
A Coldwater Christmas

Visit the Author Profile page at Harlequin.com for more titles.

GRAYSON

Delores Fossen

Chapter 1

Silver Creek, Texas

Sheriff Grayson Ryland couldn't shake the feeling that someone was watching him.

He slid his hand over the Smith & Wesson in his leather shoulder holster and stepped from his patrol truck. He lifted his head, listening, and glanced around the thick woods that were practically smothering the yellow cottage. The front door and curtains were closed.

No sign of the cottage's owner, Eve Warren.

No sign of anyone for that matter, but just twenty minutes earlier Eve had called his office to report that she had seen someone *suspicious* in the area.

Grayson knew this part of the county like the back of his hand. Along with his brothers, he had fished in the creek at the bottom of the hill. He'd camped these woods. There were a lot of places to duck out of sight....

Plenty of memories, too.

That required a deep breath, and he cursed himself for having to take it.

The front door opened, and he spotted Eve. She was a five-foot-six-inch memory of a different kind. She'd obviously known he was there. Maybe that was the reason his brain was firing warnings on all cylinders.

"Grayson," she said, her tongue flickering over her bottom lip. "You came."

That nervous little tongue flicker and the too-hopeful look in her misty blue eyes riled him. "You called the sheriff's office and asked for me," he reminded her. "You said you thought you saw someone."

"Of course." She nodded, swallowed hard. "But I wasn't sure you'd come."

Neither was he, especially since he was neck-deep in a murder investigation, but when he'd gotten her message, he'd decided not to send a deputy, that he would be the one to personally respond.

Well, respond to the call anyway.

Not to the woman.

Not ever again.

It'd been over sixteen years since he'd last seen Eve. She'd been standing in a doorway then, too. Her blond hair had been well past her shoulders back in those days, but it was short now and fashionably rumpled. The last decade and a half had settled nicely on her curvy body.

Something he decided not to notice.

Since his eyes and body seemed to have a different idea about that not-noticing part, Grayson got down to business.

"You reported someone suspicious?" he prompted.

"I did." She scrubbed her hands down the sides of her pearl-gray dress. The cold December wind caught the hem, making it flutter around the tops of her knees. "I was about to call you anyway…about something else… and then I saw him. A man. He was down by the creek."

Grayson lifted his shoulder and wondered why the heck she'd intended to call him, but he didn't ask. "Could have been a neighbor." Even though there weren't any close ones to the Warren cottage.

"I don't think it was a neighbor," Eve insisted. "I got a bad feeling when I spotted him."

Yeah. Grayson knew all about bad feelings. The one he had about this situation was getting worse with each passing moment.

"I didn't want to take any chances," she continued. "What with the murder you had here a few days ago. How are you handling that, by the way?"

She probably hadn't meant to irritate him with that question, but she did. Hell, no matter what she said, she would irritate him. But Grayson didn't want anyone, including Eve, questioning his ability to handle a murder investigation, even if it was only the third one in his twelve years as sheriff of Silver Creek.

"I heard you haven't identified the body, or the killer," she added.

"Not yet." And Grayson got back on target. "You have any idea who this person was you saw?"

Eve shook her head. "No. But for the past couple of days I've been getting hang-up calls at my condo in San Antonio. And there's been a time or two when I thought someone was following me. Nothing specific. Just a feeling. It was one of the reasons I decided to come out to the cottage. So I could get away."

Well, that explained that. Eve had inherited the cottage from her grandmother eighteen months ago, but to the best of Grayson's knowledge, this was her first visit to the place. And she hadn't just come to relax. She'd planned on calling him.

Why?

Again, he didn't ask. He kept this conversation focused on the job he'd been called out to do.

"Any reason you know of why someone would follow you or make those hang-up calls?" he asked.

Another head shake. "I've been under a lot of stress lately," she admitted. "The job. And some personal stuff. Until I saw the man, I kept telling myself that it was all in my head. But he was real, Grayson."

He mentally groaned at the way she said his name. It was intimate, the way she used to murmur it after one of their scalding hot kissing sessions.

He glanced at the woods, then the creek. "I'll have a look around," Grayson let her know. "But if you're worried, you probably shouldn't be staying out here alone."

He turned to have that look around.

"Wait," Eve called out. "Don't go. I wanted to ask about your family. How are your brothers?"

He had four living brothers. Four sets of news, updates and troubles. Since it would take the better part of an hour to catch her up on everything, Grayson settled for saying, "They're all fine."

Grayson turned again, but again Eve stopped him.

"Even Nate?" she questioned. "I heard his wife was killed a few months ago."

Yeah. That was all part of the troubles. The worst of

them. "Nate's coping." But Grayson knew that wasn't true. If Nate didn't have his baby daughter to care for, his brother wouldn't make it out of bed each morning. Grayson was still trying to figure out how to take care of that.

"And the ranch?" Eve continued. "I read somewhere that the ranch won a big award for your quarter horses."

Fed up with the small talk, Grayson decided to put an end to this. Chitchat was an insult at this stage of the game. However, when he looked back at her, he saw that she had her hands clenched around the door frame. Her knuckles were turning white.

Grayson cursed under his breath. "Okay. What's wrong?" But he didn't just ask. He went closer so he could see inside the cottage to make sure someone wasn't standing behind her, holding her at gunpoint. Because Eve wasn't the white-knuckle type. He had never known anything to scare her.

The place was small so he was able to take in most of it with one sweeping glance. There was no one in the living and eating area, and the loft/bedroom was empty, too.

Grayson looked her straight in the eyes. "Eve, are you all right?"

She hesitated and nibbled some more on her lip. "I really did see someone about a half hour ago, I swear, and he ran away when he spotted me."

Since that sounded like the beginning of an explanation that might clarify the real reason for her call, Grayson just stood there and waited for the rest of it.

"Could you come in?" Eve finally said. "I need to talk to you."

Oh, hell. This couldn't be good. "Talk?" he challenged. He was about to remind her that it was long over between them, that they had no past issues to discuss, but she kept motioning for him to come in.

"Eve," he warned.

"Please." Her voice was all breath and no sound.

Grayson cursed that *please* and the look in her eyes. He knew that look. He'd seen it when she was thirteen and had learned her mother was dying from bone cancer. He'd seen it again sixteen years ago when on her twenty-first birthday she'd stood in the doorway of the ranch and demanded a commitment from him or else.

Because he'd had no choice, Grayson had answered *or else*.

And Eve had walked out.

Now, Grayson walked in. She stepped back so he could enter the cottage, and she shut the door behind him. He didn't take off his Stetson or his jacket because he hoped he wouldn't be here that long.

It was warm inside, thanks to the electric heater she had going near the fireplace. No fire, though. And it would have been a perfect day for it since the outside temp was barely forty degrees.

With a closer look, Grayson could see the place was in perfect order. Definitely no signs of any kind of struggle or hostage situation. There was no suitcase that he could spot, but Eve's purse was on the coffee table, and her camera and equipment bag were on the small kitchen counter. Several photographs were spread out around the bag. Since Eve was a newspaper photographer, that wasn't out of the ordinary, either.

"The pictures," she mumbled following his gaze. "I was trying to work while I waited for you."

Trying. And likely failing from the way they were scattered around. "Are you in some kind of trouble?"

"Yes," she readily admitted.

Surprised, and more worried than he wanted to be, he turned around to face her. "Trouble with the law?"

"I wish," Eve mumbled. She groaned softly and threaded her fingers through both sides of her hair. That stretched her dress over her breasts and gave Grayson a reminder he didn't want or need.

He'd been attracted to Eve for as long as he could remember. But he refused to let that attraction play into whatever the hell this was.

"Trouble at work?" he tried next.

She lifted her shoulder but answered, "No."

He glanced at the photos on the table again.

"I took those at a charity fund-raising rodeo in San Antonio," she explained.

So, they were work, but judging from the casual way she'd mentioned them, they weren't the source of the worry in her eyes. "Look, I could play twenty questions and ask about a stalker, an ex or whatever. But let's save ourselves some time and you just tell me what you have to say."

She nodded, paused, nodded again. "It's personal. And it has to do with you. I need to ask you something."

Grayson braced himself for some kind of rehashing of the past. After all, he was thirty-eight now, and Eve was thirty-seven. Hardly kids. And since neither of them had ever married, maybe this was her trip back down memory lane.

Well, he didn't want to take this trip with her.

"I've been having some medical problems," she continued. But then paused again.

That latest pause caused Grayson to come up with some pretty bad conclusions. Conclusions he didn't want to say aloud, but his first thought was cancer or some other terminal disease. Hell.

Had Eve come home to die?

"What's wrong?" he settled for repeating.

She shook her head, maybe after seeing the alarm in his eyes. "No. Not that kind of medical problem."

Grayson silently released the breath he'd been holding.

"I'm, uh, going through, well, menopause," she volunteered.

Of all the things Grayson had expected her to say, that wasn't one of them. "Aren't you too young for that?"

"Yes. Premature menopause." She swallowed hard again. "There's no way to stop it."

Well, it wasn't a cancer death sentence like her mother's, but Grayson could understand her concern. "So, is that why you're here, to try to come to terms with it?"

He'd asked the question in earnest, but he checked his watch. Talking with him wouldn't help Eve come to terms with anything, and he had work to do. That included a look around the place and then he had to convince her to head back to San Antonio. It was obvious she was too spooked and worried to be out in the woods all alone.

"I don't have much time," she said before he could speak. "That's why I came to Silver Creek today. And that's why I'll need your answer right away. I know this isn't fair, but if you say no, I'll have to try to find someone else…though I'm not sure I can." She didn't stop long enough to draw breath, and her words bled together. "Still, I'll understand if you want to say no, but Grayson, I'm praying you won't—"

"What are you talking about?" he finally said, speaking right over her.

Now Eve stopped and caught on to the back of the chair. "Perhaps you should sit down for this."

The rushed frantic pace was gone, but her eyes told him this particular storm was far from being over.

"I'd rather stand," he let her know.

"No. Trust me on this. You need to be sitting."

That took him several steps beyond just being curious, and Grayson sank into the chair across from her. Eve sat as well, facing him. Staring at him. And nibbling on her lip.

"I'm not sure how to say this," she continued, "so I'm just going to put it out there."

But she still didn't do that. Eve opened her mouth, closed it and stared at him.

"Grayson," she finally said and looked him straight in the eyes. "I need you to get me pregnant. *Today.*"

Chapter 2

Eve had tried to brace herself for Grayson's reaction.

She'd anticipated that he might just walk out. Or curse. Or even ask her if she'd lost her mind. He might still do those things, but at the moment he just sat there while his jaw practically hit his knees.

Other than his slack-jaw reaction, there was no sign of the storm that she must have stirred up inside him. Not that Eve had expected him to show any major signs of what he was feeling.

Grayson was Grayson.

Calm, reliable, levelheaded, responsible.

Hot.

In those well-worn Wranglers, black Stetson, black shirt and buckskin jacket, he looked like a model for some Western ad in a glossy magazine.

A comparison he would have hated if he had known what she was thinking.

Even though he had that scarred silver badge clipped to his rawhide rodeo belt, Grayson was first and foremost a cowboy and, along with his brothers, owner of one of the most successful ranches in central Texas. That success was due in large part to Grayson.

There was nothing glossy about him.

Eve forced herself away from that mental summary of Grayson's attributes. His hot cowboy looks and ranching success weren't relevant here. It had been the calm, reliable, levelheaded and responsible aspects of his personality that had caused her to want him to father her child.

Maybe it was her desperation, but Eve had hoped that Grayson would also be cooperative. That slack jaw gave her some doubts about that though.

"When I was at my doctor's office this morning, I found out I'm ovulating," she continued. That seemed way too personal to be sharing with anyone except maybe a spouse or best friend, but she didn't have time for modesty here.

Time was literally ticking away.

"The fact that I'm ovulating is nothing short of a miracle," she continued. "The doctor didn't think it would happen, and it almost certainly won't happen again."

Grayson just kept staring.

She wished he would curse or yell, but no, not Grayson. Those silver-gray eyes drilled right into her, challenging her to give him an explanation that he could wrap his logical mind around.

There wouldn't be anything logical about this. Well, not on his part anyway. To Eve, it was pure logic.

"I desperately want a child, and I'm begging you to help me," she clarified in case the gist had gotten lost in all her babbling. "I don't have time to find anyone else. I've got twenty-four hours, maybe less."

Grayson dropped the stare, blew out a long breath and leaned back in the chair. He was probably glad that she had insisted on the being seated part.

He flexed his eyebrows. "How can you possibly ask me to do this?"

"You're the first person I thought of," she admitted.

Actually, he was the *only* person. Those Ryland genes were prime stuff, and all the Ryland males were able-bodied, smart as whips and drop-dead gorgeous with their midnight-black hair and crystal-gray eyes. Again, the looks were just icing.

Grayson wasn't just her first choice for this. He was her *only* choice.

"Don't say no," Eve blurted out when she was certain Grayson was about to do exactly that.

Now he cursed. This time it wasn't under his breath. "No," he stated simply, but it had not been simply said. There was a flash of emotion in all those swirls of gray in his eyes. "You already know I don't want to be a father."

It was an argument that Eve had anticipated, and she had a counterargument for it. "Yes, because you had to raise your younger brothers after your father walked out and your mother died."

Now *she* cursed. She should have rehearsed this. Bringing up Grayson's reckless father was not the way to earn points here even though it'd happened over twenty years ago when Grayson was barely eighteen. A lifetime wouldn't be long enough to forget or forgive that kind of hurt, and it had shaped Grayson to the very core of who he was now.

Yes, he'd been a father figure to his five younger siblings. Head of the ranch and the family. And he'd sacrificed so much for both that by the time Eve had been looking to settle down and have a family with him, Grayson no longer had anything to give anyone.

Including her.

Still, she wanted him for this massive favor.

"I'm not asking you to be a father." Eve tried and failed to keep the emotion out of her argument, but her voice broke. "I only need you to get me pregnant, Grayson. Nothing else. In fact, I would insist on nothing else."

She hated to put him into a corner as she'd done all those years ago. That had been a massive mistake. But she did need an immediate answer.

Grayson shook his head again and eased to the edge of the chair so they were closer. And eye to eye.

"I can't." He held up his hand when she started to interrupt him. "I know the difference between fathering a child and being a father. I can't say yes to either."

Oh, mercy. He wasn't even giving it any thought or consideration. He had doled out an automatic refusal. Eve had thought she had prepared herself for this, but she obviously hadn't. That sent her desperation to a whole new level. Everything inside her started to race and spin as if she were on the verge of a panic attack.

She immediately tried to come up with other ways she could persuade him. First and foremost, she could try to use their past. Their connection. They'd been close once. Once, they'd been in love.

Well, she had been in love with him anyway.

Grayson never quite let himself take that leap of the heart, and he'd certainly never said the words.

She had hoped the close-to-love feelings that he had once had for her would be a trump card she could use here to convince him. Heck, she wasn't too proud to beg.

But she shook her head.

Begging might work. *Might.* However, this was Grayson, and because in the past she had loved him, Eve owed him more than that. She reined in her feelings and tried to say something that made sense. Something that would make him see that she wasn't crazy, just desperate.

"I'm sorry," she somehow managed to say. Her breath suddenly felt too thick to push out of her lungs, and she understood that whole cliché about having a heavy heart. Hers weighed a ton right now. "When the doctor told me I was ovulating and that I probably had a day or two at most, I thought of you. I jumped right in my car and drove straight to Silver Creek."

"I'm flattered. I think." The corner of his mouth lifted a fraction.

Ah, there it was. The biggest weapon in the Grayson Ryland arsenal. That half smile. Even now, after his refusal, it made her feel all warm and golden inside.

Since he'd attempted some levity, Eve did, too, but she doubted the smile made it to her eyes. God, this hurt. She wanted this baby more than her own life, and it was slipping away as the seconds ticked off.

"You can find someone else?" Grayson asked.

"I hope." But that was being overly optimistic. She'd lost a lot of time by driving out to Silver Creek, but then she'd had no choice. She very well couldn't have explained this with a phone call. Plus, she had prayed that she would be able to convince him once they were face-to-face.

She'd obviously been wrong.

Eve felt the raw blush on her cheeks and got to her feet. "I need to hurry back into San Antonio."

Grayson stood, as well. "Maybe you can use a sperm bank or fertility clinic?"

"No." She tried to blink back the tears, but failed at that, too. "Not enough time. The doctor said it takes days, even weeks to go through the screening and get an appointment. Plus, many of the clinics are closed because Christmas is only three days away."

He acknowledged that with a shrug. "A friend then?"

The drive had given her time to consider that, as well. It was sad but true that she was seriously lacking male companionship. Heck, she hadn't had a real date in nearly a year, and her last boyfriend was married now. As for male friends and coworkers, none had fit the bill as well as Grayson Ryland.

She shook her head and hurried to the kitchen where she crammed the photos back into her bag. The pictures were yet another kettle of fish, but they would have to wait. Eve wasn't ready to give up her baby mission just yet, even if she'd failed with Grayson.

She put on her red wool coat and hoisted both her purse and equipment bag onto her shoulder. Moving as fast as she could, she shut off the heater, unplugged it and turned back around to face Grayson. Even after his refusal, she couldn't help feeling that jolt of attraction when she looked at him.

Drop-dead gorgeous was right.

And for several brief moments Eve considered tossing the little bit of pride she had left. She could just throw herself at him and try to seduce him.

But she rethought that.

Grayson would resist. He had already shown her that he had a mountain of willpower and discipline to go along with those looks.

"What will you do?" he asked.

Because she felt the tears start to burn in her eyes, Eve dodged his gaze and grabbed her keys. "Maybe I can hire a friend of a friend."

She could make some calls the second she was back in her car, but she had no idea where to start.

"Hire someone?" Grayson questioned. He stepped outside the cottage with her.

Eve nodded. She closed and locked the door before she headed for her car. It wasn't below freezing, but the icy wind sliced right through her.

"You'd hire someone?" Grayson repeated when she didn't answer. He caught on to her arm and whirled her around to face him. "Eve, listen to yourself. Yes, I know you're desperate, and this baby must be important to you or you wouldn't have come here, but you can't just hire someone to sleep with you."

"To provide semen so I can be inseminated," she corrected, maneuvering herself out of his grip. She couldn't look at him and didn't want him to look at her. Eve hurried across the yard. "I have no intentions of sleeping with anyone to get pregnant. I was serious about not having a biological father in the picture. I'll make some calls, find a donor, pay him for his sperm and, if necessary, I'll do the insemination at home."

Grayson made a sound of relief, or something. Probably because he'd thought she was indeed crazy enough to jump into bed with the first guy she ran across on the drive home. Eve's biological clock was screaming for her to do that, but she wanted a healthy baby and body.

"I want to raise a baby on my own," she continued. "And if I find someone, he'll have to agree to giving up his paternal rights."

No need to rehash the emotional baggage that had brought her to that conclusion. Besides, Grayson knew about her absentee father and the abusive stepfather that she'd had as a kid. He didn't know about the three failed relationships she'd had since leaving Silver Creek, and that included one episode of her being an honest-to-goodness runaway bride.

It was just as well he didn't know that.

Best not to spell it out that she considered Grayson and only Grayson for a life partner. He was literally the only man she trusted, even if he had crushed her heart all those years ago. And now he'd managed to do it again.

Frustrated with herself and her situation, Eve threw open the back door of her car so she could dump her bag and equipment onto the seat. She hesitated for just a moment because she knew Grayson was right behind her. If she turned around, she'd have to face him once more.

"I'm sorry I bothered you," Eve mumbled.

She turned and, still dodging his gaze, she tried to sidestep around Grayson.

He sidestepped, too, and blocked her path. She hadn't thought it possible, but he looked more uncomfortable than she felt.

"I can call the Silver Creek Hospital," Grayson suggested. "Doc Hancock might be able to pull some strings and speed up things with a sperm bank. Or I could talk to my brothers. They might know—"

"Don't involve your brothers," Eve interrupted.

Anything but that. Just talking about this would be hard enough for Grayson, especially telling them that he had turned her down. Eve didn't want to be the subject of conversation at the Ryland dinner table.

"Best not to involve anyone from Silver Creek," she added. "I'll go to a hospital in San Antonio and, well, beg." And she would. This pregnancy was going to happen, even if she didn't have a clue how she would manage it.

She stepped around him and hurried to the driver's side of the car. Since she wasn't looking at Grayson, that was probably the reason she saw the movement.

In the cluster of trees about fifty yards from her car.

"What?" Grayson asked when she froze.

Eve looked around the trees, trying to figure out what had caught her attention.

There.

She saw the man.

Dressed in a dark shirt and pants, he had a black baseball cap sitting low on his head so that it obstructed his face. He quickly ducked out of sight, but from just that quick glimpse, Eve recognized him.

"That's the same man I saw earlier, by the creek," she told Grayson.

Grayson drew his gun from the shoulder holster beneath his jacket. The metal whispered against the leather, and he moved in front of her. "Any idea who he is?"

"No." But she knew that he was hiding, and that couldn't be good.

Did this have anything to do with the hang-up calls she'd been getting? Or could it be her imagination working overtime? Everything suddenly seemed to be going against her.

"I'm Sheriff Grayson Ryland," Grayson called out. "Identify yourself."

Eve stood there and held her breath, waiting. But the man said nothing.

"You think it's a local kid playing a prank?" she whispered, praying that was all there was to this.

Grayson fastened his attention to those trees. "No. A local kid would have answered me."

True. Grayson commanded, and got, respect in Silver Creek. And that caused her heart to pound against her chest. After all, there was a killer on the loose. Eve almost hoped this was connected to the hang-up calls. Better that than having a killer just yards away.

Grayson lifted his gun, and he took aim. "Well?" he prompted, his voice loud enough that the person hiding wouldn't have any trouble hearing him. "Come out so I can see who you are."

Still nothing.

"Get in your car," Grayson instructed from over his shoulder. "I'll get a closer look."

Eve wanted to latch on to him, to stop him from walking toward those trees, but this was his job. Plus, Grayson wouldn't stop. Not for her. Not for anyone.

"Just be careful," she whispered, her voice cracking a little. Eve eased open her car door and ducked down to get inside.

The sound stopped her.

It was a loud blast, and it shook the ground beneath them. Her stomach went to her knees, and her breath stalled in her throat. For a split second she thought someone had shot at them.

But this was much louder than a gunshot.

"Get down!" Grayson shouted.

He didn't give her a chance to do that on her own. He hooked his arm around her waist and pulled her behind her car door and to the ground.

Eve glanced behind her, at the cottage, and she saw what had caused that nightmarish sound.

An explosion.

Her grandmother's cottage was on fire.

Chapter 3

What the hell was going on?

That was Grayson's first thought, quickly followed by the realization that if Eve and he had stayed inside the house just a few more minutes, they would have both been blown to bits.

Behind them, the cottage had orangey flames shooting from it, and there was debris plunging to the ground. Maybe a propane tank had exploded or something, but Grayson wasn't sure it was an accident.

After all, there was a guy hiding in the trees.

Grayson figured it was too much to hope that the two things weren't related.

Had this person somehow rigged the explosion? If so, that meant the man would have had to have gotten close enough to the cottage to tamper with the tank that was just outside the kitchen window, but Grayson hadn't heard him. Of course, he'd been so involved with Eve's baby bombshell that he might not have noticed a tornado bearing down on them. He would berate himself for that later.

Now, he had to do something to protect Eve.

Grayson took cover in front of her and behind the car door, and he re-aimed his gun in the direction of the person he'd seen just moments before the explosion.

"Get out here!" he shouted to the person.

After hearing no response to his last demand, Grayson didn't expect the guy to comply this time. And he didn't.

No answer.

No sign of him.

Grayson kept watch behind them to make sure no one was coming at them from that direction. Other than the falling debris, the fire and black smoke smearing against the sky, there was nothing.

Except Eve, of course.

Her eyes were wide with fear, and he could feel her breath whipping against his back and neck. "We could have died," she mumbled.

Yeah. They'd been damn lucky. A few minutes wasn't much of a window between life and death, and her storming out had literally saved them.

Because she looked to be on the verge of panicking, Grayson wanted to reassure her that all would be fine, but he had no idea if that was true. The one thing he did know was that it wasn't a good idea for them to be in the open like this. There could be a secondary explosion, and he needed to get Eve someplace safe so he could try to figure out what had just happened.

He glanced at his truck, but it was a good thirty

feet away. Too far. He didn't want Eve to be out in the open that long. There wasn't just the worry of a second explosion but of their tree-hiding *friend* and what he might try to do.

"Get inside your car," he told Eve, "and slide into the passenger's seat so I can drive."

"Oh, God," he heard her say.

And Grayson silently repeated it. He didn't know just how bad this situation could get, and he didn't want to find out with Eve in tow.

"Put the keys in the ignition," Grayson added when he felt her scramble to get into the car. "And stay down. Get on the floor."

No *Oh, God* this time, but he heard her breath shiver as it rushed past her lips. He wasn't exactly an old pro at facing potentially lethal situations, but he had the training and some experience during his time as sheriff. This had to be a first for Eve.

Not too many people had ever come this close to dying.

Grayson glanced behind him to make sure she had followed his orders. She had. Eve had squeezed herself in between the passenger's seat and the dashboard. It was safer than sitting upright, but Grayson knew a car wouldn't be much protection if anything was about to happen. A secondary explosion could send fiery debris slamming right into them.

He tried to keep watch all around them while he eased into the driver's seat and adjusted it so he'd fit. He needed to put some distance between the cottage, woods and them, and then he would call for assistance. Someone could take Eve to the sheriff's office, and

Grayson could figure out why all of this didn't feel like an accident.

While keeping a firm grip on his gun, he shut the car door and started the engine. He took out his phone and handed it to Eve. "Call the fire department."

She did but without taking her stunned gaze off the flames that were eating their way through what was left of the cottage. It had to break her heart to see the damage, and later the full loss would hit her.

As if she hadn't had enough to deal with for one day.

Even now, with the chaos of the moment, he still had her request going through his head.

I need you to get me pregnant.

He'd made it clear that wasn't going to happen, so the situation was over for him. But not for Eve. He had seen that determination in her eyes, and one way or another, she was going to get this dream baby. Hell, this near-death experience might even make her more determined.

"Hang on," Grayson warned her as he drove away— fast. He didn't exactly gun the engine, but he didn't dawdle, either.

The narrow road was dirt, gravel and mud since it had rained hard just that morning. With the sinkholes poxing the surface, it was impossible to have a smooth ride. But a smooth ride was an insignificant concern. Right now, he just wanted Eve out of there so he could deal with this situation on his own terms.

In other words, *alone.*

"The gas was turned off," Eve murmured. "It's been turned off for months. So what caused the explosion?"

"Maybe a leak in the gas line." And if so, that would be easy to prove.

"Call the first number on my contact list," Grayson

instructed. It was for the emergency dispatcher in the sheriff's building. "I want at least one deputy out here with the fire department. Have them meet me at the end of the road."

Once help arrived, he could hand off Eve to whichever deputy responded, and Grayson could escort the fire department and others to the scene. He didn't want anyone walking into a potential ambush.

Eve made the call, and he heard her relay his instructions to the emergency dispatcher. Just ahead, Grayson spotted the first curve of the snaky road. He touched the brakes.

And nothing happened.

Nothing!

The car continued to barrel toward the curve. So Grayson cursed and tried again, but this time he added a lot more pressure.

Still nothing.

Hell.

"What's wrong?" Eve asked.

Grayson dropped his gun onto the console between them so he could use both hands to steer. "I think someone cut the brake line."

Eve put her hand against her chest. "W-hat?"

She sounded terrified and probably was, but Grayson couldn't take the time to reassure her that he was going to try to get them out of this without them being hurt. The curve was just seconds away, and the road surface was as slick as spit. But his biggest concern was the trees. The road was lined with them, and if he crashed into one of them, Eve and he could both be killed on impact.

"Get in the seat and put on your seat belt," he told her, fastening his attention on the curve.

She scrambled to do just that, but he figured there wasn't enough time. To buy them a little more of that precious time, Grayson lifted the emergency brake lever, even though it wouldn't help much. The emergency brake would only work on the rear brake, and it wouldn't slow them down enough. Still, he had to try anything to reduce the speed.

"Hold on," he warned her.

Eve was still fumbling with the seat belt when the car went into the curve. Grayson had no choice but to try to keep the vehicle on the road since the trees were just yards away.

The right tires caught the gravel-filled shoulder, kicking up rocks against the metal undercarriage. The sound was nearly deafening, and it blended with his own heartbeat, which was pounding in his ears.

Eve's car went into a slide, the back end fishtailing. Grayson steered into the slide. Or rather that's what he tried to do, but he soon learned he had zero control. He saw the trees getting closer and closer, and there wasn't a damn thing he could do about it.

For just a split second, he made eye contact with Eve. Her gaze was frozen on him while her hands worked frantically to fasten the seat belt. Her eyes said it all.

She thought they were going to die, and she was silently saying goodbye.

Grayson didn't say goodbye back because he had no intention of dying today.

He heard the click of her seat belt, finally. And Grayson jerked the steering wheel to the left. The car careened in that direction, but not before the back end smashed into a live oak tree. The jolt rattled the entire vehicle and tossed them around like rag dolls.

Thank God they were wearing their seat belts.

He also thanked God that he was able to hang on to the steering wheel. They'd dodged a head-on collision, and the impact with the tree had slowed them down some, but they literally weren't out of the woods yet.

The car went into a skid in the opposite direction.

More trees.

Grayson didn't even bother to curse. He just focused all his energy on trying to control an out-of-control car.

And it was a battle he was losing.

There was a trio of hackberry trees directly in front of them. If he managed to miss one, he would no doubt just plow into the others, or one of their low-hanging limbs.

He fought with the wheel, trying to make it turn away, but they were in another skid, the mud and rocks helping to propel them in a direction he didn't want to go.

"There's the man we saw earlier," Eve said, her voice filled with fear.

She pointed to Grayson's right, but he didn't look in that direction. Not because he doubted her. No. The hiding man probably was there, but Grayson had to give it one last-ditch effort to get the car into the best position for what would almost certainly be a collision.

"Cover your face," Grayson managed to warn her. Because the limbs would probably break the glass.

His life didn't exactly flash before his eyes, but Grayson did think of his family. His brothers. His little niece, Kimmie.

And Eve.

She was there, right smack-dab in the middle of all of his memories.

He watched the front end of the car slide toward the middle tree, but at the last second, the vehicle shifted. No longer head-on. But the driver's side—his side—careened right into the hackberry.

Grayson felt the air bags slam into his face and side. The double impact combined with the collision rammed him into Eve and her air bag. There were the sounds of broken glass and the metal crunching against the tree trunk. The radiator spewed steam.

"We're alive," he heard Eve say.

Grayson did a quick assessment. Yeah, they were alive all right, and the car was wrapped around the hackberry.

"Are you hurt?" he asked Eve, trying to assess if he had any injuries of his own. His shoulder hurt like hell, but he was hoping it was just from the air-bag punch and that it hadn't been dislocated. He would need that shoulder to try to get them out of this crumpled heap of a car.

When Eve didn't answer, Grayson's stomach knotted, and he whipped his head in her direction. Her hands were on the air bag that she was trying to bat down, but her attention was fixed on the side window.

Grayson soon saw why.

The man, the one who'd hidden in the trees, was running straight toward them.

Chapter 4

The man was armed, a pistol in his right hand.

Eve heard Grayson yell for her to get down, but she didn't have time to react. Grayson pushed her down, her face and body colliding with the partially inflated air bag.

"My gun," he snarled.

Grayson cursed and punched at the air bags. He was obviously trying to find his weapon. When Eve had last seen it, Grayson had put it on the console, but the crash had probably sent it flying.

Oh, mercy.

That meant they were sitting ducks, unarmed, with a gunman bearing down on them. She couldn't get out of the car, not with the man so close and on her side of the vehicle. They couldn't get out on the driver's side because it was literally crunched around a tree. Thank

God for the air bags, or Grayson would have been seriously injured or killed.

Eve glanced up at the approaching man. The person
who was likely responsible for the explosion that had
destroyed her grandmother's cottage. The fear raced
through her.

Still, she felt anger, too.

This idiot had endangered them and was continuing
to do so. She wouldn't just stand by and let him shoot
Grayson and her. Neither would Grayson.

They both grappled around the interior of her car,
and Eve remembered her own gun in the glove com-
partment. It took some doing to get the air bag out of
the way, but she finally managed it. She threw open
the glove box door, latched on to the gun and handed
it to Grayson.

He immediately took aim.

The man must have seen him do that because he
ducked behind a tree. She wasn't sure if that was a good
or bad thing. If the man had stayed out in the open,
Grayson would have had a clean shot. This way, they
were still trapped.

"One of the deputies will be here soon," Grayson
reminded her.

Probably one of his brothers. Both Dade and Mason
were Silver Creek deputy sheriffs, and since Grayson
had requested backup, they would no doubt get there
as soon as humanly possible.

But that might not be soon enough.

Using his left hand Grayson continued to bat away
the air bag, but he kept his attention pinned to the tree
where the man had ducked out of sight. Eve kept watch
as well, but there were other trees near that one, and it

wouldn't take much for the man to move behind one of those closer trees and sneak right up on them.

"Who is he?" Eve meant to ask herself that question, but she said it aloud.

"I don't know," Grayson answered. "But he could be the killer we're after."

Yes. Eve was aware that there was an unidentified killer on the loose.

Thanks to the newspaper coverage, she was also aware that just a few days ago a young woman's body had been found in the creek. The woman had been fully clothed, no signs of sexual assault, but her fingerprints and face had been obliterated. That's the term the press had used, *obliterated,* and Eve had assumed the killer had done that to prevent her from being identified.

It had worked.

So why would this killer come after Grayson and her now?

Until the body was identified, and that might never happen, it wasn't likely that Grayson would be able to come up with a list of suspects.

But Eve had a sickening thought.

Perhaps the man had killed the woman in or near the cottage. Maybe he was destroying any potential physical evidence that would link him to the crime. And here she'd walked in with so much on her mind that she hadn't even considered a trip home could be dangerous. This in spite of her knowing about the murder that possibly happened just a stone's throw away from the cottage.

That oversight could be deadly.

She choked back a sob. Only minutes earlier her main worry had been getting pregnant, but for that to happen Grayson and she had to survive this. If something went wrong and he got hurt, it would be her fault because he wouldn't have been out here in these woods if she hadn't called him.

"I'll get you out of here," she heard Grayson say.

It sounded like a promise. But Eve knew backup was still a few minutes away. A lot could happen in those few short minutes.

Because she had her attention pinned to that tree, she saw the man lean out. Or rather she saw his gun.

"Get down!" she warned Grayson.

Just as the shot slammed through the window directly above Eve's head. The sound was deafening, and the bullet tore through the safety glass.

Grayson moved forward, his body and forearm pushing her deeper onto the floor so that she could no longer see what was going on.

And Grayson fired.

Eve automatically put her hands over her ears, but the blast was so loud that it seemed to shake the entire car. What was left of the safety glass in the window came tumbling down on top of her.

Grayson elbowed the chunk of glass aside and fired another shot. All Eve could do was pray, and her prayers were quickly answered. Even with the roaring in her ears from the shots, she heard a welcome sound.

A siren.

Maybe the fire department. Maybe a deputy. She didn't care which. She just wanted Grayson to have backup. Her gun was fully loaded, but Eve didn't have any other ammunition with her, and she didn't want to risk a gun battle with the man who had a better position behind the tree.

"The SOB's getting away," Grayson growled.

Eve hadn't thought this situation could get more frightening, but that did it. If he managed to escape, he might try to come after her again.

She didn't need this, and neither did Grayson.

Grayson obviously agreed because he climbed over her and caught on to the door handle. He turned it, but it didn't budge. Eve didn't relish the idea of Grayson running after a possible killer, but the alternative was worse. Besides, the gunman had quit shooting.

For now, anyway.

Eve rammed her weight against the door to help Grayson open it. It took several hard pushes, but with their combined effort the door finally flew open.

"Be careful," she warned him.

"You, too," Grayson warned back. "Stay put and try to find my gun. I figure he's trying to get as far away from that siren as he can, but if this guy is stupid and doubles back, shoot him."

That didn't help with her ragged nerves, but as Grayson sprang from the car, Eve made a frantic search for the gun. She also kept watch, blindly running her hands over the floor and seats.

The sirens got closer, and she saw the flashes of blue lights at the end of the road. Backup was just seconds away, but Grayson was already running past the tree that the gunman had hidden behind.

Her fingers brushed over the cold gunmetal, finally, and Eve snatched up Grayson's Smith & Wesson. Her hands were shaking like crazy, but she positioned the gun so it would be easier for her to take aim. But she was hoping that might not be necessary.

A Silver Creek cruiser came to a screeching stop

next to her wrecked car, and she recognized the man who jumped out. It was Dade, Grayson's brother. Like Grayson, he wore jeans and a badge clipped to his belt, and he had his gun ready. He was lankier than Grayson, but Eve didn't doubt Dade's capabilities. From everything she'd heard, he was a good lawman.

"Eve?" he asked. Dade was clearly surprised to see her in Silver Creek. Then his gaze flashed to the cottage. Or rather what remained of it. It was still on fire, but there wasn't much left to burn.

Soon, very soon, it would be just a pile of ashes.

"Someone blew up the cottage. And then he fired a shot at us," she explained. "He might be the killer you're looking for." Mercy, her voice was shaking as badly as her hands, and she tried to rein in her fear so she could point toward the tree. "Grayson went after him."

Concern flashed through Dade's eyes, and he snapped his attention in the direction where she'd pointed. "Stay here," Dade said, repeating Grayson's earlier order. "The fire crew is right behind me. And keep that gun ready, just in case."

She watched him run toward the spot where she'd last seen Grayson, and Eve added another prayer for Dade's safety, too. Like all the Rylands, she'd known Dade her entire life, and even though he was only two years younger than she was, she had always thought of him as her kid brother. That probably had something to do with all the meals she'd helped cook for Dade and the others after their mother committed suicide.

"The dark ages," she mumbled.

That's how she'd always thought of that time twenty years ago when Grayson and his brothers had basically become orphans. During the years that followed, Eve had gotten close with all of Grayson's brothers, closer than she had been with her own family.

She blinked back the tears. And here she'd endangered yet another *family* member. Heck, Mason was probably on the way, too. Before the hour was up, she might have put all three of them at risk.

Eve heard a second set of sirens and knew that the fire department was close by. She stayed in the car, as both Grayson and Dade had warned her to do, but she moved to the edge of the seat, closer to the open door, so she could try to pick through the woods and see Grayson. She still had sight of Dade, but Grayson was nowhere to be seen.

She glanced behind her at the fire engine as it made the final turn from the farm road onto the gravel drive that led to the cottage. The driver turned off the sirens, and everything suddenly went silent.

Eve could hear the wind assaulting the trees. She could hear her own heartbeat in her ears.

She also heard Dade shout, "Get down!"

And the sound of a gun going off ripped through the silence.

Chapter 5

Grayson cursed and dove to the ground.

He'd already had enough surprises today, and he didn't need this SOB firing any more shots at him. Besides, Eve wasn't that far away, and he darn sure didn't want a stray bullet traveling in her direction.

"You okay?" Dade called out. His brother had dropped to the ground, too, but was crawling toward Grayson.

"Yeah. I'm just fine and dandy," Grayson barked. "You see him?"

Dade didn't answer right away, giving Grayson some hope, but that hope went south when his brother finally said, "No."

Grayson lifted his head and examined the woods. Since it was the dead of winter, a lot of the foliage was gone, but that didn't mean there weren't plenty of places to hide.

And then Grayson heard something he didn't want to hear.

The sound of water.

Hell. This guy was in the creek, and that meant he was getting away.

Dade apparently heard it, too, because he cursed and got to his feet. So did Grayson, and they started to run toward the sound of that splashing. Of course, the splashing was long gone before they arrived on the creek bank.

And there was no sign of the gunman.

Dade and Grayson stood there, looking hard, but there was no way to tell which direction he went. If the guy was smart, he could have just floated downstream and out of sight. Of course, he could have scrambled over the outcropping of rocks on the other side of the creek bed and then disappeared into the dense woods.

"We need a tracking dog," Dade mumbled.

Yeah. And they needed their brother Mason out here on horseback. Mason was a better tracker than any dog or any of the local Texas Rangers, but Grayson intended to ask for their help, too. He wanted this gunman caught *now,* and he would use any resource available.

"I got a good look at his face," Grayson let Dade know. "If he's in the system, I think I can pick out his photo."

Though that would take time. Maybe lots of time. Something Grayson wasn't sure he had.

This guy would be back.

The question was why? Grayson was sure if he could figure that out, then he would have a better chance of identifying him and stopping another attack.

"Why don't you get Eve away from here? She's pretty

shaken up," Dade suggested. He took out his cell phone. "I'll start making calls."

Grayson started to say no, that he wanted to stay. If they got lucky with the search, he wanted to be the one to put the cuffs on this piece of slime, but Dade was right. Eve didn't need to be here. Neither did he. His brothers could handle it and handle it well. So he turned and headed back toward Eve and her car.

He spotted her the moment he came out of the thick cluster of trees. She was out of the wrecked car, talking to Dusty Bullock, the fire chief. She looked calm enough, but Grayson knew that underneath her nerves had to be raw since to the best of his knowledge this was the first time she'd experienced anyone trying to kill her.

And there was no doubt that the killing attempt had been aimed at Eve.

When she saw Grayson, Eve ran toward him, but he quickly closed the distance between them because he didn't want her out in the open.

"Did you catch him?" she asked.

Grayson shook his head and watched her expression go from shock to fear. Yeah. She understood how important it was for them to find this gunman *today*.

Since she looked ready to launch herself into his arms, or cry, he took his gun from her, reholstered it and handed Eve her handgun. She slipped it into her coat pocket. And Grayson caught on to her shoulder so he could lead her in the direction of his truck.

"I need to get you back to my office," he grumbled. Grayson hated the gruffness in his voice. Hated even more that he couldn't comfort her at a time when she needed comforting, but after the conversation they'd had in the cottage, it was best if he kept his distance.

"But what about the gunman?" she challenged. "He's still out there."

"Dade's looking for him, and we'll bring in help." Grayson stopped next to the fire chief. "Call me the minute you know what caused the explosion in the cottage."

"You're thinking it was foul play?" Dusty asked, his craggy face bunched up with concern.

"Yeah," Grayson answered honestly, though he knew that would cause Eve more panic. "I want the brake line on Eve's car checked, too, because I'm sure someone cut it."

"Oh, God," Eve mumbled.

He got her moving again, but she stopped first to retrieve her purse and equipment bag from her car. Since she looked ready to fall apart, Grayson decided to use the drive to his office to get her to concentrate on how they could bring this nightmarish day to a good conclusion.

A conclusion that would end with an arrest.

"Did you see the gunman's face?" Grayson asked. He drove away from her cottage, which would soon be taped off and processed as a crime scene.

"Not really." When she couldn't get her seat belt on after two tries, Grayson reached over and helped her. His hand brushed against hers, and he quickly pulled back. With the energy between them already on edge, it was best to avoid touching her.

And *thinking* about touching her.

Something he didn't quite accomplish.

Grayson huffed and continued. "The gunman had brownish-red hair. About six-two. Around a hundred and seventy pounds. Ring any bells?"

She shook her head. "Should it?"

"Maybe. I figure you've crossed paths with him. Why else would he want to come after you that way?"

Eve mumbled another "Oh, God," and plowed her fingers through the sides of her hair. "I don't recognize him." She pressed hard against her temples and head. "What could I have done to make him want to kill me?"

That was the million-dollar question, and Grayson had to explore all possibilities. "An old boyfriend, maybe? Maybe he altered his appearance so that you didn't easily recognize him?"

Her hands slipped from her hair and dropped into her lap. She stared at him. "You're the only boyfriend I have who's riled at me."

"I'm not riled," Grayson protested.

She huffed. "You're riled all right."

He huffed, too. "Just because I turned down your offer to make a baby doesn't mean I'm pissed off." But when he heard his tone, he realized he was. Grayson cursed. "I just wasn't expecting you to ask anything like that, okay? You surprised the hell out of me."

"Yes, I figured that out. But you can't blame me for trying. I just thought… Well, I just thought *wrong*."

She was right about that. So, why did Grayson feel so blasted guilty for turning her down? Since that was something he didn't want to think or talk about, he went back to the investigation. They were still fifteen minutes out from his office, and he wanted to put that time to good use instead of adding to that guilt trip.

"I heard you were engaged but broke things off," Grayson tossed out there. "Could your ex be holding a grudge?"

She mumbled something he didn't catch. "No. It's

true, I called things off the day of the wedding, but he's moved on and already married to someone else."

Maybe her ex-fiancé had indeed moved on, but Grayson wanted to verify that was true. Love and love-scorned were motives for a lot of crimes.

And a lot of questions.

He wanted to ask Eve why she'd waited until her wedding day to end things, but it was none of his business.

"How about a member of your ex's family?" he pressed. "Sometimes family members or friends think they need to avenge a broken heart."

She sat quietly a moment. And she didn't deny that broken heart part. "Why wait over a year to get revenge?" She shook her head again. "I was thinking maybe what happened today has to do with the killer. Maybe he was trying to destroy evidence by destroying the cottage?"

Yes. That was the next theory on Grayson's list. Perhaps the killer had left some kind of forensic evidence in or near the cottage. That was a solid reason to destroy it.

"But then why would he want to kill you?" Grayson pressed. He turned off the ranch road and onto the highway that would take him back into town. "Is it possible you know something about the murder?"

"How could I? I wasn't in Silver Creek when it happened. I was in San Antonio."

"The murder might not have happened in Silver Creek," he reminded her. "In fact, I suspect it didn't. I think the body was just dumped there."

She gave him a flat look. "Trust me, I would have remembered if I'd witnessed someone being murdered."

True. But there had to be a reason this guy was after

her. Grayson really needed to get an ID on that body because he couldn't shake the feeling that the dead woman and this attack were connected.

"We don't have an identity on the dead woman, but she was five-six and was in her early twenties." Grayson hoped that would spur Eve to remember something.

Eve nodded. "I read that in the paper. Her face and fingerprints had been obliterated." She paused. "What does that mean exactly?"

"You don't want to know." But Grayson would never forget the sight of what was left of the woman. Someone had literally bashed in her face so that none of her features had been recognizable, and then cut off the pads of her fingertips. He'd also broken off her teeth, probably so that dental records couldn't be used to identify her. "But the killer didn't obliterate her hair, and it's unique. Three colors—red, black and blond. Remember seeing anyone with hair like that?"

She shrugged. "It's possible. That type of hair isn't so rare in a city the size of San Antonio."

True. But it was the only thing he had to go on. Now it was time to grasp at a few straws. "When did you start getting hang-up calls?" Grayson pressed.

"Four days ago," she answered without hesitation.

Four days. According to the ME, that was an estimate of when the woman had been killed.

He was about to continue his questions when Grayson spotted the familiar rust-scabbed red truck barreling down the highway. It was his brother Mason, responding to the scene. Grayson didn't slow down. Neither did Mason. They exchanged a glance, and in that split-second glance, Grayson saw exactly what he wanted to see: Mason's determination to find the man who'd taken shots at Eve and him.

Sometimes keeping Mason's intense moods under control was like trying to keep a leash on a rogue bull. But it was that intensity that made Mason a good cop. Mason wasn't the sort of man Grayson would go to with his personal problems—he wouldn't get much empathy there—but for everything else Mason was the brother he knew he could rely on the most.

Grayson stopped in the parking lot of his office and turned to Eve. "I need to get your statement about what just happened and ask you a few more questions about those hang-up calls. Then I can take you to the ranch. You can stay there until we catch this guy."

She was already shaking her head before he finished. "I can't go to your ranch."

No. He didn't have time for this argument. "Look, I know it might be a little uncomfortable for you there, what with Dade and Mason around—"

"It's not that. I'm comfortable with your family. Always have been."

Grayson couldn't argue with that. Heck, his brothers had, and probably always would, consider Eve a sister. His youngest brother, Kade, often said that Eve was more like a mother to him than his own mother had been.

So what was Eve's issue?

She stared at him. "I need to get back to San Antonio, and I intend to do that as soon as I can arrange for transportation. Your reports will have to wait. I have to find a place where I can be inseminated *today*."

Grayson was sure he looked at her as if she'd lost her

mind. "Eve, someone tried to kill you," he reminded her, though he was positive she hadn't forgotten that.

Her hand was still shaking when she touched her fingers to her lips. She paused a moment, still trembling, and her gaze came back to his. "If I don't do the insemination today, I'll never have a baby. And yes, I know there's a killer out there. And yes, that killer might have been the one to take shots at us today. But I don't have time to wait for him to be caught."

Grayson broke his no-touching rule and caught on to her shoulders. He wanted to make this very clear. But for a moment he lost his train of thought when he saw the nicks and scrapes on her face. From the air bag, no doubt. But even with the superficial damage, Eve was still the most beautiful woman he'd ever seen.

He pushed that thought aside with all the rest of the carnal things that came to mind whenever he looked at Eve. She had, and always would have, his number.

Grayson met her eye to eye. "The killer could come after you in San Antonio."

She blinked, swallowed hard. "So, I'll hire a bodyguard as soon as I call the rental car company to come and get me. I want to be on the road within the next thirty minutes."

He didn't know whether to curse or try to shake some sense into her. "Eve, is this baby worth your life?"

Her breath rattled in her throat. Tears sprang to her eyes. "Yes," she whispered.

And with that, she grabbed her equipment bag and purse and got out of his truck. The bag went on one shoulder. Her purse on the other.

Well, he'd asked the question, and even though it hadn't been the answer he wanted to hear, Grayson knew it was Eve's final answer. She wasn't going to budge on this.

Hell.

That meant he had to drive back into San Antonio with her. Or else send Dade or Mason. Now Grayson cursed because he sure didn't have time for this.

He got out, slammed the truck door with far more force than necessary and followed her into the back entrance of the law enforcement building. It wasn't a huge place—especially considering how much time he spent there. It had a reception area, four offices, two interrogation rooms and a holding cell on the bottom floor. There was an apartment-style break room on the top floor where there'd once been jail cells before a new facility had been built on the edge of town.

Grayson stepped inside and heard the day shift dispatcher, Tina Fox, talking from her desk in the reception area. An area roped off with twinkling Christmas lights and a miniature tree that played annoying tinny carols when anyone walked past it. Mason had already kicked it once. Grayson was considering the same. As far as he was concerned, this was a bah-humbug kind of Christmas, and this attempt to kill Eve wasn't doing much to change his opinion about that.

Tina looked back at him and waved. From the sound of it, she was getting an update from Dade. Soon Grayson would want that update as well, but first he had to deal with the most hardheaded woman in Texas.

Ahead of him, Eve made her way to his office while she fished for something in her purse. She finally pulled out her cell phone when she came to a quick stop. Her hand and phone had been moving toward her ear, but that stopped, as well. She stood there frozen, her gaze fixed on something in his office.

Grayson cursed and hurried to pull her aside because he knew what had shocked her. The crime board in his office had photos of the dead woman. Or rather what was left of her. To put it mildly, they weren't pretty.

"Sorry about that," he mumbled. And he crossed the room to turn the board around so that the gruesome pictures would be facing the wall.

"Wait!" Eve insisted.

She walked closer, her attention nailed to the grisliest of the photos. It was a close-up view of the dead woman's bashed-in face and had been taken several hours after her body had been fished out of the creek.

"There's no need for you to see these," Grayson assured her. When he tried to turn the board again, she caught on to his arm to stop them.

She moved even closer, until her face was just inches from the photo. Eve mumbled something and then dropped her equipment bag onto his desk. Frantically, she began to rummage through it, pulling out the pictures that Grayson had seen earlier on the counter at the cottage.

"What is it?" he asked.

"I've seen her before." Her voice was all breath now. "Well, I've seen that hair anyway."

Grayson glanced back at the dead woman's hair, though the image was already embedded into his mind. He wasn't sure he'd ever be able to forget it. But the hair was certainly distinctive. Three colors. Red, blond, black, and the black was only on the ends of her choppily cut hair.

Eve continued to pull photos from her bag, glancing at each and then tossing them aside on the tops of folders and reports that Grayson had spread out on his desk. She plucked another from the bag and froze again.

Grayson looked at the shot from over her shoulder. He recognized the location—it had been taken at the indoor rodeo arena in San Antonio. There were at least a dozen people standing at the railings, their eyes fixed on the bull rider who had just been tossed into the air.

Then he saw the woman.

And her hair.

"When did you take this?" Grayson couldn't ask the question fast enough. He grabbed the picture from her so he could study it.

"Four days ago at the fund-raiser rodeo. I had these printed because I wanted to take a better look at them to see which to include in the story. But I didn't use this one." She paused. "It's her, isn't it?"

Grayson paused, too, but not because he wasn't sure. He was.

The image of the dead woman stared back at him.

Chapter 6

Eve hadn't realized she was holding her breath until her lungs began to ache. "Is that the murdered woman?" she asked Grayson.

"Yeah," he finally said, his attention still glued to that photo. "Any idea who she is?"

"No, I took dozens of random shots that day. She was just someone in the crowd."

"Yes. But if the medical examiner is right, this is also the day she was murdered." He tipped his head to her bag. "I need to look at all the pictures."

She gave a shaky nod, and while she was doing that, Grayson peeled off his jacket and tossed it over the back of his chair. Then he put the photo on his fax machine. "I'm sending it to the Ranger crime lab in Austin with a request for immediate processing."

Good. Soon he might have a name to go with that face.

Eve continued to dump pictures onto his desk, but with each one she mumbled a no. She huffed. "That's it. The only one I have of her."

"Then I'll have to get what I can from it."

He made several more copies of the picture, one that he pinned on to the corkboard with the other photos. The others, he put in his in-basket so he'd have them for other law enforcement agencies. Then he sat at his desk, placing the original picture right next to him, and he fired off that request message to the Ranger crime lab.

While he did that, Eve took herself back to that photo session. It had been routine, something she'd done dozens of times.

"Four days ago," she said softly. "That's when my hang-up calls started."

That got Grayson's attention. He stood and stared at her, and Eve knew what he was thinking. Was there something in the photo that had caused the hang-up calls, the fire at the cottage and the shooting?

Was the killer in the photo?

Eve rifled through her equipment bag and came up with a small magnifying glass. She handed it to Grayson, and he used it to zoom in. She hurried beside him so she could take a look, as well.

Unlike the rest of the spectators, the woman wasn't looking at the bull rider. She had her attention on the man wearing a baseball cap on her left. Her face was tight, as if she was angry. *Very* angry. And the man had his hand gripped on to her arm.

"I'm pretty sure that's the guy who shot at us today," Grayson mumbled, tapping his finger to the guy in the baseball cap.

Eve sucked in her breath. She hadn't gotten a good look at him, but the build was right. So was that baseball cap.

Grayson turned back to his keyboard. "I'll ask the lab to put the entire picture into the facial recognition program. It's the fastest way for us to get an ID."

Good. Eve wanted that. But she also wanted to get out of there and on the road. It was already past noon, and time was running out. She took out her cell to call for a car rental, but before she could make the call, Grayson's phone rang.

"Sheriff Ryland," he answered, and she knew from his expression that whoever was on the other end of the line was telling him something important. Was it possible the Rangers had already managed to ID the dead woman? Eve prayed they had. Because the sooner that happened, the sooner Grayson could proceed with the investigation.

"Yeah. I'll let Eve know," Grayson mumbled several seconds later. "What about the search? Any sign of the gunman?" He paused. "Keep looking."

"What happened?" she asked the moment he hung up.

"That was the fire chief." Grayson pulled in a long breath. "He said he's positive someone tampered with both your brakes and the gas line that led to the cottage. Plus, there was a tracking device on your car."

Eve had tried to brace herself for bad news. After all, it was a logical conclusion about the brakes and gas line, but it still sent an icy chill through her. So did the fact that someone had tracked her out to the cottage.

God, did someone really want her dead because she'd taken a photo?

"Do you park your car in a garage in San Antonio?" Grayson asked.

"No. I use the lot adjacent to my condo."

In other words, her vehicle had been out in the open. Not just there but at her downtown office, as well. Obviously, someone could have planted that tracking device at any time in the past four days. And during those four days, the person had no doubt watched her, plotting the best way to get the picture and eliminate her.

She held on to Grayson's desk to steady herself.

Grayson cursed, moved out of his chair, grabbed her arm and forced her to sit down. "I hope now you realize that going back to San Antonio is a bad idea."

Yes. She did. But that wouldn't stop her. "Then I'll go to Austin. I'm sure they have fertility clinics there."

Grayson didn't curse again, but the look he gave her showed the profanity he was choking back.

"I don't expect you to understand." She got to her feet and squared her shoulders. She looked him straight in the eye. "You're burned out with the whole idea of fatherhood so how could you understand that for me having a baby, *my* baby, is the most important thing in my life?"

Grayson looked her straight in the eyes, too. "Eve, what I understand is this killer knows you took his picture, and he'll do anything to get it back. I can keep you safe here in Silver Creek until we can get the picture printed in tomorrow's paper. That way, the killer won't have a reason to come after you because thousands of people will have seen his face, along with the woman he probably murdered."

She tried to shrug. Eve wasn't immune to the fear, but she wasn't giving in to it, either. "Then print the

photo, and tomorrow I can celebrate both my insemination and my safety."

He didn't answer that and just kept glaring as if
searching for the right argument to change her mind.
There wasn't an argument that could do that.

Eve adjusted her cell again, ready to make her call.
"I'll get a car rental, and on the drive to Austin, I'll
phone clinics and start begging. One way or another,
I'm getting pregnant today."

Now he cursed and shook his head. "Give me a few
minutes, and I'll drive you to Austin myself."

Eve hadn't thought the day could have any more surprises, but that was a big one, and she knew just how
massive a concession that was for Grayson.

"You can't," she argued. "You have too much to do
to babysit me."

"Save your breath," he growled. He grabbed his coat
and put it on as if he taking his anger out on the garment. He also snatched the rodeo photo of the dead
woman. "You're not the only hardheaded person in this
room. And if you can make calls on the drive over, then
so can I. If I have to, I'll run this investigation from
my truck."

He brushed past her and headed for his door, and she
heard him tell the dispatcher that he had to leave. Eve
didn't want to think of what kind of complications this
might cause for Grayson, but she knew it would. She
also knew this was another huge compromise for him.
Maybe Dade and Mason could find this gunman today
so this would all be over.

She gathered up the pictures and stuffed them into
the equipment bag. Her hand knocked against another

photo. The only framed one on Grayson's desk. It was of his maternal grandfather, Sheriff Chet McLaurin.

Despite her own horrible circumstances, she smiled when she saw the man's face. Eve had known him well, and he'd become like her own grandfather. When he'd been murdered twenty years ago, Eve had grieved right along with the Ryland clan.

She wondered if Grayson and his brothers realized that the man in the photo was the reason they'd all gotten into law enforcement. An unsolved murder could do that. It was a wound that would not heal.

Eve spotted another wound.

The silver concho hooked on to the top of the frame. She recognized it, as well. Grayson's father had given all six of his sons a concho with the double *R* symbol of their family's ranch. He'd done that, and then less than a week later, he'd left Silver Creek and abandoned the very family that he claimed to have loved.

No wonder Grayson didn't want kids of his own.

He'd witnessed firsthand that parenthood could cut to the core. Eve swore she would never do that to her child.

"Ready?" Grayson said from the doorway.

She'd been so caught up in the picture of his grandfather and the concho that she hadn't noticed Grayson was there. He had also noticed what had caught her attention.

"Yeah," he mumbled as if he'd known exactly what she'd been thinking.

Eve silently cursed the legacy that Grayson's father had left him, and she stuffed the rest of her things into the equipment bag.

"You kept the concho he gave you," she commented as they went to his truck.

He didn't answer until they were both inside the cab of his truck. "Sometimes it helps to remember how much I hate my father."

She stared at him. "How could that possibly help?"

"It's a reminder that sometimes the easy way out can hurt a lot of people."

He didn't look at her when he said that, and if Eve hadn't known him so well she might have thought that was a jab at her decision to go through with this insemination. But since she did know him, she figured he was talking about his family duties. For Grayson, family came first, and that hadn't always been easy for him.

"Mason put a bullet in his concho," Grayson said under his breath. He drove out of the parking lot and onto the road that would take them out of town and to the highway. "Then he nailed it to the wall directly in front of his bed so he could curse it every morning when he woke up."

Eve sighed. So much hurt caused by one man. Their father, Boone Ryland. "I remember Dade told me that he threw his away."

"Yeah." And for a moment, Grayson seemed lost in those bad memories. The dark ages. However, his cell rang, and he morphed from the wounded son to steely sheriff.

"Sheriff Ryland," he answered. He put the phone on speaker and slipped it into a stand that was mounted to the dashboard. He also kept watch around them as they passed the last of the town shops.

"It's me, Dade. I just got off the phone with the Ranger lab. They got a match on the photo."

"Already?" Grayson questioned.

"It wasn't that hard. Her name is Nina Manning, age

twenty-two, from Houston, and she had a record for drug possession and prostitution. There's also a year-old missing person's report complete with pictures."

"Nina Manning," Eve repeated. It didn't ring any bells.

"Is Eve still with you?" Dade asked.

Eve looked at Grayson and waited for him to answer. "Yeah. I have to drive her, uh, somewhere. But I want to know everything that's happening with the case. Any sign of the gunman?"

"No. But Mason's out here. If the guy's still in the area, Mason will find him."

Eve doubted the gunman was still around. Heck, he'd probably parked his car on one of the ranch trails and was now probably long gone. Or maybe he was looking for her. Despite the importance of Dade's call, that caused her to look in the rearview mirror. No one was following them. The rural road behind them was empty.

"Were the Rangers able to identify the other man in the picture who had hold of Nina's arm?" Grayson asked.

"There was no immediate match."

Grayson shook his head. "I think he's the guy who tried to kill us today so we need an ID."

"The Rangers are still trying," Dade assured him. "But they did get a match on the man to the woman's right. His name is Sebastian Collier."

Now that rang some bells. Eve had seen the surname many times in the newspaper, mainly in the business and society sections. "He's related to Claude Collier, the San Antonio real estate tycoon?" Eve asked.

"Sebastian is his son," Dade answered. "And sonny-boy has a record, too, for a DWI and resisting arrest.

Guess his millionaire daddy didn't teach him to call the family chauffeur when he's had too much to drink."

Eve picked up the photo that Grayson had brought along, and she zoomed in on the man to Nina Manning's right. Sebastian Collier looked like a preppy college student in his collared cream-colored shirt and dark pants. It certainly didn't seem as if he was with the woman with multicolored hair.

But then Eve looked closer.

Sebastian's attention was certainly on Nina. His eyes were angled in her direction, or rather in the direction of the grip the other man had on Nina's arm. Sebastian looked uncomfortable with the encounter.

"Keep pushing the Rangers," she heard Grayson tell his brother. "I want that other man identified. I also want someone out to question this Sebastian Collier." He looked at his watch, mumbled something in disgust. "I'll try to get to San Antonio myself as soon as I'm sure Eve will be safe."

Dade assured Grayson he would do everything to get a name to go with that face in the photo, and he ended the call.

Eve hadn't missed Grayson's mumble of disgust, and she was positive she was the cause. He wanted to be in the heat of this investigation, but here he was driving her to Austin instead. She turned to face him, to tell him that he could just drop her off in Austin and leave. Not that it would do any good—he would insist on staying. But she had to try. This investigation was important to both of them.

However, before she could launch into another argument, she heard the sound.

It was a thick, hard blast.

At first she thought maybe they'd had a blowout. But the second sound was identical.

"Get down!" Grayson shouted.

Just as a third blast ripped through the truck window.

Chapter 7

Grayson slammed his foot onto the accelerator to get Eve and him out of there, but it was already too late.

He heard the fourth shot, and he also heard Eve repeat his shouted command of *get down*. But he couldn't duck out of sight. He had to fight to keep them alive. He pushed Eve down onto the seat so that she wouldn't be hit with the bullet or the broken glass.

But the bullet didn't crash through the glass.

It hit the tire.

Grayson's stomach knotted, and he felt his truck jerk to the right. He fought with the steering wheel and tried to stay on the road, but it was impossible. The now-flat tire and metal rim scraped against the gravel shoulder.

"Hang on," he warned Eve.

They were going to crash.

He couldn't avoid that. However, the crash was the

least of Grayson's worries. Someone had shot out the tire, and that someone was no doubt waiting for them. That meant Eve was in danger all over again, and Grayson cursed the bastard responsible for that.

There were no trees near the road, thank God, but there were clusters about a hundred yards off the road. That's probably where the gunman was hiding. And then there was the creek directly in front of them. He didn't want to go there because there were some deep spots in the water that could swallow them up.

"We have to jump," Grayson told her, and he pumped the brakes to slow the truck as much as he could. However, he didn't have much control of the vehicle.

Jumping was a risk, but the greater risk would be to remain inside so the gunman would have an easier chance of killing them. Besides, there was that potential for drowning.

Eve didn't answer, but she nodded and caught on to the door handle.

"When you jump out, run toward the trees to the right," he added. "And grab my cell phone."

Grayson took out his gun. Eve grabbed the phone.

"Now!" He barreled out at the same time as Eve, and he hit the soggy ground ready to fire. The truck gave Eve some cover for just a few seconds, until it plunged nose-first into the creek.

The gunman fired, the shot kicking up mud and a clump of grass several yards in front of Grayson. Grayson returned fire, a single shot, praying it would buy Eve enough time. He could hear her running, but he had to do everything to keep the gunman's attention on him.

Grayson spotted the gunman, or rather the sleeve of his jacket. He spotted Eve, too. She had ducked behind an oak and had taken out her own gun from her coat pocket. She leaned out and took aim at the gunman.

What the hell was she doing?

That knot in his stomach twisted even harder. She had purposely left cover, the very thing he didn't want her to do. Grayson frantically motioned for her to get back. But she didn't. She fired. Her shot slammed into the tree where the gunman was hiding. The bullet didn't hit him, but it caused the man to jump back.

Even though Eve's diversion could have been deadly, it was exactly what Grayson needed because he scrambled toward Eve and dove behind the tree. He also caught on to her and pulled her deeper into the woods. He damn sure didn't want her to get hurt trying to protect him.

"Stay back," Grayson warned her in a rough whisper. But he soon realized that staying back might be just as dangerous as staying put. That's because the gunman was on the move. He dropped back into the thick patch of trees. The SOB was trying to circle behind them.

Grayson had faced danger alone and had even faced it with other lawmen, but being under fire with a civilian was a first. And to make matters worse, that civilian was Eve. He wished he could go back in time and save her from this.

He repositioned Eve behind him and went deeper into the woods as well, but not toward the gunman. They needed to get into a better position, so with Eve in tow, he started moving, going at a right angle. He tried to keep his steps light so that it wouldn't give them away, but that wasn't easy with the dead limbs and leaves littering the grounds.

Eve and he ran, until he lost sight of the road and truck, and he didn't stop until he reached a small clearing.

Another shot came at them.

It wasn't close, at least twenty feet away, but the gunman had sent it in their direction. However, Grayson now knew the gunman's direction, too.

He moved Eve to the right, and they followed the thick woods until they reached the other side of the clearing. Grayson glanced back at Eve to make sure she was okay.

Her breath was gusting now, she was pale, but she didn't appear to be on the verge of panicking. There was some fear there in her eyes, but there was also determination to get out of this alive.

Eve motioned across the clearing, and Grayson saw the gunman duck behind another tree. He caught just a glimpse of the man's face, but Grayson was more convinced than ever that this was the same person in the photo with the dead woman. Grayson hadn't had many doubts left that this was connected to the photograph Eve had taken, and he certainly didn't doubt it now.

The gunman continued to work his way to his right, and Grayson did the same. It was a risk taking Eve deeper and deeper into the woods, but he had to figure out a way to stop this guy. Preferably alive. But he was more than willing to take him out if it meant Eve and he could get out of there.

When they'd made it all the way to a new section of the creek, Grayson stopped and waited.

He didn't have to wait long.

Grayson spotted the gunman just as the man spotted them.

The gunman lifted his weapon, but Grayson was already braced for the attack. He shoved Eve back, took aim and fired before the gunman could. It was a sickening sound of the bullet slamming into human flesh.

A deadly thud.

Clutching his chest, the man flew backward and landed among the dense underbrush.

"Is he…dead?" Eve whispered.

"Maybe." The moments crawled by, and Grayson waited. Watching. He looked for any movement, but he didn't see it. "Stay here."

Eve caught on to his arm and looked ready to launch into an argument about why he should stay put, but her gaze dropped to his badge. Resignation went through her eyes as a worried sigh left her mouth. "Be careful."

"That's the plan," he mumbled, and he headed in the direction of the fallen gunman.

He kept watch on Eve and tried to push aside all the other things that crept into his mind, but Grayson knew once this threat was over, he had a dozen other things to deal with—especially Eve.

Grayson reached the spot he'd last seen the gunman, and he cursed. The gunman was still there, in the exact place where he'd taken his last breath. His gun had dropped from his hand.

"He's dead," Grayson relayed to Eve.

She started toward him, practically running. "You're sure?"

Grayson leaned down and checked for a pulse, but that was just to keep everything straight for the reports he'd have to write up later. "Yeah."

Eve was nearly out of breath by the time she made it to him. She took one look at the man's ash-white face, and she shivered and leaned against Grayson.

He'd seen death before, maybe Eve had, too, but it was different seeing it like this. She was trembling hard now, and there were tears in her eyes, so he took her arm and led her away. There was no need for her to see any more of this.

"Why did he try to kill us?" she whispered, her voice clogged with emotion.

Grayson didn't know for sure, but he figured it had something to do with the dead woman in the photos. Maybe this gunman had killed her. "I'll find out," he promised Eve.

Since she looked ready to collapse, Grayson pulled her into his arms. She didn't put up a fight, probably because there was no fight left in her. This had taken, and would continue to take, a lot out of her. Grayson regretted that, but he didn't regret that this guy was dead.

Or that he was able to give some small comfort to Eve.

She was still trembling, but her breathing started to level. What she didn't do was move away, and Grayson was thankful for it. He hated to admit it, but the shooting had shaken him, and being this close to Eve was giving him as much comfort as he was hopefully giving her.

Even now, under the worst of circumstances, he couldn't help but notice how nicely Eve still fit in his arms. Her body practically molded against his.

"We're not bad people," she mumbled. "This shouldn't happen to us."

Yeah. But Grayson knew that neither good nor bad had anything to do with this. The dead man was likely trying to cover up a murder, and in his experience people would do anything and everything to avoid jail.

She pulled back and stared up at him. Their gazes connected, and that *fit,* too. He could read her so well and knew the tears were about to spill again. She had a good reason to cry, and later he would lend her his shoulder, but for now, he had things to do.

"This guy might not be the one who killed Nina Manning. He could be just a triggerman," Grayson explained, trying to keep his voice void of emotion so that she would stay calm.

He failed.

Despite her leveled breathing, Eve still looked anything but calm. So, to soothe himself and her, he brushed a kiss on her temple and then eased back so that she was no longer in his embrace.

"The only way we make this better," Grayson whispered to her, "is to end it. I have to find out why this man came after us."

Eve's bottom lip trembled, and she nodded. Seconds later, she nodded again. "I'm not weak," she assured him. Something he already knew.

"You just saw me kill a man. There's nothing weak about your reaction. Truth is, I'm shaking inside." And that was the truth. Killing didn't come easy to him, and he hoped like hell that it never did.

Another nod. Eve blinked back tears and reached out to him, but neither of her hands was free. She had her gun in her right hand. The cell phone in the other.

He took the cell from her and motioned for her to move even farther away from the body. "I'll call Dade," he let her know. And he tried. But the signal was so low that the call wouldn't go through. Grayson sent him a text instead and gave Dade their location.

Eve slipped her gun into her pocket and pulled her coat tightly against her. It wasn't freezing, but it wasn't warm, either. Besides, she was battling adrenaline and nerves, and that was no doubt contributing to the trembling.

"What now?" she asked.

Grayson took a deep breath before he answered. "We wait."

She blinked. "For how long?"

He heard the unasked questions, and he knew she wouldn't like the answers to any of them. "The text will eventually get through to Dade, and he'll come after us."

"Good." Her face relaxed a little. "Then we should walk back to the road to meet him."

Grayson glanced back at the body. "The coyotes won't leave a fresh kill alone for long. I need to preserve the crime scene as much as possible because I need an ID on this guy."

Eve started shaking her head. "But I need to get to Austin."

He nodded and settled for saying, "I know."

"No. You don't know." She huffed and blinked back more tears.

Hell.

Well, at least she wasn't shaking so hard, but this was about to get ugly.

"You don't know," she repeated, and she just kept on repeating it until the words and the tears got the best of her. She sagged against a tree.

"Eve," he said reaching out to her, but she just moved away.

Her breath broke on a sob. "I've made some terrible mistakes in my life. First, giving you that ultimatum. And then I promised my heart and life to a man I didn't love. I'm the Typhoid Mary of relationships, Grayson, but I know I'm meant to be a mother."

She was. Grayson didn't doubt that. Heck, she'd practically been a mother to his youngest brother. Grayson,
however, didn't have a good track record. And he tried
one last time to convince Eve of that.

"I'm not the man you want to father your baby," he
insisted.

She opened her mouth to say something, but Grayson didn't want her to tell him something along the
lines of his being the only man she wanted for that job.
He couldn't hear that. Not now. Not with Eve falling
apart like this.

"I sucked as a father," he continued, trying to snag
her gaze. Eye contact might help her see the determination. "My brother Gage is dead."

"Gage died doing a job he loved," she clarified. "You
couldn't and wouldn't have stopped him from joining
the Justice Department any more than he could have
stopped you from being sheriff of Silver Creek."

Maybe. But that didn't change things. Besides, Gage
was just one of his failures.

"Dade has got so much rage inside him. Nate's just
one bad day away from needing professional help. And
Mason? Hell, I wouldn't be surprised if he hunted our
father down just so he could kill him in cold blood."
Grayson paused because he had to. "That's the kind of
family I raised."

Now she made eye contact, and the jolt was like a
head-on collision. Grayson had hoped she would see his
emotion, and maybe she did, but he saw hers in complete vivid detail. The pain. The need.

The hopelessness of her situation.

"If I helped you," he managed to say, "I'd just screw
things up again."

She swiped away the tears and stared at him. "If you don't help me, I'll never know what it's like to be a mother. I'll never have a part of my life that I want more than my next breath." She walked closer. "Grayson, you would have no responsibility in this, other than having sex with me. I swear, *no responsibility.*"

He had to say no. Had to. And Grayson just kept repeating that.

But he knew the reality here.

Even if Dade got the text and responded right away, it would be an hour or more before they could get this body out of the woods. Grayson would need another vehicle since his truck was in the creek. It would be nightfall or later before he could get Eve to a clinic in Austin. Since it was just three days before Christmas, it was likely the clinics had already closed for the day. Maybe for the rest of the holiday week.

Still, Grayson had to say no.

Didn't he?

"Don't think too much," she whispered, walking closer.

The cold air mixed with her breath and created a misty fog around her face. It seemed unreal. Like a dream. And Grayson had had so many dreams about her that he nearly got lost in the moment.

Oh, man.

She could still make him burn.

Eve stopped, directly in front of him. So close he could take in her scent. She leaned in and put her mouth to his ear. She didn't touch him. Didn't have to touch him. Her scent was enough. He fought to hang on to the denial he intended to give her, but it was a battle that Grayson knew he was losing.

Worse, he *wanted* to lose.

"Just consider this a big favor for an old friend," she whispered.

A friend? Eve was plenty of things, but she wasn't a friend. Whatever she was, she was pulling him closer. And closer.

"Please," she said. Just that one word. Her warm breath brushed against his mouth like a kiss.

He looked into her eyes and didn't look beyond that. Yeah. He could say no. He could turn and walk away.

But that wasn't what Grayson was going to do.

What he did was exactly as Eve had said. He didn't think too much. He didn't look beyond this moment and the bad mistake he was about to make.

Grayson cursed and pulled her to him.

Chapter 8

Eve was too afraid to ask Grayson if he was sure about this. She was too afraid to delay even a second because she couldn't risk that he would change his mind.

This had to happen, and it had to happen now.

Grayson was obviously with her on the *now* part. He slid down, his back against the tree, and he pulled her down with him.

Eve's breath was racing already. Her heart pounded against her ribs so hard that it felt her bones would break. She was trembling, scared and cold, but she pushed all those uncomfortable things aside and pressed her mouth to his.

Big mistake.

She felt him stiffen, and the air between them changed. He'd agreed to the sex, to the making a baby part, but

that stiff mouth told her that he wasn't ready or willing
to go back to where they'd been.

"All right," she mumbled, hoping the sound of her
own voice would steady her nerves.

It didn't, but Eve didn't let raw nerves or Grayson's
steely look get to her. She worked fast, sliding up her
dress and moving onto his lap in the same motion. She
didn't meet his gaze. Didn't want to. This was already
difficult enough without seeing the proof of what he
was thinking.

And he was no doubt thinking this was a big mistake.

Eve didn't let him voice that. She knew what she
had to do. She'd had years of experience making out
with Grayson. After all, they'd had their first kiss when
she was fifteen, and they had spent years driving each
other crazy.

She knew how to make him crazy.

Eve didn't kiss him again, but she put her mouth
right next to his ear. He liked the breath and heat. He
liked the pressure and the touch of her tongue there.
Well, at least that's what used to fire him up. She had
another moment of panic when she realized that her
mouth might not have the same effect on him as it had
back then. He might push her—

Grayson made a slight, familiar sound.

If she'd been any other woman, she might not have
even heard the catch in his chest, the small burst of
breath that he tried to choke back. But Eve heard those
things, and she knew exactly what they meant. This
was still a fire spot for him. So were her hands on his
chest. Since his shirt was already partially unbuttoned,
she ran her fingers through his chest hair. And lower.

Grayson liked lower.

Still did, apparently.

Because by the time she trailed her fingers from his stomach and to the front of his jeans, she found him already huge and hard. She pressed her sex against his.

Eve suddenly didn't feel so cold.

A thought flashed through her head—this was like riding a bicycle. Well, better actually. Her body knew exactly what Grayson could do to her, how he could make her soar. And fall. That wouldn't happen now. It couldn't. She had to keep this as clinical as possible. He was merely a sperm donor here and not her lover.

Eve fumbled with his zipper and finally managed to lower it. No thanks to her hands. She was trembling. So was her mouth, but that didn't seem to affect the kisses she lowered to his neck.

She reached to take off her panties, but Grayson latched on to her hand. His grip was as hard as the part of him she was pressed against.

Her gaze snapped to his, and again Eve was terrified that he was stopping this. But Grayson didn't look her in the eyes. He made another of those sounds, a growl from deep within his throat, and he grabbed her with his other hand. He turned her, shoving her back against the tree. The impact and her surprise nearly knocked the breath out of her.

Grayson seemed to have no trouble breathing. He yanked off her panties and pushed his hips between her legs. He was on his knees now, and the weight of him pinned her to the tree.

For just a moment, she registered the rough bark against her back and bottom. His raw grip. The harsh profanity he was mumbling. Then, he thrust into her.

One long stroke that was nearly as rough as the hold he had on her wrists.

Her body gave way to his sex. Welcoming him. Yes, he was rough, and the thrusts inside her didn't become gentle, either. Of course, he knew her body as well as she knew his. And Grayson knew her. Gentle didn't work for *her.* She had always been in such a hurry to have him that she had begged for hard and fast.

Exactly what he was giving her now.

The man knew what he was doing, that was for sure. He'd learned to make love with her. He knew how to bring her to climax within seconds. Normally, Eve would have gladly surrendered to that climax. She would have surrendered to Grayson, but she instinctively knew that would make the aftermath even worse than it already would be.

And it would be *bad.*

This would cut her off from Grayson forever. Once he'd had time to apply his logical no-shades-of-gray mind to this, he would feel that she'd manipulated him. And she had. Later, Eve would deal with it, too. But for now, she pressed her mouth to the spot just below his ear. She whispered his name.

"Grayson."

The trigger, he had once called it. To finish him off, all she had to do was say his name. It had just the effect she knew it would.

He thrust into her one last time and said her name, too. *Almost.*

"Damn you, Eve," Grayson cursed.

And he finished what he'd started.

Chapter 9

Grayson got up as soon as he could move. He fixed his clothes and then put some distance between Eve and him. He couldn't go far, but even a few yards would help.

He hoped.

Behind him, he could hear Eve milling around. She was also mumbling. Grayson didn't want to figure out what she was saying. He didn't want to figure out anything except why he'd snapped and done the very thing he'd sworn he wouldn't do.

"If you're waiting for me to say I'm sorry, then you'll be waiting a long time," Eve let him know. "Because I'm not sorry, and I hope you're not, either."

Oh, he was. Sorry and stupid. But that wouldn't change what had happened. There was no way he could justify having sex with Eve. Yes, she might get pregnant. She might finally get that baby she wanted, but that put him right in a position he didn't want to be.

He didn't want to be a father.

Of course, the odds were against Eve having conceived. Grayson had no idea of the stats, but even with her at the prime time of the month, this had to be a long shot.

Hell.

That bothered him, too.

He wanted Eve to have this chance at motherhood, but Grayson wanted what he wanted, as well. Too bad he couldn't quite put a finger on what he did want. Nor did he have time to figure it out. His phone beeped, and he glanced down at the message as it came onto the screen.

"Is it Dade?" Eve asked, hurrying to his side. She was still fixing her clothes, and she smelled like sex. Looked like it, too, Grayson noticed when he risked glancing at her. He looked away as fast as he could.

"Yeah." Grayson worked his way through the abbreviations Dade had used in the message and gave her a summary. "He used my cell phone to pinpoint our location and will be here soon."

She made a sound of relief. So different from the sound she'd made just minutes ago when he'd taken her against the tree. The memory of it flashed through his head, and Grayson knew that memory would give him no peace.

His phone beeped again, and there was a new message from Dade. "He wants me to take a picture of the body," Grayson relayed to Eve. "As soon as we have a better signal, I can send it to the Rangers and they can feed it through the facial recognition program."

Something that Grayson should have already thought of, but then he'd had sex with Eve on his mind.

He cursed himself again.

"Wait here," he ordered, and Grayson walked across the woods to the body. Even the mini break from Eve might help because right now his stomach was knotted even harder than it had been in the middle of the attack.

The dead man was still there, of course, sprawled out among the clumps of dried leaves and fallen tree limbs. Grayson snapped a couple of pictures and checked the signal. Still too weak to send the photos, but he made a mental note to keep checking. He made another mental note not to do any more looking at Eve. No thinking about Eve. No more need for her that was generated below the belt.

Hard to do with her standing there in that body-hugging dress.

"Thank you," she whispered when he went back to her.

He didn't want to hear this. "Don't," Grayson warned. "Don't say anything." He wasn't a man who dwelled on regrets, but by God he could make an exception.

She stepped in front of him and forced eye contact. "Thank you," Eve repeated, and she leaned in pressed a chaste kiss on his cheek.

His cheek!

Here his body was still burning for her, and she had risked giving him a brotherly kiss like that. The woman really was playing with fire.

Grayson stepped back and fastened his attention on the area where the dead man was. "Did I hurt you?" he growled.

"No." Eve answered it so quickly that she'd probably

anticipated the question. Which meant he'd been too rough. Grayson shot her an over-the-shoulder glance to let her know that.

She shrugged. "I don't mind a little rough. But you're aware of that."

Yeah, he was. He knew every inch of her body and could have gotten her off with just a touch. But Grayson had tried to keep the pleasure factor out of this. For him that was impossible. His body was humming, and well satisfied, even though his brain was confused as hell.

"How long before you know if this worked?" he asked.

"I'm not sure. I'll have to ask my doctor." She hesitated. "I figured I wouldn't call you or anything with the results. I thought it would be easier that way. Is that okay?"

Was it? Grayson didn't have a clue what was okay. His brain was a mess right now. "Yeah," he settled for saying.

She pulled her coat around her and shivered. Eve was obviously cold, but Grayson intended to do nothing about that. He'd already done enough for the day.

"I don't want you to tell your family about this," she insisted. "As soon as we're out of here, I'll leave so you won't have to see me."

He gave her another look that was probably more scowl than anything else.

She huffed. "Grayson, I'm not stupid. I know what's going on in your head, and you'll want to put as much distance between us as possible."

True. But distance was going to be a problem until he figured out why the man had wanted her dead. Grayson was about to remind her of that when he heard Dade call out to them.

"Over here!" Grayson answered. With Eve right behind him, he went in the direction of his brother's voice.

Eve raked her hand through her hair, trying to fix it, and she brushed off the bits of leaves and twigs from her coat. Grayson tried to do the same.

He soon spotted Dade, and he wasn't alone. Deputy Melissa Garza was with him. Mel, as she liked to be called. And Grayson was thankful Dade had brought her along.

"You okay?" Dade asked when he was still a good twenty yards away.

Grayson nodded, but he was far from okay. He tipped his head to the body. "Single gunshot wound to the chest, and he bled out. It's the man we chased into the woods behind Eve's cottage."

Mel began to trudge her way through to the dead man, but Dade stayed on the path that led directly toward Grayson. As his brother walked closer, he glanced at both Eve and him. Not an ordinary glance but a suspicious one.

"I have the photos," Grayson said showing Dade his cell. Best to get Dade's suspicious mind back where it belonged—on the investigation. "Is the medical examiner on the way?"

"Yeah. He and his crew are right behind us." Dade volleyed more glances between the two of them.

"Good. Mel can stay with the body, and you can get Eve and me out of here," Grayson instructed. "I want to get the photos to the Rangers."

Dade called out Grayson's instructions to Mel, and the deputy nodded.

"Are you really okay?" Dade asked Eve as the three of them headed back toward the road.

"You mean other than the raw nerves, the tear-stained cheeks and adrenaline crash?" The corner of her mouth lifted. "Yes, I'm okay."

Dade hooked his arm around her shoulders. "I wish you could have had a better homecoming." He shifted his attention to Grayson but didn't say anything. Dade's left eyebrow lifted.

Grayson ignored him and kept on walking. Thankfully, they soon reached a spot where the cell signal was stronger, and he fired off the photos. If the dead man had a police record, then it wouldn't take the Rangers long to come up with an ID.

It took a good ten minutes for them to get back to the road where Dade had a cruiser waiting. Dade helped Eve into the front passenger's seat, closed the door and turned back around to stare at Grayson.

"Don't ask," Grayson growled in a whisper.

Dade lifted his shoulder. "Hey, you got my vote if you're getting back together with Eve."

"It's not a vote." Grayson cursed. "And what part of 'don't ask' didn't you understand?"

"The *don't* part." Dade smirked as only a younger brother could manage to do.

Grayson cursed some more. "Look, I'm in a bad mood. The kind of mood where I'd love to beat someone senseless. My advice? Stay out of my way, or that someone will be you." He threw open the door and climbed into the driver's seat.

As soon as Dade got in, Grayson sped back toward town. His mood improved a little when he saw the ME's van approaching from the opposite direction. That meant Mel wouldn't have to stay out there very long, and that was good. He needed all his deputies back at the station so he could figure out what the heck was going on.

"Any idea how the dead man tracked you down?" Dade asked from the backseat.

Grayson was about to say no, but then he groaned. "Probably a tracking device. He put one on Eve's car, we know that, and I'm guessing he put one on the truck, too."

Eve made a small gasping sound of surprise.

"I'll have someone check when they fish your truck from the creek," Dade assured him. But Grayson heard the hesitation in his brother's voice. Dade was no doubt wondering why Grayson hadn't thought of the possibility of a tracking device before he'd driven the truck away from his office.

Grayson didn't need another reason to put some distance between Eve and him, but there it was. He was thinking like a rookie, and the stakes were too high for him to make another mistake.

This mistake could have gotten Eve killed.

He wouldn't forget that.

Since Eve was shivering, Grayson decided to turn up the heat, though the adrenaline was probably more responsible than the chilly temperature. Eve apparently had the same idea because she reached at the same time he did. Their hands collided. And she pulled back as if he'd scalded her. Ironic, since just a half hour earlier he'd been deep inside her. Still, it was good they were in agreement about this no-touching thing.

"Uh, I'm guessing Eve's in protective custody?" Dade wanted to know. It sounded like a loaded question.

Eve turned in the seat to look at Dade, and Grayson nodded. "She can stay at the ranch."

"At the ranch?" She shook her head. "That's probably not a good idea."

Yeah. He was in agreement with that, too. The sex against the tree had only created more tension and friction between them, but there couldn't be any more mistakes.

"You might not have to be there long," Grayson explained. "We just need to tie up some loose ends on this case." He looked in the rearview mirror so he could see Dade. "Any more news on our DB, Nina Manning?"

"Still waiting on the preliminaries. Once we have the next of kin identified, we can talk to them, as well."

Grayson shook his head. "You said there was a missing person's report filed on her a year ago. Who filed that?"

"Her mother, Theresa Manning. She was a single parent, no record of the father, and Theresa died about a month ago. Yeah," Dade added when Grayson glanced at him in the mirror. "Theresa was diabetic and died from an insulin overdose. Could have been an accident, but I asked the Houston cops to look into it."

Yes, because the timing was suspicious.

Grayson's phone buzzed, and he saw the caller was from the Texas Ranger lab. "Sheriff Ryland," he answered and put the call on speaker so Dade could hear.

"Ranger Egan Caldwell," the man identified himself. "I have a match on the photos of the dead man."

Grayson released the breath he'd been holding. "Who is he?"

"Leon Ames. He has a record, obviously. Seven years ago for assault with a deadly weapon. He spent two years in a Bexar county jail and is still on probation."

Well, prison hadn't rehabilitated him, that's for sure. "He tried to kill me twice today, and he's in the photograph with the dead woman, Nina Manning. Is there a connection?"

"Nothing obvious, but he's got a history with the other man in the photo, Sebastian Collier."

"How?" Dade and Grayson asked in unison. Eve leaned closer to the phone and listened.

"Leon Ames works...worked for Sebastian's father, Claude. He was a handyman at their San Antonio estate."

Handyman. That was an interesting word, considering the photograph with the dead woman and the attempts to kill Eve and him.

"I'm faxing you the rest of the report," the ranger continued. "For what it's worth, I don't think Leon Ames was working alone. From everything I can see, he was nothing more than a lackey."

"What makes you think that?" Grayson asked.

"A large sum of money deposited into his bank account the day after the murder. Twenty thousand dollars. We can't trace the money because he made the deposit in cash. My guess is that money was a payoff for services rendered."

Grayson suspected as much. "So, who hired Leon—Claude or Sebastian?"

"Either is possible," the ranger answered. "But I think all roads in this investigation lead to the Colliers, and that you'll find a killer at the estate."

Chapter 10

Eve needed a friendly face, and she saw one the moment Grayson pulled to a stop in front of the Collier estate. His brother, Lieutenant Nate Ryland, was there waiting for them on the sidewalk in front of the towering black-iron fence that fronted the equally towering Collier estate.

Nate smiled, his dimples flashing, and the moment she stepped from the car, he pulled her into his arms. "Even under these circumstances, it's good to see you," Nate whispered.

"It's good to see you, too." And Eve meant it. She'd never felt more at home than in the arms of a Ryland, and Nate was no exception.

She inched back to meet his gaze and return the smile. The Ryland DNA was there all right, etched over his perfectly chiseled face, black hair and storm-gray eyes. But Nate was smooth around the cowboy-edges in his dark blue suit, which was a job requirement for San Antonio P.D. Like the rest of the Ryland clan, he was more at home in Wranglers and on the back of a horse.

Would her baby be the same?

Her baby, she mentally repeated. And she felt her smile deepen. Yes, a pregnancy was a long shot, but it was possible that she was well on her way to getting the child she'd always wanted.

"Eve?" Nate said, drawing her out of her daydream. "You okay?"

"Of course. I was just distracted for a moment." Eve stared at him, and her smile faded when she remembered what Nate had gone through. "I'm sorry about your wife's death," she whispered.

Eve was even sorrier that she hadn't gone to the funeral or spoken to him about it before now. Nate had always felt like a brother to her, and she'd let him down at a time when he no doubt needed all of his friends. "How are you handling things?"

His smile faded, too. "It's, uh, complicated," he mumbled. Nate's gaze swung in Grayson's direction, an indication to her that this conversation was over. "Are you ready to do battle with the Colliers?"

"Considering their hired gun tried to kill us, yeah, I'm ready."

Nate gave a crisp nod. As a lieutenant, he'd no doubt done his share of interrogations. He was also a cop with some clout when it came to handling an investigation.

And Grayson.

If Nate hadn't had some influence, Eve wouldn't have been allowed to tag along. As it was, she'd practically had to beg Grayson to let her come. He'd wanted to tuck her safely away at the ranch. Eve wanted to be safe, but she didn't want that at the expense of learning the truth. She had taken the incriminating photo, and she wanted to confront the person responsible for what was going on.

"Anything I should know before we go inside?" Grayson asked his brother.

"Well, they haven't lawyered up. But I doubt that means you'll get a lot of cooperation, especially when you link the dead woman to their now dead employee."

Eve hoped Nate was wrong. She wanted answers today so she could start distancing herself from Grayson. She couldn't keep leaning on these Ryland shoulders.

"So, Claude and Sebastian know that Leon was killed?" she clarified.

"They do. And when I spoke to them over the phone, I also told them that Leon tried to murder both of you." Nate walked toward the gate and flashed his badge at the monitor. Seconds later, the gate creaked open.

"I'd like to handle the interview myself," Grayson insisted.

"Figured you would. But if we learn anything we can use to hold either one of them, I need to make the arrest since we're not sure where this murder occurred."

An arrest. Eve hoped that would happen, and then things could finally get back to normal. Well, maybe. If she was indeed pregnant, then nothing would be *normal* again.

Nate shot her a glance. "And I hoped you would say as little as possible. I want them to see you, so they'll know that the picture you took is no longer a reason to come after you. That's the only reason I'm allowing you in the middle of a murder investigation."

She nodded, mumbled a thanks.

"Eve knows the rules," Grayson said, and it sounded like a warning. He walked ahead of them toward the porch that stretched the entire width of the three-story house. There were dozens of white columns, each of them ringed with fresh holly, and a five-foot-tall vertical wreath hung on the door.

Nate fell in step alongside her. "Did something happen between you two?" he asked.

What—did she have a big sign stuck to her back proclaiming that she'd had sex with Grayson? Of course, *sex* was a very loose term for what had happened between them. It had seemed more like a biology experiment.

And that, she reminded herself, was exactly what she'd asked of Grayson.

No strings attached. No emotion. No discussion.

Well, she'd gotten all of that. He had hardly said two words to her when they'd gone back to the sheriff's office to change his clothes. Or on the drive from Silver Creek to her San Antonio condo so she could get a change of clothes, as well. Ditto for more of his silence on the drive to the Collier estate.

And that was just as well.

He was making it easier for her to walk away.

"Nothing happened," she lied.

Nate made a sound that could have meant anything and joined Grayson on the porch as he rang the doorbell. Eve stayed just behind them. A maid wearing a uniform opened the door, and without saying a word, she ushered them through the marble-floored foyer and into a sitting room where two men waited for them.

The room was decorated in varying shades of white and cream. A stark contrast to the floor-to-ceiling Christmas tree that was practically smothered in shiny blood-red ornaments. After the real blood she'd seen today, the sight of those ornaments twisted her stomach a little.

Eve recognized both men in the room—Claude from his photos in the newspapers and Sebastian from the picture she'd taken of him at the rodeo. Both men were dressed in suits. Claude's was black. His son's, a dark gray. Both men were sipping something from cut-crystal glasses that looked and smelled expensive.

"Sheriff Grayson Ryland," he said, stepping ahead of Nate and her. "This is my brother, Lt. Nate Ryland from SAPD, and Eve Warren."

"Ah, Ms. Warren, the woman who took the photo in question," Sebastian quickly supplied. He crossed the room and shook all of their hands. His expression and greeting were friendly enough, but Eve wondered just how long that would last.

The friendly demeanor didn't extend to the other Collier in the room. Claude was a carbon copy of his son, but he was at least twenty pounds thinner and his scowl bunched up his otherwise classic features. His navy blue eyes were narrowed, and he watched them as if they were thieves about to run off with the family silver. He also didn't ask them to sit, probably because he hoped this would be a short visit. Or maybe he was just naturally rude.

"Yes, I took the picture," Eve answered when Sebastian continued to stare at her. "How did you know about that?"

That question earned her scolding looks from Nate and Grayson, who obviously didn't want her involved in this questioning, but Sebastian only flashed that thousand-watt smile. A smile that probably worked wonders on his business associates, but to her it felt slimy.

Just like the man himself.

"A journalist friend told me," Sebastian volunteered. "I understand it was going to be printed in tomorrow's newspaper. But then you managed to ID the unfortunate victim."

"Yes," Grayson verified. He kept his gaze pinned to Sebastian. "Mind explaining what you and your *handyman* were doing in the photo with Nina Manning?"

Sebastian opened his mouth to answer, but his father's voice boomed through the room. "Leon Ames is not my handyman. I fired him three days ago."

Grayson and Nate exchanged glances. "Why?" Grayson demanded.

Claude shrugged as if the answer wasn't important. He responded only after Grayson continued to stare at him. "Erratic behavior," Claude finally supplied. The man couldn't have sounded snootier if he'd tried. "I expect impeccable behavior from my employees, and Leon didn't live up to that."

"How so?" Grayson pressed.

Claude blew out an irritated breath. "If you must know, he used one of the family cars to run a personal errand. I questioned him, he lied about it and I dismissed him. End of story."

Grayson matched the irritated breath response. "No. It's not the end of it. Because the day before you fired him, Leon and your son were photographed with a woman who was murdered."

"I can explain that," Sebastian offered, still sounding very cooperative. "I went to the charity rodeo, and I ran into Leon and the woman. I believe they were lovers."

"Lovers?" Grayson again. "Leon was twice her age."

Claude flexed his eyebrows. "Then, maybe *lover* isn't the right term. I think the woman was a pro. She was hitting up Leon for cash."

Since Nina did indeed have a record for prostitution, that could be true, but Eve wasn't about to believe him. Sebastian almost certainly wouldn't admit if he'd been the one who hired Nina for her *services.*

"Tell me everything you remember about the meeting," Grayson demanded, looking directly at Sebastian.

Sebastian took a sip of his drink and gave another nonchalant lift of his shoulder. "As I said, I went to the charity rodeo so I could make a donation and ran into Leon. The woman was with him, and they seemed to be, well, cozy."

"In the picture they appeared to be angry," Grayson fired back.

"That came later." Sebastian didn't hesitate. "The woman's attitude became less friendly when Leon refused to give her money."

Grayson stepped closer to Sebastian. "Did she say what the money was for?"

Sebastian shook his head. "I didn't listen to their conversation, Sheriff. The woman was obviously low-rent. Probably high on drugs. Once I realized that, I moved away and let them finish their discussion. I didn't want to be seen in that kind of company."

"Did it seem as if Leon knew Nina before this meeting?" Nate asked.

"I'm not sure." Sebastian finished his drink in one gulp.

"You should be talking to Leon's friends about that," Claude interrupted. "I won't have my family's good name dragged through the mud for the likes of Leon Ames."

Grayson gave him a flat look. "I don't suppose you have the names of Leon's friends?"

Claude's mouth twisted as if he'd tasted something bitter. "I do not make it a habit of delving into the personal lives of my employees." He slapped his glass onto the table. "And that's the end of this interview. Anything else goes through our family attorneys."

Sebastian gave an embarrassed smile. "I've already told you everything I know."

"Not quite." Despite Claude's rude dismissal, Grayson stayed put. "When's the last time you saw Leon and the dead woman?"

"Probably just a few minutes after Miss Warren here snapped the photo. I left, and I have no idea where they went." Sebastian checked his watch. "Now, if you'll excuse me, I need to get ready for our guests. We're having a small Christmas gathering here tonight."

"If you remember anything else about the encounter with Nina and Leon," Grayson said to Sebastian, "I want you to call me." He extracted a business card from his jacket pocket and dropped it on the glass end table. "I'll also need you to go to SAPD and give a written statement."

Sebastian groaned softly. "Please tell me that can

wait until after the holidays. Christmas is only three days away."

"And SAPD will be open all day," Grayson fired back. "A woman is dead, and she deserves justice. I need that statement and anything else you can remember about Leon's friends."

"Of course," Sebastian finally agreed, but he was no longer so cordial. His mouth tightened.

Both father and son turned to walk out, but they stopped when the sound of a woman's high heels echoed through the room. They all turned in the direction of the sound, and Eve spotted a curvy blonde in a plunging liquid-silver dress, who was making her way toward them. She, too, had a drink in a crystal highball glass, and she was teetering on five-inch red heels that were the exact color of the Christmas ornaments.

"Claude, you didn't tell me that we had guests." She clucked her tongue and smiled first at Grayson. Then Nate. She didn't even spare Eve a glance.

"They're not guests," Claude snapped. "They're cops. And they were just leaving."

"Leaving?" The woman gave a quick fake pout. "Well, let me introduce myself. I'm Annabel Collier, Claude's wife." Her cherry-lacquered smile went south when she glanced at Sebastian. "And I'm his stepmother."

Eve hadn't studied the background info on Annabel, but she was betting that stepmother and son were close to the same age. Annabel was clearly a trophy wife.

A drunk one.

"The maid was about to show them out," Claude reiterated, and just like that, the maid appeared in the doorway of the sitting room.

"I can do that," Annabel volunteered. She hooked her arm through Grayson's, and Eve didn't think it was her imagination that the woman pressed the side of her double Ds against Grayson's chest.

"Isn't the estate beautiful this time of year?" Annabel babbled on. Some of her drink sloshed onto the floor and the toes of those red stilettos. "I love all the sparkles and the presents. Claude is very generous with presents, you know. I peeked, and all I can say is five carats, platinum setting." She punctuated that with a drunken giggle.

Behind them, Eve heard Claude mumble something, but both Sebastian and he stayed put as Annabel escorted Grayson to the door. Nate and Eve followed, and Eve wondered if she could trip the bimbo who was hanging all over Grayson. Since Grayson and she weren't together, it didn't make sense to be jealous, but Eve felt it anyway.

Annabel threw open the door, and the cold December wind poured into the foyer and rustled the shimmering gold wreath. Despite her strapless dress she stepped onto the porch with them. She glanced over her shoulder, and when her gaze returned to them, she was a changed woman. No bimbo smile, and her sapphire-blue eyes were suddenly intense.

Eve was too dumbfounded to do anything but watch, which was probably a good thing.

Annabel plucked something from her cleavage and pressed it into Grayson's hand, which she pretended to shake. "The Colliers have secrets," she whispered, her bottom lip trembling. "Deadly ones."

Annabel giggled again, sliding right back into the persona of the drunken trophy wife. "Happy holidays," she told them as she stepped back inside. She gave Grayson one last pleading look, and then shut the door.

"What was that all about?" Nate mumbled.

But Grayson didn't answer. He hurried off the porch and toward the car. So did Nate and Eve. He waited until they were outside the gates and away from the security cameras that dotted the fence.

Then Grayson opened his hand so that Nate and Eve could see what Annabel had given him.

Eve stared it and shook her head.

What the heck was going on, and why had Annabel given them *this?*

Chapter 11

Grayson was several steps beyond exhaustion, but he kept his eyes on the road. It was nearly dark, and the temperature had dropped, and the last thing he needed was to wreck another car today.

"Anything?" he asked Eve again.

It was a question he'd asked her several times since they'd left San Antonio nearly a half hour earlier. Most of that time, Eve had been using the laptop that she'd picked up from her condo so she could view the pictures.

Pictures on the tiny memory card that Annabel had given them.

Grayson had already emailed a copy of the card's contents to the crime lab in Austin, but he wanted to have a closer look for himself as to what Annabel had considered important enough to pass along to a sheriff who was investigating her husband and stepson.

Eve shifted the laptop to a position so that Grayson could see. He glanced at the screen and saw the thumbnails of the photographs. There were dozens of them.

"Annabel obviously likes to take pictures, but I think I finally have them sorted," Eve mumbled. She tapped the ones in the first row. "These are shots taken in what appears to be Claude's office. My guess is Annabel took them with a hidden camera mounted somewhere in the room because the angle never changes."

"Anything incriminating?" Grayson asked.

"Hard to tell. Claude's obviously having a discussion with this dark-haired woman, but there's nothing sexual going on. I think they're arguing."

Grayson agreed. Everything about their body language conveyed anger, not romance. "I need to find out who that woman is." And the crime lab could maybe help with that.

"Well, I think we can rule her out as a mistress. Claude seems to prefer women half his age, and this woman looks to be about fifty." Eve enlarged the photos on the next row, and she made a sound of surprise.

"What?" Grayson asked. He didn't want to fully take his eyes off the road, but Eve's reaction grabbed his attention.

"There are a dozen or more shots taken in a hotel lobby. An expensive hotel, judging from the decor. And there's Nina." She pointed to the next series of pictures. "Nina's not alone, either. Both Claude and Sebastian are there with her."

Eve met his gaze. "That means Sebastian lied about never having seen Nina."

Yeah. Annabel had been right about family secrets. Was this what she'd meant?

"Is a lie enough to arrest Sebastian?" Eve asked.

"No. With his money and connections, we need more. We need a motive." Grayson turned off the highway and onto the ranch road that would take him home.

She huffed and pushed her hair from her face. Eve was obviously exhausted, too. Even with the watery light from the laptop screen, he could see the dark circles beneath her eyes. He could also see how damn attractive she was, and he wondered if there was ever a time he wouldn't look at her and think just that.

"Maybe Sebastian and Nina were lovers?" Eve tossed out there. She was obviously unaware that he was sneaking glimpses of not just the photographs but of her. "Maybe Sebastian snapped when he found out his lover also had a romantic interest in his father?"

Grayson shook his head. "That doesn't look like a lover's encounter. Even though it's possible that one or both had sex with her, and Nina was trying to blackmail them. After all, Claude did say he wouldn't have his family's good name dragged through the mud. Maybe this was his way of making sure that didn't happen."

And Claude could have hired Leon to kill a blackmailing Nina.

But then why was Sebastian in the picture?

Better yet, why had Annabel given him this incriminating evidence?

Grayson wasn't sure, but he intended to find out. He'd already requested a more detailed background check on Nina and all the Colliers, including Annabel.

"There are some pictures taken at the charity rodeo," Eve let him know. "Not mine. These are ones that Annabel or someone else shot. High angle, zoom lens. She was probably in the top seats of the stadium."

Maybe so that the men wouldn't notice her, which meant that Annabel probably knew she was snapping pictures of something incriminating.

"Did she photograph the encounter with Leon, Nina and Sebastian?" Grayson asked.

He took the last turn to the ranch and could see the lights of the sprawling two-story house just ahead. Sometimes, he took home for granted. But not tonight. It was a welcome sight.

"Not that I can readily see," Eve answered, her attention still nailed to the computer screen. "I need to enlarge the photos and study them."

"Later." The pictures were important, perhaps even critical, but he wanted to get her settled into the guest-room first. He'd already called the housekeeper, Bessie Watkins, to let her know they were on the way so that she could prepare the guestroom.

Eve looked up as if surprised to see they were already at the ranch. "Wow," she mumbled.

That reaction was no doubt for the Christmas lights. There were hundreds of them lining the fence that led all the way to the main house. Even the shrubs had been decked with twinkling lights, and there were two fully decorated Christmas trees on each end of the porch.

"Bessie did this," Grayson explained. "For Nate's daughter, Kimmie. It's her first Christmas."

Grayson felt a tightness in his chest. Because it was a Christmas that his niece wouldn't be able to spend with her mother. It made him even more determined to keep Eve safe. And he'd taken measures to make sure that happened.

The ranch was huge, over three thousand acres, but it was equipped with a full security system that monitored all parts of the house and property. There were also at least a dozen ranch hands in quarters on the grounds.

Then, there were his brothers.

Mason and Dade were still at work in town, but soon they would return for the night. Nate, too, even though Kimmie and he lived in a separate wing of the ranch house. The youngest, Kade, was at his apartment in Austin where he worked for the FBI, but he could be at the ranch in an hour if necessary.

Grayson hoped it wouldn't be necessary.

He stopped the car in the circular drive and looked around. It was pitch-dark now, but there were enough security and Christmas lights for him to see that no one was lurking around, ready to strike. Still, he didn't want to dawdle. Grayson grabbed the suitcase that Eve had taken from her place in San Antonio. She latched on to the laptop, and they hurried up the flagstone porch steps.

Other than the Christmas lights, there was no glitz here like at the Collier estate. The porch was painted white, and the rocking chairs weren't just for show. They used them often.

"You're finally here," Bessie said the moment she threw open the door. And despite the laptop between them, Bessie hugged Eve. "Girl, you are a sight for sore eyes."

"It's great to see you, too, Bessie," Eve answered.

"I got a room all made up for you." Bessie caught on to Eve's arm and led her across the foyer. Not marble, but Texas hardwood.

The furnishings here and in the rest of the house leaned more toward a Western theme with pine tables and oil paintings of the various show horses and livestock they'd had over the years. One of Dade's girl-friends had joked that it was cowboy chic.

Eve glanced around and took a deep breath. She was probably thinking things hadn't changed much since she'd last been here. Grayson's thoughts went in a different direction. As always, she looked as if she belonged there.

Under different circumstances, she would have.

But it hadn't been different circumstances since his father had walked out on his family twenty years ago. Since then Grayson hadn't wanted a wife or a family. Of course, that hadn't stopped him from having sex with Eve in the woods.

Later, he'd have to figure out how to deal with that.

Bessie directed Eve toward the stairs to the right of the entry. "I can run you a bath. And then you can have something to eat. I made chili and pecan pie, your favorites."

Eve looked back at Grayson as if she expected him to rescue her. "I need to go over these pictures," she insisted.

Grayson took the laptop from her, balancing it in his left hand since he had her suitcase in his right. "The pictures can wait a few minutes. Besides, I'm starving. Take your bath so we can eat."

That wasn't exactly true. Eve and he had grabbed some fast food on the way out to the Collier estate, but Grayson knew he could get Eve's cooperation if she thought the dinner and bath breaks were for him and not her.

It worked. Eve didn't argue.

While Bessie chattered away about the Christmas dinner plans, she led Eve into the bathroom of the guest suite. Grayson deposited Eve's suitcase in the bedroom and went to his suite directly across the hall so he, too, could grab a quick shower.

Grayson tossed his clothes and Stetson onto the bed and hurried because he wanted to get back to the pictures. He also needed to find out the status of the background checks on Annabel, Claude, Sebastian and Nina. However, he wasn't nearly as quick as Eve because he had barely dried off and put on a pair of clean jeans when there was a knock at the door.

"It's me," Eve said, but she didn't wait. She threw open the door just as Grayson was zipping his jeans.

"Oh, sorry," she mumbled. Her hair was wet, no makeup, and she was wearing a dark green sweater top and pants. She wasn't wearing shoes but rather a pair of socks.

She fluttered her fingers behind her as if indicating that she was about to return to her room so he could finish dressing. But she stayed put with her gaze pinned to his bare chest and stomach.

She pulled in her breath and held it for a second. "You have a scar," she whispered.

For a moment Grayson had thought that breathless reaction was for his half-naked body. It's a good thing it wasn't.

And he was pretty sure he believed that.

She walked toward him, slowly, leaned down and touched the six-inch scar that started at his chest and ended on his right side. "How did it happen?"

"I broke up a fight at the cantina on the edge of town. Didn't see the switchblade until it was too late."

Another deep breath. "You could have been killed." Her voice was suddenly clogged with emotion.

Yeah. But Grayson kept that to himself. He also

caught her hand to move it off his stomach, but somehow their fingers ended up laced together.

And neither of them pulled away.

Their eyes met. She was so familiar to him, but those eyes always held a surprise or two. Sometimes they were a misty blue. Other times, the color of a spring Texas sky.

Grayson cursed that last analogy.

He was a cowboy, and the last thing he should be doing was thinking poetic thoughts about the color of Eve's eyes.

His thoughts weren't so poetic when it came to the rest of her.

Grayson knew exactly how she looked beneath those winter clothes. He knew how much she liked it when he kissed her belly. And the inside of her thighs. He knew the way she smelled. The way she tasted. The sounds that she made when he was driving her hot and crazy. And it was because he knew all those things that he had to back away.

But he didn't.

They stood there, gazes locked, as if paralysis had set in and neither could move. Eve's breath became thin. Her face flushed. She glanced at his bed, and Grayson knew exactly what she was thinking.

He'd made love to her in that bed.

Things had been different then. Ten years ago they'd remodeled the house and turned all the bedrooms into suites. But the black lacquered wrought-iron bed was the same. It'd been his grandfather's, and Grayson had staked claim to it twenty years ago after his grandfather had been killed. He'd gone through several mattresses in those twenty years, but the bed itself had remained unchanged.

No telling how many times Grayson had sneaked Eve up to his room. To this very bed.

In the beginning, neither had had a clue what they were doing. They had followed their instincts. Did the things that felt good. And plenty of those times, he'd had to kiss her hard and deep to muffle the sounds she made when she climaxed.

Grayson could hear those sounds now echoing through his head.

He couldn't help but respond to those memories. To the touch of her fingers linked with his.

Part of him, the part straining against the zipper of his jeans, started to rationalize that he could put her on that bed again. He knew how to get those sounds from her. Knew the delicious heat of her body.

"Mercy," she mumbled, but it didn't have any sound. She shook her head. Moistened her lips.

He wanted to hear her voice. Those sounds. But most of all, he just wanted to kiss her.

"It would be a mistake," Grayson said more to himself than her.

"Oh, yeah. A big one." But she inched closer. So close that he tasted her breath on his mouth. That taste went straight through him.

Something inside him snapped, and he latched on to the back of her neck and hauled her to him. Their mouths met, and he heard the sound all right. A little bit of whimper mixed with a boatload of relief.

Grayson knew exactly how she felt.

Helpless. Stupid.

And hot.

"Should I close the door and give you time alone?" someone snarled from the doorway. It was his brother Mason.

Eve and Grayson flew apart as if they'd just been caught doing something wrong. Which was true. They couldn't lust after each other. Sex against the tree to make a baby was one thing. But real sex would turn their status from *it's complicated* to *it's damn impossible.*

"Well?" Mason prompted in that surly noninterested way that only Mason could manage. "You need time to do something about that kiss or what?"

"Did you want something?" Grayson fired back at his brother.

Mason lifted the papers he had in his hand and dropped them onto the table near the door. "Background reports on the Colliers and the dead girl. You should read them. There's some interesting stuff in there." He tipped his head to the laptop. "Anything with the photos?"

"Not yet," Eve and Grayson said in unison.

If that frustrated Mason, he didn't show it. He turned but then stopped. "Good to see you, Eve." From Mason, that was a warm, fuzzy welcome.

"It's good to see you, too." Eve's was considerably warmer. Strange, most people steered clear of Mason, but Eve went to him and planted a kiss on his cheek.

Now Mason looked uncomfortable. "Yell if you need me." And with that mumbled offer, he strolled away.

Both Eve and he hurried to the reports that Mason had dropped on the table, and Grayson snatched them up. There were at least thirty pages, and with Eve right at his shoulder, they started to skim through them. It didn't take long for Grayson to see what Mason had considered *interesting stuff.*

There was a photo of Claude's first wife, Cicely, and it was the same woman in the photos taken in his office. So that was one thing cleared up. Claude's ex had visited him. Nothing suspicious about that. Since she was the mother of his son, they would always have a connection.

That required Grayson to take a deep breath because he couldn't help but think that one day, soon, Eve and he might have that same connection.

"Cicely had twins," Eve read, touching her finger to that part of the background. "Sebastian and Sophia."

This was the first Grayson had heard of it, but then he'd only had a preliminary report of Sebastian before the interview at the Collier estate.

Grayson read on. "When Sophia was six months old, the nanny, Helen Bolton, disappeared with her, and even though Helen turned up dead three months later, Sophia was never found."

On the same page of the report, there was a photo of baby Sophia that had obviously been taken right before she went missing.

"You have a scanner in the house?" Eve asked, her attention nailed to the picture of the baby.

"Sure. In my office."

Eve grabbed the laptop and headed up the hall. She practically raced ahead of him, and the moment they were inside, she fed the picture into the scanner and loaded it onto the laptop with the other photos they'd gotten from Annabel.

"What are you doing?" Grayson wanted to know.

While she typed frantically on the keyboard, Eve

sank down in the leather chair behind his desk. "I have age progression software. It's not a hundred percent accurate, but it might work."

Grayson watched Eve manipulate the copied image of the baby, and soon it began to take shape. The adult version of Sophia Collier appeared on the screen.

Grayson cursed under his breath. The hair was different, but there were enough similarities.

"Oh, God," Eve mumbled. She leaned away from the laptop and touched her fingers to her mouth. "Do you see it?" she asked.

"Yeah." Grayson saw it all right.

And it meant this investigation had just taken a crazy twist.

Because the dead woman, Nina Manning, hadn't been Claude's mistress as they'd originally thought. She was Sophia Collier, Claude's missing daughter.

Chapter 12

"I wished you'd stayed at the ranch," Grayson mumbled again. He kept his attention pinned to the San Antonio downtown street that was clogged with holiday shoppers and traffic.

Eve ignored him. She'd already explained her reasons for tagging along for this visit to Cicely Collier. She wanted the truth about the dead woman, and when that happened, the danger would be over. She could go home and, well, wait until she could take a pregnancy test.

It had been less than twenty-four hours since Grayson had agreed to have sex with her, but she'd read enough of the pregnancy books to know that conception could have already happened.

She could be pregnant.

Despite everything else going on, Eve smiled and slid her hand over her stomach. Even though it was a long shot, she wanted to hang on to the possibility as long as she could.

Even if she couldn't hang on to Grayson.

That kiss in his bedroom had felt so much like old times, and as stupid as it sounded, it had felt more intimate than the sex. It had been real, not some gesture that she'd had to talk Grayson into doing.

And that's why it couldn't happen again.

She could coax him into kissing her again. Maybe even talk him into coming to her bed. But he would soon feel trapped, and he would blame himself—and her—for feeling that way. She cared for him too much to make him go through that. Grayson already had enough duty forced on him in his life without making him feel even a shred of obligation to her. More kissing would make him feel obligated.

"You okay?" Grayson asked.

She glanced at him and realized he'd seen her hand on her stomach. "I'm fine."

He seemed suspicious of her answer, but he didn't press it. Nor would he. A discussion about the baby was off-limits for both of them, and Eve was thankful for it. Conversation wasn't going to help with this matter. No. The only thing that would help was to put some distance between them.

The voice on the GPS directed them toward another turn, and Grayson drove into the upscale San Antonio neighborhood. Of course, she hadn't expected Cicely to live in a shack, but it was obvious the woman had done well in the divorce settlement.

Grayson parked in the driveway of the two-story Victorian-style home. It was painted a soft buttery yellow with white trim, and despite the fact that it was the dead of winter, the lawn was as pristine as the house.

"I have a warrant for Cicely's DNA," Grayson explained, grabbing the large padded envelope that earlier he'd put on the backseat. "I can compare it to Nina's. If it's a match, we'll have proof that Nina is really Sophia Collier."

"What about Claude's DNA?" Eve asked.

"There's a warrant for that, too. Nate's over there now collecting it."

Poor Nate. She doubted Claude would make the process easy. For that matter, maybe Cicely wouldn't either, especially when they told her that her long-lost daughter was likely dead. Murdered, at that.

Eve was bracing herself for the worst.

Grayson and she got out of the car and went to the door. Unlike at the Collier estate, Cicely already had the door open and was waiting for them.

Cicely looked exactly as she had in the photographs that Annabel had taken of her in Claude's office. Her short, dark brown hair was perfect, not a strand out of place, and she wore a simple olive-green wool suit. She was nothing like Annabel, her curvy young replacement, but it was easy to see that Cicely had once been stunningly beautiful.

"Sheriff Ryland," Cicely greeted. Her nerves were there in her voice and the worry etched on her face.

"Mrs. Collier. This is Eve Warren. She's helping with the investigation."

"Yes." She stared at Eve and repeated it. "Sebastian called and told me that Ms. Warren had taken a picture that you have some questions about."

Cicely stepped back, motioning for them to enter.

She didn't say anything else until she led them into a cozy room off the back of the foyer. The painting over the stone fireplace immediately caught Eve's eye. It was an oil painting of two babies. One was definitely Sophia, and she guessed the other one was Sebastian.

"My children," Cicely explained, following Eve's gaze. "Won't you please have a seat?" She motioned toward the pair of chairs.

There was a gleaming silver tray with a teapot and cookies on the coffee table. Cicely sat on a floral sofa and began to serve them. Eve sat across from her.

"Sebastian dropped by earlier, and we had a long chat." Cicely's hands were trembling when she passed Eve the tea that she'd poured in a delicate cup painted with yellow roses. "He's worried. And so am I. You think Sebastian had something to do with Nina Manning's death."

"Did he?" Grayson asked. He waved off the tea when Cicely offered it to him and sat in the chair next to Eve.

"No." Cicely's pale green eyes came to Eve's. "But of course, that means nothing. I would say that because he's my son."

Eve was more than a little surprised that a mother would admit that. Of course, despite her comment about *being worried,* maybe Cicely and Sebastian weren't that close.

Grayson took out the warrant and the DNA kit from the envelope and handed them to Cicely. "I need a sample of your DNA."

Cicely's forehead bunched up, and for a moment Eve thought she would refuse, but she only refused the warrant. She pushed it aside, took the swab and without questions, she used it on the inside of her mouth.

"It's not necessary, you know," she said, handing the kit back to Grayson.

Yes, it was, and Eve figured Grayson was about to tell her why. Eve held her breath.

"Mrs. Collier—" But that was as far as Grayson got.

"Yes," Cicely interrupted. "I know that Nina Manning is…was my daughter."

Eve didn't know who looked more surprised—Grayson or her.

Cicely took a sip of tea, but her hand was trembling so much that some of it sloshed into the saucer. "I've already done the DNA test, and I can provide a copy of the results if you need them."

Grayson stayed quiet a moment. "How long have you known that she was your daughter?"

Cicely dodged his gaze. "About a month."

"A month?" Grayson mumbled something under his breath. "And you didn't think you should tell the police that your kidnapped daughter had returned?"

"I considered many things but not that." Cicely let the vague comment hang in the air for several seconds. "About a month ago, Nina showed up here and claimed to be Sophia. She said that as a baby she'd been abandoned at a church and had been raised in foster care. I didn't believe her, of course. Not until I got back the results from the DNA test."

Cicely blinked back tears. "I thought my daughter was dead."

After twenty-two years, that was reasonable, but Eve knew if she'd been in Cicely's shoes, she would have never stopped looking. *Never.*

"What happened when you found out Nina was telling the truth?" Grayson asked.

Balancing her cup on her lap, she picked at a non-existent piece of lint on her jacket. "I begged her to come home. It was obvious that she needed help. Rehab. Counseling. Did you know that she'd been selling her body to support her drug habit?"

Grayson nodded. "She had a record."

Cicely pulled in her breath as if it were physically painful to hear her suspicions confirmed. "She refused my help. She only wanted money, and I didn't want to hand over cash because I knew she'd just use it for drugs. So I called Claude to see if he would help me convince her to go to rehab."

Grayson and Eve exchanged a glance.

"Claude knew that Nina was your daughter?" Grayson asked.

"Of course," Cicely said without hesitation. "What? Did he deny it?"

"He did," Grayson confirmed.

Her mouth tightened. "Well, apparently he wasn't just a weasel of a husband, he's also a weasel of a father." She practically dumped her teacup onto the table and got up. She folded her arms over her chest and paced. "Did you meet his new tart of a wife?"

"Yes, we met Annabel." Grayson didn't say a word about the photos Annabel had provided. Without them, it might have taken a lot longer to make the connection between Nina and Sophia. However, Eve wasn't sure that had been Annabel's intention.

"Annabel." Cicely repeated the name like it was a profanity. "You can put her at the top of the list of suspects as my daughter's killer. She probably hired her lapdog, Leon Ames, to murder my baby in cold blood."

Eve set her tea aside also. This conversation was

definitely loaded with bombshells. "Why would Annabel do that?" Eve wanted to know.

Cicely rubbed her fingers together. "Money, plain and simple. Claude's dying, you know?"

Grayson shook his head. "You're sure?"

"Positive. Sebastian told me all about it. Claude has a malignant nonoperable brain tumor. Probably has less than two months to live. And when they put Claude in the ground, the tart will inherit half of his estate. If Sophia had lived, the split would have been three ways. Apparently, that wasn't enough money for her."

Mercy. If that was true, then Cicely had not only just given Annabel a motive but Sebastian, as well. After all, Sebastian certainly hadn't volunteered anything about the dead woman being his sister. In fact, he'd lied to Grayson from the very start.

"I need to re-interview Claude and Sebastian," Grayson said, standing.

"Annabel, too," Cicely insisted. "She's the one who had my baby killed, and I'm going to prove it. I want her surgically perfected butt tossed in jail."

Cicely wasn't so shaky now. She looked like a woman on a mission of revenge.

"You need to stay out of the investigation," Grayson reminded her. "If Annabel is guilty, I'll figure out a way to prove it."

Cicely didn't respond, and Eve wondered just how much trouble the woman would be. She wasn't just going to drop this.

"You can see yourselves out," Cicely said with ice in her voice. She'd apparently worked herself into a frenzy and was no longer in the hostess mode.

Grayson and Eve did just that. They saw themselves

out, but Eve was reeling from what they'd just learned. Reeling and frustrated.

"I thought by now we'd have just one suspect," Eve whispered to Grayson on the way to the door. "Instead we have two—Annabel and Sebastian."

"We have four," Grayson whispered back, and he didn't say more until they were outside. "Claude might not have been so happy to see his drug-addicted, prostitute daughter return to the family fold."

True. He had a thing about keeping mud off his good name. "And the fourth suspect?"

Grayson opened the car door for her, and she got inside. "Cicely."

Eve shook her head. "You think she would kill her own daughter?"

"I don't know, but I'm going to find out." He shut her door, got in behind the wheel and drove away. He took a deep breath. "I could drop you off at SAPD headquarters while I re-interview the Colliers."

Eve gave him a flat look. "I'm going with you."

Grayson matched her look and added a raised eyebrow. "There could be a killer in the house."

She wasn't immune to the fear, mainly because Eve believed that one of the Colliers was indeed a killer. But she was stuck on this investigation treadmill until Grayson made an arrest. Eve wanted to confront the danger head-on, and the sooner that happened, the better.

Grayson mumbled something about her being stubborn and grabbed his phone. "Then I'll have Nate bring the Colliers into the police station."

Eve didn't have to guess how this would play out. "They aren't going to like that."

"Good. Because I don't like the lies they've told us.

Plus, I'd like to see how Claude reacts when I show him the memory card his wife gave us."

Eve almost felt sorry for Annabel. *Almost*. But then, Annabel did have a strong motive for murder—her soon-to-be-dead husband's money. And it was as if Annabel was trying to put the blame on either Claude or her stepson with those pictures she'd taken.

Grayson made the call to Nate, and while he was arranging the follow-up interview with the Colliers, Eve grabbed her laptop because she wanted to continue studying the photos. Before she could do that, however, she noticed the email from her doctor, Alan Stephenson.

The message was simple. "I've been trying to reach you. Call me."

Eve automatically reached for her cell, only to remember she didn't have one. It was in Grayson's truck, which had gone into the creek. She hadn't checked her answering machine at the condo either, mainly because Grayson had been in such a hurry to get her out of there.

"I need to use your phone," she told Grayson the moment he ended his call with Nate.

"Anything wrong?" he asked.

"I'm not sure." Eve took the cell and frantically pressed in the phone number at the bottom of the email. A dozen things went through her mind, most of them bad. Had the doctor been wrong about her ovulating? Had she put Grayson through all of this for nothing? Her heart broke at the thought of her being too late to have a child of her own.

She got the doctor's answering service first, but Dr. Stephenson had left word to put her call through to him. Moments later, the doctor picked up.

"Eve," he greeted, but she could hear something in his voice. This was not good news.

"I got your email. You've been trying to call me?"

"Most of yesterday afternoon. I found a private sperm donor, but as you probably already know, it's already too late. I'm sorry."

Her lungs were aching so she released the breath she'd been holding. "I found a donor." She didn't look at Grayson, but she sensed he was looking at her.

"That's wonderful." The doctor sounded both surprised and relieved. "Did you use artificial insemination?"

The image of Grayson in the woods flashed through her mind. "No. There wasn't time."

The doctor cleared his throat. "Well, the old-fashioned way works, too."

And was a lot more pleasurable. But Eve kept that to herself. "I know it's probably a long shot."

"Maybe not. Having sex when you're ovulating substantially increases the odds. Come in next week, and I'll run a test. We should be able to tell if you're pregnant."

Everything inside Eve began to spin. "Next week? That soon?"

"That soon," the doctor assured her. "Call the office and make an appointment. I'll see you then."

The doctor ended the call, and Eve just sat there and stared at the phone. It was exactly the news she wanted. The doctor was hopeful that she had conceived, and she wouldn't have to wait long. Seven days. That was it. And she would know if Grayson and she had made a baby.

But she immediately shook her head. She couldn't think of this as Grayson's baby.

Only hers.

"My doctor can do the pregnancy test next week," she relayed to Grayson, though he was looking at everything but her now.

He didn't respond. Which was just as well. Best not to mention pregnancy tests or the baby again because if this interview with the Colliers went well, maybe Grayson could make an arrest. Then, they would go their separate ways.

That stung.

But it was necessary. A baby had to be enough. She couldn't go weaving a fantasy life with Grayson when the last thing he wanted was to raise another child.

Eve cursed the tears that sprang to her eyes, and then she cursed Grayson for being able to detach so easily. She glanced at him to see if he'd had any reaction whatsoever to the test news, but he was volleying his attention between the street ahead and the rearview mirror.

That wasn't a detached look on his face.

"What's wrong?" she asked, turning in her seat to follow his gaze.

He reached inside his jacket and drew his gun. "Someone's following us."

Chapter 13

Next week

The timing of Eve's pregnancy results should have been the last thing on Grayson's mind, but he was having a hard time pushing it aside.

"That dark blue car is the one following us?" Eve asked. She apparently wasn't thinking baby tests, either. She had her attention on the vehicle behind them.

"Yeah." It wasn't right on their tail, but the blue car had stayed several vehicles back and had made the last three turns that Grayson had taken.

"Can you see the driver?" she asked.

"No." The noon sun was catching the tint of the windows at the wrong angle, and Grayson couldn't even tell how many people there were in the car. Heck, he wasn't positive they were even being followed.

So Grayson did a test of his own.

Without signaling, he took a right turn so quickly that the driver behind him honked. But Grayson got his answer. The blue car made the same turn.

"What now?" There was a tremble in Eve's voice, and it had been that way since she'd spoken to her doctor. But now it was heavy with concern.

"We drive to SAPD headquarters as planned." Grayson only hoped the car followed them into the parking lot so he could confront this moron. Of course, he didn't want to do that with Eve around, but maybe he could get her inside the headquarters building first.

Grayson made his way through the side streets and spotted the SAPD parking lot just ahead. He pulled in, heading straight toward the drop-off that would put Eve just a few yards from the front door.

"The driver didn't turn," Eve relayed.

A glance in the rearview mirror verified that. Maybe this idiot hadn't wanted to risk arrest, but that didn't mean he wouldn't follow them when they left. Grayson would have to take extra precautions. He damn sure didn't want someone trying to shoot out their tires again.

"I'll park and be inside in a minute," Grayson told Eve and was thankful she didn't argue with him about that. The instant he came to a stop, Eve hurried inside the building.

Nate was there, just inside the door waiting for her, and Grayson caught a glimpse of Nate pulling her into his arms for a hug. It was ironic. His brothers had always loved Eve, had always thought of her as part of the family. How would they react if it turned out that she was indeed pregnant with his child?

Grayson groaned.

Maybe the better question was, how would *he* react?

Well, next week he'd know. By then, he'd hopefully have Nina Manning's killer behind bars and would be able to have some time to think this all through.

He parked and went inside to join Eve and Nate who were waiting for him in the reception area.

"Eve said someone was following you?" Nate asked.

"Yeah. But he apparently got cold feet. I got a description but not the plates."

Nate's forehead bunched up. "When you get ready to take Eve back to the ranch, I'll have one of the cruisers accompany you. That should deter anyone from following or launching another attack."

You'd think, but this investigation was twisting and turning too much for Grayson's liking. He just wanted it to end so that Eve could be safe.

"Sebastian Collier is already here," Nate announced, leading them through the headquarters toward the interview rooms. "Claude and Annabel are on the way."

"Did they give you any hassle about coming?" Eve asked.

The flat look Nate gave her indicated they had. "Claude says he'll sue us for harassment."

Grayson figured the man would use that threat, but if the DNA proved that Nina was his biological child, then that might get SAPD authorization for a search warrant to start going through not just the Collier estate, but Claude and Sebastian's financials. After all, someone had paid off Leon Ames, and Grayson was betting it was a Collier. Unfortunately, if they used cash, then the financial records might be a dead end.

"Eve and I can watch through the two-way mirror in the adjacent room," Nate suggested. Both Grayson and he looked at Eve, and she opened her mouth, probably to argue.

"Give yourself a break from the stress," Grayson told her, and he dropped his gaze to her stomach.

Her eyes widened and just like that, she nodded. Yeah, it was a dirty trick considering she might not even be pregnant, but there was no reason for her to go a second round with this pack of jackals. Just being in the same room with them spiked his blood pressure.

Nate maneuvered them through the maze of halls until they reached the interview room, and he took Eve next door. Sebastian was seated, but he didn't offer the smile and warm welcome that he had earlier.

"I'm assuming this is important?" Sebastian asked. Everything about his body language revealed his impatience and annoyance. His face was tight, and his breath was coming out in short bursts.

"It's important," Grayson assured him. He didn't sit. He wanted to stand so he could violate Sebastian's personal space and make him even more uncomfortable. "Did you have someone follow me a few minutes ago?"

"Please." Sebastian stretched out the syllables. "I have better things to do, like last-minute shopping. Tomorrow's Christmas Eve." He stared at them, and then he mumbled a profanity under his breath. "Look, I don't know why I'm suddenly a suspect, but I did nothing wrong."

"You lied to me."

The staring match continued, and Sebastian was the first to look away. More profanity came. "About two weeks ago Nina Manning called me and asked to meet her. She claimed she was my long-lost sister. The timing was suspicious because her call came less than twenty-four hours after my father found out he was dying."

Grayson reserved judgment on the suspicious part. "Did you meet with her?"

"Yes. At a hotel in downtown San Antonio. I didn't believe her. I thought she was running a scam, but because I didn't want her upsetting my father, I was prepared to pay her off. Then, my father showed up, and after they argued, Nina ran out."

Well, that explained Annabel's pictures. "How did your father know about the meeting?"

"Nina called him, too. I guess she figured if she couldn't get the money from me, then she'd get it from my father."

Something about this didn't sound right. "If Nina wanted money, why did she run off after the so-called argument?"

"Because she was a drug-addicted, lying little witch," someone said from the doorway. It was Claude, and Annabel was by his side. Both looked about as thrilled to be there as Sebastian was.

Sebastian got to his feet. "You should sit, Father."

"I don't intend to be here that long," Claude fired back. "My attorney is on the way, and I've already put a call in to the mayor. I will not be treated like a common criminal." He aimed that remark and an accompanying glare at Grayson.

"Besides, Claude isn't well enough for this," Annabel added. The words were right, but the emotion didn't quite make it to her eyes. No glare for her, but she did look uncomfortable.

"A woman is dead," Grayson stated, looking at Claude. "She was last seen alive with your son and former employee. That employee tried to kill me and the woman who photographed Nina Manning." He paused. "Or maybe I should call the dead woman Sophia Collier."

"Never!" Claude's voice boomed through the hall, and with his index finger pointed at Grayson, he stepped into the room. "That piece of trash has no blood of mine in her."

Grayson shrugged. "Your ex-wife thought differently. She believed Nina was Sophia."

Annabel huffed. Now, there was real emotion. "Of course Cicely would believe that. She's mentally unstable, you know."

"She is," Sebastian agreed.

Grayson glanced at Claude to see if he had a comment about his ex, but Claude's jaw was so tight that Grayson figured he wasn't capable of speaking. Grayson made a mental note to do some digging to see if Cicely was indeed suffering from any form of mental illness.

"Since Nina's paternity is in question, we needed the DNA sample from you," Grayson told Claude.

"Which I gave," Claude spat out. "But there's no test that will convince me that she was my Sophia."

"Your son must have thought it was at least possible," Grayson disputed, "because he met with her again at the charity rodeo."

"I didn't meet with her," Sebastian insisted. "I already told you she was there with Leon. I simply ran into them."

Grayson just looked at them, waiting for an explanation he could actually believe—because he didn't buy the running into them story. His stony look didn't stop with just Sebastian, either. When Grayson let his intense stare stay on Annabel, her breath began to tremble, and she actually dropped back a step, probably because she thought she was about to be outed about the memory disk she'd given him. And Grayson considered it, but if either Sebastian or Claude was the killer, then that might make Annabel the next victim.

There was a soft knock, and since the door was still open, Grayson didn't have any trouble seeing who'd made the sound.

Cicely.

She was holding her leather purse in front of her like a shield, and she looked at them as if trying to figure out what was going on. Grayson knew how she felt.

"By any chance were you the one who followed Ms. Warren and me?" Grayson asked.

"Yes." And Cicely didn't hesitate, either. "I wanted to see if you'd run to Claude and tell him everything I said to you." She gave a smug nod. "But instead you ordered him to come here. Did he deny it?" Cicely asked, sliding her venomous gaze at Claude.

Claude had some venom of his own. The veins on his forehead and neck started to bulge. "If you're talking about that woman claiming to be Sophia, of course I denied it. She wasn't our daughter."

"I told you that I did a DNA test," Cicely said between clenched teeth.

"A test that could have been faked," Sebastian interrupted. "You're so eager to find your long-lost daughter that you're willing to believe anything."

"I faked nothing, and neither did Sophia." Cicely was so angry now that she was shaking, and she opened her purse and snatched something from it. Something encased in a plastic zip bag. She slapped it onto the table.

Grayson walked closer to see what it was. He'd expected a photo or something else that might shed light on this.

But it was a diamond bracelet.

Grayson frowned. "Is this connected to the investigation?"

"It is." Cicely pointed to Annabel. "She gave the bracelet to Sophia as a bribe to get her to leave."

Annabel, Sebastian and Claude all disagreed, and they weren't quiet about it, either. "I've never seen that bracelet before," Annabel insisted. She reached for the bag, but Cicely snagged her wrist.

"Sophia said you gave it to her and demanded that she sell it and use the money to get out of town. I sealed it up because I'm betting the police can find your DNA on it."

Maybe. But that wouldn't prove anything other than perhaps Annabel had told him another lie. It didn't mean she was a killer.

"How did you get the bracelet?" Grayson asked Cicely.

And with that one simple question, the room fell silent, and all eyes were on Cicely.

Cicely lifted her chin as if insulted by the implication of the question. "When Sophia came to my house, she had the bracelet with her and said it was a bribe from Annabel. She also said she was scared, that she thought Annabel would kill her if she didn't leave town and not try to stake a claim to her rightful inheritance."

"It's only a rightful claim if she was my sister," Sebastian tossed at her. "And she wasn't."

That started up another round of accusations, and

Cicely was loud and liberal with the name calling—
especially the names she called Annabel.

"Shut up!" Grayson practically yelled. And he turned
back to Cicely. "Why would Sophia leave the bracelet
with you?"

Cicely didn't jump to answer that. In fact, she swallowed hard. "She didn't say, exactly, but I think she
knew something bad was going to happen to her. I think
she wanted me to have it so I could prove that Annabel
was her killer."

Annabel gasped and caught on to Grayson's arm. "I
didn't kill her. I…" But she didn't finish, and the grip
she had on his arm melted away. "I didn't kill her," she
repeated.

Sebastian moved closer as if checking to make sure
Annabel was okay. When his attention came back to
Cicely, his eyes were narrowed. "Mother, why don't you
tell the sheriff about your association with Leon Ames?"

"Association?" Cicely pulled back her shoulders. "I
don't know what you mean."

"Really?" Sebastian challenged. He walked toward
his mother. Slow, calculated steps. "Leon visited you
often. In fact, he visited you in the past week."

Cicely didn't deny it, and when she tried to look
away, Grayson got right in her face. "Is it true?"

The woman finally nodded, prompting an I-told-you-
so huff from Sebastian. Neither Annabel nor Claude
seemed surprised with Cicely's admission, which meant
they had likely known.

"Leon was my friend." Cicely's voice was practically
a whisper.

Friend. That was an interesting relationship, especially considering Leon worked for Claude. Of course,

that didn't mean he hadn't been secretly working for Cicely, as well. Since Grayson believed that Leon had likely killed Nina, now he had to figure out who had given the man orders to kill.

"Leon was your lover and would have done anything for you," Sebastian accused. He was smirking when he looked at Grayson. "My mother has an affinity for associating with lowlifes. That's probably why she was so eager to believe that woman when she claimed she was Sophia."

That put some fire back into Cicely, and she opened her mouth, probably to verbally blast her son into the next county.

But a sound stopped her.

A gasp.

Not just any ordinary gasp, either. It was as if all the air swooshed out of Claude's lungs.

"Sebastian," Claude managed to say. A split second before he clamped his hands to the sides of his head and dropped to the floor.

Chapter 14

Eve got out of Grayson's car and made her way up the steps of the ranch house. Despite the fact that someone had tried to kill them twice today, her nerves were no longer firing on all cylinders.

Thank God.

The bone-weary fatigue was no doubt responsible for that. The Christmas lights helped, too. Hard to think of murders and attacks when there were hundreds of multicolored lights twinkling around her. And then she stepped inside and knew this was the main source of her calmer nerves.

For reasons she didn't want to explore, the Ryland ranch always had and always would feel like home to her. So many memories, and they flooded through her, easing away the rest of the tension.

Grayson walked in right behind her. He had his

phone sandwiched between his ear and shoulder, a place it'd been during most of their drive from San Antonio back to the ranch. Along the way, he'd gotten several updates on the investigation.

And Claude.

Judging from the part of this particular conversation, Grayson was talking with Claude's doctor.

When the man had first collapsed at the SAPD precinct, Eve had thought he was faking it so he could put a quick end to the interview. But after he'd been rushed to the hospital in an ambulance, the doctors had informed Grayson that Claude's condition was critical. So, no more interviews until the man was stable. Whenever that would be.

"Claude is still touch and go," Grayson relayed to her when he ended the call. "He might not make it through the night." He slapped his phone shut and pulled in a long, weary breath.

Eve understood that weariness. She wasn't fond of Claude, but if he died, he might take his secrets to the grave. Especially one secret.

Had he been the one responsible for Nina's death?

Or did that guilt lie with Sebastian, Annabel or even Cicely?

"What about the DNA results?" Eve wanted to know because she'd heard Grayson's phone conversation with Nate about that, as well.

Grayson shook his head. "Nothing yet, but we should have preliminary results in an hour or two." He used the keypad on the wall to arm the security system. "Nate's also checking to see if anyone else, including Cicely, ran a DNA test on Nina."

She thought about that for a moment. "But Cicely

said she'd done the test. Why would she lie about something like that?"

"Who knows? I'm still working that out, but I'm not ready to believe anything a Collier says."

Eve agreed. All of them seemed to have something to hide, but the DNA results might be a start toward learning the truth. If Nina was indeed Sophia, then that only strengthened Sebastian and Annabel's motives for murder. They might not have wanted to split Claude's estate three ways.

Still, there were some things Eve hadn't been able to grasp. "I understand why Claude might have had Nina killed," she commented. "With his elitist attitude, he would never admit to having a drug addict daughter. But what about Cicely? She seems more than willing to admit that Nina was hers. So, why would she kill her?"

"Seems," Grayson emphasized. "That's why I want to see when and if Cicely ran the DNA test."

Ah, Eve got it then. Because the test could have been a cover-up. Nina could have confronted or even attempted to blackmail Cicely, and Cicely could have refused to believe this was her long-lost daughter. Cicely could have had Nina killed out of anger. However, the woman wouldn't look like a major murder suspect if she told everyone that she knew Nina was truly Sophia.

If Cicely had done that, it was a smart move.

"Anyone home?" Grayson called out. When no one answered, he headed for the kitchen, and Eve followed.

She immediately spotted the note from Bessie on the double-door stainless-steel fridge. "Mason called. He and Dade are staying in town to work on the case," Grayson read aloud. "Nate and the baby won't be home, either. Haven't heard a peep from Kade. Dinner's in the fridge and I'm headed out for girls' night at my sister's place in Saddle Springs. Give Eve a good-night kiss for me." Bessie had added a smiley face.

The woman's attempt at humor didn't cause either Grayson or Eve to smile. But it did give Eve an uneasy feeling because she realized that Grayson and she were alone in the house. She glanced at Grayson, and his quick look away convinced her that he was aware of it, as well.

"You'll need to eat," he reminded her.

"You, too," she reminded him right back.

But neither of them moved. They both stood there, staring at Bessie's note, while the air zinged around them. For a moment Eve wondered if Grayson might act on that good-night kiss after all, but he mumbled something about being hungry and pulled open the fridge door.

There was a large baking dish with lasagna on the center shelf. She was suddenly starving. She knew from experience that Bessie was an amazing cook, but Eve decided both Grayson and she could use a little space to clear their heads. After all, in the past twenty-four hours, they'd nearly been killed and had then gotten embroiled in a murder investigation.

They'd also had sex.

Even the fatigue couldn't erase the too-familiar tingling she still felt. And that was another huge reason for a little head-clearing space.

"I think I'll take a shower before I eat," Eve told him.

Grayson didn't have time to respond because his cell phone rang. Eve waited just a few seconds to make sure it wasn't critical, but when she realized it was the youngest Ryland, Kade, calling for an update about the investigation, she excused herself and went to the guest suite.

Eve intended to head straight for the shower, but she saw the photo album on the guest bed. The leather cover had probably once been white but had aged to a rich cream color, and it was thick, at least three inches.

"Here's your Christmas present. Thought you'd like copies of some old memories," was written on the sticky note attached. "Love, Bessie."

She was reasonably sure she didn't need any more memories or copies of memories, but Eve sat on the edge of the bed and opened it. The first picture was of Boone and Marcie Ryland, Grayson's parents, on their wedding day. They were both smiling, and there were no hints of the troubles to come nineteen years later when Boone would walk out on Marcie and his six sons. A few months after that, Marcie would take her own life.

What a waste. So many lives had been changed because of Boone's departure. Especially Grayson's. If he hadn't had to raise his brothers, he might have wanted a family of his own. But it hurt Eve too much to dwell on that particular *if*.

Eve turned the page to Grayson's baby picture— probably taken when he was no more than a day or two old. She smiled. If she was indeed pregnant, then this was a glimpse of how her baby could look.

She flipped through the pages, each of them snapshots of time. Grayson's first horseback ride—barely a toddler in the saddle. His first day of school.

And then Eve was in the picture—literally.

Nearly all the subsequent pages had photos of her with the Ryland family. Christmas. Easter. Birthdays. She'd been a part of them. Always engulfed in those strong arms that had always given her so much love.

She ached to be part of that again but knew it was

lost forever. The ultimatum she'd given Grayson all those years ago had sealed her fate and separated her from him, and his family, forever.

Or had it?

Her mind began to spin with the possibility of her baby being part of this. Not permanently part of the family but maybe visits so the baby would know his or her bloodline.

But she forced herself to stop.

She'd made the deal with Grayson—if he got her pregnant, that would be it. No strings attached. So, her fate was sealed. Her baby's fate, too. One way or another, she would leave as soon as it was safe.

Eve blinked back tears, but more followed. She was still swiping them away when the house phone rang. She glanced at the caller ID screen and saw that it was Annabel Collier. Since this could be important, she lay the album aside and hurried downstairs.

Grayson was in the kitchen where he was already talking to Annabel, and he had put the call on speaker. "I'm listening," he said to Annabel.

Annabel didn't say anything for several seconds. "I'm not sure how to say this."

Grayson huffed. "Try," he insisted. He looked at Eve then, and his right eyebrow slid up, questioning her about something. When she shook her head, Grayson went to her and touched her cheek. Or so she thought. But not a real touch. He wiped away a stray tear.

"You okay?" he mouthed.

Eve moved away from him, and thankfully didn't have to explain anything because Annabel continued.

"I lied to you," the woman confessed.

Grayson didn't huff this time, but he looked as if he wanted to do just that. "Which lie would that be?"

"About the diamond bracelet. It was mine. I figured you would discover that when you had it tested so I decided to come clean. I gave it to Nina, hoping it would convince her to leave."

Now Eve was the one to huff. The Colliers were certainly free with their lies, and she didn't think it was a coincidence that the lies seemed to be attempts to prevent them from being charged with murder.

"Then Cicely was right." Grayson took out a plate of heated lasagna from the microwave and handed it to Eve.

"Cicely was trying to make me sound guilty. That's the only reason she had the bracelet. She wants to incriminate me."

Eve got them both out some silverware and paper napkins and sat at the counter. Grayson got out two longneck beers and his plate. He looked at her. Studied her. Maybe trying to figure out what had caused those tears.

"The question you should be asking yourself is how Cicely got that bracelet in the first place," Annabel went on. "Because I seriously doubt Nina freely gave it to her. That bracelet was worth thousands, and a druggie like Nina wouldn't have handed it over without a fight."

"Are you saying Cicely killed Nina and took the bracelet?" Grayson didn't wait. He sat and started to eat.

"Yes, that's exactly what I'm saying." But then Annabel paused. "Or maybe Sebastian killed her and gave the bracelet to his mother. He could have done it to try to incriminate me, too."

"Sebastian," Grayson repeated. "I wondered when this conversation would turn to him."

"What do you mean?" Annabel accused.

He had a gulp of beer first. And another look at Eve. "I mean your husband is dying. By tomorrow morning, you could be a wealthy widow—thanks to your huge inheritance. If Sebastian were out of the picture, you'd have double the wealth and no pesky stepchildren around to cash in on their daddy's will."

Annabel made a sound of outrage. "I didn't kill anyone!" she practically shouted.

"Maybe. Can you say the same for your husband?" Grayson challenged.

Silence. The moments crawled by, and Grayson continued to sip his beer. The glances at her continued, too. What didn't happen was a denial from Annabel about her husband's innocence.

"If Claude recovers, you'll have to ask him that." Annabel's voice was no longer hot with anger. It was ice-cold and impatient.

"I will," Grayson assured her. "Now, tell me why you gave me the memory card with the photos."

She paused again. "Because I knew something wasn't right when Nina showed up. Claude and Sebastian were having secret conversations. And Cicely kept calling. I didn't know Nina was going to die, but I thought I might need proof."

"Proof of what?" Grayson pressed.

"That I didn't have anything to do with her, her life or her death."

"Well, the pictures don't prove that." Of course, they did prove that all their suspects had had close contact with a woman who was murdered. Even if Annabel hadn't taken the pictures herself, she had certainly been aware of them.

"I didn't kill her," Annabel insisted. "Now that I've told you about the bracelet, we have nothing further to discuss." And she hung up.

Without taking his attention off Eve, he leaned over and pressed the end button on the phone. Since his stare was making her uncomfortable, Eve focused on the square of lasagna in front of her.

"Why are you looking at me like that?" she finally asked.

Grayson opened his mouth. Closed it. And the staring continued.

Eve decided she'd just spill it. "I was crying because I'd been looking at a photo album that Bessie gave me for Christmas. Old memories," she settled for saying.

"Oh." And judging from his tone, that was not the answer he'd expected. "I thought maybe…well, I thought you'd learned you weren't pregnant."

Now, it was her turn to say "Oh." He'd seen the tears and assumed the worst. Or maybe in his case, the best—that maybe she'd gotten her period. However, that wouldn't be just bad news. It would break her heart.

"No." Since the lasagna suddenly wasn't settling well in her stomach, Eve got up so she could put it back in the fridge. "I won't know until next week."

"Okay." He nodded, repeated it.

She could feel his regret. His doubts. And Eve was just too tired to go there. She whirled back around to remind him that from here on out he wasn't part of her life.

But Grayson stood and whirled around at the same time, and they practically smacked right into each other.

Eve started to move back, way back, but Grayson caught on to her arm, anchoring her in place. She could have shaken off his grip, of course, but she didn't.

"I can't do this," she managed to say.

His eyebrow came up again, and he was obviously waiting for an explanation of what specifically she couldn't do, but Eve hesitated one second too long, and in that second she got caught up in Grayson's eyes. His scent.

His touch.

She'd never been able to resist him, never, and apparently tonight was no different.

"I can't, either," he answered. Though she had no idea what he meant by that.

She soon learned though.

Grayson leaned in and put his mouth on hers. It was just a touch, barely qualifying as a kiss, but this was Grayson. He could make her melt with a simple brush of his mouth and she'd forget all the arguments she had going through her head about why she couldn't do this. Kissing would only lead to more complications.

Still, Eve moved closer.

She hooked her arm around the back of his neck and eased him down to her. His mouth pressed harder, and that barely-a-kiss became a real one.

He snapped her to him, body to body, and took her mouth the way he always had. He was clever and thorough, and any thought of resisting him flew right out of her mind.

In fact, she did the opposite of resisting.

Eve got even closer, sliding her hands down his back and adjusting their positions so that the kiss turned to full body contact. Yes, there were clothes between them, but she knew his body so well that she had no trouble filling in the blanks of how it would feel to have him naked against her.

"You still can't?" he mumbled against his mouth.

She couldn't answer because the kiss turned French and scalding hot. If she'd had breath left to speak, she wouldn't have used it to state the obvious because clearly she *could*.

Couldn't she?

This wouldn't be lab sex for the purpose of getting her pregnant. This would be like old times. And then what?

Eve forced herself to consider *then what*.

Grayson cursed, and for a moment she thought he had reached the same *then what?* roadblock that she had. It took her a moment to realize he was cursing because his phone was ringing. She hadn't heard it over the roar in her head.

"It's Nate," Grayson let her know after he glanced down at the screen. He flipped the cell open and jabbed the speaker button. He also leaned against the kitchen counter and tried to level his breathing.

Eve did the same, though it would take more than some deep breaths to get back to normal.

"Please tell me you have good news," he greeted Nate.

"Well, it's news," Nate explained. "I'll let you decide if it's good or not. Just got the preliminary DNA results, and Nina Manning was indeed Sophia Collier."

So there it was—the proof that at least some of the Colliers weren't going to like because that proof was also motive.

"I did a statewide search of labs that had tested Sophia's DNA," Nate continued, "and I couldn't find any record that Cicely had requested a test."

Another lie, and Eve was betting that Cicely would just lie again when Grayson questioned her about it.

Eve huffed. Would they ever learn the truth so that Sophia's killer could be brought to justice and so that she could finally get on with her life?

She looked at Grayson and felt his kiss still burning her mouth. Maybe getting on with her life wasn't even possible. That kiss had proven that she would never get Grayson out of her blood and out of her system.

Never.

"But someone else did request a test on Sophia's DNA," Nate added. That caught Eve's attention. "That happened just three days before Sophia was murdered."

"Who?" Grayson and Eve asked in unison.

"Sebastian," Nate answered.

Eve saw the surprise in Grayson's eyes. Sebastian had denied that Nina was his sister, but yet he obviously knew the truth because he'd had her DNA tested.

"You're positive about this?" Grayson pressed.

"Positive, and I have proof. Sebastian tried to cover up the payment for the test by using cash, but the lab has 24/7 surveillance. We have footage of him going into the lab and then picking up the results."

"What kind of a timeline are we looking at for this? Did Sebastian have the DNA results before Nina was murdered?" Grayson wanted to know.

"Oh, yeah," Nate assured him. "He had them all right. Less than twenty-four hours after he got the results that confirmed Nina was his sister, someone killed her."

Grayson shook his head, mumbled something. "Then

as far as I'm concerned, that makes Sebastian Collier our number-one suspect."

Eve agreed, and judging from the sound he made, apparently so did Nate.

"So what do you want me to do?" Nate asked Grayson.

Grayson didn't even hesitate. "Pick up Sebastian and put him in a holding cell. I'll be at SAPD first thing in the morning to read him his rights and arrest him."

Chapter 15

Grayson downed the shot of whiskey. It was strong stuff, Mason's private stash, and it burned his eyes and throat. What it didn't do was clear his head.

But then, that was asking a lot from a shot of whiskey.

The details of the case kept running through his head. Thoughts of Eve kept running through his body. Neither would give him much peace tonight, even though the house was whisper-quiet and would likely stay that way because it was going on midnight.

"Midnight," he mumbled.

Since he had an early-morning trip to SAPD to question and arrest Sebastian, he should be sleeping. Heck, Eve probably was. She'd called it a night well over an hour ago.

Good thing, too, because before her good-night Grayson had been on the verge of resuming the make-out session that Nate's call had interrupted.

He shouldn't have touched her.

And he damn sure shouldn't have kissed her.

He should have just walked away and let fate sort out the details of what was to come in the next week or so. But the sight of those tears in her eyes had shaken him. Grayson considered himself a strong man, but he wasn't strong enough to keep her at arm's length when she'd been crying.

He poured himself another shot and took it in one gulp. Still no relief. So he gave up on the whiskey and headed out of the den and to his bathroom for a shower. He stripped along the way, dropping his clothes on the bedroom floor, and he kept the water ice-cold.

That didn't work, either.

There was a furnace of heat in his body, and there was only one cure for what he felt.

Eve.

Damn her. Damn *him*.

Grayson knew that pretty much any woman could satisfy his body, but there was only one woman who could satisfy *him*. And that was Eve.

For most of his life, she'd been what had fired him up and cooled him down—sometimes in the same minute. She'd been the one woman he couldn't get out of his head. And no amount of whiskey or cold water was going to cure that. No. There was only one cure, and she was right across the hall.

Grayson cursed and put on his jeans. No sense trying to talk himself out of jumping off this Texas-size cliff. He was going to jump all right, and this could be a fall that would hurt for the rest of his life.

He didn't knock on the guestroom door. Didn't want anything to slow him down and stop him. Well, that was the plan anyway, but his mouth went dry when he spotted her. Not asleep as he'd thought she would be. No. Eve was wide-awake, lying in bed, the ice-white covers draped loosely over her breasts and the rest of her.

Grayson shut the door. And went to her.

"The right thing would be for me to go back to my room," he told her.

Her mouth trembled slightly and turned into the hint of a smile. "Grayson, for once in your life, don't do the right thing, okay?"

She caught on to his hand, pulled him closer. Grayson obliged and leaned down for a kiss. He'd kissed her a thousand times, maybe more, but each time always felt like the first. That punch hit him hard in the chest and then below the belt.

How could he want anyone this much?

And worse, why would he want her this much even after he'd had her?

Grayson kept the kiss simple, though his body was revved up way past the kissing stage. Still, he needed this. The feel of her mouth against his. The sweet silk of her lips. Her taste. He needed it all, and apparently Eve did, too, because she kept inching him closer.

The covers shifted, and the sheet slipped off her breasts. No bra. Just Eve's bare breasts. He met her gaze and saw the little spark there.

Grayson used just the tip of his index finger to draw the covers down. He got an interesting show as he revealed every inch of her. Bare stomach. Bare hips. He heard himself choke back a groan.

No panties.

"I like to sleep naked," she whispered.

"I like that you like to sleep naked." He tried to chuckle. Failed at that, too.

"No." Eve tightened the grip on his hand. "Don't you dare have any doubts about this."

Oh. He had doubts, but he wasn't going to do anything about them. Grayson did what he did best. He took control of the situation. He raked back the rest of the covers, exposing every bit of Eve's naked body.

Yeah, she was beautiful.

He hadn't had to see her naked to remember that, but this trip down memory lane was a good one.

Grayson put his knee on the bed, the feather mattress giving way to his weight. He let himself ease into a fall and kissed her on the way down until his body was pressed hard against hers. The fit was right. Perfect. And it created pressure in all the right places.

"Jeans," she mumbled and fumbled for his zipper.

Grayson let her deal with that so he could make some headway with what he'd started. And what he'd started was a full-body kiss.

He trailed the kisses down her throat to her breasts. Yeah. That taste hadn't changed. He took her nipple into his mouth, and the zipper fumbling stopped, just as he figured it would. Eve moaned, arched her back and shoved her fingers into his hair to pull him closer.

"Yes." She repeated it and wrapped her legs around him.

His jeans were still between them, but Eve got the position and the pressure just right for this to go to the next level.

"Make me crazy, Grayson," she whispered and then laughed, low and husky.

He was too involved in the kissing to laugh, but he smiled when he slid his body through her leg lock and kissed her where she really wanted to be kissed. Right in the center of all that wet heat.

But Eve didn't stay on just the receiving end. She ran her hands over his shoulder and into his hair. Her legs caressed his back...and lower.

She knew exactly how to drive him crazy, too. And how to pleasure him. After all, they'd spent their teen years making out in his truck. Kisses only, at first. Lots of kisses.

Then, the touches.

He'd given Eve her first climax with his hand in her panties. They'd lost their virginity on her seventeenth birthday. They'd both been clumsy and awkward. But they'd both learned a lot over the years.

"Too crazy," she let him know when she was close to climaxing.

She caught on to him, pulling him back up so she could go after his zipper again. She wasn't playing this time. She was hot and ready so Grayson helped her, and she used her feet and hands to work the jeans off his hips.

"Commando," she said when she noticed he wasn't wearing his usual boxers. She smiled when she looked down between their bodies and no doubt saw that he was hard as stone. "That's my Grayson."

She froze and got that deer-in-the-headlights look. As if she'd crossed some line and tried to take them back to a place they could never go again. And maybe she had with that *my Grayson*. But he didn't care a flying fig about lines. He'd crossed the biggest line of all just by coming into her room.

He pinned her hands to the bed. Pinned her body, too. She would want his full weight on her so Grayson obliged, and he pushed himself inside her.

Mercy.

The pleasure was blinding.

It was like coming home for Christmas.

Eve arched her back and pressed her head against the pillow. She rocked her hips into his, causing him to go deep and hard into her. He was probably too rough. That thought was just a flash, and soon he couldn't think at all.

He moved inside her. Faster. Harder. Deeper. Until she was so close to climax. Until everything was a blur.

Everything except Eve.

Everything inside him pinpointed on her. Just her. The primal ache clawed away at him. This need as old as man. The need to take and claim.

But there were other needs, too.

And it was that need that sent Grayson in search of a kiss. He wanted the taste of her in his mouth when he lost all reason. When she slipped over the edge.

Eve came in a flash, when Grayson was deep inside her, when his mouth took hers.

Grayson said her name. It came from a place deeper than the primal need that had brought them to this point.

Somewhere in his brain, it registered that this was going to complicate the hell out of things. But that was only a split-second thought. Eve's legs tightened around him. She pulled him closer, and her climax brought on his.

Grayson felt his body surrender. Felt that slam of pleasure that was beyond anything he ever deserved to feel. Something so perfect. So amazing.

So Eve.

Chapter 16

"**Y**ou did what?" Grayson snapped to the person on the other end of the phone.

Eve thought the caller might be Nate, but she wasn't sure, and she couldn't tell from the conversation what Grayson was snapping about now. But there was no doubt, he was snapping.

Eve stared out the car window, sipped her coffee and debated—again—what she should say to Grayson once he had finished this call. Or if she should say anything. After all, he certainly hadn't volunteered much about coming to her bed for one of the most amazing nights of her life.

In fact, he had avoided the subject.

Of course, he'd been on the phone most of the morning and during the entire drive from the ranch to San Antonio. So that was his excuse, but she had to wonder, if it hadn't been for the calls, would he have come up with another reason for them not to talk?

"You're positive this isn't some kind of ruse so Sebastian can escape?" Grayson demanded.

Mercy, that didn't sound good, and she didn't think it was a good sign when Grayson turned off the interstate two exits before the one for SAPD headquarters. Grayson had been on his way to arrest Sebastian, but there had obviously been a change of plans.

"No," Grayson continued. Except that wasn't a bark or a snarl. He mumbled it. "Eve's with me. There wasn't anyone at the ranch to stay with her. The ranch hands have already left for their Christmas break."

Even though he practically mumbled that part, too, she heard the frustration. Grayson hadn't wanted her to come along when he questioned Sebastian. He'd wanted her tucked safely away at the ranch, but both Dade and Mason were still in town working the details of Nina's murder. Or rather Sophia Collier's murder. And with Bessie and the ranch hands off the grounds, Grayson had reluctantly brought her along to arrest and interrogate Sebastian.

Not the ideal way to spend Christmas Eve.

Of course, the danger was almost certainly over for her now that the photos she'd taken were in the hands of the authorities. Sebastian had no reason to kill her. Well, unless he was hell-bent on getting some kind of revenge because she'd inadvertently incriminated him, and now that he was in police custody, even that wasn't possible.

She hoped.

This could all be over soon, especially if Grayson managed to get a confession from Sebastian. Or if something hadn't gone wrong with his arrest. Judging from

Grayson's sour expression and change of direction, that wasn't just possible but likely.

Grayson slapped his phone shut and took the turn for San Antonio Memorial Hospital.

Her heart dropped.

"Is someone hurt?" she asked and then held her breath.

He shook his head. "Claude's doctor doesn't think he'll last much longer so he requested the family's presence at Claude's bedside. That includes Sebastian."

Since Claude was critical, the doctor's request was reasonable, or at least it would have been if Sebastian weren't a murder suspect.

"An SAPD officer is escorting Sebastian," Grayson let her know. "They should arrive at the hospital any minute now."

And that explained why Grayson took the final turn toward San Antonio Memorial. It wasn't a large hospital but was in one of the more affluent neighborhoods of the city. No surprise about that, considering Claude was a millionaire many times over.

"Did Nate say if Claude was talking?" Eve asked.

"He's lucid." Grayson paused. "And he wants to see me."

Strange. Claude certainly hadn't wanted to see Grayson when he'd been ordered to SAPD headquarters. "Do you think he'll make a deathbed confession?"

Grayson's scowl deepened. "Maybe. But if he does, it'll probably be for one reason—not to tell the truth, but to save his son."

Of course. With Claude dying, it wouldn't matter if he confessed to a murder he didn't commit. But then, it was possible that he had indeed killed Sophia since there was no tangible proof that Claude knew she was his biological daughter. And even if he had known, he could have killed her when he realized she wasn't the darling little girl he wanted in his family.

There was no street parking, just a multilevel parking garage so Grayson drove in and looked for a spot. He took the first one available, at the back of the second level.

Grayson glanced around. So did Eve. And somewhere amid the glancing, their gazes collided.

There.

Eve saw it in his eyes then—the conversation he'd been avoiding all morning.

"Do I need to apologize?" Grayson tossed out there like a gauntlet.

She thought about her answer. "No. Do I?" She tossed that proverbial gauntlet right back at him.

He cursed, looked away and scrubbed his hand over his face. "I'm the one who went to your bed."

"And I could have said no," Eve reminded him.

But that was a lie. She'd never been able to say no to Grayson, and she wouldn't have started last night. Still, this had caused more tension between them, and that's the last thing they needed when they were within minutes of facing the Colliers.

And facing a possible pregnancy.

Eve certainly hadn't been thinking about getting pregnant when Grayson had climbed into bed with her. She'd been thinking about making love with him, but now that it was the morning after, she knew that last night had increased her chances of getting the baby she'd always wanted.

However, it hadn't helped her *relationship* with Grayson.

She could feel his uneasiness, and she had to do something to diffuse it.

"What happened between us doesn't have to mean anything," she settled for saying, but those words hurt. Because it sure as heck had meant something to her. It meant that Grayson had still wanted her enough to risk plenty by coming to her like that.

He looked at her, as if he might dispute her not-mean-anything offer, but he only shook his head. "We'll talk about this later."

Eve caught on to his arm when he started to bolt. "No need." That hurt, too, but she had to give Grayson an out. He'd done her a huge favor by having sex with her, and she didn't want him to feel guilty or tormented.

She leaned over and brushed a chaste kiss on his cheek. "I already know how you feel about fatherhood, about a lot of things." Eve had to take a deep breath before continuing. "And I know when this investigation is over, your life can get back to normal."

Something flashed through his metal-gray eyes, and his face tightened. For a moment she thought they might have that blowup they'd been skirting around all morning. But he didn't toss out any more gauntlets or launch into an argument. He eased her hand off his arm and stepped from the car.

Eve could only sigh and do the same.

The garage wasn't just dank, it was cold, and Eve pulled her coat tighter against her. She had no scarf or gloves. She'd forgotten to pick those up when they'd been at her condo the day before, and women's clothing was in short supply at the Ryland ranch. Eve had made do with the gray pants and sweater that she'd packed, but she had been forced to wear the same red coat that had survived their trek through the woods.

Ahead of her, Grayson pulled the sides of his buckskin jacket together, as well. No festive red for him. He was wearing his usual jeans and dark shirt. Practically a uniform for him. He'd also worn his badge and shoulder holster, of course, which meant because he was armed, they would have to go through security inside.

She fell in step alongside Grayson as they walked to the elevator that would take them into the hospital, but they didn't get far before Grayson stopped. He lifted his head and looked around, just as he'd done when he had first parked. She looked, too, but only saw the sea of cars in the dimly lit space.

"Is something wrong?" Eve asked.

Grayson didn't answer. He glanced around again and caught on to her to get her moving to the elevator. It was clear he was hurrying now, but Eve didn't know why.

"I got a bad feeling," Grayson mumbled.

That put her on full alert because she knew from experience that Grayson's instincts were usually right.

And they were.

The sound zinged through the garage. It wasn't a blast. Eve wasn't sure what it was until the window shattered on the car next to them. Then she knew.

Oh, God.

Someone had fired at them.

Grayson cursed and shoved Eve to the side between two parked cars. He followed, moving directly in front of her, and in the same motion, he drew his gun.

What the hell was happening now?

The danger to Eve should be over. Finished. She was no longer a threat to Sophia's killer since her photos had gone public. Obviously, the shooter wasn't aware of that.

Because another shot came right at them.

Not a loud blast but more like a swish. That meant the gunman was using a weapon rigged with a silencer.

This had to be connected to Sophia's murder. They couldn't be that unlucky to now be the victims of a random attack. Maybe someone didn't want them hearing whatever deathbed confession Claude was likely to make. If so, then it was even more vital that Grayson speak to the dying man.

Grayson pushed Eve flat on the concrete floor and tried to pinpoint the origin of those two shots. He also tried to spot the gunman. There was no sign of anyone, but he thought maybe the shots had come from a black van on the other side of the parking lot. It wasn't a huge space, only about fifty feet across, but with the vehicles jammed together, there were plenty of places for a would-be killer to hide.

"Call Nate and tell him we need backup," Grayson told Eve. Without taking his attention off that black van, he grabbed his phone from his jacket pocket and handed it to her.

Another shot.

This one smacked into the headlight of the car right next to them. The glass shattered, flying through the air, and Grayson had to duck down and shield his eyes.

Almost immediately, he heard footsteps.

Behind him, he also heard Eve call Nate and request assistance, but Grayson shut out what she was saying and concentrated on those footsteps. Someone was running, and he caught just a glimpse of that someone before they ducked out of sight.

The person was dressed head-to-toe in black and was wearing a black baseball cap that obstructed the shooter's face.

It could be anyone.

And that *anyone* ducked between two other vehicles— a white pickup truck and a red sports car.

"Nate's on the way," Eve relayed. "He said he'll seal off the exits to the garage and do a silent approach."

Good. He needed his brother because this situation could get more dangerous than it already was. If anyone came out of that elevator, the gunman would probably shoot to kill so there'd be no witnesses to this attack. Plus, someone driving into the garage could also become a target. Right now though Grayson's biggest concern was Eve, and getting her safely out of there.

He lifted his head a fraction and listened for any sound of movement or more footsteps. None on both counts. Just Eve's too-fast breathing, and she was mumbling something that sounded like a prayer. She was obviously terrified, and it didn't help that this was the third attempt to kill her. In fact, it was probably worse now because she might be pregnant.

But Grayson pushed that thought out of his mind.

He needed to focus, and he couldn't do that if he thought about the baby he'd possibly made with Eve.

The next shot got his full attention. It didn't slam into the car as the others had. This one was aimed at the ground, and it ripped through the concrete just a few feet in front of them. The shooter had obviously gotten himself in a better position to deliver a fatal shot.

Grayson needed to throw him off-kilter as much as

he could. That wouldn't be easy since he only had his sidearm. There was extra ammunition in his car, but that was yards away and would be too dangerous to try to reach. That meant he had to make every shot count while maneuvering the gunman as far away from Eve as possible.

Grayson waited for the next shot, and he didn't have to wait long. It, too, tore into the floor and sent a cloud of debris and dangerous concrete bits right at them. He ducked out of cover for just a second and then fired in the direction of the shooter.

He hit the red sports car.

The shot bashed into the front end, and almost immediately the alarm went off. It was a piercing roar that was almost deafening. And worse. It blocked out any sound of the gunman's footsteps.

"Stay down!" Grayson warned Eve when he felt her move behind him.

He knew for a fact that she didn't have her gun with her because he'd talked her out of bringing it. Now, he wished he hadn't. He didn't want Eve up and returning fire, but it would have been nice to have the extra ammunition.

Even with the distraction of the car alarm, Grayson saw where the next shot landed. This one hadn't been aimed at them but rather the overhead lights. The gunman took out the ones near the elevator and stairwell, plunging that area into total darkness.

That could be good or bad.

Good because Nate would likely make his approach using the stairs, and the darkness would help conceal him. But that same darkness could also conceal the shooter if he tried to escape. Grayson didn't want this SOB to get away. He wanted to end this now.

Two more shots came at Eve and him, one right behind the other.

The gunman had moved again. This time to the right. Hell. The gunman was moving toward those stairs. Not only would that give him an escape route, it would also give him a better angle to fire more of those lethal bullets.

"What's going on up there?" someone called out. "I'm the security guard for the hospital."

"Sheriff Grayson Ryland. We're under fire. Stay back!"

But the words had no sooner left Grayson's mouth when he saw something out of the corner of his eye. To his left. There was a man in a dark gray uniform. The security guard, no doubt. He had his weapon drawn and had ducked down a little, but he was still making his way toward them.

The gunman obviously saw him, too.

Because a shot went in that direction.

The guard dove to the ground, but he was literally out in the open and therefore an easy target. Grayson had to do something, so he came out of cover, estimated the position of the shooter, and sent a bullet his way.

Because of the blasted car alarm, he couldn't tell if the gunman even reacted. Maybe he'd managed to hit the bastard, or at the very least maybe he had gotten the guy to back off so the guard could scramble to safety.

"You need to get down!" Eve snarled, and she put her hand on his back to push Grayson to the ground again.

It wasn't a second too soon.

The next bullet that was fired would have slammed right into him if Eve hadn't pulled him down with her.

However, Grayson didn't have time to thank her because everything seemed to happen at once. Another shot went toward the security guard who was trying to scramble away.

And then there was the movement in the stairwell.

For one horrifying moment, Grayson thought it was the gunman getting away. But this person wasn't dressed all in black.

It was Nate.

His brother was sneaking up the stairs, trying to get a drop on the gunman. But it was dark, and Nate was out of position. Unlike the gunman, who was probably only a few feet away.

"Watch out!" Grayson yelled to his brother.

But it was already too late.

Grayson couldn't hear the shot that the gunman fired, but he saw the end result.

A bullet slammed right into Nate's chest.

Chapter 17

Eve screamed, but the sound of her voice was drowned out by the blaring car alarm.

Her scream didn't warn Nate in time. Neither did Grayson's shouted warning to his brother. And because they'd failed, she watched in horror as the bullet hit Nate.

He flew backward from the impact.

"Oh, God." And Eve kept repeating it like a hysterical mantra.

Had he been killed?

She thought of his baby daughter, Kimmie, who would be an orphan if Nate died. And it would be partly her fault. If she just hadn't taken that damn picture then there would have been no attempts to kill her. All of this had started because of that.

Eve automatically bolted toward Nate so she could help him, but Grayson latched onto her and pulled her back to the ground. Good thing, too. Because the shots came at them again. This time, however, they were non-stop. Frenzied. They pelted into the cars on either side of them and the concrete floor in front of them.

Eve covered her head with her hands, but she couldn't stay behind the shelter of the vehicles for long. "We have to help Nate," she shouted, though she was certain that Grayson already knew that.

Because Grayson was practically lying on top of her, she could feel the rock-hard muscles of his body, and his chest was pumping from the adrenaline. His gaze volleyed between the stairwell and the area where the gunman was likely hiding. He was primed and ready to fight, but he would also do whatever it took to save his brother.

Eve couldn't see Nate, nor could she hear him, but she prayed he'd somehow managed to survive the gunshot and the fall. Either could have been fatal.

She saw some movement at the other end of the parking lot and spotted another uniformed security guard on the stairwell. He had his gun ready, thank God, but he didn't seem to be in any better position than Grayson was to stop this. Still, he might be able to do some good if the shooter moved.

Finally, the shots stopped. Maybe because the gunman had to reload. Or, God forbid, maybe because he was escaping. The thought of that sickened Eve. She didn't want a killer to get away.

But right now, Nate was their first priority.

Grayson eased off her and inched toward the car to their right. He was probably thinking of making a run to the stairs, but she prayed he wouldn't do that. He could end up like Nate, or worse.

Since she still had Grayson's phone, she called nine-
one-one to report an officer down, though someone was
likely already aware of that. She doubted that Nate had
come alone. But she immediately rethought that. Maybe
that's exactly what Nate had done. Maybe he'd rushed
to help his brother and her and hadn't considered the
consequences.

She would have reacted the same way if it meant
saving Grayson.

The moment she ended the call, Eve saw Grayson's
gaze swing to the left. And she soon saw why. The
first security guard was crawling toward them. She saw
the blood on his shoulder and knew that he, too, had
been shot. They had to get an ambulance up here right
away, but that couldn't happen until the gunman had
been stopped.

Grayson latched on to the guard and pulled him next
to Eve. The man was clearly in pain, and even though
he was clutching his gun, he had both it and his hand
pressed to the wound. It didn't take medical training
to know he'd already lost too much blood. Eve pushed
aside his hand so she could apply some pressure.

"Wait here," Grayson ordered. "Use the gun if you
have to." His eyes met hers, and she could see that it
was indeed an order.

But, God, what was he going to do?

Please.

She didn't want him out there in the open, making
himself an easy target. She wanted him to stay behind
cover, even though cover didn't mean safety. Not with
those bullets flying everywhere.

Her heart was pounding against her chest now, and
her breath was so thin that she felt light-headed. Despite

the cold, there was a fine mist of clammy sweat on her face. She felt sick, but she tried to fight off the feeling of dread. They would survive this, somehow, because there was no other alternative. It couldn't end here for Grayson and Nate.

Grayson took the gun from the security guard and handed it to her. Eve latched on to it, but she was shaking her head. "You can't go out there."

He shook his head, too. "I don't have a choice. This has to stop."

That was it. No other explanation. Grayson maneuvered around her and the guard and went behind them. He disappeared when he ducked around the front of the car to her right.

Well, at least he wasn't going to charge out into the center of the garage. He was obviously trying to get to the stairwell, and maybe the security guard could provide some backup. However, that still meant Grayson was moving closer and closer to the gunman, and she was betting the gunman would be looking for them to do just that. Shooting Nate could have all been designed to draw Grayson and her out into the open.

If so, it had worked.

Eve couldn't hear what the security guard was mumbling, but he squirmed, his face tightening in pain. She pressed harder on the wound to try to stop the flow of blood, but she also kept watch of the area near the black van where the last shots had originated.

"This is Sergeant O'Malley, SAPD." The man's voice boomed from a bullhorn. It sounded as if he was at street level. "Put down your weapon and surrender."

Backup. Thank God. But since there was no response

from the shooter, Eve doubted he would just do as the sergeant had demanded.

By her calculations it'd been a minute, maybe more, and the gunman hadn't fired. Eve had no idea if that was good or bad, but it was certainly easier to think without those bullets bashing into the cement and other cars.

And because it was easier to think, tears sprang to her eyes.

Eve blinked them back. She couldn't give in to the worry and fear, but she was terrified for Grayson. For Nate. For this wounded security guard whom she didn't even know.

But who was out there doing this?

Sebastian? Maybe. But only if he'd managed to get away from his police escort. Of course, either Claude or Sebastian could have hired a gunman. It was possible Claude wasn't even in critical condition but instead had orchestrated this to get Grayson and her into a position so they could be killed.

That brought her back to why again.

If they could just figure out who'd fired shots at them, then knowing the *who* would tell them the *why*.

Eve finally spotted Grayson again. He was seven cars over to her right and was inching his way to the stairwell. She held her breath, waiting for another shot.

Nothing.

The seconds crawled by so slowly that she could feel them ticking off in her head. Finally, she saw some movement in the stairwell.

Nate.

Thank God he was moving. However, he wasn't just moving. He had his gun aimed and ready and was making his way back up the stairs. Not easily. He, too, was wincing, and Eve soon realized why. His shirt was open, but there was no blood. Only a Kevlar vest.

Relieved, she let out her breath in a rush. Nate hadn't been shot. The impact of the bullet had probably knocked him down the stairs. He looked shaken up but very much alive.

So that was one prayer that'd been answered.

The security guard moved again, the muscles in his body going stiff, and Eve looked down at him to see what had caused that reaction. His eyes were wide and not focused on her.

But rather behind her.

Oh, God.

That was the only thought that had time to form in her head because Eve felt a hand grip on to her shoulder. She didn't have time to move. There was no time to react.

Before someone pressed the barrel of a gun to her head.

Grayson's heart went to his knees.

This couldn't be happening.

He'd had just a split second of relief because his brother was alive, but that relief went south in a hurry when he saw Eve. She was no longer where Grayson had left her—crouched with the injured security guard between the two cars. She was standing now.

And she wasn't alone.

Someone was behind her, their arm curved around Eve's neck, and that someone had a gun pointed directly at Eve's head. The person had a second gun next to Eve's neck. Both weapons were positioned to deliver a fatal shot.

Grayson couldn't see the person's face, only the black baseball cap. But he could see Eve's. The color had drained from her cheeks, and she was looking around as if trying to figure out how to escape.

But Grayson didn't want her to move.

Not with that gun pressed to her head.

"Drop your weapon and surrender," Sergeant O'Malley called out again.

Grayson was thankful for the backup, but he didn't want the sergeant's demand to make this bad situation worse.

He took aim, and with his attention nailed to the gunman's hand, Grayson inched closer.

"There's no need to do this," Grayson shouted. "Let her go."

If the gunman responded, Grayson didn't hear it. He wished like the devil that the car alarm would stop. He had to try to negotiate Eve's release, and it was hard to do that when he couldn't hear what was going on.

"Eve is no threat to you," Grayson tried again, all the while moving closer.

He didn't have a clean shot, not with the gunman using Eve as a human shield, but he needed to get as close as possible because it was likely this SOB was planning an escape. After all, Eve was still alive, and there had to be a reason for that. The gunman had taken her hostage.

But why?

Grayson was certain he would soon learn the answer, but he hoped he wouldn't learn it too late. Eve couldn't die. She just couldn't. Someway, somehow, he had to put himself in a position where he could save her.

He glanced over his shoulder at his brother. Nate

wasn't following him but instead had crouched down and was making his way to the other side of the garage toward the black van and the red car with the blaring alarm.

Good move.

His brother might get a better angle on a shot that way, and Nate could also possibly block an attempted escape. The second security guard could help with that, too, since he was covering the other end of the garage. Grayson couldn't let the gunman get Eve out of there because once he no longer had any use for a hostage, the shooter would almost certainly kill her.

"The security guard needs medical attention," Grayson shouted to the gunman. Since the guy wasn't moving, he wanted to try a different approach. "Why don't you end this now so we can get an ambulance up here?"

Still nothing. But the guy was moving a little and looking around. Grayson didn't like the edgy movement because it proved the gunman was nervous and way out of his comfort zone.

Grayson stopped but kept his gun lifted and aimed. "Step out so I can see you." And he tried to make it sound like an order. Hard to do with that gun right at Eve's head.

"What should I do?" she mouthed.

But Grayson shook his head. He didn't want her to do anything. Not yet anyway. But if it came down to it, he hoped she could drop out of the way so that Nate or he would have a clean shot.

Grayson glanced around to see the best way to approach this, and while he was still studying the situation, just like that the car alarm stopped. Maybe the battery had given out or perhaps Nate had managed to disarm it. Either way, it was now deadly silent.

The gunman lifted his head, just a little, and even though Grayson still couldn't see his face, he didn't think it was his imagination that the guy wasn't pleased with the silenced alarm. But Grayson was certainly thankful for it. Maybe now he could hear this bozo's voice and figure out who he was dealing with. If it wasn't Sebastian, then maybe one of the Colliers had hired a triggerman.

"SAPD has the building surrounded," Grayson tossed out there. "You can't escape. But what you can do is let Eve go, and we can talk about a peaceful surrender."

No answer, but he hadn't expected one.

The guy finally moved. Well, he moved the gun away from Eve's head anyway, and for a moment Grayson thought he might surrender. He didn't.

He lowered the gun, pointing it down to the floor, and he fired.

Hell.

Grayson couldn't see exactly what had happened, but judging from the look of sheer horror on Eve's face and from her scream, the gunman had shot the security guard at point-blank range.

Things had just gone from bad to worse.

The gunman moved again, quickly this time. He put the gun back against Eve's head and he pushed her forward. He followed with the front of his body pressed to Eve's back.

The gunman was heading for that black van.

Nate was there, somewhere. Hopefully, in a position to stop a getaway attempt.

"You won't be able to drive out of here," Grayson warned.

But he'd barely had time to issue that warning when the gunman shifted his weapon.

He fired at Grayson.

Grayson jumped to the side, just in time, and he landed hard against the concrete floor. His shoulder jammed, the pain shooting through him, but he ignored it and came up ready to fire.

The gunman fired first, and the shot pinned Grayson down behind the back of a small truck.

"I have to kill you, you know," the gunman said.

Or rather the gunwoman. Because that was a female voice. A familiar one.

"Cicely?" Grayson spat out. She was the last of the Colliers that he had suspected. "Why the hell are you doing this?"

"Because you all have to die." Cicely's voice was eerily calm, but there was nothing calm about her expression when she met his gaze over Eve's shoulder. "Step out and die like a man, Sheriff Ryland. The other one, too." She tossed a look in Nate's direction. "And that other security guard."

She was just going to kill them all?

Why?

"Your son is in custody for Sophia's murder," Grayson tossed out there. He was testing the waters, trying to get Cicely to talk. And he was also hoping to distract her.

What he didn't intend to do was surrender.

"That's a mistake. He didn't kill his sister." Cicely's voice broke on the last word. "I know because I did it."

Eve gasped, and that was pretty much Grayson's reaction. "You killed your own daughter?"

A hoarse sob tore from Cicely's mouth. "It was an accident, but I don't expect you to believe that."

"I do." And Grayson wasn't lying. He did believe her. "Why did you do it?"

With Eve still in a body lock against her, Cicely continued to inch toward the black van. "I'll tell you, but it won't save you. Nothing will."

Grayson would prove her wrong, somehow.

"I begged Sophia to come home to me, but she just laughed. She wanted money, you see. Claude's money and mine. She didn't want us. Didn't want to be family again."

"So you killed her?" Eve asked in disbelief.

Cicely jammed the gun harder against Eve's head. "I told you that was an accident," Cicely practically yelled. "Sophia said her foster mother confessed to her who she really was—a Collier. The foster mother wanted to try and get money out of us. But Sophia gave her an overdose of insulin to get her out of the way."

Grayson didn't think Sophia's motives were pure, that she did that in order to protect her biological parents. "Sophia did that so she wouldn't have to share the cash with her foster mother?" he asked.

Cicely nodded. "Then, when Sophia and I were arguing, I pushed her, and she fell and hit her head." Another sob. "I had Leon dispose of the body. But Leon remembered that someone at the rodeo had been taking pictures. Pictures that would link him to Sophia. And eventually link her back to me. Leon tried to get them back from Eve, and then you killed him."

"Because he tried to kill us," Grayson reminded her. "Eve did nothing wrong. She was only doing her job when she took the pictures."

"Yes, but I couldn't have the police thinking Sebastian had anything to do with this. He's innocent, you know." She pulled in a shaky breath. "Now step out, Sheriff, and drop your gun so I can do what I have to do to protect my son."

"You mean so you can kill me," he answered flatly.

Eve frantically shook her head. "Stay put," she told Grayson.

Cicely fired at shot at him. "If you stay put or hold on to your gun, I'll make it painful for Eve. You're not the sort of man to cower behind a car while the woman you love is screaming in pain."

Grayson ignored that *woman you love* part and got ready to move. He would leave cover. There was no question about that. He wouldn't let this insane woman hurt Eve. But he couldn't just let Cicely kill him either, because he had to live so that he could rescue Eve. He wouldn't do her any good if he was dead.

"I'm coming out," Grayson let Cicely know. He glanced over at Nate who was ready to fire, as well.

Grayson slid out his gun first, not too far away. He needed to be able to reach for it. And then he stood.

At the exact moment that Eve shouted, "No!"

Eve rammed her elbow against Cicely and darted to the side. But Grayson didn't have time to get off a clean shot. Because Cicely darted to the side, too, and the woman didn't release the grip she had on Eve.

Grayson yelled for Eve to get out of the way, but the sound he heard turned his blood to ice.

The sound of the shot that Cicely fired.

Not at Grayson. Nor at Nate.

Grayson's world tipped on its axis when the bullet slammed into Eve.

Chapter 18

Eve heard the shot.

She also heard Grayson call out to her.

But she couldn't answer. She couldn't do anything except slide to the floor.

The pain was instant, searing, and it sliced through her right side like a red-hot stiletto. She grabbed at the fire and felt the warm blood against her fingers.

She'd been shot.

That fact registered somewhere in her mind. It also registered that she needed to tell Grayson to get down so that he, too, wouldn't be shot. But Eve couldn't make herself speak.

Was she in shock?

Or worse, was she dying?

Ironically, she could deal with the thought of her death, but not of Grayson's. She didn't want his life to end here in this cold, dank garage.

Because she was in love with him.

Always had been. Always would be.

And that's why she had to save him. At least one of them had to make it out of here alive.

"Eve?" Grayson called out. "Are you all right?"

She tried to answer, but Cicely was still beside her, crouched down, with a gun in each hand. She jammed the gun to Eve's head again.

"Tell him to come to you," Cicely demanded.

Eve shook her head. She had to do something to buy a little time. "They'll put you in jail," she managed to say to the woman who'd just shot her. "They'll give you the death penalty. All of this will be for nothing."

"No," Cicely quickly disagreed. Her eyes were wild, her gaze firing between Grayson and Nate. "Annabel is tied up in that black van. When the Rylands and you are dead, I'll shoot her and make it look like a suicide. I've already forced her to write the note, and trust me, it'll be no hardship killing that bimbo witch. She stole my husband. And my life. She deserves to die a thousand deaths."

Oh, God. Cicely wasn't just crazy, she was smart. If Eve couldn't fight back and stop her, Cicely might just get away with this. Worse, Cicely was trying to maneuver herself into a better position to kill again.

Cicely tucked the gun she'd been holding in her left hand into the waist of her pants. That meant she could use that hand to put a tight grip around Eve's neck. Cicely wasn't choking her, exactly, but it was close. Eve was already light-headed enough, but it was obvious Cicely was going to do anything to force Eve to cooperate.

"Tell the sheriff to come to you," Cicely repeated. "And make sure he's unarmed."

She would die before she did that because Cicely

intended to kill them all anyway. Eve wouldn't be the reason Grayson took a bullet.

"You're not just killing me," Eve whispered. "I'm pregnant. You're killing my child, too. Maybe a daughter. It would be like killing Sophia all over again."

Cicely blinked, and with that blink Eve saw the hesitation in the woman's eyes. Her gaze dropped to Eve's stomach and then to the blood on the side of Eve's gray sweater. It wasn't much more than a split second of time, but that brief lapse was all that Eve needed.

She latched on to Cicely's wrist.

It was risky, but at this point anything she did or didn't do was risky. All she knew was that every drop of blood she lost put Grayson, Nate, her possible pregnancy and herself in danger. Besides, Cicely had killed both Sophia and the security guard, and Eve knew she wouldn't hesitate to kill again.

Cicely made a feral sound, part scream and part groan, and she struggled to throw off Eve's grip. Eve held on and tried to wrench the gun from Cicely's right hand. Of course, the woman had a second gun that she could use, but Eve would deal with that later. For now, she needed a weapon so she could fight back.

"Eve?" Grayson called out.

The sound of the struggle must have alerted him because Eve heard his frantic footsteps. He was running to try and save her.

Or maybe running to his death.

Eve clamped onto Cicely's gun because she knew that Grayson's life depended on it.

Grayson cursed, and even though Eve couldn't see him from her position, he was close by. Cicely was aware of that, too, because she bashed the gun against Eve's head and then pointed the weapon at Grayson.

Cicely fired.

The fear and adrenaline slammed through Eve, and despite the blow Cicely had delivered to her head, she kept fighting.

"Grayson!" Nate called out.

Nate sounded terrified, and that spiked the fear inside Eve. Did that mean he'd just witnessed his brother being shot?

Oh, God.

Eve couldn't risk thinking about that now. She had to stay in the fight. Despite the pain and the fear, she had to keep fighting.

"Come closer and he dies," she heard Cicely say, and she let go of Eve.

Eve swiveled around and realized Cicely was talking to Nate as he approached them. He had obviously retrieved his weapon and now had it trained on Cicely.

But Cicely had her gun aimed at Grayson.

Another smart move because Nate wouldn't do anything to risk his brother being killed.

Nate froze, but he didn't lower his gun, and he glanced behind him at the stairwell. Hopefully, there were backup officers there and ready to respond.

And then there was Grayson.

He, too, was ready to respond, but he was no longer the calm, collected lawman. Grayson said her name.

Eve.

It was a hoarse whisper filled with concern. No doubt from the blood.

"I'm okay," Eve said to him, even though she had no idea if that was true. She might have lost the chance to be a mother, but worse, she might lose Grayson. "I'm so sorry," she managed to say.

He shook his head. "For what?"

Too many things for her to say here. Besides, there was nothing she could say that would allow them to go back and undo everything. This was their fate, and unfortunately it was in the hands of a crazy woman hellbent on covering up the murder of her own daughter.

"Eve needs a doctor," Grayson told Cicely. "End this now."

"It ends when you're all dead." But Cicely didn't sound as convinced of that as she had just moments earlier. She glanced at Eve. "I didn't know about your baby. If I had, I would have found a way to leave you out of this."

"Baby?" Nate mumbled. That obviously shocked him, but he didn't take his attention off Cicely.

Later, Eve would have to explain.

If there was a later.

The pain shot through her side again, and Eve felt the fresh trickle of warm blood. Grayson noticed it, too, because she saw his body tense. He was getting ready to have a shoot-out with Cicely. And he could no doubt kill her. But could he do that before she fired a lethal shot at him?

Eve couldn't take that risk. She had to do something, and she used her own body. She kicked at Cicely, and she put every ounce of her strength behind it. The heel of her shoe connected with the woman's shin, and Cicely howled in pain.

It wasn't much of an attack, but Grayson made the most of it.

He dove at Cicely, his muscled body ramming right

into the woman, and he slammed her back into the adjacent car.

Cicely made a gasping sound, fighting for the air that Grayson had knocked from her, but that didn't stop her from trying to aim her gun at his head.

"Watch out!" Eve shouted.

Grayson latched on to both of Cicely's hands and bashed them against the car's body. Her gun clattered to the floor, and Grayson snatched the other weapon from the waist of her pants. He tossed it on the floor, as well.

Nate moved in and kicked both of Cicely's weapons away, but even unarmed, Cicely didn't give up. She continued to fight until Grayson turned her around and pushed her hard against the car's fender.

A sob racked through Cicely, and she went limp.

"Take Cicely," Grayson immediately told Nate. "I'm getting Eve to the E.R."

He kept his forearm on Cicely to hold her until Nate switched places with him. Grayson didn't waste a second. He scooped Eve up in his arms.

"How bad?" he asked.

She wanted to lie. Eve wanted to tell him that everything would be all right, but the fight had taken the last of her breath. She opened her mouth, but no sound came out.

Grayson raced to the stairwell where the other officers were pouring up the steps. One of those officers latched onto Cicely, yanked her hands behind her back and cuffed her.

Grayson looked down at Eve as he ran toward the E.R. doors. He was so worried. And scared. She realized that was the first time she'd seen fear in Grayson's eyes.

Everything started to move in slow motion, and the edges of her vision turned gray. At first. Then, darker.

She fastened her gaze on Grayson and fought to keep her eyes open. But she failed at that, too.

Her eyelids fluttered down, and the last thing Eve saw was Grayson's face.

Grayson was afraid if he stopped moving, he would explode.

So he turned and once again paced across the surgical waiting room of the San Antonio hospital. It didn't help his raw nerves, nor did it ease the massive knot in his stomach, but he couldn't sit and wait as his brothers were doing.

Nate and Dade were on the far side of the room. Nate was on the phone, but both Dade and he were staring at a TV where *It's a Wonderful Life* was playing. Grayson doubted they were actually watching the movie, but they were trying to maintain a calm, business-as-usual facade. For his sake no doubt.

They knew he was ready to explode.

Mason, being Mason, didn't even attempt a facade. He was in a chair on the opposite side of the room, and he was glaring at anything and everything—including Jimmy Stewart on the screen. He was especially glaring at the hall where a nurse had appeared earlier to tell them that Eve was finally being taken to surgery.

Two hours.

That's how long it'd been since Eve had been in the hospital. Grayson hadn't known that one hundred and twenty minutes could feel like a lifetime, but he damn sure knew it now. Every one of those minutes had crawled by.

"She'll be okay," Nate assured him.

Dade mumbled his agreement, but it didn't sound remotely convincing. Mason's glare deepened.

The glare wasn't for Eve. Mason wasn't fond of too many people, but he cared as much for Eve as Grayson's other brothers did. No, this glare was for Cicely, for what the woman had nearly done to Eve. But the good thing in all of this was that Cicely was locked away at the SAPD facility and couldn't come after any of them again.

"Claude Collier's condition has stabilized," Nate reported when he ended the call. "Annabel's still being checked out over in the E.R., but she's going to be okay. Just some bruises and scratches from where Cicely attacked her and stuffed her in the van."

It was the wrong attitude for a lawman to have, but Grayson didn't give a flying fig about the Colliers. He only wanted good news about Eve.

At the sound of footsteps in the hall, his brothers stood, and Grayson turned to see Dr. Andrew Masters making his way toward him. Grayson had met the lanky no-nonsense doctor briefly when Eve had first been rushed into the E.R.

Grayson narrowed the distance between the doctor and him. "Is she okay?" he asked. But he wasn't sure he could take hearing any bad news.

The doctor nodded. "Eve should be fine."

"Should be?" Mason growled, taking the tone and the words right out of Grayson's mouth. "What the hell does that mean?"

The doctor gave a weary huff and looked at Grayson. "Physically, she'll be all right. The surgery didn't take long at all."

"Then what did?" That growl came from Dade. "It's been two hours."

"She had to be examined and prepped. The bullet

entered her right side and made a clean exit. It didn't hit any vital organs, which makes her a very lucky woman."

Lucky. Yes, she was, but Grayson didn't feel so lucky. Eve had come damn close to dying.

"You said *physically* Eve will be all right?" Nate questioned.

Dr. Masters glanced at Grayson. A funny kind of glance. Had Eve told him about the possible pregnancy? No doubt.

She might not have actually mentioned that Grayson could be her baby's father, but the doctor wasn't an idiot. He had almost certainly put one and one together when he's seen Grayson's reaction to her being shot.

"Eve wants to see you," the doctor said to Grayson. "But don't stay long. I want her to get plenty of rest." Then, he turned that authoritative gaze on the rest of the Rylands. "You can all come back in the morning."

The trio looked as if they might argue, but Nate finally caught on to his brothers' arms. "Grayson will see to Eve," he reminded them.

Yeah. He'd done a stellar job of that in the past forty-eight hours, hadn't he? He'd had sex with her, twice, and had nearly gotten her killed.

Grayson took a deep breath and followed the doctor to the post-op room at the end of the hall. Everything in the room was watery white, including Eve. There wasn't a drop of color in her cheeks. Still, she managed a smile of sorts when she saw him.

"You've got five minutes," the doctor instructed, "and then I don't want her to have any more visitors until tomorrow. Don't worry. After what Eve's been through, she'll sleep during that time anyway."

Grayson prayed that was true, that she would sleep

with no nightmares. He stood zero chance of that happening for him. Every time he closed his eyes, he would see the attack. It would torment him, and he would try to figure out what he could have done to prevent it. In his nightmares, he would stop Cicely's bullet from hitting Eve.

But saving her from that bullet was a day late and a dollar short.

"You look worried," she mumbled. Her words were slurred, and her eyes bleary.

"I am worried." Grayson walked closer. She looked too fragile to touch, but he skimmed his fingers down her arm, barely making contact with her skin. "The doctor said you were going to be okay."

"Yes." The half smile faded. "It's too early to know if that's true."

"The baby," he whispered.

She gave a shaky nod. "The trauma probably put an end to any pregnancy."

Of course. Her body had been through a lot. Too much. He didn't know much about the biology of conception, but the blood loss and the shock from the attack could have caused her body to shut down.

Being shot was hardly conducive to making a baby.

"Dr. Masters said I should brace myself for the worst," she added. "So that's what I've done."

It made him ache to hear her say that, to see the resignation in her exhausted eyes.

"I'm sorry," Grayson said, because he didn't know what else to say.

She lifted her chin, though it was shaky, too. "I just wanted to thank you, for everything. That's why I asked to see you."

That hurt, as well. And it also riled him to the core.

Grayson didn't want to be thanked for doing a half-assed job at protecting her. "Don't—"

"I know. You don't want to talk about it." She pulled in a slow breath and fought to keep her eyes open. "That's okay."

No. It wasn't *okay*. Far from it. He should tell her...

But tell her what, exactly?

Tell her that he wasn't sorry about sleeping with her? That was a moot point now that the gunshot wound had compromised her already slim chances of getting pregnant.

Maybe he should explain to her that he was sorry he hadn't stopped Cicely from shooting her? Or that the only thing he wanted was for her to be happy? She deserved happiness. She deserved a lot more than he could have ever given her.

But Grayson didn't say any of those things. He just stood there, looking at Eve, and knowing he couldn't do or say anything to make it better.

"Go home to your family." Her voice had no sound now. Even though her eyes drifted down, she smiled that sad half smile again. "Have a good life, Grayson."

The words went through him like ice. Like the dark cold he felt deep within his soul when he thought he'd lost Eve in that parking garage.

Because the words sounded like a goodbye.

And Grayson knew that's exactly what it was.

Well, he had his answer. Eve might have been groggy from the surgical drugs, but he hadn't seen any doubt in her eyes, and she damn sure hadn't asked him to stay.

Have a good life, Grayson.

With those words slamming through his head, Grayson did as Eve wanted. He walked away.

Chapter 19

The pain seared through her when she eased off the hospital bed and into the wheelchair, but Eve tried not to react visibly. She didn't want Dr. Masters to see the pain on her face because he would only give her more hassle about leaving. And there was no way she wanted to spend the rest of Christmas day in a hospital.

Besides, if she stayed, she would go stark-raving mad. Every moment she was in that bed, she thought of Grayson and of the life that she'd nearly gotten to have as a mother.

"You know how I feel about this," the doctor grumbled. It was a paraphrase of the grumble he'd been doling out since she'd insisted on going home.

So yes, she did know how the doctor felt. He wanted her to stay put one more day, even at the risk of her sanity. However, the moment he signed the release papers, Eve snatched them from his hand.

Dr. Masters gave her a flat look. "At least tell me you'll be with family or friends, that you aren't going home alone."

"I won't be alone," she lied.

His flat look intensified. "You told the nurse to tell the Rylands that you couldn't have any visitors, that you were in too much pain."

"I lied about that." And that was the truth.

She had told that lie not because of the pain. Well, not the physical pain anyway, but she couldn't bear the thought of saying goodbye to Grayson again. Once she was home and had recovered, she would email his brothers and thank them for, well, for being there when it counted most.

Dr. Masters scribbled something on another piece of paper and handed it to her. "A script for pain meds and antibiotics," he explained.

The antibiotics were a necessity but not the drug for pain. The pain was right there, stabbing through her, but she didn't want to put any more drugs in her body in case there was the minuscule chance that she might be pregnant.

Yes, it was a pipe dream, but Eve was going to hold on to it until a pregnancy test proved otherwise.

"I can't talk you out of this?" the doctor asked. He grabbed the back of her wheelchair when Eve tried to wheel herself toward the door.

"No. I've made up my mind."

He gave a heavy sigh, followed by a nod, and he stepped behind her so he could wheel her toward the door. With any luck, the taxi she'd called would be waiting and could take her to her condo. She'd also phoned the super because she didn't have her keys. He had promised to meet her there and let her in. Then she could get some cash to pay the taxi driver.

"What should I tell the Rylands when they show up?" Dr. Masters asked.

And they would show up. "Tell them I made a miraculous recovery and that I'm spending the holiday with friends."

The doctor made a sound of disapproval but wheeled her out anyway.

"The taxi is meeting me at the back of the building," she let him know.

Another sound of disapproval, but he went in that direction anyway. Eve looked over her shoulder. No sign of Grayson. And she tried to convince herself that was a good thing.

The tears came anyway.

She blinked them back and realized that the pain in her side was nothing compared to the piercing ache in her heart. Damn her. She had known not to get too close to Grayson, and she'd done it anyway.

Again.

The doors slid open as they approached, and the cold wind nearly robbed her of her breath. So did the man who stepped out onto the walkway. Not Grayson.

Dade.

He was there, right next to the taxi that was waiting for her. Dade smiled, flashing those killer dimples that had probably coaxed many women into his bed. The dimples had never worked on Eve because to her Dade would always be the brother she'd never had.

"I asked at the front desk," Dade explained, "and

the nurse said you were checking out early. Since I didn't see you out front, I figured I'd check back here." He tipped his head to the taxi. "Going somewhere?" It was a friendly enough question, but there was concern in his voice.

"I need to get home." Eve kept it at that. She gave the doctor a nod of reassurance that all was well, and he went back inside.

"Right. You need to get home," Dade repeated. He blew out his breath as if resigned to the fact that they weren't going to have a real discussion here. "Want me to drive you?"

She shook her head. "It's Christmas and you should be with your family. The taxi will get me home just fine."

Another nod. He reached in his jeans' pocket, pulled out something and walked closer. "Your Christmas present," he announced. "Sorry, but I didn't have time to wrap it." Dade caught on to her hand and dropped something into her palm.

A silver concho.

Eve knew exactly what this was. One of the silver conchos that Boone Ryland had given to all six of his sons before he'd walked out on them and their mother.

She looked at Dade and shook her head. "I thought you threw yours in the creek."

Dade shrugged. "I had this one made for you a while back but never got around to giving it to you. I figured this was a good time."

Her mind slipped back to all those years ago, and she could see the hurt teenager whose father had run out on him. The concho was a reminder of both the pain from that loss and the family that Boone Ryland had made.

"Thank you," she managed to say despite the massive lump in her throat.

"I always thought you should have one," Dade added. "And if you decide to throw it in the creek, put a bullet in it or drape it around a picture frame, it's your right." He stooped down so he was eye level with her, and he caught on to her shoulders. "Eve, you're a Ryland, and you belong with Grayson."

The tears threatened again, and she hoped that Dade thought the cold wind was responsible. "I can't have Grayson," she said. She put the concho on her lap so her hands would be free to wheel the chair to the taxi door.

But Dade took over. "Because Grayson's too stubborn and proud."

"No. Because he's Grayson." She managed a smile when Dade helped her into the back of the taxi. She made sure she had hold of the concho, and then closed her hand around it.

Dade brushed a kiss on her forehead. "I can't do anything to change your mind?"

She didn't even have to think about this. "No."

Eve had seen Grayson's reaction the night before. He felt guilty for her injury and guilty that the bullet had almost certainly cost her a baby. That guilt would eat away at him, and he would come to her and try to make things right.

Eventually, they'd land in bed again.

And eventually the old feelings and wounds would resurface, and Grayson would resent her for forcing a relationship on him that he didn't want.

"I can tolerate a lot of things in life," she whispered to Dade. "But I refuse to be the person who brings Grayson Ryland to his knees. I love him too much for that."

Thankfully, Dade didn't argue. He didn't question her or her logic. He simply smiled, shut the taxi door and waved goodbye.

Eve pressed her hand and the concho to her heart, hoping it would ease the pain. But that was asking a lot from a little piece of silver, even if this piece of silver was one of the most precious gifts she'd ever received. She definitely wouldn't throw it in the creek or put a bullet in it. She would keep it close to her heart.

Eve waited until the driver was out of the parking lot before she broke down and cried.

Chapter 20

Grayson cursed. He'd actually punched a singing Christmas tree and rammed it into the trash can.

He'd thought it was a reasonable reaction at the time. The tree was stupid, sitting on the dispatcher's desk at the sheriff's office and bursting into that same tinny "Jingle Bell" tune every time anyone walked past it. Well, Grayson was tired of it. Plus, it was nearly two weeks past Christmas, and if he'd had any holiday spirit, it was long gone.

Still, he'd punched a Christmas tree.

And that's when he knew this had to end.

His mood was well past the surly stage, and even the usually even-tempered Nate had demanded that Grayson *do something*. Grayson hadn't needed to figure out what his brother meant. He knew.

He had to see Eve.

So he'd forced himself into his new truck and started driving.

However, now that he was parked in front of her condo in San Antonio, Grayson was rethinking his impulsiveness. He probably should have called or emailed first. Heck, he darn sure should have sorted out his feelings and what he wanted to say to her.

What if she told him to take a hike?

That wasn't the only worry on his mind. Still, he had to see for himself that she was okay, that she had recovered both physically and mentally from the shooting.

He was about to get out of his truck, when the front door to her condo opened, and Eve backed out. She had on jeans, a dark red sweater top, and she was dragging something.

A Christmas tree.

Not a fake singing one but a real one with dry, browning branches. No ornaments, but there were a few strands of silver tinsel that caught the cold January wind and the afternoon sun. Since she was struggling with it and since he was pretty sure she shouldn't be twisting and turning her body like that, Grayson hurried over to help her.

She must have heard his footsteps because she let go of the tree and whirled around as if she'd expected to be attacked.

Hell.

She'd been having those nightmares about the shooting.

But her expression quickly went from alarm to a smile. Not the weak half-assed smile that she'd given him in the hospital. This was a real one. An Eve smile that lit up her whole face. That smile caused him to freeze.

Oh, man. She was beautiful. Always had been, always would be. And he would always feel as if it he'd been sucker-punched when he saw her.

"Grayson," she said on a rise of breath.

"Eve." His voice didn't sound any steadier than hers.

They stood there, staring, waiting. And because Grayson had to have something to do with his hands, he grabbed the trunk of the dead tree.

"Where do you want this to go?" he asked.

She motioned toward the Dumpster at the end of the parking lot where there were several other discarded Christmas trees. "The recycling truck is supposed to pick them up today," she let him know.

Grayson headed in that direction, and Eve followed along beside him. He looked for any signs of pain or limited movement, but there weren't any.

"I'm okay," she assured him as if reading his mind. "I had my post-op check up last week, and the doctor said I was healing nicely."

"Good." He cursed himself when he repeated it.

Grayson didn't hurry because he didn't want Eve to hurry to keep up with him, but he didn't dawdle, either. It was cold and blustery, and despite her *healing nicely* remark, he didn't want her outside any longer than necessary—especially since she wasn't wearing a coat. He tossed the tree next to the others and headed back.

"Would you like to come in?" she asked. The invitation was tentative, like her body language. She wasn't fidgeting exactly, but it was close.

"Yeah. I'd like to talk." And say what exactly, Grayson didn't know.

Well, except for asking her the results of the pregnancy test she'd taken. Of course, if by some miracle that result had been positive, she would have already told him.

Maybe.

And Grayson had to accept that maybe she had already written him out of her life. It seemed that way in the hospital.

Eve walked into the condo ahead of him and shut the door once he was inside, but didn't sit. She stuffed her hands into the back pockets of her jeans, causing her sweater to tighten across her breasts.

Something he shouldn't have noticed.

However, he also noticed her necklace. Not an ordinary one. It was a familiar concho with the double *R* brand of his family's ranch.

"Dade gave it to me for Christmas," she said, following his gaze. "He had it made years ago."

Funny, his brother hadn't mentioned a thing about seeing Eve or giving her a Christmas present. After Eve had left the goodbye note at the hospital, Grayson had thought all the Rylands had respected her wishes to be left alone.

Apparently not.

And he would take that up with Dade when he got home.

"The concho doesn't have bad memories for me like it does for you and your brothers," Eve explained. She shifted her weight, glanced away. "When I see it, I don't think of your father leaving. I think of all the memories of when he was there. When things were good."

Leave it to Eve to find the silver lining.

Grayson reached out and slid his fingers beneath

the concho pendant. But it wasn't just the pendant he touched. His knuckles brushed against her breasts. She made a slight shivering sound and stepped back. Grayson let go of the concho and stepped back, too.

"Sorry," she mumbled. But then her chin came up. "I guess it's stupid to apologize for an involuntary response. I'm always going to feel an attraction for you, Grayson, and saying I'm sorry won't make it go away."

No. But admitting the attraction only reminded him that he felt the same about her. Not that he needed a reminder. Just seeing her had the heat sliding through him.

"Always?" he questioned. Oh, yeah. This was playing with fire all right.

She met his gaze head-on. "Always."

Their gazes held, and so many things passed between them. Questions. But very few answers, only the obvious one about this simmering heat. Yes, it would always be there.

"How are you, really?" he asked.

The corner of her mouth lifted. "Well, I'm not in any shape to haul you off to my bed, but I'm healing."

That didn't cool him down. Oh, man. He was stupid to keep at this, but Grayson had no choice. He needed to get to the bottom of this once and for all.

"Do you want to haul me off to your bed?" he asked.

He didn't quite get the reaction he'd hoped for. Eve huffed, and her hands came out of her pockets and went on her hips. "Yes. Happy now?" She didn't wait for his answer. Not that he had one. "What's this visit really about?"

He didn't have an answer for that, either. But he knew he sure as hell needed one. Grayson couldn't go back to kicking Christmas trees or to his nonstop surly mood. He had to resolve this situation once and for all.

"Well?" she prompted. She wasn't tapping her foot, but it was close.

Grayson tried to wrap his mind around his feelings, but Eve huffed again.

"I'm in love with you," she tossed out there like profanity. "I've tried not to be, but I can't make my feelings go away. So, there! Learn to deal with it." Another huff. "Would you like to know what I've been dreaming about for the past two weeks?"

Not the shooting. Grayson prayed it wasn't that.

"About *you*," she tossed out, as well.

Grayson was relieved. Sort of. "I've dreamed about you, too."

He had to gather his breath because he knew these next few minutes would be the most important of his life. Everything was about to change.

And it all hinged on Eve.

"I'm in love with you, too." He said the words fast, like pulling off a bandage, and he was surprised that it hadn't hurt one bit. Just the opposite.

Grayson felt relieved.

That relief didn't extend to Eve, however. Her eyes widened. Her mouth dropped open. "When did you realize that?" she asked.

"A long time ago. It just took me a while to get around to saying it." And because it'd taken him too long, he decided to repeat it. "I love you, Eve."

She didn't say a word. She just stood there, mouth open, and then the tears sprang to her eyes. Grayson moved first, but she was faster. Eve launched herself into his arms.

He took things from there.

Grayson kissed her, and for the first time in his life, he didn't hold anything back. He loved her, and he wanted her to know that. He must have succeeded because the kiss quickly turned fiery hot.

Eve coiled her arms around him, pulling him closer, but Grayson kept things gentle. Or at least he tried. Hard to stay gentle with the kiss going French and with Eve pressed against him. It wasn't easy, but Grayson pulled back to remind her of her injury.

"You're not in any condition for sex," he reminded her.

"Maybe not our normal version of sex." She put her mouth right against his ear because she was obviously a twisted woman who knew that would torture him in the best kind of way.

Grayson groaned and gladly gave in to the torture. He lifted his hands in surrender while she went after his neck.

Oh, yeah.

Eve knew every inch of his body, and within seconds had him rethinking that no-sex-right-now rule.

She pulled back slightly, met his gaze and gave him a nudge with her body that had his eyes crossing. "But remember, I'm in love with you," Eve confessed, "and we can find a way to make this happen."

He froze. And Eve noticed. She went stiff, too, and some panic raced through those jeweled blue eyes. "I was talking about sex when I said we can find a way."

"Were you?" he challenged.

More panic. She stepped back, as she'd always done in the past because she didn't want to put him in a corner. Well, Grayson was sure of two things—he was crazy in love with Eve, and he wanted to be in that *corner*.

He caught on to the silver concho pendant again, and because he wanted to hear that little shiver of arousal, he let his fingers trail over her right nipple.

He smiled when he heard the sound.

And then Grayson let go of the pendant and dropped to his knees.

Eve's sexy shiver turned to a gasp. "What are you doing?"

Grayson didn't even have to think about this. "I'm asking you to marry me."

The room was suddenly way too quiet. No more shivery sounds. No gasps. Eve just stared at him, and for one horrifying moment, he thought she would turn him down.

She certainly didn't say yes.

"Why are you asking me now?" she wanted to know.

Grayson had to release the breath he was holding so he could speak. "Uh, is that a trick question?"

"No." Eve was quick with that assurance but not with the answer to his proposal.

He shrugged. "I thought it was obvious. I'm asking because I love you. Because you're already part of the family, but I wanted to make it official. And because I want you in my bed every night."

She stared at him, as if waiting for more.

What?

That wasn't enough?

Grayson eased her down to her knees so they were face-to-face and so he could kiss her. She apparently needed a reminder of that love she'd professed for him just minutes earlier.

The kiss was long, satisfying and left them both breathless. "Say yes," he insisted.

But she didn't. She pulled back again. "Is this about the attempt to get me pregnant?"

"No." And he hoped she could see that was the honest to goodness truth. "This is about being in love with you. We can discuss the details of our future later, but for now I need an answer, and I need that answer to be yes. Because I can't imagine living the rest of my life without you."

Now, she made a sound. No shiver, but a melting sigh, and her smile returned. Eve slid her arms around him.

"Yes," she finally said. "Because I can't imagine living without you, either."

Grayson wasn't sure which he felt first—relief or happiness, but it was the happiness that filled every part of him.

Eve had said yes!

He wanted to whoop for joy and celebrate, but first he needed another kiss. Their mouths met, barely a touch at first, but in their case familiarity bred lust because this kiss quickly turned scalding hot.

Grayson wanted to tell his brothers about the engagement, but after a few more of those kisses, he knew his brothers would have to wait. Right now, he wanted to make love—gently—to his fiancée.

He got up, scooped Eve into his arms and headed for her bedroom. The kisses didn't stop. In fact, they got more heated as Eve pressed her mouth to his chin and then his throat.

"Wait!" she said the moment he eased her onto the bed.

Hell. That wasn't a word he wanted to hear. "You

can't take back your yes," he let her know. "You're marrying me." And he hoped she didn't argue.

"I didn't mean wait about that. Of course I want to marry you. I've wanted that since I was sixteen."

And that made Grayson smile.

He eased them onto the bed and then rolled her on top of him. "Then why did you say wait?" But his gaze dropped to her side. "Oh. Second thoughts about sex?"

"No." She made it sound as if he'd lost his mind. "I want sex. Trust me, I really want to have sex with you. But I have to tell you something first."

Her smile faded until she looked anything but happy.

Grayson froze again. In fact, he was reasonably sure that every muscle in his body locked up so he couldn't move. "What's wrong?"

"Uh…" And a moment later, she repeated it. She also licked her lips and bunched up her forehead. "The test was, well, it was positive."

It took a few seconds for that to sink in through the worry and the haze in his mind. "You're pregnant?" And that was something he thought he'd *never* hear himself ask Eve.

She nodded. Swallowed hard.

Eve eyed him as if he were a stick of dynamite about to go off. "I should have told you the minute you got on your knees, but I was so surprised. And happy. The only thing I could think of was saying yes. I didn't think that this baby could change everything."

He caught on to her arm. "Wait a minute." The thoughts and words were flying at him so fast that it took Grayson a moment to speak. "You think a baby could change the way I feel about you?"

She blinked back tears. "Does it?"

Oh, man. He had some explaining to do. Grayson decided to start that explanation with a kiss. He gently pulled her down to him and did just that.

"Yes, it changes how I feel about you," he admitted. He slid his hand over her stomach. "It makes me love you even more."

Her breath swooshed out and she snapped him to her. Probably too hard. But Grayson couldn't make himself let go of her.

"But this messes up the plans you had for your life," she reminded him.

"Screw the plans." In fact, he was looking forward to a little chaos, especially the kind of chaotic love that a wife and a child would give him. He hadn't realized until now that having Eve and this child gave him something he'd never had—completion.

His life would be complete with them.

He wouldn't just have brothers. Wouldn't just be part of the Rylands. He would have his *own* family.

"So you're happy?" she asked.

Grayson wanted no room for doubt. "I'm the happiest man on earth." And he pulled her into his arms so he could hold her and kiss her.

He could have sworn he felt everything in the universe go into some kind of perfect cosmic alignment.

Or maybe that was just his heart.

Either way, this was right. No, it was better than that. It was perfect.

And Grayson wanted to hold on to Eve and his baby like this forever.

* * * * *

Love Harlequin romance?

DISCOVER.

Be the first to find out about promotions, news and exclusive content!

 Facebook.com/HarlequinBooks

 Twitter.com/HarlequinBooks

 Instagram.com/HarlequinBooks

 Pinterest.com/HarlequinBooks

 YouTube.com/HarlequinBooks

ReaderService.com

EXPLORE.

Sign up for the Harlequin e-newsletter and download a free book from any series at
TryHarlequin.com

CONNECT.

Join our Harlequin community to share your thoughts and connect with other romance readers!
Facebook.com/groups/HarlequinConnection

HSOCIAL2021